SO-ARE-567

Mary Wallace

Mary Wallace has said of this, her first novel: "There's an old fairy tale about a magic pot that cooked soup on request—and kept right on cooking because no one knew the magic words to make it stop. The soup overflowed the pot, filled the kitchen, and flooded the street. That was my experience in writing *Reason for Gladness*. The book was written simply because it was *there*, demanding to be put down on paper. I cannot even say that I created the characters; it would be nearer the truth to say that they created themselves and came to me, somehow, from somewhere."

Mary Wallace probably underestimates the scope of her own original artistry, but in any case, the wonderful O'Nolans will soon come to have *"the welcome familiarity of old friends . . . Brendan has an otherworldly quality that is endearing as well as exasperating . . . Readers will chuckle, will recognize the rich, warm relationships that develop."*

—*Library Journal*

Reason for Gladness

Mary Wallace

AN AVON BOOK

ACKNOWLEDGMENT

Special thanks to the teacher of Irish
who assisted me with the Irish language
used in this book—a teacher who prefers
to remain anonymous.

The song, "I Wish I Had the Shepherd's Lamb,"
is from the book, *Folk Songs of England,
Ireland, Scotland and Wales,* edited by William
Cole. Copyright, 1961, by William Cole and
Norman Monath. Reprinted by permission of
Doubleday & Co., Inc.

AVON BOOKS
A division of
The Hearst Corporation
959 Eighth Avenue
New York, N. Y. 10019

© Copyright 1965 by Mary Wallace.
Published by arrangement with Funk & Wagnalls Company, Inc.
Library of Congress Catalog Card Number: 65-21938

All rights reserved, which includes the right to
reproduce this book or portions thereof in any
form whatsoever. For information address
Funk & Wagnalls Company, Inc., 360 Lexington Avenue,
New York, N. Y. 10017.

First Avon Printing, January, 1967

Cover illustration by Carl Cassler

Printed in the U.S.A.

To Muriel Fuller

1

HOME today.

Home today at half-past one.

Anne had not slept for thinking of it. Light reflected through the hospital window had laid a shining silver parallelogram on the wall beside her bed. Sleepless through the hot August night, she amused herself by using the lighted space as a screen, projecting upon it like magic-lantern slides the pictures her mind drew one by one out of her heart's store.

Within those bright borders she framed the children's faces: sometimes each alone, sometimes all together as if grouped for a snapshot, crowding a little to make sure they would all be within the margin of the film. The baby's face, too, she framed there, a face so like a flower. . . . "Well it is," he had said, "that already we had chosen the name Rose for this one. . . ." And, over and over again, *his* face, of all most beloved.

So strong, so proud a face. Young—he was only thirty-one—yet a face that bore the stamp of a thousand years. Incredibly, he could trace his ancestors that far back. They lived in him—you could sense them, you could see them— a shadowy line stretching into the past. And beyond them, beyond the named and known, beyond the thousand years, the line stretched away more shadowy still into time, into an era so remote that it had had its moment of presentness before there had been a scroll or even a stone tablet on which to record it.

Sometimes, framed there in silver on the wall, the face wore a stern, cold look, but with gentleness under it, such

gentleness as could be guessed at only by someone w.
felt the coldness melt under his smile, or had seen all
great strength of his hands leashed in some infinitely del.
cate act—caring for a baby or smoothing the hair back
from the forehead of a sick child.

From the bright patch on the wall he smiled at her, and
there was no darkness anywhere then; nor was there any
loneliness when she could bring back the sound of his
voice, in its curiously beautiful way speaking words of
comfort.

"Not must you worry, *a chroí na páirte*. So has God
willed it, my dearest, that between the two of us joy and
goodness shall always be greater than anything that touches
us from the world outside our door. Too much reason have
we for gladness, to dwell long in our talk or in our thought
on that which would cast a shadow or cause us to feel re-
proachful of God's will because not is it always within our
power to understand why certain things are one way and
not another."

"I should be with you." This was the pain. "You should
not be so alone."

"Alone? Five times over," he answered, "are you waiting
for me there at each day's end. Not am I alone. Even
through the night is there one who makes sure that your
place beside me in the bed is not left empty."

At this she could laugh.

"Brendan?"

"Brendan would it be. That weak I am that a three-year-
old child can work his will upon me with the greatest ease.
But did he only ask, 'Please, Father?' I think then I might
be able to answer, 'Better it is for you, Brendan, to sleep
alone in your crib, which is no farther away, as you know,
than the reach of my hand.' But when it is *'Má's é do thoil
é, má's é do thoil e, 'Athair?'* not can I then find it in my
heart to refuse him. And none but myself to blame, for
having taught him his first words in Irish."

He could cheer her with his words; he could fill her
heart to overflowing. But it had been a cruel time just the
same, this week during the summer of 1941. Cruel to be
parted from him when her love and her faith and her pride
in him could at least have been solace, though they could
not be help.

Painfully, there in the hospital, so far from him, so un-

8

able to help, she had forced herself to read each day's account of the hearing, because only by fully reading could she fully share; and today, at the very end, had come that single little bright sword-flash of triumph, which the paper plainly begrudged him yet did not deny: "O'Nolan's testimony could not be shaken."

There it was. So little a thing, but so rich with meaning.

He stood alone, but stronger than any, stronger than all. Against the slanting of the newspaper accounts, which even made sport of the way he talked; against the attacks of those who sought to show him motivated by self-interest, a publicity seeker; against the testimony of others, who swore that his charges were without any validity at all; against powerful, unknown influences; against threats of suit for defamation of character, threats of arrest for criminal libel, threats of summary dismissal from the Department—against all this he stood alone. In every way they knew, by every means at hand, they tried to break him down, but they could not make him change one word. She knew the look he would turn on them: cold, rock-hard, and inscrutable. Steadfastly, without compromise, without alteration, he resisted them, and there at the end were those significant six words: "O'Nolan's testimony could not be shaken."

At eleven o'clock she got up, offered the newspaper to the young woman who shared the room, and drew the curtains around the bed. Then, taking her clothes from the small traveling bag he had brought last evening, Anne dressed.

"Aren't you the lucky one!" The young woman laid the paper down when the curtains were pushed back again. "Here you are, going home today. And poor me, stuck for a week!"

Anne smiled at her. They had not, up to that time, engaged in conversation. The young woman had been brought in late the preceding afternoon and, except for a brief period during visiting hours, had slept straight through. Since breakfast, she had been preoccupied with many little complaints and calls for attention. She was pretty, petulant, and very young.

Anne asked sympathetically, "Your first?"

"Oh, no. My second. Only one more to go, thank heavens! We decided on three," the girl explained. "I'm having them as close together as possible, so as to get it over with while I'm still young enough to have some fun after I've got all that out of the way. Being near one age," she added, "they'll be good company for one another."

"Yes," Anne said.

She sat on the edge of the bed, taking a small mirror from the drawer of the bedside stand and glancing in it briefly while she drew a comb through her hair.

The girl watched her.

"What's your score?"

"Six."

"Not really! Six children? You couldn't possibly! How old were you when you married, for pity's sake?"

"Eighteen."

"And had you one every year?"

"I've been married for eleven years," Anne said, leaving the arithmetic to be worked out in any combination the girl selected.

"Are you a Catholic?"

"Yes."

"Well, I guess that explains it. I believe in planned parenthood myself."

Anne thought of saying, "So do we. *We* planned to have as many as we could." But she didn't; it would sound contentious, even perhaps a little boastful.

"I don't see how anyone dares have a big family these days," the girl went on. "My husband only makes six thousand a year. We could never afford it."

We afford it on less than that, Anne thought, but again remained silent.

"The way we see it, it's better to have just two or three and be able to give them more advantages. After I get my third one over with, I can go back to work. We'll be pretty well fixed then. Do you work?"

"No."

"I shouldn't imagine you could. It must be pretty hard to find a sitter willing to take on six."

"Yes, I suppose it would be."

"You must be terribly tied down."

"I never thought of it that way," Anne said.

"Well, better you than me. I could never stand it. I'd like to see anybody sell that 'Woman's place is in the home'

10

line to *me*. Men would like to go back to it, though. They don't like us competing. Is your husband that way?"

"My husband has a great many old-fashioned ideas," Anne said.

Like honesty, she was thinking. And standing on principle, even if he must stand alone. And giving his children the greatest advantage of all—the advantage of being wanted, each and every one, not just the ones who come at a time that "suits."

"Oh, *men!*" the girl said, putting all the trials of womanhood into the word, and with that word dismissing the subject. "I'm dying to ask you a very personal question. Would you mind?"

More personal, Anne wondered, than the ones you have already asked?

"No, not at all."

"What do you use on your hair? I'm not asking to be catty," she said quickly. "If you only knew how hard I've tried to get mine to come out that color. But look at it. Like straw! Yours is beautiful. Just beautiful."

Poor child, Anne thought. How far from true values must one be to be envious of another's bleached hair? The truth would surely hurt her.

"I'm sorry. I can't help you. I don't use anything."

"You mean it's natural? Almost platinum blond, and *natural?* Oh, no! How lucky can you get? And that lovely shadow-wave—the way it lifts there on each side, away from your temples, like two silver wings—that's natural, too? And the way the ends curl under? And you do nothing, I suppose, but nothing, except run a comb through it, oh so casually. I don't believe it! You *must* have some fabulously wonderful hairdresser somewhere. You have, haven't you?"

Anne laughed.

"Not unless my two little girls qualify. They love to play with my hair. It's more fun than brushing their dolls' hair, especially as the dolls would soon be bald. They both have their father's hair, dark red. Their first question when they learned they had a little sister was 'Is she a blonde?' I don't know whether they hoped she would or wouldn't be."

"You make it sound like fun," the girl said, almost suspiciously, as if there must be a trick about it. "Having girls, I mean. Both mine are boys."

11

"I have three boys," Anne said. "They're fun, too."

"Don't you find them a great handful? Getting into mischief, and talking back, and fighting, and everything?"

"Their father keeps them in line," Anne said, thinking of three-year-old Brendan, with his seraphic little face and beguiling use of his father's native speech, usurping her place in the bed while she was gone.

The girl's next question took her by surprise.

"You're American, aren't you?"

"Oh, indeed, yes."

"I heard your husband talking last evening," the girl said. "I saw him, too, and is he ever something to see! You must look wonderful together, because you're fairly tall, too."

"Only medium. Five six."

"Well, that's good enough. Better than being a shorty like me. I'm only five one. I get so sick of always having to buy junior clothes. . . . But what I started to stay, I heard your husband talking last evening. At first I just put him down as Irish, with a strong brogue, but then two or three times I thought he said things to you in a foreign language."

"He did. In Irish."

"No kidding! You mean the Irish language is still really being used? I guess I just don't get around much. I thought all those writers like James Joyce and George Bernard Shaw wrote in English."

"They did. But my husband, though he was born in this country, spent most of his life on the west coast of Ireland. On the Arran Islands, actually. In the places where he lived as a child, more people used the old native speech than English. He speaks both."

"I suppose that accounts for it," the girl said. "I mean, for the rather odd and unusual way he has of speaking. You're going to think I'm frightfully inquisitive and without any manners at all, and the truth is I am, and I guess I haven't. I know your name is Anne, I heard your doctor call you that this morning. But what was it *he* called you? I couldn't make it out."

"You probably heard him call me Awineh Nee Vreeain."

"Awineh . . . ?"

"My maiden name was Anne O'Brien. In Irish that is *Áine Ní Bhriain*. He has always called me that."

"How charming."

12

The girl frowned in perplexity. "You know," she said, "it's rather a coincidence your mentioning the Arran Islands. I remember reading just the other day about someone from the Arran Islands—who could it have been? . . . Oh, I know. That policeman who kicked up all that fuss, charging there was police protection of all those gambling places and bawdy houses and what not. There's hardly been anything else in the paper all week. And not a word of truth in it, they say. All made up. All lies. He just wanted to get his name in the paper. Can you imagine anyone stirring up a hornets' nest like that, just for publicity?"

Anne stood up, with a light, free movement, as if she had suddenly been freed of something that had been weighing her down.

"I can imagine somebody doing it for quite other reasons," she said.

The calmness of her own voice surprised her. But it should not, she realized, because she felt no anger or resentment toward this child, whom she pitied. Far from feeling anger, she felt pure gratitude for the opportunity it gave her to stand beside him, though so small an opportunity and so far removed. The sympathy of friends, the indignation of those who saw truth pilloried, were hard to bear. But this was joy.

"You spoke, a few minutes ago, of the advantages you hope to give your children. Is there a greater advantage a father can give a child than the example of his own integrity, his own courage? If he had no other reason—this man you were reading about—I think that would be enough. How else," Anne asked, "could he meet the eyes of his children and not turn his own eyes away?"

The girl was pitiably ignorant and her sense of values was awry, but she was not unintelligent. "You are his wife."

"There is no other thing," Anne said, "that I could acknowledge with so much pride."

But a little later, sitting outside on the shaded balcony, she found that she was trembling. She did not feel quite so strong as she should. She had been careful not to let anyone know, because if they knew they might not let her go home. And she had to go home. The trouble and the worry had upset her, but she would be all right once she was home.

She heard the lunch carts coming off the elevators, but

she did not go back to her room. Best not to eat anything now. Best just to wait. Very soon he would come for her. Or if something prevented—if the trouble wasn't over after all, and he couldn't get away—he would send someone for her. Her father or her brother. Whatever happened, he would not forget the day or the hour—or her.

Don't think about the trouble, she told herself. Think about the children. Think how Nora will make a great event of the homecoming. Nora will make them all take baths and put on fresh clean clothes immediately after lunch, and then for an hour afterward forbid them to move hand or foot, for fear they might get dirty again, or might not be right there, ready and waiting, lined up on the front walk when the car stopped at the curb.

Think of the children. . . .

Brendan had disappeared. One minute he was there, the next minute he was gone. No one knew where. In the blinking of an eye he had vanished.

"I thought he was with you," Aunt Nora said to the girls, accusingly.

"No, he isn't with us, Aunt Nora. We thought he was with you."

"Paul, have you seen Brendan?"

"Isn't he here? I thought he was right here."

"Patrick!"

The piercing call from the foot of the stairs produced upstairs the sound of a door jerked violently open and slamming back against a wall.

"What!"

"Where is Brendan?"

"How should *I* know? *I'm* up here. *He's* down there!"

"He isn't! He's disappeared! He was here just a minute ago, and now he's gone. And I must leave. I'm going to be late for my appointment as it is. Come down at once, Patrick, and find him. At once!"

"I can't! I haven't anything on but a towel!"

"Why haven't you?"

"Because you told me to take a bath, and I don't take a bath with my clothes on!"

"Well, you're taking entirely too long!"

"It takes longer," came the bitter response, "when you've only got cold water!"

14

The door that had banged open banged shut.

"Brendan is a very troublesome child, Aunt Nora," seven-year-old Peggy said primly. "He hides. He does it all the time. To get attention."

"That child is being hopelessly spoiled," Aunt Nora said, peering distractedly behind the living-room sofa. She tried a feeble ruse. "Brendan, we know where you are. Come out, now. Come out at once. *Brendan!* . . . Oh, I do think you girls could have kept an eye on him. I'm going to be very late."

"But, Aunt Nora," Peggy countered with pious reproach, "you told us to watch out the window for Mother. We couldn't watch out the window and watch Brendan *both.*"

"He has to be somewhere in the house or yard," Katie said, with the logic of her almost-nine years, "because we would have seen him if he had gone out front. Besides, the latch is on the gate and he can't work it."

"Usually he hides under a bed," Peggy volunteered, without volunteering to make an under-the-beds search. "But one time he hid in the laundry basket under all the clean clothes. We didn't find him for hours that time, because he went to sleep. Mother got awfully scared and called Father, and Father got off from work and came home, and when Brendan heard Father's voice he woke up—and there he was!"

"Was he punished?"

"Why, no, Aunt Nora. He was so *happy* to see Father home in the middle of the afternoon."

"One time he hid in the kitchen closet behind the ironing board," Katie remembered. "It's the only closet there's any use looking in, because it's the only one with a light, and he can reach the chain. He'd never hide in a *dark* closet. I'll go look."

Six-year-old Paul offered a contribution.

"One time he hid in the cellar, in the coalbin. You should have seen him *that* time, Aunt Nora!"

"And one time in a bureau drawer——"

"And in the back shed——"

"And in my doll house——"

"Well, he must have exhausted all the possibilities," Aunt Nora said. "At least you know where to look. . . . Well! Are you *here,* finally, Patrick?"

Patrick, having a cold passion for justice, resented the

15

implication that he could have dressed and come downstairs any faster, especially after having to look fruitlessly for clean clothes and finally being obliged to put on one of his two good white shirts and the brand-new, very light-colored pants that had been reserved for starting back to school next week. On top of this was the initial offensiveness of being required to bathe and change his clothes when he hadn't been the least dirty in the first place. A number of stinging retorts came to mind, but he repressed them. ("Not would I hear again, Pádraig, of your speaking discourteously to your Aunt Nora. A good woman she is, and in kindness and love she set her own affairs aside to come here and help us in your mother's absence, though not even is she blood kin to us, but wife to your mother's brother, your Uncle Paul. Not will son of mine repay her with insolence and unfriendliness. Do you keep these words in mind.") He contented himself with asking, "What's all the fuss?"

"We can't find Brendan. I did think, Patrick—— Oh, my! *should* you have put on those new trousers?"

"They're all I have," Pat said, "except my Sunday suit."

"They're so light. I don't know what your mother was thinking of. They'll show every little spot of dirt."

"They're for school," Pat said in defense of his mother; and in defense of himself, "And I never get dirty anyway."

Aunt Nora, realizing that she had on her hands rather more than she could manage even when dealing with one thing at a time, decided against pursuing this line.

"I did think, Patrick, that I could depend on you to watch your little brother. Your father said——"

This was too much.

"*You* said I should go take a bath!"

"Patrick O'Nolan, do you want me to tell your father how rudely you speak? I should think," Aunt Nora said, "that you would have a little clearer recognition of your responsibility, a big boy like you. Ten years old! You're old enough to understand things. Your poor father, with all this trouble he's been having, and your poor mother, coming home from the hospital with a new baby, and not knowing at all what the future holds, and then to find Brendan missing. . . ."

"All right, Aunt Nora." Patrick squared off to meet his responsibility, and with it to accept the blame. "I'm sorry.

16

I should have taken him upstairs with me. But you don't have to wait. I'll find him. All I have to do is think."

"What you have to do is get busy and look for him, young man! What earthly good will it do to *think?*"

"I'm smarter than he is," Pat said coldly. "Do you imagine he could think of any place to hide where I can't think of looking for him?"

Aunt Nora was won by this logic. There was also something in the very look and manner of her nephew that won her—such a fine, strong boy, big for his age, so handsome with his golden hair and blue eyes and healthy coloring, so capable and dependable, so like his father in so many ways . . .

"Pat, dear," she said, "I know I can depend on you. Certainly, if your father trusts you, I can. And I simply must go now, but as soon as I get to the doctor's office, I'll telephone to know how you've made out. And unless you find Brendan in a very few minutes, or unless your father and mother come very soon, you are to go next door and tell Mrs. Moran. Do you understand?"

Pat said, "Yes, Aunt Nora."

He meant that he understood. Certainly he didn't mean that he would enlist the aid of old Mrs. Moran in looking for Brendan.

When Aunt Nora had gone, Pat folded his arms and pinned his younger sisters and brother with a stare. "All right. Which one of you knuckleheads saw him last?"

"Peggy did," Paul said at once.

"Paul did," said Peggy.

"What did you do to him?"

"Nobody did *any*thing to him."

"What did you say to him?"

"Paul said——"

"Peggy said——"

"One at a time! *You.*" Pat leveled a finger at his sister. "What did you say to him that made him go off and hide?"

"*I* didn't say anything," Peggy denied virtuously. "But Paul told him Mother wouldn't have any time to bother with *him* any more, now with a new baby."

Paul promptly retaliated. "You did so say something! You said Mother likes girls better than boys anyway!"

"And *you* said he couldn't sleep in the crib any more, in their room, because the baby would have to have it. You said Father was going to make him sleep in the attic, with the squirrels and the mice and the spiders!"

"I didn't say *mice!* And *you* said thousand-leggers!"

"Well, *I* say I ought to knock your heads together," Pat shouted, "till your brains, if you had any, would spill out all over the floor! Now get busy and look for him!"

"Where?"

"Everywhere!"

"I'm not going to," Peggy said, beginning to sniff. "I'm not going to get all hot and dirty crawling around on the floor looking under beds and bureaus. It would just serve him right if nobody *ever* found him!"

"You won't get half as dirty *crawling* around as you'll get being *dragged* around if you *don't* crawl! Now hike upstairs! And you"—to his brother—"take the cellar and the attic. And you"—to Katie—"go over the whole downstairs. I'll look outside. *Move!* It's quarter after one!"

But after everyone had covered his own appointed territory, and then had changed around and covered everyone else's, and then had assembled again, still they were only four. Feelings that had at first been merely of vexation were fast changing to alarm.

"He's simply *not* in the house. We've been up and down and all over a dozen times, and he's simply *not*. Pat"— Katie had been flushed from the exertion of the search, but now suddenly she was pale—"Pat, what are we going to do?"

"Keep looking, of course."

"But where? There's nowhere else to look. We've all looked in every possible place, and he's simply *gone*. Maybe," Katie said in an awful whisper, "maybe he's been kidnapped!"

And both girls began to cry.

Pat felt a chill go through his blood, but he said angrily, "You're nuts! He's right here somewhere, and I could find him if you'd just shut up and let me think!"

"Aunt Nora said we should go tell Mrs. Moran———"

"Well, we're *not* telling Mrs. Moran, or anybody else! You go back in the house and go through every room again, inch by inch. Hike, now. On the double!"

When they had gone back inside, Pat stood thinking. He had a heavy feeling in his stomach, and this interfered a little with the clarity of his thoughts. The heavy feeling was the weight of his responsibility, for was he not his brother's keeper?

"In your charge do I leave the younger ones, Pádraig, it being so that your mother and myself must both be away from this house, and no one but yourself to care for them between the time your aunt must leave and the time of my return. Know I well that I can put full trust in you to watch over them and see that none comes to harm, and this is a matter of much satisfaction to me and much pride. Not is it so that every man can depend in this way upon a son but ten years old."

His father depended on him. How could he face his father unless he found Brendan?

He forced his mind to go once more over every possible hiding place, making careful mental notes of each one that could sensibly bear re-examination.

He had looked under the front porch. Enough light came through the lattice so that he could see plainly; Brendan wasn't there. Nevertheless he looked again.

He had looked under all the bushes along the side of the house and along the fence, lifting the low-sweeping branches of the spirea to make sure. He looked again.

There was a wooden stoop at the back of the house, but no possible way of getting under it. He had put a flashlight to the cracks between the boards, anyway. There was nothing; it would be a waste of time to look there again.

At the end of the yard, backed up to the board fence along the alley, was a tool shed, six feet square. He looked in here again. It contained a lawn mower, a wheelbarrow, a rake, a pick and two shovels, some shingles left over from the new roof on the kitchen shed, two peach baskets (empty), a tricycle with one pedal missing, and a few hand tools hanging from hooks along the sides. Everything was very neat (it had to be, it was his assignment to keep it that way), and there was nothing a child, even a very small child, could hide behind or under. He closed the door.

The tool shed was set on a three-inch-high concrete foundation on the two sides and back. Purposely, for the rat-hunting convenience of the family cat, the foundation had not been extended across the front.

Against the shed, in the shelter of the east side, was the box which housed the family dog. The box was empty. Dinty, half-Irish terrier and half anything else, seldom used it in the summer, preferring to dig his way under the tool shed and lie in a cool clay cave underneath. He had recently devoted a good deal of time and energy to enlarging his summer residence, and there was a mound of loose earth directly in line with the tool-shed door. Pat had earlier kicked some of it away in order to get the door open.

Now Dinty stood before the door with his tongue hanging out and his somewhat less than half a tail wagging.

"Yeah, it's all right for you," Pat said, "to mess the place up. But I'm the one who's going to have to cart that stuff away."

Dinty, offering neither apology nor sympathy, continued to wag his tail. His interest was not in Pat's prospective labors, but in the enlarged entrance he had made to his ground cellar.

"Jesus, Mary, and Joseph!"

This was said strongly but only slightly above a whisper, because the use of these names out of their proper context received, if overheard, active paternal discouragement.

Dinty, at the same moment, put his nose to the hole and sniffed, the loud, woofing sniff that usually went with his examination of a rat hole or of a turtle safely withdrawn from him within its shell.

Pat shouted, "Come out from under there, you little rat! *Come out!*"

A muffled wail came back to him. Entreaty and terror were in it.

"I can't! Oh, Pat, I can't! Get me out, Pat, please get me out!"

Pat lay flat on his stomach and turned the beam of his flashlight under the tool shed. Far back in Dinty's cave, beyond Pat's reach, was his missing brother. Brendan had crawled under the shed as far as he could go. He couldn't turn to either side—the excavation at its far end was neither wide enough nor deep enough for turning unless he first backed up. And he couldn't back up, because a stout splinter had him firmly hooked by the seat of his shorts.

Pat raged: "It serves you right! I ought to leave you there! I'm *going* to leave you there! Till Pop comes home! And boy, will he give it to you this time! You just wait!"

"Oh, Pat, please get me out!"

"How can I? I can't reach you! And *I* can't crawl under there, the hole's not big enough!"

20

"Get me out, Pat, please get me out!"

"Well . . . wait," Pat said—unnecessarily, since Brendan's predicament certainly allowed no alternative—"I'll have to dig."

He got a shovel from the tool shed and set to work. Dinty's pile of loose earth was easy enough to move, but when he started on the ground under it, hard-packed by the going in and out of feet, and bone-dry from the summer's drought, digging was another kind of labor entirely. He had to use the pick. It was heavy, and took all the strength he had to swing it hard enough to make any impression on the packed earth. When he had a little of the surface broken, he went back to using the shovel.

And all the while came the piteous though muffled sound of Brendan's crying.

Pat said, "Oh, shut up!" but he jammed the shovel savagely against the ground and stood on it with both feet, jumping up and down to make it bite in.

His clean white shirt, already spotted with clay, was now plastered to his body with sweat. After a feverish ten minutes of digging and sweating and panting and resting (while Dinty spelled him and showered him with earth), and then digging again, he had enlarged the hole to a size that he thought would, by tight squeezing, permit him to crawl under. He lay flat again and managed to squirm his way into the cave far enough to reach his brother's feet. He tugged, but neither the splinter nor the shorts would yield. He worked his way farther under, until he had a hand on the seat of the shorts. He pulled, he jerked, he twisted, he said a few forbidden words—and the shorts came away from the splinter.

He took firm hold of his brother's ankles, one in each hand, and pushing with his elbows, started inching backward, snaking his body out. It was a laborious and infuriating exit, earning him sore elbows and sore knees and a painful bump when he lifted his head too soon. But, presently, he was out. He could breathe again. He struggled to his knees and pulled.

And there, presently, was Brendan also, once again in the light of day, a sorry sight indeed, covered from head to foot with damp bright orange clay, and raining tears of combined fear, remorse, relief, and gratitude.

Pat, still on his knees, gave a moment's vengeful thought

to spanking him, good and hard. Instead, he found himself thinking: Poor little guy! and—perhaps because he was still on his knees—saying a wordless little prayer of thanks to God for having found him.

Wordlessly, then, he got to his feet, reached down and took a tight grip on the waistband of the once-white shorts, lifted his little brother off the ground, and, wasting no time trying to set him on his feet—for at this point his legs were rubber—lugged him, helplessly dangling, to the house.

Katie met them at the back door, with a gasp and a flood of exclamations.

"Oh, my goodness! Where on earth . . . ? Pat, your new trousers!"

"Oh, sure," Pat said in bitter resignation, "I'll get whatfor. Go run water in the bathtub. Quick, will you! They'll be here any minute!"

Katie didn't stand to argue, but she called back as she ran, "There's no hot water, Pat. He'll yell murder!"

"Cold water was good enough for me," Pat said grimly. "Let him yell!"

At a point halfway home, pulling over to a shady spot beside the curb, Tadhg O'Nolan stopped the car.

"A thing or two it would be well for us to speak of," he said, "while yet we are alone. Then I think we will have little need to speak of it again."

Anne waited, very still. If she turned her head, she thought she would not be able to bear what she must read in his face, what she had heard in his voice—the hurt and the bitterness that were all he had won from his lonely fight. She kept her eyes, instead, on the face of the baby sleeping in her arms. The flower-face of the baby. . . .

"The matter which has been troubling us," he said, "is at an end. Not will it at this time be investigated further. Those against whom the slanderous charges were made are cleared. That one who made the charges, thoroughly has he been discredited. So the matter rests. But they are deemed good and kindly men, all of them, and in their charity it has been decided that none will take action against the accuser for the damage he misguidedly sought to work against them. Not is he to be called to answer for his slanders before a court of law. Not is he to be dismissed from the Department; for very just and generous, it is

22

stated, they all are, with compassion in their hearts, and not would they wish to see a man thrown out of work who has a wife and six children dependent upon him. Decided it is, then, merely to transfer that blundering, bullheaded fellow, O'Nolan, to another District."

"Tadhg. . . ."

He saw her close her eyes against tears, and was ashamed to know that he was causing her pain. He spoke sorrowfully, then, the bitterness gone from his voice.

"Do I ask you to forgive me, Anneen, for the hurt I have given you. And not do I mean the hurt of this moment alone, but all the hurt. So it is that when a man is set on doing according to his own way, it can sometimes be a cruel thing to others, even to those he holds most dear and could not wish to hurt."

"Tadhg . . . please . . . you have never hurt me. Never, never by anything you have ever done, never by anything you could ever do."

"A difficult and uneasy time it has been for you, you with the hour on you for the baby's coming and so much worry and grief besides. Only this can I ask you to believe: not could I do otherwise. Even had I known it must turn out this way—all for nothing, all a mockery—still could I not have done otherwise."

"Dearest, I know. Please believe, I know. Please believe that I would not have wanted you to do otherwise."

"*Creidim.* I believe. We have talked of it before; not would it be needful that we talk of it again, except that certain things must be known and faced. It is better, I think, that you know them now than that you become aware of them later and so have cause for later grief. . . . I have destroyed our future."

"*Destroyed?*"

"Not do they keep me on, as you must realize, for the reasons they said. They keep me on to silence me. Did they discharge me, and did I go before the Civil Service Commission with appeal, then would it all be aired again, and not could any say it might not take a turn, somewhere, to their disadvantage. But within the Department I can do nothing more. In another District, O'Nolan will be little threat to them. Care will be taken that no matter of policy, no deviation from the fixed rule, comes to his attention, for it is known now that he is uncooperative and not to be trusted. All this that has been in the newspapers will soon be forgotten; already has it lasted beyond the interest of most. So, too, will O'Nolan be forgotten, except by those who will keep his name on their blacklist. There will be no more advancement. What I am now—a sergeant of police—that I will remain. No more than that, to the end of my days."

"The examinations, Tadhg? You were first, you were highest. . . ."

"That will make no difference. A man who fails to qualify in any one respect can be passed over, no matter how he qualifies in other ways. It yet remains a matter of discretion. And favor."

"You do not have to stay. There are other fields. . . ."

"The blacklisting would reach out, I think, to the other fields, for there were some in very high places who interested themselves unduly in this matter. Did I give up a sure livelihood to seek an unsure, it might be at even greater cost. With the children to think of, I have not the right. Enough harm has been done. To take further risk I cannot."

"Whatever you do," Anne said, "I know it will be the best thing, the right thing."

"It is your love that speaks, Anneen, and not your reason. But I think I have greater need of your love than of your reason. By majority definition 'the right thing' and 'the best thing' can have much difference between them. Even some whom I hold to be my friends counseled that to do 'the right thing' was a fool's course, and better would it be did I look less to what was going on around me and more to which side of my bread has the butter on it. Stay clear of it yourself, they said, if you do not like it, but take care that you get in no one else's way. There is no percentage, they said, in being too honest. But not is O'Nolan a man who can be told. Even yet," he added with a grim smile.

"Tadhg, *I* cannot be told that the right thing and the best thing are not the same. And we have so much, dearest. We are so rich, so blessed by God."

"We are that," he agreed, "and I know it well. But responsibility goes with the blessing. To raise a family we must have money, and of money there will never be but enough to carry us through from the year's beginning to its end. There is war in Europe. Before this year is out, I think, we will have entangled ourselves in it also. The cost of living will go up, a little higher each year. We will have enough, *buíochas le Dia!*—thank God—to keep good food on our table and good shoes on our children's feet. But many things, many comforts and pleasures that I would see you have, many things the children will see that others have and they have not, will remain beyond the limits of what we can afford. This is part of the cost I have put on you and on them. And a bitter thing it may seem to some of them, when they are old enough to understand."

"When they are old enough to understand," Anne said, "they will see only the wonderful thing you have given them. They could not fail to see, and be your children. Dearest, it is not *your* fear of the future that makes you talk this way. And for me, where could I find a safer place in all the world than at your side?"

He smiled at her then. His face changed, and the whole day changed.

"*Áine Ní Bhriain,* it is time we go home. The children are waiting to see this small one."

And there they were. While the car was yet half a block away they could be seen standing on the front porch steps: Katie and Peggy and Paul.

But this was not the scene Anne had framed in the silver parallelogram last night.

Something was wrong with the picture. Was something wrong with . . . ?

She murmured anxiously, "Pat and Brendan?"

The three were at the gate when the car stopped, and an instant later they were through, shouting, "Mother! Mother!" Their father came around the car, opened the door for her, took the baby from her arms, and the children converged.

She gathered them in, all three at once, hugging them close.

"Darlings, darlings. How wonderful to see you. How wonderful you look. How wonderful to be home again!"

But where . . . ?

There. Just coming out the door. On the porch. Now coming down the steps. Now coming down the walk. Now waiting, just inside the gate.

Something very odd about them, surely.

Brendan had a thoroughly scrubbed, uncommonly rosy look. His hair, which was baby-soft and still a little long (his mother so loved the bright halo of red-gold curls that she had not yet been able to make herself run the clippers really close when she trimmed it), was wet, and had been given so vigorous a slicking-down that only the very ends of it were beginning to recover, springing up again in myriad little rings. He was spotless in white T-shirt and light tan shorts. He was poised on his toes, like a bird about to take flight. His hand was clasped tightly in Pat's, but it did not appear that he was clinging to his brother, rather that he was being clung to. His eyes were wide, beseeching, and blue-shadowed, as they became when he cried; they were dry of tears, but they seemed to his mother to be fearfully asking a question, to be seeking confirmation in her face of something he must know, yet dared not ask.

If Brendan had a fresh-out-of-the-bathtub look, what Patrick was fresh out of his parents could not guess. He wore, even more conspicuously than his earth-soiled, bath-splattered clothes, a very curious expression, at once challenging, defiant, self-satisfied, and resigned. The thought crossed his father's mind that calculated and open defiance of his Aunt Nora's passion for extreme cleanliness might explain his appearance; and if this were so, the further thought crossed his mind that he and his oldest son would in short order have a little set-to that would establish once and for all the unacceptability of conduct of such nature and for such reason.

Patrick met his father's sternly questioning eye with a bold and belligerent look, but in it there was also a little spark of laughter, as he made an all-but-imperceptible motion of his head downward toward Brendan.

Between son and father a message passed. It was not unusual that it could pass in this way, for their understanding of each other was intimate beyond any ordinary understanding, and many and many a time they passed their messages back and forth without need of words, without need even of change of expression, only their eyes meeting. Between them the unspoken could be as surely known as a man's own thought knows and understands itself.

Tadhg O'Nolan looked then from his oldest son to his youngest.

"A Bhreandáin," he said at once, for all that needed to be known of the strange appearance of these two was completely clear, "you it is who must be first to see *do dheirfiúr nuabheirithe,* your newborn baby sister, for closest is she to you, she being now the youngest and you the next to youngest. Now when you have first greeted your mother, who begins to grieve for thinking that no longer do you love her or have need of her after these many days, that even may you have forgotten her altogether and know not who she is . . ."

This was the signal. Pat released his hold, and the little boy ran to fling himself into his mother's welcoming arms.

After the reaffirmation of mutual maternal and filial devotion, his father sat on his heels on the front walk and gently folded back the edges of the little blanket.

"Now do you come here to me," he said, "for a question I would ask of you. Look."

Breathless with delight, Brendan looked.

"A Bhreandáin, nach í an bláth í? Is she not the flower? What name would best be on her, do you think?"

"Bláth?" the little boy asked doubtfully.

"A very special flower she is," his father said. "The fairest of them all. Would you not think she should be called by the name of the fairest flower of all?"

"Róis," Brendan whispered.

" *'S í sin a h-ainm.* That is her name."

Lightly but securely cradled, the baby lay in the curve of one arm. Tadhg O'Nolan put the other, strong, safe, and loving, around his little son, and there, when he stood up, was Brendan enthroned in the place he loved best to be.

Knowing that nothing would frighten him now, and counting on Pat not to tell (unless, of course, he was asked) whose fault it had all been, the children chorused the story.

"Brendan hid, Father."

"Under the tool shed——"

". . . in Dinty's hole."

"We couldn't find him——"

"He couldn't get out——"

"Pat had to dig him out, Father."

". . . and give him another bath."

But Brendan was safe. From his special refuge, from his impregnable fortress, he could smile at them. What they said now, what they had said before, mattered not at all.

Nothing could reach him now. Nothing could hurt or frighten or bewilder him. He was safe. In the one place where he was always safe. In the place he would always run to and always find open. In the place he loved.

He held no grudge, and when he forgave he forgot. He no longer remembered that it was Peggy and Paul whose fearful words had struck terror to his heart—such terror that he had been driven to bring on himself the second terror, the terror of Dinty's hole.

Safe on his father's arm, he blessed them with his smile.

2

BRENDAN ran up and down the yard.

He ran on his toes, so lightly that it could almost be imagined his feet never touched the ground at all. Light as a fairy, his mother thought fondly, watching from the end of the yard where she was taking down the clothes. Fast as the wind, thought Brendan exultantly, as on his way down the yard he raced ahead of the swirling little gusts that blew in from the street and opened paths through the fallen leaves, lifting them and sending them spinning.

So effortlessly did he run that he still had breath for singing.

Over and over he sang:

> *"Is Ó! goirim, goirim thú,*
> *Is grá mo chroí gan cheilig thú.*
> *Is Ó! goirim, goirim thú,*
> *'S tú peata beag do mháthar!"*

His baby sister Rose tried to run, too, but she was so very young—only fourteen months—that her running was limited to a few steps in pursuit of him, first one way and then the other, as he dodged around her and raced by.

The leaves were from Mrs. Moran's big catalpa tree next door. But they were his, all his; she said he could have them. All the beautiful, golden, heart-shaped leaves were his. To run through. To pile into a bed when he was tired of running. To take up singly, choosing the most perfect, the most golden, and marvel at the tracery of the veins, wondering what it would be like to be as tiny as the very tiniest ant, and follow all those little crisscrossing roads around and about over the leaf. You would get lost. You would never find your way home again. He was glad he wasn't an ant on the leaf. He was glad he was Brendan, who owned the leaf.

Lying there on a pile of leaves, he made up a little chanting song to them:

"Oh, leaves, leaves, leaves,
  Do you know is coming fall?
  Yes, said the leaves, we know;
  For there are no more strawberries,
  Or raspberries, or huckleberries.
  Winter is coming.
  In the summer will come more.
  In the summer will come more.
  In the summer. . . ."

The day before yesterday his father had taken him into the country. They had walked along a road—not a street, but a road made of yellow earth with leaves scattered over it. They had stood on a wooden bridge that had no railing, and had looked dizzily straight down to the glittering golden sand and pebbles over which the water ran. And on a high bank there were bushes growing, with bright red leaves and a few dried-up dark purple berries, though it was late, his father said, to find huckleberries still clinging to the bush. Next year they would go back in the summer, when he could eat the berries. He imagined them having a sweet, strange, dark purple taste, like nothing he had ever tasted; and they would be warm on his tongue, picked fresh from the bushes growing there in the sunlight on the high grassy bank beside the yellow road. . . .

He jumped up and put a leaf on Rosie's head, and told her it was a fairy's hat. He told her if she kept it on, she'd be able to see the fairies who lived under the bridal-wreath bushes. Rosie crept around looking under the bushes, but the leaf fell off and she couldn't see the fairies. He pointed them out to her—there, and there!—but she couldn't see them.

"Keep looking!" he told her, and began running again.

"Is Ó! goirim, goirim thú. . . ."

Mrs. Moran had come out to take the dry pieces from her wash line also, and she and his mother stood talking over the fence.

"Thank you, Mrs. Moran!" he called out as he flew past. "Thank you for the leaves!"

"That child seems made of light," Mrs. Moran said wonderingly. "Seventy I am and six months over, and never did I see the like of him before. And is it Irish he's singing, now for a fact? . . . Only fancy that! And here I am, an old woman and myself born in County Cork, and not understanding a word of it. Brendan!" she called. "Come tell me what you are singing!"

Brendan paused in mid-flight.

"It's 'The Shepherd's Lamb,' Mrs. Moran."

"And can you sing it for me in English?"

"Yes, but it isn't nearly so pretty in English."

"Well," said Mrs. Moran, "here I am, just a poor old body who doesn't understand any but English. Sing it for me, won't you?"

Brendan sang:

> " *Oh, I hail you, I hail you!*
> *You are my own heart's love so true.*
> *Oh, I hail you, I hail you!*
> *You are your mother's little pet!*"

"I think *you* are your mother's little pet!" Mrs. Moran said.

"No! Rosie is my mother's little pet!" Brendan took flight again, calling back, "I'm my father's little pet!"

"Bless the child!" said Mrs. Moran. "He's the great one for his father, is he? What a time they must have together, talking between themselves."

"Yes," Anne said, "they have all the rest of us at a disadvantage."

"And did none of the others pick it up so, from their father?"

"None of the others picked up anything but The Lord's Prayer. And you can hardly say they picked it up," Anne amended, laughing. "They learned it under considerable duress."

"Well, there," said Mrs. Moran. "That's more than most people can do, say a prayer in two languages. And are they all over their sickness now and back in school this morning?"

"They're all back. Pat wasn't out, he had mumps his first year of school. And the girls were lucky, their swelling lasted only two days. Paul was quite sick, though. He was the last one, and it seemed to hit him hardest."

"Well, that's the way. I remember some of mine were awfully sick with the mumps. But it's better for them to have all those things while they're little. *That* blessed lamb will be next," Mrs. Moran predicted, watching Brendan run through the leaves.

"I dread the thought," Anne said. "He's so especially pitiful when he's sick. By contrast, I suppose." Her eyes followed the small, flying figure. "And he's been riding so high," she added, "all this week, with his father home."

"That's it, now," said Mrs. Moran. "And what a pity for the two of them that this Grand Jury thing breaks right into his vacation."

"Yes," Anne said.

"With the jury already sitting for two months," Mrs. Moran said indignantly, "wouldn't you think they'd have called him sooner, or else waited? And on top of that, having him served with a subpoena, the same as those that are mixed up in it! My Bill says there wasn't any need of that! He says they just wanted to make it look as if he was mixed up in it, too. He says they knew very well Tadhg would come if he was just asked, himself being the very one who started the whole thing off a year ago. Well, some good may come of it for him at the end."

"He doesn't think so, Mrs. Moran."

"How not? With all the raids and arrests they've been making, and the changing around of police, and the closing up of those gambling houses and other places, and the whole town the better for it—there's many will be grateful when they remember it was him that started it all."

"The ones who will remember," Anne said, "won't be the ones with cause to be grateful."

"There, that's it," Mrs. Moran agreed. "And all tied up with politics the way it is, there's bound to be some of the guilty get clear of it. My Bill says it's just the little ones they'll send to jail. The big ones don't even get their names mentioned in the paper. Bill says some of the big ones are right there doing the investigating, when it's them should be investigated. And some of them are running the city, he says. He says if we knew who really owned those places, or if we knew who it was had really been taking in the protection money, then we'd really know something. But he says that won't come out."

"No," Anne said, "that won't come out."

"Well, at least," said Mrs. Moran, "now since they opened it up again, everybody knows that everything he told them last year was true, in spite of the way they covered it all up then. You just wait, dearie. Nothing lasts but for a while, and one of these days things will take a turn. You know the old saying: The honest man will get what he's entitled to. God will reward a fine young man like your husband. Now you just mark my words."

A car stopped in front of the house. They heard Brendan's glad shout as he passed them, *"Tagann m'athair!* Comes my father!" and watched love put wings to his already flying feet.

"Dia's Muire dhuit, Dia's Muire dhuit, a Athair!"

As he asked the blessing of God and Mary on his father, Brendan climbed on the gate, flinging himself recklessly up and over into the arms that reached for him.

His father, making the standard reply, asked the blessing of Saint Patrick, also.

"Dia's Muire dhuit is Pádraig, a Bhreandáin."

"Céad míle fáilte, 'Athair! A hundred thousand welcomes!"

"Go mairidh tú. May you live."

Rosie came out from under the bushes, having forgotten, if she had ever known, what it was she had been looking for. Drawn by the same magnet, she also ran toward the gate, needing to pick herself up only twice on the way.

Tadhg O'Nolan came down the yard holding a child on each arm. In the double encounter his hat had been pushed back on his head to a carefree angle, which had the effect of belying the strain of the weary and frustrating hours.

Anne wasn't deceived. Her heart ached with her love for him, and with her helplessness.

"And is it over so soon?" Mrs. Moran asked. "We didn't think to see you home so early. We thought it likely they might keep you yet another day with their questions."

"Not is it over." He made light of it with his smile. "Not has it even begun. From half-past eight till half-past one did I but keep a chair warm for them in the anteroom, and then was I told to come back tomorrow."

"You haven't had lunch, then," Anne said.

"Níl ocras orm," he answered, and looked at his son. *"A mhic,* now do you tell your mother what I said, for not has she good Irish as you have, and already she may be thinking to hurry in and fix *an béile mór*—a big meal—for me."

"Níl ocras ar m'athair," Brendan said to his mother, and wondered why they laughed.

"Better would it be did you tell her in English," his father suggested.

"My father isn't hungry," Brendan said.

"Tell her: *Ba mhaith liom cupán tae amháin agus ceapaire cáise.*"

"My father would like a cup of tea and a cheese sandwich."

"Má's é do thoil é."

"Please."

"The wonder of it!" Mrs. Moran exclaimed. "That precious child understands every word you say!"

"Is Éireannach é."

"I am an Irishman," said Brendan.

"Bless the child!" said Mrs. Moran.

" *'Athair*"—Brendan pointed to the golden carpet over the yard—"Mrs. Moran gave me the leaves. All the leaves!"

"Go gcúití Dia léi é!" his father said at once. "May God reward her for it! The saint she is, in her kindness."

"I expect God looks for better things than that to hand out His rewards for," said Mrs. Moran. "It's more reward than I deserve, just to watch the glad time he's been having."

"There is none so glad as Brendan when Brendan is glad," Tadhg O'Nolan answered, looking with laughing tenderness into his son's face, "and none so sad as Brendan when Brendan is sad."

He set the little boy down.

"Go you now," he directed, "and gather the tools we will need, and when I have had my bite of lunch, we will mend the front porch with new boards. That much time have we left of the day."

Golden was the time left of the day. The bright sun came slanting in to the place where they worked, and the bright wind came blowing, and to Brendan's ears the sounds of hammer and saw were music.

Five blows drove each nail down. He sang to the rhythm of the hammer:

"A haon—a dó—a trí—a ceathair—a cúig!
Is fear—láidir—m'athair-se—'slaoch—cruaidh!"

Sometimes his father, "the strong man and hard warrior," teased him by striking a nail only four times, so that he must hold back the "*a cúig*" already on the tip of his tongue; or by striking an extra blow, making him quickly add, "*a sé!*"

There were many things he could do to help. He had each tool ready and near to his father's hand, as needed. He held the nails and doled them out one by one. He stood on the boards to hold them steady while his father sawed, or he supported the ends so they wouldn't drop too soon under the sawing and split the wood. But between times, while his father took measurements or did some careful work with chisel or plane to make two boards fit together so neatly that no one could see the patch, he amused himself with the brace and bit.

His father let him have one of the old discarded boards and told him he could make as many holes in it as pleased him, but he must be sure to have another old board under it, so that the auger did not by accident go through and make a hole in one of the new boards, where no holes must be. Kneeling, Brendan leaned all his weight on the brace and turned it round and round, and round and round —and it took a lot of turning to make a hole, much more turning than when his father did it. While he turned he sang, making up words to match the turning:

"Round and round Mt. Everest comes,
Higher and higher the sun rises day,
Round and round the sun comes night,
Faster and faster the world goes round,
Tipple, topple, goes the world!"

Tadhg O'Nolan, listening, paused in his work to note the words of this curious song on a scrap of paper. Only so could a man capture and hold what was as elusive and fleeting as a wild bird's song, and in another moment would be gone from memory, gone out of time, as the dew from the leaf or warmth from an October afternoon when the sun goes down.

He had tucked the scrap of paper away in his shirt pocket and had again taken up mallet and chisel, when his attention was caught by a car stopping at the curb. Two men got out and came across the sidewalk to the gate. He knew them well—they were men from his old Police District, men he had long worked beside but had not seen in the past year, since his transfer. He got to his feet and waited. Over his mind a cold stillness settled. He watched them open the gate and walk up to the porch, and he let them be the first to speak the words of greeting.

"How are you, boy?"

The heartiness was overemphasized. The friendliness was false. His ear caught both notes plainly.

His little son—perhaps hearing the same false note, or perhaps merely frightened of strangers—came quickly to stand close beside him, slipping a small, anxious hand into his.

"Long time no see," the visitors said. "How's the world been treating you?"

They put out their hands, and because ancient customs of hospitality required it, Tadhg O'Nolan shook hands with them and returned their greetings.

They leaned against the porch railing and talked of the weather, and Adolf Hitler, and the progress of the war, and whether or not F.D.R. would run for a fourth term. He listened, made an occasional comment for politeness' sake, and waited. Brendan, deciding that the intrusion was without element of danger and that listening to the conversation was far less enjoyable than working with the brace and bit, went back to making holes.

"I hear they're having you up before the jury," one of the men said at last. "Tomorrow, is it?"

"Today it was to be."

"Oh, today. Didn't they get to you?"

"Not did they."

Into his mind the thought came: Because it was desired by someone that you get to me first.

"Well, it looks like you're still the star witness, Sarge. But

I guess," one of them said with a knowing look, "you'll soft-pedal it this time."

"What is asked me, will I answer."

"Oh, sure. But by this time there must be a lot you've forgotten."

"Not am I a man who forgets."

"Oh, come off it. Last year's dead. It couldn't be deader. You aren't going to muck through all that ancient history, are you?"

"That which is history is already a matter of record."

"That's where you're wrong. They tell me those old files got lost, somehow. It beats all," the man said with a grin, "how careless the office help is nowadays."

"Not have the newspaper files been lost."

"I don't think the newspapers would do the jury much good, even if they could use them. The newspapers only printed portions of your testimony, not the whole transcript. And they were polite about a lot of names. Hell of a lot of names they just couldn't bring themselves to mention, they were so polite. Well, I was brought up on the idea it pays to be polite. Ever think it might pay you?"

"Had you other business with me?" Tadhg O'Nolan asked coldly, picking up his saw.

"Don't go getting on your high horse, Sarge. We're old friends, aren't we? Just old friends trying to look out for your interest. Like to see you get ahead. Best man on the Force. Hell of a note if the best man on the Force never got to be anything higher than a desk sergeant. Fellow told me there's going to be a lot of vacancies away up there when they get through firing all the top brass that's been tarnished by this little ruckus. Wouldn't be a bit surprised to see you step right into one of them. Wouldn't be surprised if a little bonus went along with the job, too. Maybe as much as five G's. You're a family man, Sergeant. You think a lot of your family and you'd always want to do right by them, wouldn't you?"

"Also would I wish to do right by any who attempt to suborn a witness."

The two men laughed.

"You always did use big words, Sergeant. Like we told you, we're just old friends. Just trying to show you the angles, for old time's sake. Suborn? Not us. You're too smart a cop to think you could make that stick, on your unsupported word against the two of us. You've got a witness," said one of them, looking down, "but I'm afraid he'd leave your story as full of holes as he's going to leave your porch."

"Well," said the other, "you'll see us around, Sergeant. We expect to be downtown bright and early tomorrow morning ourselves. Think it over and look us up. Just give us the old high sign, and I think maybe we can put you in touch with a fellow you'd like to talk to."

As the visitors went down off the porch, one of them turned to say, "We've only showed you one side of the coin, Sergeant. Bear in mind that it has a reverse side also."

"To whomever sent you, do you take back the word that O'Nolan answers with the reverse side of his hand!"

The men laughed heartily without mirth, unlatched the gate, and let themselves out of the yard.

Four young O'Nolans, slipping past, let themselves in and came up on the porch.

The girls, vying with each other to be first to reach their father, reached him simultaneously, one on each side. Paul took a quick inventory of the short pieces of new wood sawed off the ends of the boards, wondering if he could have them to build something with. Pat looked to see how much of the old flooring needed to be removed and replaced, and estimated that he and his father could easily finish the job by supper time.

Tadhg O'Nolan stood watching the car until it was out of sight. The voices of the children broke against him like waves running on a stony beach.

"Father, we had an arithmetic test and I got a hundred—even after being out two weeks!"

"Father, Winnie Ring is having a Halloween party, and we're invited. May we go? Oh, please, may we go?"

"We saw where a big tractor-trailer jackknifed and upset, and about a million dozen eggs all over the street!"

"Hey, for Pete's sake!" This was Pat, staring down at the handiwork of his youngest brother. "Look what this little goof-nut has done! Made a hole right down through the porch!"

It was true.

The three-quarter-inch bit had gone clear through the old

38

discarded board and right on down, neat as you please, through one of the brand-new boards that his father had just laid.

Brendan looked at it in horror. His father had warned him that he must be careful. His father had said that he must have *two* old boards, one on top of the other. And he hadn't remembered about the two boards. While the men were there, talking, he had been carried away by his zeal, by his song, by his delight. He had just kept turning and turning, and he hadn't noticed that the brace going round and round, and round and round, had driven the bit round and round through the thickness of two boards instead of only one.

The gold edges of the day were dulled. The sun wasn't shining so warmly on the porch any more. The wind had a chill to it.

Tears filled his eyes. He looked up. He whispered, " '*Athair?*"

The look he saw on his father's face struck him numb with bewilderment and fear. He had never seen so strange, so cold a look. He knew the dreadfulness of what he had done, he knew he must meet his father's displeasure. On two or three occasions he had met it before, and it had rocked his world, even when it had been no more than a word or two of stern reproof. Never on any occasion had his father's displeasure been so great that it overshadowed his love.

Until now.

Now he saw only a terrible anger. Cold and hard as stone, his father's face had a look on it that seemed to take him far away, far beyond anywhere, farther than could ever be measured or known, though he was standing right there on the porch. Katie and Peggy stood one on each side of him, their arms around him, and his around them; yet he seemed, in some terrifying way, to be far away from Katie and Peggy, too, as if he didn't know he was standing there between them, holding them close.

"Look at that!" Pat said. "Just look! You'll have to take all six of those new tongue-and-groovers out to get at it!"

Now his father looked down. Brendan, watching fearfully, could see him come back, slowly, from that far place; and just when he thought he could no longer bear it—the terrible, cold anger, the unlovingness—his father looked up from the hole in the board, looked up just high enough to meet his eyes.

Then everything about the awful moment changed. The coldness melted like ice in a summer sun. Warmth came back, first into his father's eyes, then into the gold October day. His father's arms around the girls suddenly tightened and he hugged them close.

Then his father laughed. Oh, it was wonderful laughter, rich and reassuring.

"A family man!" his father exclaimed. "Did they say it themselves, those two, and the true word they spoke! A man would wish to do right by his family, they said. Well would he indeed, and it be such a family as mine! *A Bhreandáin*"—he held out his arms, and with a little whimpering sound of relief and joy Brendan ran into them—"not will we concern ourselves about the hole. So it has been told me—and was it not yourself who told it me?—that the Little People who live under the bushes beside the house through the summertime, have winter residence beneath our porch, where they are snug and safe from the cold rains and the snow. When the sun moves low across the south, will it then come shining in here all day long, and very grateful will they be, I think, for the spot of sunlight you have given them, to cheer them through the weary winter months."

"*'Athair*"—this thought was so entrancing that Brendan's mind leaped at once to lay hold of it as his own, and to expand and embellish it—"I'm almost sure it was really the Little People who were turning the brace. I was just holding it."

Everybody laughed except Pat, who strongly disapproved of this line.

"Well, you sure handed him a nice out on *that* one!" Pat said witheringly, his disapproval very plain.

They went back to work, to finish the repair of the porch before the day ended. Pat came to help, after he changed his clothes. His father marked the boards and Pat sawed them, and the work went fast. Brendan handed nails. Between times he kept peering down the hole, wanting to see what the little spot of sunlight looked like, but he couldn't see anything.

40

"Of course not, dopey!" Pat said. "You're covering up the hole!"

Brendan went down off the porch and peeped through the little squares of the lattice, shielding his eyes from the outer light with his hands. And sure enough, there it was— a little oval disk of sunlight in the semidark of the cave under the porch. He didn't see any fairies, but then on such a beautiful day, of course they'd still be outside under the bridal-wreath bushes.

He didn't touch the brace and bit again. It was too risky. Even the fairies might not be able to get him off a second time.

Besides, he was tired. Kneeling beside his father, taking nails out of the bag and passing them one by one, he began to feel very sleepy. Very sleepy and somehow a little queer. The sun was still bright, the day was still warm and not as windy as it had been, yet every now and then he shivered.

He got so very sleepy that he began to sway, and once he almost lost his balance. When this happened, his father put out a hand to steady him, and then laid the hand against his forehead.

For another moment they knelt there side by side, looking at each other, reluctant to put the unhappy truth in words.

"*A mhic mo chroí*, son of my heart," his father said sadly at last, "there is fever on you."

"*Níl fiabhras orm, a Athair*," Brendan pleaded. "*Níl. Tá codladh orm*. I have no fever. I am just sleepy. Isn't that all, '*Athair?*"

With thumb and finger tip Tadhg O'Nolan gently touched his son's neck, at a spot on each side, just below the ear, just behind the jawbone.

"Doesn't it hurt you there?"

"I was just wondering if it did," Brendan said piteously.

His father laid the hammer down and got to his feet.

"Do you come now, my son. *Tá sé i n-am codlata dhuit.* For you it is bedtime."

"Will I be very sick, '*Athair?*" Fear shadowed the question.

"*Beidh an Naomh Mháthair Dé ad' choimhdeacht.* The Holy Mother of God will be watching over you."

Brendan put his arms around his father's neck and his

41

head on his father's shoulder. The last thing he saw, as he was borne into the house, was that the sunlight was gone from the porch.

When he fell asleep, the golden leaves of the catalpa tree went blowing through his dreams.

3

IN THE fall of 1943, soon after he was twelve years old, Patrick O'Nolan declared himself a free and sovereign state. Not, to begin with, in so many words. Rather it was by the contumacy of act and deed that his new independence was proclaimed.

Pat held certain truths to be self-evident, among them his own natural superiority to most, and the qualifications that entitled him to stand second to none. That he should be prevented from taking his rightful place in the world until he reached a designated, wholly arbitrary age by the calendar was, as he saw it, a discriminatory form of nonsense, and he set himself stoutheartedly to overthrow this outworn and senseless tradition.

Self-willed he had always been, and defiant when thwarted. Conflict with constituted authority had flared as early as his second year, when he had learned to plant his feet, fold his arms, and say *"Won't!"* Even at that age he had not yielded to argument, to coaxing, to threat or to the implementation of the threat. He had not yielded, in the true sense of the word, at all. It had been necessary physically to overpower him and bear him bodily from the field, to him an outrageous act of aggression against a sovereign entity. The folded arms, the firmly planted feet, the belligerent readiness to make his stand against any odds, became the symbol of his statehood, persisting through the years.

On earlier occasions his defiance had been for a reason: when, for example, told to do something he objected to doing, or forbidden to do something he wished to do, or questioned for the truth (which he always gave boldly) concerning some piece of mischief, or punished for some disobedience or other unseemly behavior. Now the defiance was purely for its own sake: to establish his position, to demonstrate his self-evaluation. It was a matter of pride. He was willing to suffer for it, as the martyrs for their faith.

The shards of old established rule lay all along the new path on which he so willfully and obstinately set his feet. To a large extent, from this point on, he made his own rules.

It began with the breaking of what he indignantly and contemptuously termed his "yard arrest."

The young O'Nolans had always been yarded. They lived too late to enjoy freedom of the streets, even the streets of the immediate neighborhood, clean and essentially respectable though it was.

Their own mother, as a child in this same neighborhood, had known and enjoyed all the little pleasures that spell freedom to a city child: the dallying walks home from school; the sidewalk games; turn after turn around the block to the humming of roller skates; the summer nights, gathering in little groups on someone's front steps or walking up and down from the house to the corner, safely within sight of parents who were all sitting out on the little porches enjoying the cool dark, and whose voices reached down to the street in fragments of conversation or laughter, reassuringly near yet not intruding on the children's sidewalk world. But all that was over. The neighborhood had changed, not so much within itself as by the encroachment upon it from all sides of hazards that had belonged, in their mother's childhood, only to *other* neighborhoods, comfortably distant.

Automobile traffic was the greatest hazard, the one that took the largest toll, though it was not the most fearful. Parents who nostalgically remembered that old sweet freedom of the sidewalk world in the after-school and early-evening and all-day-Saturday hours, found that they must deny it to their children. The speeding car and the hit-run driver had invaded that world. More dreadful still was another invader whose numbers seemed yearly to increase: he might be your own neighbor's adolescent son or a "cured" habitual offender, you never knew, you couldn't recognize him on the street; but when one day some little girl didn't come home from school and searchers found her body in the cellar of an empty house, then you knew he was there.

Invading, too, were the gangs of juvenile hoodlums from other neighborhoods, roaming the fringes of this. Once in a while some boy coming home after dark was set upon by one of these packs and viciously beaten. The neighborhood boys, gathering on the street corners in little groups, secretly began recruiting their own gang, to be ready for the others when they came. Secretly they armed themselves, as the enemy did, with switchblade knives and blackjacks and short pieces of chain, anything that could be easily concealed in their pockets, including, inevitably, two or three small revolvers. The outside-of-the-neighborhood gangs had made no foray in recent weeks, so there had been no outbreak of juvenile hostilities; but the weapon supply carried its own suggestion of other uses. From time to time someone getting off a bus or trolley car at a lonely corner was knocked down and robbed. From time to time some storekeeper—often an old woman who kept a little tobacco or candy shop—was held up at gunpoint by boys with stockings pulled over their heads. From time to time a car left parked with the keys in it was stolen, to be discovered later, abandoned or wrecked somewhere on the other side of town.

Anne had lived in a row house, with the freedom of the street; her children, denied the freedom of the street, had at least the compensation of a yard, where grass and flowers and a cherry tree could grow, and games could be played, and a dog could be kept.

The section of the city in which they lived had been developed at the turn of the century, when it lay next door to open country. Space had been plentiful, then, and the developer, building one entire block of houses himself, six on each side of the street, to spur the sale of his building lots, had allowed generous clearance between the houses. Perhaps he had foreseen a day when that block, set in the very heart of row houses crowding all around, would be like a clearing in a forest. To each of the four corners he had allotted 100 by 150 feet of ground, and on each he had built a durable, three-story, ten-room house. When young Tadhg O'Nolan (twenty, in love, and newly returned from the land of his ancestors to the land of his birth) went house-hunting in 1930, the corner house he chose was as sound as the day it was built. Real-estate values were down —it was during the Depression—and a thirty-year-old house, sound but a little shabby and quite out of fashion, found few takers. The O'Nolans had been able to purchase it very reasonably, and a few years later, when values went up again, they could have sold the side yard for half as much as they had paid for house and all. Down the street, on the next corner, the property owner had done this, and a new house had been built, not ten feet away from the wall of the old. But what then of the children, with most of the yard gone and streets unsafe? "Not is the land for sale," said Tadhg O'Nolan, thinking not only of three-year-old Patrick and two-year-old Katie already playing in the yard, but of the baby not yet walking, and the one not yet born, and the others who would follow in their time, God willing.

The yard, then, increasing in importance as time went on, had doubled in importance by the time Pat was twelve. Other children could enjoy the benefits of the yard, as many as cared to, but the O'Nolans could not, except by special permission, go out unaccompanied except to school. Patrick himself was guardian of the gate.

But Patrick, after his twelfth birthday, ceased altogether to regard himself as a child. All the old, long-established rules, still applicable to his younger brothers and sisters (whom he pointedly referred to as "the kids"), ceased therefore, as he saw it, to apply in any way whatsoever to him. His only connection with them now (in his own mind) was as a law-enforcement officer: it was his duty to see that the others obeyed the rules. He, himself, would go and come as he pleased. He was the young lord of the house, and his own man.

One of the fixed rules made it mandatory that all walking to and from school must be together. No travel by singles or even by pairs was permitted. The four school-age O'Nolans traveled as one.

Pat did not, on that historic day when he fired the first shot from his embattled position on the bridge, flout this rule. His sense of responsibility was too strong for that. He walked home as usual with Katie and Peggy and Paul, seeing them safely inside the yard, where his responsibility could rationally be considered to end. He then went upstairs and changed his clothes. This also was a rule, and this also he obeyed—because he chose to. He was careful of his clothes for reasons of economic necessity (which he fully understood, being no longer a child) and of personal fastidiousness, which was by nature deeply ingrained. But when he had changed his clothes and come downstairs again, he announced to his mother, with studied casualness: "I'm going out."

This should not, of course, have been under any circumstances a declarative statement, but an interrogation in which the word *may* should have occupied a conspicuous position. But his mother was never too demanding about form—she preferred to interpret the spirit in which a thing was said, and as the casual tone in no way suggested deliberate intent to substitute an announcement for what should have been a request, she passed over this slight irregularity and said, "To the store, Pat?"

There was a little variety store two blocks over, and occasional afternoon sorties upon it, for school supplies or other items when someone had a bit of change to spend, were permitted.

"Brendan would love to go with you. His grandfather gave him a quarter today for reciting the *Salve Regina* in Irish. He has been living in a dream all afternoon, thinking of all the things he's going to buy with it. Have you time to take him with you?"

"I'm not going to the store."

"Where then, darling?"

"Just out."

The spirit in which this was said could not be interpreted in any way but one. Peggy and Paul looked at each other in astonishment.

Anne said, "Pat, I have to know where you're going."

"I can't tell you," Pat answered. "I don't know myself." And he went out.

He was home five minutes ahead of his father, after having been gone almost two hours. His mother gave him one hurt and anxious look, and then avoided looking at him again. She said nothing before supper, and through the meal she was very quiet. Pat knew she was nervous and unhappy because she would have to tell his father what he had done. For this he felt no resentment. It was her duty to tell; she would be guilty of concealment and dishonesty if she didn't. He was opposed on principle to concealment and dishonesty, and certainly wouldn't look for them or wish for them in his own mother. He had chosen his course with full awareness of its consequences. He had no intention of trying to escape the consequences by saying he was sorry and he wouldn't do it again, because he *wasn't* sorry and he *would* do it again, and was fully prepared to say so even if it won him a double dose. He knew what he was in for, and that he had no one to charge it to except himself. He accepted the charge.

His father, being a perceptive man, knew as well as Pat did that there was reason for the quietness. He also read the looks of the children, who kept sending quick and covert glances across the table in the direction of their oldest brother. The glances revealed a wide range of feeling, from simple curiosity to a deep anxiety that halfway through the meal could contain itself no longer and found release in tears.

This was Brendan. He had listened to the talk of the others before supper; he knew that Pat had done a forbidden thing for which he was certain to be punished, and the thought of Pat being punished—Pat, whom he worshipped as a junior god—was more than he could bear. When one of his appalled glances was intercepted by his father, the awfulness of impending doom overwhelmed him, and he put his head down and wept quietly into his plate.

This brought the matter out of the realm of shadow into the hard white light.

"Now is it time, I think," his father said, "that some explanation be given me of the curious atmosphere which surrounds this table."

The explanation was given briefly, for Anne preferred to let the details of the incident rest between them. She did not, as she knew she might, wish to make things any harder either for her son or for her husband, by following Brendan's example and allowing her tears to show.

"When you have finished your supper, Pádraig," his father said, with what might have been deceptive calm if Pat had not very well known that calm would make the ultimate carrying out of sentence no lighter, "you will go upstairs."

Subsequently, upstairs, Pat's explanation of his conduct made the whole little escapade completely understandable, though not in any degree excusable. His father listened

48

carefully, without anger, to the explanation. He weighed it, he asked a few questions.

"Where did you go?"

Pat knew better than to answer "Nowhere." Vagueness of speech was not tolerated by his father, who used words for their meanings and saw to it that his children did the same. Knowing this, Pat had ready a short but roughly comprehensive description of his itinerary.

"To the drugstore. From there up past Kinney's garage as far as the avenue. Then around the ball park and home."

"Two hours would it take you then, to walk so far?"

"Part of the time I just stood around."

"Alone?"

"Mostly. I met a couple of fellows I know. We talked a little. Some kids were playing ball on Hanlon's lot. I watched for a while."

"And had you pleasure in doing this, Pádraig?"

"I wasn't looking for pleasure. I just wanted to do it, that's all. I have a right to do it!" Pat said, flaring.

"A very questionable right, is it not, that one? A right to disobey your father?"

"It's your own fault!" Pat's arms were already folded, his feet already planted; further expression of defiance could only be added by the set of his jaw and the belligerence of his tone. "It's your fault for trying to make a lot of rules that only a baby *wouldn't* disobey!"

"*Trying* to make rules, do you say?"

"Well, okay, making them! I don't say it's not all right for the kids," Pat conceded. "But I do say it's not all right for me!"

"Not can I suppose," his father said, still without anger but with very plain meaning, "that you think to get away with it, Pádraig."

Pat answered with injudicious triumph, "I *got* away with it! I did it, didn't I! Oh, sure, I know. Well, go ahead, see if I care!"

"Now, Pádraig, I think I can make you care. . . ."

"I'll go again tomorrow!" Pat said recklessly. "I'll go any time I want! You can't stop me!"

"Tomorrow it may be so," his father answered, "that you will go again. But I think the next day you will not wish to go."

The first round, it might be said, had ended in a draw.

Thereafter, through that fall and winter, ensued a long war, in which sharp attack and counterattack alternated with periods of quiet and accord. Pat, being no fool, did not push his campaign to a point which might have resulted in complete rout of his forces. His resolve had been to do as he pleased. He had made no committments to himself at the outset as to what his pleasure must be at any given time or in any given circumstances, so there was in no sense any admission of faintheartedness, much less of defeat, if at any time it better pleased him to stay than to go.

He waged a war of attrition, and he knew that in the end he must win, because time was on his side. There could be no other outcome. Whether or not he had been premature in asserting his independence and in establishing (to his own satisfaction) his equality and his separate and sovereign rights, it would have the same end: his father must eventually grant him formal recognition. They both knew it. The knowledge won no relaxation of parental authority and no remission of the fixed price he must pay for defiance of it, but it provided him with an underlying sweet foretaste of triumph, which was balm to his soul.

His father made one concession.

"Now if you must persist in this course, Pádraig, not are you longer forbidden to do so. But mistake me not. Do you, when you come home from school, go off in this manner which you well know displeases your father and grieves your mother, you will be punished. *I* will punish you. But, if you must go, then so it is, you must go. Not do I forbid it, for not will I have you go again with the sin of disobedience on your soul, that God must also be obliged to punish you for that you have set yourself against His commandment to honor thy father and mother."

This did not, of course, cause Pat to increase the frequency of his after-school expeditions. On the contrary it caused a falling off, as his father had known it would; for defiance that had as its prime motive the pure (or impure) satisfaction merely of a wish to defy, lost much of its savor with the technical lifting of the ban. To lose the peculiar satisfaction of disobeying, yet to retain the consequences, made the continued following of this particular course seem merely silly. Pat saw a clean, brave line of demarcation between something that might be termed foolhardy, such as his recent conduct, and something that could only be

50

termed foolish. It was not in him to be foolish. It became necessary, therefore, to review his position and revise his strategy.

The next step, obviously, was to leave the house *after* supper. But this presented much greater difficulty, required much greater finesse, and would, indeed, have appeared quite hopelessly impossible to any but the most determined and the most ingenious.

His father was home in the evening. True, there were occasions, occurring perhaps once in two weeks, when he wasn't. Physically, it would have been the easiest matter in the world to bide his time until one of these occasions turned up and then simply walk out of the house, unopposed, as he had been walking out after school. However, there were other obstacles to this course, three in fact, and all insurmountable. First, if he did that, the defiance would still have the character of being directed first-hand against his mother, whom he had neither reason nor wish to defy. *She* was not the one who made the rules, nor the one who enforced them. There was no satisfaction to be drawn from defying his mother; it required no courage, no proud front; and far from being an act that he could boast of, it was a shabby thing of which he would feel ashamed. To leave the house at night in his father's absence, then—and this was the second obstacle—would not be *boldly defiant*. It would merely be sneaky. And Pat despised a sneak.

But the third and greatest obstacle was that to leave the house at night in his father's absence would be a negation of responsibility and a breach of trust. For years, on such nights, it had been his responsibility to wait up with his mother. "Will it be late," his father used to say, "before I return. Do you wait up, Pádraig, in case your mother has need of you, and that she does not sit alone." It became so much a matter of understanding between them that for a long while now it had ceased to be necessary to issue the instruction directly, for part of the pattern of life was that he would wait up with his mother on nights when his father must be away. Even as recently as two weeks ago, with the rebellion in a most flagrant stage, his father had left the house one night without a word to remind him of his obligation; without even a look that could be called a look, for their eyes had met so fleetingly that no one else could have been aware of their having met at all. His father depended on him to stay; knew he would stay; completely trusted him to stay. To leave the house at night, in his father's absence, therefore, was unthinkable.

So it was necessary to lay very careful groundwork for his next move.

Having laid it, he came into the living room one evening about seven-thirty; came through it, rather, for it was plain that he was on his way to the front door. His father was sitting in the big chair under the lamp. Only Brendan was with him, perched on a stool close beside the chair, with a book which was a part of the evening ritual. (Brendan had not yet started school, nor was the book one that he would learn to read in school when he did, for it was a collection of the Ossian legends of Finn MacCumhail, and it was printed in Irish. He and his father were reading it together aloud, his father pronouncing each word slowly and distinctly, and Brendan's soft, musical little voice following one syllable behind.) Anne was upstairs putting Rosie to bed. The other children were still gathered around the dining-room table, doing their homework.

The stage was well set. Patrick, on his way through the living room, with superb nonchalance spoke to his father in passing.

"I've finished my homework. I'm going out for a while."

He knew he would be stopped before he reached the door, knew it so well that he stopped a fraction of a second before his father spoke. He knew, too, exactly how his father would play out the little scene, dignifying it with polite question.

"What errand takes you, Pádraig?"

"No errand."

"Where is it you go, then?"

"Nowhere special. Just out."

"For no reason?"

"For the reason," Pat said with great deliberateness, "that I want to. That's all."

This sounded so absurd even to his own ears, that for a moment he thought his father would surely laugh, and he was torn between wondering whether, if that happened, to be affronted and angry—as his dignity would demand—or to throw in the towel and laugh along with him. Conflict between them ended many times in laughter. He almost hoped it would end that way now, even though, if it did,

52

he would have the whole thing to plot and plan all over again another night.

But his father didn't laugh. His eyes were very blue, very bright, as concealed laughter made them; he seemed to weigh the advisability of laughing and to decide against it.

He said, "Not does that seem to me sufficient reason."

"It doesn't have to," Pat answered, honestly trying to sound merely reasonable, rather than insolent. He didn't feel insolent toward his father. All he wanted was to establish himself as an equal. "I'm the one who's going."

His hand was now on the doorknob. Again he felt close to laughing, this time at the expression of shock on the face of his little brother, who was too great a coward, himself, to say "Boo!" to a goose, although if it came to that, Pat thought, he'd certainly say "Boo!" to a goose before ever he'd dream of saying "Boo!" to his father.

"Take off your jacket lad," his father said, "and sit you down. Not is it a night for going out to walk around without purpose, even had you consent of your father to do so. Raining a bit it is, and cold, for yet is the spring early. Better would it be did you stop here with us, if your homework is finished, and much would your brother enjoy having you listen while he reads of Finn MacCumhail."

Here his father smiled down at Brendan, and Brendan turned one of his ecstatic looks upward, joy leaping in him at the thought of having Pat there to hear him read.

Kindly, so kindly, his father was offering him the opportunity to back down from his declared intention and yet save face; was asking him, in a roundabout way, not to force the issue, not to make him take action to put down the insurrection still another time. So many times had he already taken action, had there not been enough of it?

Pat was tempted. He didn't really want to go out. It was, as his father had said, cold and rainy. Even if he went only as far as the drugstore, two blocks down and two blocks back, it would be an uncomfortable walk and one answering no need except his need to show off, his need to say, "Nobody's telling *me* what to do!"

He fully realized that he had chosen a position very hard to defend. His father, on several occasions, had patiently pointed out to him its weaknesses.

"Much trust have I always had in you, Pádraig, to do only what is sensible and right. Not is there any fear on me

53

now that you would do wrong, did you have freedom to run the streets as you please. You I trust, my son, but not do I trust the streets; too much do I see every day of the evil that is there. When I say I must know where you go and what reason you have for going, it is not to belittle you, or to deprive you of any right; it is because I see too much of what happens to those who go and come without other reason than to do as they please, answerable to no one. . . ."

"True son of mine you are," he had said another time. "Little need have you to explain these things to me. Harder it may be, I think, for you to explain them to yourself than to me. At just the age you are now, when my father died—and as big and strong I was as yourself—did I then hold that I was equal to any man in the village, and set myself to do a man's work and take a man's responsibility. Had anyone said, 'Not so, Tadhg O'Nolan, you are too young; now must you bide at home with your mother while others go to gather in the nets,' that one would I have scorned. . . . But that was in another place and time, my son, and another way of life altogether than you know here. Though little more than twenty years ago it was in fact, as well might it have been two thousand."

It had been hard, very hard, not to weaken when his father talked this way; not to yield, not to abandon his campaign, which by such talk could be made to seem wholly uncalled for and wholly unworthy. The curious power of his father's speech, the spell it could cast over the unwary listener, was a thing he must stubbornly and coldly set himself to resist. He must remind himself that he was fighting for a Cause, for a matter of self-respect, for recognition of a basic right.

Stubbornly and coldly, then, he set temptation aside. He folded his arms, faced his father squarely, and said, "I'm going out. If you don't want me to go, you'd better lock me up. There's no other way you can stop me."

His father sat looking at him for a long moment. Pat tried to read his face, but it was masked. No message was exchanged in that long look, and Pat wondered guiltily if the reason he could not read his father's face was that his own duplicity stood in the way, clouding the understanding that usually was so intimate a thing between them.

His father no longer appeared to be amused, but neither did he appear angry. Certainly he was not approving, yet neither did he seem to condemn. There was no surprise to be read in his look. There may have been curiosity. But nothing was clear.

At the end of the long moment he rose to his feet.

"*Tá go maith*," he said. "Very well, Pádraig. I will come upstairs with you, and can we find a key to turn the lock on your door, will it then be as you wish. Such have I heard of before," he went on blandly, "there being now and again those who come to police stations asking to be locked up, for that they cannot trust their own actions. A curious thing has it always seemed to me, yet can I see how there might be wisdom in it. Brendan"—he had caught an anxious, upturned look—"do you wait right here but a few minutes, and when I have done your brother this small favor which he requests, then will we get on with our reading."

They went upstairs. The old-fashioned locks on all the doors could be worked by the same key. They found one, and Patrick went into his room. His father gave him another of those unreadable looks, courteously wished that God might give him a good night—"*Go dtugaidh Dia oíche mhaith dhuit, a mhic*"—and closed the door.

The key turned in the lock.

Pat stood against the door and listened to the footsteps going down the stairs, across the lower hall, and into the living room. He waited a little longer, and heard his mother's footsteps follow the same course. He tried the door gently to satisfy himself that his father had indeed locked it, for his little *coup* would lose much of its effectiveness unless the door was really locked. It was. He waited another five minutes, not by guesswork but by the clock. By then, he estimated, his father and Brendan would be deeply engrossed in their nightly reading.

He went to the window. He had waxed it, and now it slid up easily and silently.

He was ready to proceed as planned.

The big oxheart cherry tree grew not far from his window. It had been planted long ago, even before the house was built, and the branch that he would use for his escape was stout and strong. Earlier in the day he had climbed the tree and made fast a short piece of rope. No one had seen him put it there, and since it hung down only a few feet, he did not think it would be noticed even if anyone happened to look up. He had made a knot at the end as a precaution against its slipping through his hands, but had not been able to give himself the additional insurance of any more knots along the length of it, for it would then have been too short to be reached from the window. As it was, he could just draw the end of it within reach of his hand by means of a broomstick with a hook in it.

With the rope in his hand he was prepared to swing out, and then either to pull himself up and get a leg over the branch to which the rope was attached, or to swing over and get a foothold on a lower branch that forked out from the trunk. Either way, he could then climb down the tree. The only dangerous part was the first swing out from the window sill. He hadn't practiced, partly for the reason that there had been no opportunity, but chiefly for the reason that he felt once would be enough. His body weight, thrown with abrupt force entirely on his arms, would be a severe strain. There was also the possibility of swinging too far and smacking up against the tree trunk. He had reviewed these hazards coolly and concluded that neither offered more than would be termed calculated risk.

Pat leaned out the window and looked down. The night was wet and black. His mother was through in the kitchen; no light shone from the kitchen window into the yard; no one could see him come down out of the tree. Directly below, the cement walk that led from the front porch to the rear of the house gleamed wetly in the light from the street lamp.

He took his broomstick and fished in the rope. To his surprise—for he had not thought the temperature had dropped so low—he found it coated with ice. This was an added risk, and he stood frowning while he considered it. His hands would slip on an ice-glazed rope. If his hands slipped, he might not be able to pull himself up the rope high enough to get a leg across the branch. This would leave him only the alternative of swinging to the fork. The tree also would be ice-coated, and this was a further hazard; but you met increased hazards by exercising increased care, not by abandoning an undertaking. To abandon the undertaking, after contriving to get himself locked in his room, would be to look a complete fool, and if he must choose between risking a fall or looking a fool, there was only one choice.

56

Gloves would help, so he found a pair.

He climbed through the window, sat for a moment astride the sill while he made sure of a good grip on the rope just above the knot, took one quick look down, and swung out.

The drop put a hard pull on his arms and gave his right shoulder a bad wrench, a little worse than he had been prepared for. There was one moment—and no denying it was a frightening moment—where his entire weight was borne by his left arm alone, and only the tight grip of one hand (and the knot) saved him from falling.

It would now be necessary, if he was to swing a leg over the branch, to pull himself a little higher up the rope. He couldn't do it. The glaze of ice permitted him no hold. Each fresh grip left him exactly where he was, at the very end, at the knot.

He gave that up, after a few futile attempts, and tried swinging over to the tree, reaching for the fork with his feet. He was below it. Try as he might, he could not, on his tiring arms, swing his body high enough to let him reach the fork. On every try he encountered only the main trunk, coated with ice and offering no foothold. The next lower branch came out on the far side of the tree. There was nothing, absolutely nothing on this side, except the two branches that he couldn't reach.

Despite the gloves, his hands were now numb with cold, his arms were aching, and he knew it was only a matter of seconds until he would lose his hold and fall. He was twelve to fourteen feet above the ground, with not even sod beneath him to land on, only the concrete walk. He could break both legs. And he could lie there, only Heaven would know how long, because as far as anyone knew he was safely locked in his own room, at his own ridiculous suggestion.

He was without self-pity. Far from it; the thought that flashed across his mind as he hung there was the very opposite: *It serves you right!*

This was his punishment. Not for disobedience. He had staunchly convinced himself that he had a right to disobey. And not for deceit. He had not said he *would* remain home if he was locked in his room. He had merely said there was no other way to stop him from going out; he hadn't said *that* way would stop him. Even if this was splitting hairs, it had at most been intended as a temporary deceit. He had planned to come walking in the front door, openly, brazenly, and in triumph. He had planned to say, "I said I was going out, didn't I? Well—I went!" That would have erased the deceit. His father would have understood, would have seen that as a trick it was no different from a card trick or a gambit in a game of chess.

The thing he was ashamed of and saw his present predicament as just retribution for, was a deeper thing than disobedience or a temporary ruse. He had violated the understanding that existed between his father and himself. He had met his father's eye, and they had not exchanged a message. He had been so intent on his little trick that he had destroyed the lines of communication: the special, secret, private wire that was all their own. Nothing would be the same again. Even if his father would still trust him, nothing would be the same. Something that had been complete was broken. A piece would always be missing. . . .

He couldn't reach the tree. He couldn't hold on to the rope much longer, his hands were too cold, his arms too tired.

Out of the dark below him his father's voice said, "Just let go and drop, lad. I'll catch you."

Pat made a little sound—half a moan, half a sob, of protest and gratefulness combined—let go and dropped.

His father's strong arms closed around him and let him down gently until his feet touched the ground.

The arms remained around him for another little fraction of time—only an instant, but it could have been hours or years, for surely hours or years would be needed to tell so much.

He said, "Pop, . . ." but that was all he could say.

He didn't care what happened next. He didn't care if his father took a strap to him, as he had said he might soon have to do. He didn't care. . . .

Because nothing was different. Nothing was spoiled. It was still there—intact, complete, inviolate—the understanding, the sharing, the bond that made them almost one person. It would always be there.

The arms released their enfolding grip, but one remained around his shoulders, turning him about and starting him toward the back door.

"Well planned it was, Pádraig," his father said, "and but

for circumstances beyond your control you could have managed it nicely. Do not take the failure hard. Not would anyone have thought the rain might freeze, so late on in the year. Do you come in with us now, for the evening is yet early, and still does Brendan wait to read his story. The patient little one he is, to wait so long."

4

IT HAD been a bad week.

To begin with there had been a terrific row between Patrick and Aunt Nora the very first day. Pat had taken the vacuum cleaner apart to repair it. He had very carefully placed the parts on a piece of newspaper on the kitchen floor, all in line exactly as he removed them, so that he would know exactly how to put them back after he replaced the worn-out bearing and reached the point of reassembly. He had to go up to the avenue for a replacement part, and to several shops before he found it. He was gone the better part of an hour. When he returned, he found that Aunt Nora, in a fever of cleaning and tidying the kitchen, had gathered up the whole neat little array of nuts, bolts, shafts, spacers, bushings, and bearings, and dumped them willy-nilly into a shoebox. Pat, who had some hard lessons behind him and still some hard ones ahead before he was to learn full self-control, neither kept his voice down nor chose his words carefully. The upshot of it was that Aunt Nora, very much upset (as much by realizing, though not admitting, that she was in the wrong, as by being told so in extremely rude language), sought refuge in a crying spell which left her with a sick headache and Peggy with a note to be put in her father's hand as soon as he came in the door that evening.

The next day was not much better. Pat in a rage was hardly any more unbearable than Pat in a grim, cold, unspeaking calm. Also, he hadn't repaired, and didn't repair, the vacuum cleaner. Aunt Nora, being allergic to dust, couldn't sweep, nor would she allow Katie to sweep. The house, as a consequence, began to acquire a somewhat grubby look, which was salt in the wounds laid open by Pat the day before.

On the third day, Brendan fell off the roof of the kitchen shed.

This was Paul's fault, primarily. He had snatched away a brand-new, never-used bird's nest that Brendan had found on the ground under the mock-orange bush. When Brendan cried to have it back, Paul said, "Birds' nests belong in trees," and gave it a toss in the general direction of the cherry tree. It fell short, landing on the low roof of the kitchen shed. "Go get it, crybaby," Paul said, and went back to his own favorite pastime of pretending that his express wagon was a heavily loaded tractor-trailer, which he was taking on a grueling transcontinental run, just now on his way through the high and dangerous passes of the Rockies.

Brendan had never been forbidden to venture on the shed roof—it had never occurred to anyone that he might—so technically he was blameless in the matter. Some responsibility rested on the girls, commissioned by Aunt Nora to play the role of informers if Paul teased Brendan; but Peggy was virtuously occupied with entertaining Rosie at the time, and Katie was upstairs making the beds. No responsibility, fortunately, rested on Pat, who had his orders to stay with the vacuum cleaner until he figured out the assembly of the scrambled parts and put them back together again. Pat was inside the shed, working at this task, at the very moment Brendan was on top of it. The sound of footsteps over his head took him outside in a hurry, but too late.

The roof of the shed could be reached only by means of a ladder if you were any less nimble than a monkey or a squirrel, or if you were too heavy for the grape arbor to take your weight. Brendan, who did not belong in either of these categories, climbed up the grape arbor, which was a trellised affair with a slat top over which the vines grew to make a shelter of cool greenery all summer long. Standing on the slats, he was able to seize hold of the rainspout that came down from the roof of the kitchen itself, and by means of it to pull himself up and over. The shed roof had a low pitch, and to walk up to where his bird's nest lay presented no difficulty at all.

Brendan retrieved the nest and retraced his steps, walking

backward. The nest was the littlest, loveliest thing, no more than three inches across, woven of the finest, softest, driest grasses, and lined with a mat of hair. Absorbed in his delighted study of it, he backed to the edge of the roof—and kept right on going.

The slatted top of the arbor that had supported his weight on the way up, let him through with a splintering crash on the way down. It broke his fall, however, and he settled into a tangled net of grapevines and broken slats, badly scared, somewhat scratched and bruised, and so snarled in the vines that he could do nothing but lie there helplessly until Pat freed him. He was still clutching the bird's nest.

On the fourth day, Paul and Peggy were assigned the very pleasant hot-weather chore of hosing down the front porch and the walk. They made a thorough and excellent job of it—and left the water running when they finished. Not only did the meter conscientiously record a steady two hours of consumption, but the stream flowed under the porch and right on down into the cellar, made its way under what was left of the winter's coal supply, and emerged to collect finally in a hideous black pool in the middle of the cellar floor.

No one noticed until Pat came home from his Saturday-morning job of making deliveries for Mr. Shaeffer, the druggist. They all sat down to the noon meal, and in the moment's silence while they waited for Brendan to say grace (his special duty ever since at the age of three he had learned to say it in Irish), Pat heard the faint sound in the pipes that told him water was running somewhere. *"Beannaí sinn, a Thiarna*—" began Brendan. "Is the hose on?" asked Pat, raising his head to sweep the company with a fiercely accusing look that sent Paul running for the door and quite destroyed Peggy's appetite for lunch.

A man can stand just so much. In his own home he is entitled to find peace at the end of his day's work, especially if his work is of a kind that brings him into hourly contact with those who wantonly disturb the peace: the foolish, the troublesome, the dishonest, the desperate, and the wicked.

Police Sergeant Tadhg O'Nolan summoned his children before him and laid down the law in somewhat harsher terms than he would have used in a calmer moment; but he was a man driven by an accumulation of torment, and

62

if he spoke with more severity than was justly warranted, and made a certain threat which he could not possibly have meant to carry out, covering as it did any offense and any offender, he could later ask God to forgive him for that once in a while a man's tongue runs ahead of his reason.

"Now has there been enough," he said, "of hearing each night that this or that has happened, such as no man should be compelled to expect of children whose intelligence has never been doubted and whose instruction has never been neglected. Plain is it to me that such steps as I have taken through this week to promote seemly behavior among you have been insufficient. Hear you this promise, now. Do I come home tomorrow and learn that any untoward thing has occurred, no matter what the nature of it and no matter which one of you may be the guilty party, *will I then put a strap on that one,* without fail and without further warning and without first listening to argument that not would it have happened so, or so, had it not been for other circumstances being such, or such."

Here his eye chanced to fall on Rosie, from whom it moved away again very quickly and on up the line to one upon whom it could more sternly dwell. On the face of that one he perceived a faint but suggestively mocking grin. Disregarding it, he went on:

"Now if it be a thing that you cannot without risk of misconduct do other than sit on chairs here in the middle of this room, then must you do so; for not again will I hear of such happenings as have been related to me each day, as if you had set yourselves one and all to establish a record of mischance and wrongdoing."

Now his eye traveled down the line again as far as Brendan, who wore a look of such wide-eyed alarm as might be called for had his father changed, within his sight, into a visitant from some nether world.

"*A Bhreandáin,*" he said, "do you know well the song you learned to sing to your mother's playing, before she went to the hospital to fetch your brother John?"

"*Tá eolas agam air, 'Athair,*" Brendan whispered.

"Since you know it, then do you come sing it for us," his father said, putting out his hand and with a sudden, all-embracing smile dismissing, for the time, all that had been done that week and all that had been said this moment past, making of it all a thing that need no more be spoken of or thought about for the rest of the evening. "Your sister Katie will play the music, and though you may cause us to weep for the poor little *maidrín*, better it is that we weep for the little dog than for a continuing unfriendliness among us, such as should not exist between a father and the children of his heart."

Sunday morning dawned with every promise of being a day of complete tranquillity. The five youngest O'Nolans went decorously to an early Mass in company with their father, who must be on duty every alternate Sunday, and that day at the Station by eight. Pat, serving as altar boy at ten o'clock, would not leave the house for another hour and a half. Sometime in the interim Aunt Nora would arrive.

The childen all wore their Sunday look (the middle four with the added grace of having just received Holy Communion), and when their father lined them up for a few parting words they looked so blameless and pure that he could not bring himself to remind them of the threat he had made the night before, it being a threat which he could neither wish to carry out nor wish to have them truly believe he would carry out, although it was for this purpose he had made it.

Therefore, when he had lined them up and looked them over, he refrained from making any reference to the assorted misfortunes and misbehavior of the past few days. He said to them instead:

"Now is it the beautiful lot you are. Proud can be the man who fathered you, and great joy can he take in knowing that your conduct is ever of such nature as to reflect utmost credit upon the quality of your upbringing."

They saw the laughter and the love in his eyes, and on that signal the girls closed in on him with a rush. He lifted Rosie to carry her with him as far as the front gate, and then saw the agony of longing in Brendan's eyes. Brendan was six, too old to be carried around like a little one . . . well, soon enough would he be too old. . . .

Brendan rode to the gate in triumph on the other arm.

The morning passed quietly and without incident. But after lunch, a whole, long, empty Sunday afternoon stretched ahead, and there was a good deal of differing opinion and discussion as to how most circumspectly, least dangerously, yet withal pleasantly to spend it.

Katie wanted to pick cherries. To Katie this project represented no hazard: she was active and agile by nature, liked best to be doing something that involved use of her physical powers, and curiously preferred that it be, whenever possible, a utilitarian pursuit. Aunt Nora had said she would put the cherries up tomorrow if somebody picked them today. They were fully ripe and the robins were hard at work on them. Katie didn't begrudge the robins a fair share, but she saw the cherries as God's gift to the O'Nolans as well as to the robins, and conscience told her it was wrong to let God's gifts go to waste.

Peggy and Paul, however, strongly vetoed the suggestion, feeling that the inherent risks were too great. They also felt that picking cherries very closely approximated work. To pick cherries to eat, right then and there, was one thing, but once you had your fill, who wanted to pick baskets and buckets full? Besides, it was too hot. But again, coming back to the main point at issue, climbing around in the cherry tree, or up and down the ladder, would be just a plain, downright invitation to trouble. Suppose one of them fell and was hurt?

"If one of us fell and was hurt," Katie argued, "Father certainly wouldn't . . . well . . . not anyone who was *hurt*."

They agreed, probably not. But suppose he held the others at fault, for complicity?

"*You* pick cherries, if you want to. *We're* going to play gin rummy."

Two against one decided the matter. Katie and Peggy and Paul sat on the front porch and played gin rummy.

Brendan wouldn't even do this. Brendan refused to budge out of the house at all. He took his father's suggestion at its literal worth, moved his hassock into the very center of the living room, where he could not possibly come into accidental contact with anything that could be knocked over, tripped over, stepped on, spilled, broken, torn, or damaged in any way whatsoever, and spent the afternoon huddled there, reading.

Only Pat and Rosie put in their time in what was for each an entirely normal manner. Pat busied himself putting up an outside aerial for a short-wave radio he had built. Rosie took a nap.

Aunt Nora, between periodic checks on all of them, merely rested until four o'clock, when she began preparations for an early supper of sliced ham, potato salad, deviled eggs, and pickled beets.

And, at four o'clock, nearly everyone else yawned and stretched and, bored with what they were doing, began wishfully thinking about doing something else.

Katie deserted the gin-rummy session and wandered around into the side yard, to stand looking upward into the cherry tree, wondering how much of the delicious cream-and-crimson fruit the birds would have left by the time she might be able to start picking the O'Nolans' share.

Rosie, waking from her nap, came downstairs flushed and sleepy-eyed, heard the voices of Peggy and Paul on the front porch and ran out to join them. Presently these three wandered around into the side yard also.

Brendan, timorously venturing at last to leave his stool and step across the encircling, invisible barrier which discretion had inscribed around the very center of the living room, betook himself to the kitchen. He always walked lightly, on the balls of his feet; this time his fairylike (some called it catlike) step took him into the kitchen as silently as a shadow, giving Aunt Nora such a start that she nearly dropped the plate of deviled eggs.

"My goodness, Brendan, I never heard you come! You ought to———" She was going to say "knock," but it seemed so extremely absurd to tell a child he ought to knock before coming into the kitchen of his own home that she amended it to "speak before you come right up behind a person like that, or at least walk so people can hear you."

She thought he looked hurt, or perhaps only hungry. The second possibility was the easier one to do something about, so she handed him a deviled egg, forgetting that he never ate them. He accepted the offering with a smile (Such a sweet smile! That child would surely grow up to be a saint.) and a polite *"Buíochas, Áintín Nóra,"* which she knew by this time meant "Thank you," though what in the world Tadhg meant by teaching that child to speak as much Irish as English was something she would never know.

Brendan went outside then, slipping in his elfish way out the back door.

Pat was engaged in driving a half-inch copper rod deep into the ground, a foot or so away from the wall of the house. It was his third try. Two other times he had gone down against rock and had been obliged to pull the rod out again and move it to a different spot. In addition to this vexatious circumstance there was the need to tap it down lightly and carefully, for a strong or careless blow would bend it. He didn't appreciate his half-circle of spectators. He said impatiently, "Would you mind staying far enough back so I can breathe?" But other than this, he ignored them.

He had been on the kitchen roof—the ladder was still propped against the side of the house—but that phase of the operation was finished and all that remained was to attach the ground wire after he drove the rod as deep as he wanted it.

Katie asked, "Are you through with the ladder, Pat?"

"Yeah, I guess."

"May I have it?"

"Help yourself."

Katie pulled at the base of the ladder, moving it back, letting the other end slide partly down the wall of the house. She *could* swing it around, now, and put it up against the cherry tree. She knew perfectly well she could. But . . .

"Pat, will you move it over against that first branch for me?"

"Look, for Pete's sake!" Pat was having troubles of his own. He was on rock again, and the hammer, glancing off the rod, had caught his thumb. "Can't you see I'm busy? *You* move it if you want it moved! You're always boasting you can do anything I can do!"

"I am not always boasting," Katie said indignantly. "And I never said any such thing. I said I can do anything *a* boy can do. I didn't mean you, and you know it. Anyway, I *can* move the ladder," Katie said, "but sometimes it wants to tip, and I thought——"

"You thought if it's going to get away from anybody, and fall and get busted, and anybody's going to get their hide tanned, you'd rather it was me."

"Pat, I never. All I thought was it wouldn't *get* away from you."

Pat started his rod in a new place.

"What a bunch of yellow-bellies! Pop's got you all too scared to move a finger!"

"I'm not!" Katie said defensively. "I've been wanting all afternoon to pick cherries. And what's more, I'm going to. And I don't *want* your help, thank you. I'm perfectly capable of moving the ladder, and I'd *rather* do it myself!"

Katie was tall for her eleven years, strong, self-reliant, resourceful, and—in regard to most things—courageous. She knew exactly how to get under the ladder at the highest rung she could conveniently reach, push it upright, balance it, give it a half turn, and let it come down again to rest against the tree. It was a very simple matter. She had done it before. She could do it again.

But something happened.

It may have been the apprehension in the voices of Peggy and Paul, adding to her own apprehension, making her hands unsteady and her judgment momentarily unsound.

"Don't do it, Katie."

"If that ever gets away from you, watch out! Boy-oh-boy!"

"Katie, it's tipping!"

"The window!"

Katie cried out in desperation, *"Pat!"* but the ladder was listing badly, and before Pat could reach it, it was out of hand and falling, the kitchen window directly within the arc of its travel.

The end of the ladder ripped through the screen at the top of the window frame and smashed the glass of the upper sash. Simultaneous with its descent was Aunt Nora's scream within the kitchen and Peggy's without. The window was partly open, and the ladder on its way down broke through each of three successive cross pieces of the double sash, showered broken glass inward over the kitchen table on which supper had been laid out, and finally came to rest, not on the window sill, which was low, but on the edge of the table itself. The impact first sent deviled eggs and pickled beets flying off their plates into the air, and instantly thereafter caused the two far legs of the table to lift ten inches off the floor. Everything that hadn't previously bounced off now slid off, except the big bowl of potato salad, which chanced to be near the edge of the table and directly in line. The salad, inextricably mixed with the crushed remains of the bowl, was all that remained on the table of the O'Nolans' Sunday-night supper.

Outside, Paul yelled, "I *told* you to watch out!" Brendan

stood transfixed with horror. Katie, white as death, closed her eyes, clasped her hands, and prayed.

When Aunt Nora, shaking with mingled fright and fury, pulled herself together enough to make her way outside, Pat was drawing the ladder back from the window.

With magnificent calm, Pat said, "I'm sorry, Aunt Nora. It slipped."

"Slipped!"

Aunt Nora tried to keep her voice down to a terrible whisper, on account of the neighbors, who were gaping from their windows and over the fences to see what had been the cause of this shattering of the Sunday-afternoon quiet. She even managed to call, with a ghastly kind of cheerfulness, to Mrs. Moran next door, "Just a broken window! Nothing serious!" And then in the whisper again:

"Slipped! Patrick O'Nolan, do you know what you've done?"

"Busted the window," Pat said.

Katie started to say, "Aunt Nora——" but Pat turned on her fiercely.

"Shut up! I don't need anybody making excuses for me! Shut up!"

"Come into the house," Aunt Nora commanded, by a heroic effort achieving a false but deadly calm. "Come into the house, all of you. And I will have nothing touched," she said. "I want your father to see exactly what you have done! Exactly!"

They filed into the house.

The torn screen, the smashed window, were only introductory to the havoc they found inside. Even Pat was momentarily appalled, at least until he realized that the spatter of bright, rich, purplish red over everything wasn't anyone's blood, but only the juice from one pint jar of pickled beets.

"I will have nothing touched!" Aunt Nora said again. "Your father will be home within the hour. I intend to stay right here until he comes. Go into the living room, all of you, and wait."

Tadhg O'Nolan sat late in the big chair under the reading lamp that night.

Sick at heart he was, and without reason. Not so. He corrected the thought. Sick at heart he was, and not could he

69

single out the reason, or name it, or quite see it clear. For the reason was made up of many things. Not one alone that could press so upon him, but one added to another, piling up.

Áine Ní Bhriain would soon be home. *Arú amáireach,* the day after tomorrow, she would be home. But too pale she looked. Too thin. Too much of her strength had gone to the child, another like himself, a great boy, John, weighing ten pounds at birth, and already demanding more than she could give him, the first one that must be put on the bottle instead of to the breast. Not would she admit to feeling unwell, or weak, but only tired, because in the hospital she could not rest for worrying that she should be home. When she was home, then would she rest—this she promised him—for there was the whole long summer yet ahead, and the two girls old enough now to share the housework and help her with the younger ones. It was so, he could see it; the hospital was a lonely place for her, she fretted more than she rested, so much did she long to be home.

Now he would have to tell her, but he would wait yet a little, that he had been transferred again. The fourth time it was, since the trouble three years ago, and no reason given. But he knew the reason, which was twofold. First it was to keep him feeling uncertain and insecure, no sooner fitting into one place than taken out of it and sent to another. They would tire of it one day, he thought, and forget him, and then he might have peace. The other reason was to make it seem that he was shifted because in some way he failed to give satisfaction. The least that might be thought was that he would not work in accord with his fellows; for in someone's hand, so he had heard, big and black across his record the single word *Uncooperative* was written. More than this, it was standard practice that one suspected of dishonesty, of having friends in a District, whom he favored or protected, would be transferred; and this they had in mind also, to make it seem that such suspicion attached to him. There was always bad feeling at the start in a new District, for no ranking officer wanted in his command one who was thought to be dishonest or known to be a troublemaker. And each time, just when resentments and hostility were giving way to awareness of the truth, and even sometimes to friendship, then he would be moved again and have it all to do over.

70

It was a small thing. Not did it touch him inside, for inside was the strength that God had put there to meet all such things and resist them, as the rock that was the homeland of his people had for thousands of years resisted the onslaught of the sea. It was enough if a man knew in his own heart that he kept faith with himself and with other men, and with those he loved, and with God.

Not was the notice of transfer, then, which had come to him yesterday, enough in itself to give him this heavy and sorrowful feeling. It merely added to the weight.

Was it the children then?

Had he been less than just? Was it conscience that pressed upon him with such heaviness, to keep him sitting here instead of seeking his bed, as the children had long since sought theirs?

Much had he been troubled through the day by remembrance of the harsh words he had spoken. A man of sense and justice, a careful man, a good father, does not threaten a child with more than he could wish to carry out. If a man must threaten, then must he at the same time guard his tongue, that his threats remain within reason. Was it excuse for him that he was feeling concern for their mother, or that he had been angered by notice of the new transfer? Not was it excuse. Such concern was a thing to be kept within himself. Such anger a thing to be left behind him at the Station at the end of the day.

Something about the happening had troubled him from the start. Something had seemed not quite understandable, not quite right. An accident, it had been. Not accident in the course of doing something forbidden, or of some piece of mischief, or of foolishness, but accident in the course of a useful and proper act. When before had he ever punished one of them for accident? But . . . this will I do, he had said, no matter what, and without listening to argument. When before had he ever refused to listen to argument? Did not Pádraig always argue, and did his father not always listen, and sometimes accept the argument and sometimes not, or sometimes accept half and reject the other half?

Odd it had seemed to him at the time that with so much cause for argument, Pádraig had not argued, had not tried to explain what happened, and how, and why, showing that in fact he was not to blame and so should not be punished. "The ladder slipped," was all he had said.

71

Slipped?

Odd, too, had been his manner. Not defiant. Not angry at injustice, which there had surely and plainly been, and which he had surely and plainly known. In the very relief it had been to know that the perpetrator of the outrage had been Pádraig and not one of the others, there had been injustice. For there was no problem, then, no need that he must fail to abide by his own word. Well could that tough young one take it, as they both knew, and, reading each other's thought, there had been the look that said, "You're damned glad it's me."

With this much, at least, he could console himself: not had it been more than token punishment. Severe he could be and must be when a thing was wrongdoing. A few weeks ago, with vexation on top of vexation leading to sudden, uncontrolled anger, Pádraig had turned his small brother Brendan upside down in a bucket of water. A bad time that had been, and might have been worse, with the little one taking in some of the water. But very different was such a matter from a thing that happened by accident, and a thing to which a curious doubt attached. . . .

Pádraig had gone downstairs whistling, and without being told had set himself to the work of cleaning up the kitchen, with help of Peggy and Paul; and then had removed a screen from one of the dining-room windows and put it in place, so that the house would not be open to night-flying insects and prowling cats and others that wander in the dark.

They had for supper the bacon and eggs that would have been for breakfast; and for the children the shadow had lifted, so that almost did it seem a lark to them to be frying bacon and eggs at seven o'clock in the evening instead of seven in the morning.

All but Katie. Very pale and quiet Katie had been, and had eaten no supper, but had gone early to bed.

Hardly above a whisper her answers were given, when he questioned.

"I'm just not hungry, Father. . . . No, I'm not sick. . . . No, Father. I'm just tired. It was so very early when we got up this morning."

So there it was. There was the answer. There was the doubt and the question resolved. Fogged indeed must his mind have been, not to have seen at once. . . .

He sat downstairs in the living room, all others in bed and the house quiet, only the hall light burning and this one lamp beside his chair. And it seemed to him that he was waiting.

When he heard a stair tread creak under the foot of someone coming quietly, so quietly, down, he knew that this was what he had been waiting for.

Katie came into the living room. Over her nightgown she wore an old striped pajama top of her brother's in place of a bathrobe, which she did not own. The jacket was too large for her; the sleeves came down over her hands, making her look little and lost. Her long, dark-red braids hung over her shoulders, and around her face little loose ends of hair escaping from the braids (as if she might have lain for hours turning her head from side to side on her pillow) made a soft frame. She had been crying; her eyes were testimony to it, red-rimmed and still brimming with tears that waited only their time to fall. She came like a sad little ghost to stand before his chair.

"*A Cháitlin, a iníon*, Kathleen, daughter, can you not sleep?"

"Father," she whispered, "Father, there is something I must tell you . . . and I cannot bear to."

"Not must you, *a mhúirnín*, my darling, for it is a thing I know."

She dropped to her knees before him and buried her face in his lap, and the tears came.

"Oh, Father, Father, I have done such wrong. I let Pat take the blame. I let Pat be punished."

He stroked her hair.

"Not was it so great a wrong that your brother holds it against you. It was his wish."

"I was afraid," Katie sobbed. "I was so afraid."

"For that the wrong is mine," he answered with pain in his heart. "Not had you true cause to fear."

"But you said, Father, you said—"

"Not would I have done so. Not would I have punished you, the good one that you are, always the first to do for any other, always ready with your help and your love."

"You said anyone . . . anyone."

"A bitter thing it is that I spoke as I did. A wrong it was, and I have asked God to forgive me. You do I ask to forgive me also."

"Oh, Father, I have nothing to forgive you for, and I love you so. But how can I be forgiven? How can I? I cannot even ask."

"I think you have but little need to ask, my heart's darling, for the fault is less yours than mine, as God knows, and for that reason has He already forgiven you without your asking. But when you make Confession of it, then will your heart be freed of the burden which it now carries."

"I am so cowardly," Katie sobbed, "so wicked. Pat is so good, so brave, and I let him be punished."

"The good brother he is to you and the good son to me, and this I say because it is plain to me that he acted to spare us both. Now must you not cry more, for it is over and done with. Not did I hurt him that he would call hurt, *buíochas le Dia!* And you and all of us witnessed how little he was troubled, that with no unkindness in his heart toward anyone he set himself to clearing away all signs of the trouble, that we all might forget, and have our supper, and none be the worse for the happening. Well pleased is your brother with himself, I think, and just cause has he to be so. Not often has a lad opportunity to be a hero. Selfish would it be of us, would it not, to wish that he might have been deprived of such opportunity, for that you and I could then sleep tonight with clearer conscience?"

He sat smoothing his daughter's hair as he talked, drawing one of the braids gently through and through his fingers. Under the spell of his voice and his touch she had stopped crying, and presently, after a little silence, she raised her head.

Suffering was still on her face, but on it also was an illumination, a glory.

"Father, I am going to be a nun!"

He looked at her with tenderness, but in a searching way, for he had always seen in the strong lines of her face a great resemblance to his mother, who once having set her mind upon a course would never turn from it.

"Great joy will it be to all of us," he said, "if when you reach an age for making such decision, you find your decision then the same as now."

"I know it will be, Father. I know it!" The radiance of her purpose shone all around her. "I will serve God every day of my life, and every day of my life Pat will be first in my prayers!"

74

"And as needful is he as deserving of your prayers," her father answered, smiling, "the brash one that he is. Come now, *a inîon dhîlis*—my dear daughter, do you sit here on your little brother's hassock and tell me from start to finish of all that happened this day, for not is it as clear to me as I would have it be."

Katie did not appear for breakfast. She was still sleeping, Peggy said; she had been sick at her stomach last night, just after they went to bed, and: "Shall I call her, Father?"

"Not so. Let her sleep."

Pat had moved the table to the other side of the kitchen, and was engaged in removing the jagged fragments of glass from the window sash. The others stood watching. When their father came, they all took their places at the table, which Peggy had laid with a minimum of breakfast requirements: a bowl of cornflakes, a knife and a spoon at each place, and in the middle of the table a quart of milk in the bottle (the milk pitcher had been broken), sugar in a coffee cup (the sugar bowl had been broken also), a jar of apple jelly, a loaf of bread in its wrapper, a slice of margarine, and the electric toaster.

An uneasy silence descended. It had something to do with Katie's not being there, and something to do with the way their father's eye passed from one to another of them around the table just after they sat down. They kept their eyes lowered and attended strictly to the business of eating, with only a glance sliding across the table now and again from one to another, each wondering if the other knew what was wrong now.

When no one wanted any more cornflakes or toast (and no one had been very hungry), an undefined expectancy kept them waiting for what was obscurely but certainly known to be coming.

Their father did not appear angry, but sometimes it was hard to tell, for he could look at them with a look that pierced their deepest thoughts yet gave not the faintest indication of his own.

"Now a question I would ask," he said at last. And into the unbreathing silence that dropped over the table, he dropped the question: "Which one among you knows who broke the window?"

No one spoke. After waiting a moment, he supplied the answer.

"Each and every one of you. Is it not so?"

Still no one spoke.

"And is there not one among you," he asked, "in whom I may put trust to tell the truth?"

There was more sternness in the last question than had been in the preceding ones, and Peggy and Paul burst in in unison with, "Pat said——" but there they stopped, drawn from meeting their father's eye to apprehensively seeking their brother's.

"One at a time would I hear you speak," their father said. "Margaret?"

"Pat said we mustn't tell!" Peggy was indignant, defensive, and ready to cry. After all, none of it was *her* fault. *She* hadn't touched the ladder. *She* had better sense. "He said if I told, he'd . . . he'd cut off all my hair, with the clippers!"

Eyes of father and oldest son met briefly. They parted, and the next testimony was called for.

"Paul?"

Paul was indignant, defensive, and a shade vindictive.

"Pat said he'd knock my teeth down my throat!"

Again the brief meeting of glances.

"Brendan?"

"Pat said if I . . ."

What had begun as an obedient whisper trailed off inaudibly as Brendan made the mistake of looking at his brother, and then found that he could not look away.

"Now must you look at me, Brendan, and not at your brother."

Brendan began again, "Pat said if I"—he made what appeared to be a supreme effort to wrench his gaze away and realign it in the right direction, but failed—"if I told it was . . . was Katie, he'd . . . he'd . . ."

Again the faint voice trailed off, first to a painful whisper and then to silence.

His father asked, "Do you fear your brother?"

"Oh, no, Father! Oh, no! *Níl. Níl eagla orm.*"

"I would know what threat was made to you, Brendan. Now must you tell it me."

"Pat said he would stand . . . stand me on my head in . . .

in a bucket of water," Brendan managed to bring out, and at the very end he was able to turn his eyes away and look at his father. He burst into tears. "But I'm sure he didn't mean it, *'Athair*."

This time the exchange of looks between Patrick and his father lasted somewhat longer than before. Pat, though inwardly shaken, held his own with outward steadiness, and in a moment the probing glance moved on to the last remaining witness.

Rosie was not yet three. She did not know quite what was wrong, or why. Her father, who had never been known to look at her without a smile, was looking at her now without a smile, and she found that very strange and disturbing. Everything was very strange and disturbing. The table not being where it belonged. The wide-open window. Breakfast over, but everybody still just sitting around. And Katie not there. The strangeness, the wrongness, suddenly all gathered into one thing: *Katie not there*.

Taking everyone by surprise, Rosie half jumped, half fell from her stool. She ran around the table to Pat. She began to cry. She pounded on Pat's knee with her small, clenched fists. She screamed, "Is Katie dead? Is Katie dead?"

Pat said, "Of course not, you little idiot!"

"You said Katie would die! You said! You said!"

"Well, she didn't," Pat answered desperately. "She's upstairs. Go see for yourself!"

Rosie ran from the kitchen, leaving a strained silence behind her. When the silence was no longer to be borne, Pat broke in upon it with angry defiance.

"All right. So I told her Katie would die if you put a strap on her. And it's true! She would!"

"The fine thing it is," his father said, "to threaten and frighten your brothers and sisters, and make liars of the lot of them!"

"I didn't make liars of them! I told them if you asked, they'd have to tell the truth. But I told them if you didn't ask, they were to keep their big mouths shut! That's all. It isn't lying, just to keep your mouth shut!"

"Circumstances there can be," his father replied, "when it closely approaches. And the threats you made—was it your intention, then, to carry out your threats, did they not do according to your will?"

77

"*You* set the example, don't you?" Pat demanded. "It was *your* intention to carry out *your* threat, wasn't it? Or did you just mean to scare the hell out of everybody, unless it happened to be me?"

"Do you tell me off, Pádraig?"

"You can try the shoe on for size," Pat said with deliberate insolence, "if you want to. And if it fits you, I guess I can put *my* foot in it all right!"

His father agreed with an emphatic "You can that!"

He looked at the clock.

"But a minute or two remains," he said, "before I must leave. Do the rest of you go now into the yard, for your brother and I have words to say that concern but the two of us."

When they were alone he said, "Do you know what I am going to do now, Pádraig?"

Pat carefully balanced one spoon on the arched handle of another.

"I've got a pretty fair idea."

"And what would that be?"

"Put it on me again, I guess."

He could rock the top spoon, like a seesaw.

"And what would that be for?"

"For lying to you, and threatening the kids."

"And would you deserve it, do you think?"

A violent, angry motion sent the spoons skidding across the oilcloth.

"For Pete's sake! What's the idea of the third degree? And what difference does it make what I think anyway? You're the one has the say about it!"

"Not do I recall that you lied to me, Pádraig." His father appeared to be making a studious effort to remember. "Is it so, then, that you lied? Nothing do I remember that you said of this matter but that the ladder slipped. As the truth, did I take it, for that it was yourself who told it me, and not before did you ever tell me untruth. Was it not so, then?"

"It was so, all right." Pat allowed himself a faint grin. Just what this line was leading to he didn't know, but when his father started hamming it up, he knew it couldn't be leading to anything he wouldn't like. "But I let you think it was me, and I guess you'd say that's the same as a lie."

"Would I so," his father answered, "in most circumstances. But did you point to an elephant and tell me it could fly, that would I call nonsense, but not would I call such nonsense a lie."

Pat, unable to see what a flying elephant had to do with it, said nothing and waited.

"Not so, Pádraig. Not did you guess correctly, just now. That which I am going to do is another thing altogether. I am going to apologize to you. Do you take it, then, by these words, that I apologize. Can you not say what the apology is for?"

The answer to this would appear to be obvious, but Pat knew that whatever his father was being, he wasn't being obvious, so the answer must be something else.

"Well, I know what it's *not* for," he said. "Because even if I didn't have it coming for what happened, I know darn well you figure I had it coming for letting it happen. So it's not for that."

"Not is it for that," his father agreed. "And for still another reason is it not for that. The bold and brave one you are, and not would I think I must apologize for that I was helpful in providing you with this excellent opportunity to prove it." The tone was smooth and grave, but Pat looked for the smile that was always deep in his father's eyes when he used this tone, and it was there. "*Ní hé sin é,* not is that it. Something there is that I should have known. Can you not say what I should have known?"

"Pop . . ."

"You have guessed it correctly, my son. Much do I blame myself for that the knowledge came to me so tardily of a thing I should have known at once—that had you been the one who moved the ladder, *not would it have slipped.*"

5

THE WHOLE trouble, Aunt Nora said, was that Brendan read too many books.

Every time you saw him he had his nose in a book. And such stuff as he read! All those fairy stories and ghost stories, the Irish ones especially—good heavens! It was no wonder the child was afraid to walk across the yard after dark, and had bad dreams which woke him up crying and screaming—and woke everybody else up too.

"You ought to regulate his reading, Anne," Nora said disapprovingly to her sister-in-law. "There are such perfectly lovely books for children nowadays. Educational and everything, and without anything in them to scare a child out of his wits."

Anne, appearing to agree, said, "I know. They've expurgated a lot of the old ones. Even Mother Goose."

"And a good thing. Some of those old rhymes are really quite horrible, you know, and weren't even meant for children in the first place. Oh, I know, they never hurt *us* any, but times are different. They know so much more now about what goes on in a child's mind, and what's suitable for them to read, and what they take the most interest in, and all that."

"I can't imagine a child taking the least interest in Little Miss Muffet," Anne said, "without the spider."

"Well, but it shouldn't frighten her."

"I've never seen the watered-down version," Anne said, laughing. "What does it do now? Teach her the correct way to hold her spoon?"

Nora laughed, too, but she didn't yield her point.

"Just the same, I think it's a very bad thing for a highly imaginative child to have his head crammed-jammed full of ideas about every kind of fairy and ghost and goblin and other supernatural being that was ever invented. Do you know what he asked me the other day? If I had ever seen a *banshee* with any color hair except red. Just as if you might as likely as not be meeting banshees any old time, shopping at the supermarket or waiting on the corner for a bus! And when I told him I had never seen a banshee at all, he said in the most matter-of-fact way—even in the most *comforting* way, because I guess he didn't want me to feel bad about it—'Oh, you probably have, Aunt Nora, but you just didn't know she was one.' Then I made the mistake of humoring him: I asked how you tell. And he went into a long explanation about it being rather difficult sometimes, but how he can always tell by their eyes. He explained in great detail that their eyes are longer and narrower than an ordinary person's, and slanted, and the color of sea water; and that instead of being able to see yourself reflected, you *look right through their eyes.* But you must be awfully careful not to, he said, because that's one of the ways they 'get' you. Once you've looked into their eyes, you've seen things no mortal man should see, and after that you aren't satisfied to be just a mortal man, you keep getting more and more like them, and finally you go off and live with the *Slooa Shee.* The fairy people, indeed! And really, Anne, I know very well he wasn't even repeating something he had read, but just making it up out of whole cloth as he went along. And that's really quite untruthful, you know. He should be corrected."

"I don't think he means it untruthfully," Anne said. "It's . . . he believes his own stories, you see."

"Anne, he insisted to me the other day that a leprechaun lived in the tool shed all last summer. Now you don't really think he believes *that,* do you?"

"Yes, in a way. He created that leprechaun last summer for companionship. He had to believe in him, or creating him would have failed of its purpose."

"But, Anne, he's eight years old. No eight-year-old child today believes in fairies. And as for believing something that he knows very well he has just made up himself . . . well, I'd be worried if he were mine. And why on earth should he create a leprechaun for companionship, with all the brothers and sisters he has?"

"I think it's probably an eight-year-old leprechaun," Anne said. "I'm afraid he's rather lonely sometimes, poor little boy. He's three years away from anyone else, in either direction. It's rather like living on his own little island."

"The others should be made to include him, Anne."

"Oh, they do, whenever it's feasible. But Paul is nearly twelve and so grown-up. He was busy every minute last summer with his bicycle repair business, and he wouldn't allow Brendan to touch anything or even come near. It was understandable, of course, because Brendan does have a talent for mishaps. Unfortunately it came just at a time when Rose had deserted him, too. Rose has always loved his stories—she used to sit and listen by the hour—but last summer, after she made the discovery that a little brother was ever so much more fun than a doll, she appointed herself full-time keeper of John, and poor Brendan was left rather at loose ends. That's when the leprechaun came to live in the tool shed."

"Well, I don't think it's good for him, Anne. He ought to have real friends his own age, not imaginary ones."

"I know."

"And I don't understand why he hasn't," Nora said. "He's such an *outgoing* child, so generous and good-natured and everything. It's hard to understand why he doesn't make friends at school. I suppose it's because he's so timid."

"And so very vulnerable," Anne said. "At school, the boys his age devote all their playtime energies to physical combat—pushing and tripping and wrestling, and snatching caps and books, and dividing into rival factions that war upon each other. He doesn't like it, so, of course, he's a perfect target for both sides; and he hasn't an idea in the world what to do about it, how to give anything back or stand up for himself. That's why he'd rather play alone, with make-believe friends."

"I don't think, Anne," Nora said, dropping her voice a little to indicate that what she was about to say was strictly between the two of them, "I really don't think that talking Irish the way he does helps him any. It just makes him seem odd to the other children, and you know how they instinctively resent any child who's different. I really don't

82

know what Tadhg was thinking of, to start it. It's much more of a handicap than it is an asset—thinking in two languages, the way he does. If it were a language he could ever possibly have any use for, like Spanish or German, there'd be some justification. But *Irish?* Why, the only reason that language ever survived at all was that there were places so cut off from everything, or so backward, that the people just didn't know any better. Oh, yes, there's all that business of trying to revive it, but even in Ireland it's really no earthly use to anybody. So what in the world is the sense of any child over *here* learning to speak it? I'm sure it must interfere with Brendan's schoolwork, because it can't help but confuse him. Sister Mary Clare told me herself how when she calls on him to explain or tell about something, he keeps trying to make it clearer by slipping in Irish words and phrases, and, of course, all the other children laugh. She says he's very stubborn about it—he keeps insisting that the Irish word says it better. And she's having the same trouble with him that the others had—reciting his prayers in Irish. I wouldn't be surprised if he even makes his Act of Contrition in Irish, when he goes to Confession! Oh, I know it's a great satisfaction and pleasure to his father, but I do think it makes things hard for the child, Anne. It's so important for a child to be like other children. So much easier for them to adjust."

"There are compensations," Anne said, thinking of Brendan's passionate delight in sharing this very special thing with his father. "I think it is of greater value to him to be close to his father than to make a better adjustment at school. It means so much to him, to both of them. I often think it must help Tadhg get through the day, just having it to look forward to."

Anne bent her head over the sewing in her lap, to conceal the tears that came without warning, but a break in her voice had already given her away, and her sister-in-law said quickly, "There, dear. I didn't mean to upset you. No child ever had a better father, and I have no right at all to be critical."

"It isn't anything you said, Nora. It's just . . . if they would only let him alone."

"Anne, you don't mean he's been transferred again?"

"Just yesterday."

"It's persecution!" Nora O'Brien said indignantly. "It's

out-and-out persecution! Isn't there *anything* he can do about it?"

"Nothing except resign. If he had only himself to think of, that's what he would do, I guess."

"It just makes you think there's no justice in the world at all," Nora said. "All that testimony he gave before the Grand Jury that time—yet never a bit of credit to him! Never anything out of it for him at all, except to be harassed and hounded and badgered for years on end. I'll never understand how such a thing can be."

"There were some very important people involved in it, Nora."

"Yes. And they should have gone to jail, like the others. Instead, here they are—running the city! And eternally taking out their spite on a man they're not fit to wipe the shoes of!"

"He cost them a lot of money," Anne said. "Hundreds of thousands of dollars annual income from those places."

"Well, it just makes me sick, Anne. It just simply makes me sick. Is he very upset?"

"He isn't upset at all. You would never know, here at home, that anything is ever wrong away from home. He just says, 'It is as God wills.' Well"—Anne smiled—*"he* says '*Bíonn sé mar is toil le Dia.*' Either way, it's very comforting."

"Oh, you both have such strong characters," Nora said. "If it were me, I'd be fretting and fuming and making a nervous wreck of myself. Yes, and of everybody else, too. But here you are, you poor dear, just going along in your usual way, taking care of a husband and seven children and half the other people in the block besides. . . . Oh, don't try to tell *me*. I know all about your going over half a dozen times a day to see if Mrs. Sheppard needs anything."

"She's bedridden, Nora."

"With neighbors on each side of her. But *they're* too busy. And I know all about your having the two Mahoney children here all last week, as if you didn't have enough to take care of with your own!"

"Their mother was in the hospital. You take care of my children when I'm in the hospital."

"That's different. We're family. You've been doing entirely too much, Anne, and not getting your proper rest. It worries me that you look so tired all the time. From what the girls tell me, you never even get an unbroken night's sleep, with Brendan having these nightmares. Oh, I know, you'll answer right away that he can't help having the nightmares. But I wonder. Perhaps I'm being very callous, but I wonder if some of it isn't just put on, to get attention. Considering how he makes things up. . . ."

"The fear isn't made up," Anne said.

"Well, he should certainly be forbidden to read after he goes to bed, Anne."

"He is."

"But the girls say——"

"I know. But it's very hard to catch him at it. He hears the first step on the stairs, and then it's too late. Tadhg did manage to surprise him the other night, and what do you suppose he was reading? You've guessed it—an Irish prayerbook. Well, of course, that took care of *that*."

"Does anyone ever look under the mattress," Nora asked cynically, "for what he is really reading? It isn't prayerbooks giving him those bad dreams."

"No, but the dreams don't seem to be connected with his reading. The dreams started after he and Paul moved up to the third floor. He was very happy about it at the time; he loved the new bookshelves and the built-in desks. But then, when he'd wake in the night, the room was strange to him, and he felt so very far away, even though our room is right at the foot of the stairs. That's when he began having the dreams. It's always the same one. He dreams that he's alone and lost in a great empty place, an endless desert of white sand. He runs and runs in it, calling for his father. When he's exhausted, he falls, and the sand lets him sink down, like water, and closes over him."

"Poor child! But don't you see, Anne, that if it weren't for all the reading he does, he wouldn't even know such a thing—a desert of white sand—let alone dream about being lost in it."

"For Brendan," Anne said with pitying tenderness, "any place is a desert, I think, if his father isn't in it."

She closed her eyes for a moment, opened them and looked at her watch, folded her sewing and put it away.

Nora asked anxiously, "Anne, dear, are you all right? You're so pale, and that's the third time I've seen you look at your watch. Are you . . . ?"

"Yes."

"Oh, my. And here I sit, worrying you with my talk. Well, I won't ask if you're sure, because you've certainly had enough experience. Let's not waste any time then, dear. You're always very calm, but I get nervous. Now don't you do a thing. We'll just let John sleep, shall we? Rose is up there with him, and I'll slip over and ask Mrs. Moran to come in and sit till I get back. I'll bring your bag downstairs, dear, and your coat and things. Now, you just wait."

"I promised to call Tadhg," Anne said.

She disliked calling the new number. He might not answer, himself, and she would have to ask for him, or perhaps have to ask someone to give him the message. She prayed that he would answer. He was desk sergeant, and they couldn't take that away from him without cause, but who could say they might not manufacture cause?

She felt almost sick with relief when the familiar, firm, beloved voice answered the first ring. It came to her over miles of telephone wire, but there was no mistaking it—in all the world there were not two such voices.

"Tadhg."

She could hear other people talking, their voices sounding loud and quarrelsome. He was busy. She must be brief.

"I'm going to the hospital now, Tadhg. But it will be hours yet, not before you come off duty, I'm quite sure."

She didn't want him to ask to be relieved, only the second day at the new Station. It wouldn't look well. It might be resented. They might refuse.

But there had never been a time when he hadn't come, and she knew he would come now; nothing would stop him.

The firm voice, the voice that made everything safe, everything right, said, "Do I leave here then within the haif-hour, *Áine Ní Bhriain*." And no less firmly, but with a deep tenderness that spoke to her across the miles, not caring that others heard, for he made his own world wherever he was: *"Go dtéir slán, a chroí istigh, agus go dté Muire Bheannaithe leat.* May you go safe, dearest, and may Blessed Mary go with you."

It seemed to Anne that the other voices fell silent as he spoke. She could picture whoever was there staring at him in surprise, partly for the unexpectedly foreign speech, but even more for that unabashed note of tenderness so out of place in the surroundings. She knew those stares, she had

86

seen them often. Even better she knew the high, cold look with which he would meet them, a look that only the bravest could meet without flinching. But for the brave, if they could see, there was the hidden smile, the wonderful warmth of friendliness that he never withheld from any who sought it.

Anne felt her heart grow light. When Nora came looking for her, she was in the kitchen, counting out cookies on a plate. Two apiece—no, three today—for Katie, Peggy, Paul, and Brendan when they came home from school, and for Rose, and one for John. None for Pat, who was beyond the cooky-on-a-plate stage ("For Pete's sake, Mother, if I want any I'll get them myself!").

Was there anything she had forgotten? She took a careful look around. Anything she meant to do? Anything she meant to tell Nora? Oh, yes!

"Saturday is Katie's birthday, Nora. I ordered a cake from Nagel's. Pat will pick it up. And I told her she could invite two friends for the afternoon, and have the cake and hot chocolate, but she and Peggy must do all the fixing and the washing up; they understand there must be no extra work for you."

"My goodness, as if it would be any work to fix a little chocolate. Now don't you worry about a thing, Anne. You just go and have this baby and get it over with, and then you settle yourself for a good long rest. You need it. I don't at all like the way you look."

"Nora, you're so good to us, so good; what would we do without you?"

"Oh, now, it's my pleasure. Don't go making out it's anything special. Are you ready?"

One more look around. Surely there was something she was forgetting?

"I just want to write a note and leave it here on the table for the children. They may be home before you get back. I just want to tell them . . ."

Tell them what? How much she loved them? How she would miss them? To be good? To be careful? To be no trouble to their aunt?

"I'll be right there, Nora."

It was on the way home from school that Brendan encountered the banshee.

Paul and Peggy were walking very fast because it was very cold. Now and then they turned around and called impatiently to him to hurry, whereupon he ran to catch up. The rest of the time he trailed them.

When it happened, he had stopped to look in a store window at a fascinating display of Christmas candies, and ornaments, and Peggy and Paul were nearly half a block ahead. It was a double window, two separate windows, really; you entered the store by way of a narrow walk between them, and the door was set well back. He had gone all the way up to the door, looking in the window on one side, and intended to retrace his steps looking in the window on the other side, and then run. But when he started out toward the sidewalk again, there was the . . . well, he was almost sure it was a banshee.

She was tall, and she was wearing a green coat that fitted tight at the waist and then flared out all around, and had a little upstanding collar of short brown fur, and a narrow band of the same fur around the bottom. She had long red hair—the most beautiful hair he had ever seen—falling in soft waves down over the fur collar and over her shoulders. She was standing there looking into the store window, not at the things in the window, but at her own reflection, and she was drawing a golden comb through her beautiful long red hair.

Brendan was frozen with fear. He didn't dare try to go past her; the walk was so narrow he would almost have to brush against her if he tried to pass. He didn't dare go into the store; they would think he wanted to buy something; they would come to wait on him, and he couldn't buy anything, he had no money. Of course, he could tell them he was just looking. It would certainly be the safest thing to do. He had just about decided on this course, when she slipped the golden comb into her handbag, and turned away and left.

But she walked in the direction he had been walking. She was between him and his brother and sister.

Peggy and Paul looked back when they reached the corner. They saw him coming and called, "Hurry up, pussyfoot!" but they didn't wait. They should have waited for him to reach them before they crossed the street. That was the rule, because he was known to be absent-minded. When

88

he was thinking about something else, he walked across streets without even knowing they were there.

He couldn't run, because *she* was in between and he was afraid to pass her. Even away out by the curb, he'd be afraid to pass. He hoped she would turn at the corner and walk in another direction, but she didn't. She crossed the street, as Peggy and Paul had, and kept right on.

When he reached the corner, the daring thought occurred to him that if he went down one block, running as fast as he could, and then over the next street, and then back again to this one, he could outdistance her.

He ran like the wind. But the cross street was longer than he had estimated, and when he had raced over the paralleling street, and looked up—there *she* was, just crossing over.

There was nothing for it, then, but to run another block. Desperation speeded him. He *must* get there ahead of her this time, he *must* rejoin Peggy and Paul; he was disobeying his father, he wasn't allowed to be on the streets by himself, he had no sense of direction, he was certain to get lost.

Breathing hard, he made it to the corner.

Peggy and Paul had reversed their direction and were all the way back at the last intersection, looking—he supposed—for him.

But there *she* was, not ten feet away and coming toward him. . . .

He turned in panic and raced back the way he had come. *And she followed.* He ran another block. And another. He got his second wind and kept on running, changing his direction at every corner to throw her off his trail. When at last he stopped, he had no idea how far he had come, and no idea where he was.

He rested a minute or two, and then started walking. The houses and stores were unfamiliar. The names of the streets were unknown to him.

He was lost, and it was getting colder every minute, and before long it would be dark.

He was afraid to ask anyone how to get to his own street. They would know he was lost, and they might . . . well, he didn't know what they might, but he was afraid. Once a patrol car with two policemen in it passed him, and the policeman on the passenger side looked at him a little suspiciously, he thought, but before he could summon the courage to call to them and tell them he was lost, the car was too far down the street. He could have wept with regret for his indecision, because they probably knew his father, and they would have taken him home.

After going up one street and down another for a long while, he met an old lady with a great yellow cat—at least he thought it was a cat—on a leash. The cat had such long hair that it trailed on the pavement, and enormous round yellow eyes. A bell on its collar tinkled as it moved. He stopped to stare at the cat, and the cat stopped to stare at him, flattening itself on the sidewalk and glaring fiercely with its great eyes. The old lady said, "Come on, Horace," and at first Brendan thought she was speaking to him, mistaking him for someone else, but then he realized she was speaking to the cat. It was faintly reassuring, because it didn't seem to him that a cat named Horace could be a very dangerous cat, and certainly not a supernatural one. He felt emboldened to ask the old lady if she could tell him where Emerton Street was. She answerd, rather vaguely, that she thought it was "up that way" a few blocks. Then she asked, "Are you lost, little boy?" And he said, "Oh, no, I just wondered how far it was." And he thanked her, and walked in the direction she had pointed.

A biting wind caught him at every street corner. He was chilled through and through, and he started to shiver. And Emerton Street wasn't "up that way." At least, he didn't come to it.

The sun went down, and lights began coming on in the stores and in some of the houses. By the pale wintry sunset he knew which direction was west, but as he didn't know whether he was north or south of home, he didn't know whether he should keep the sunset on his right or his left. He kept on walking.

It was getting on to supper time. In a little while his father would come home and learn that he wasn't there, that he hadn't stayed with Peggy and Paul, that he had willfully disobeyed, first by hanging back and then by running off, and that now he was lost, and that instead of being able to sit down and eat his supper, his father was going to have to go out in the cold and the dark and search the cold, dark streets. His father would be angry with him.

He began to cry. He kept his head down so people passing by wouldn't see that he was crying, and now he not

90

only didn't know which way he was walking, but couldn't even see, blinded as he was by tears. Fear, even colder than the cold December air, took possession of him. The fear that took possession of him in his dreams.

Just when he thought the fear must make him take to his heels again, anywhere at all, just so he ran, and just when in his mind (as in the dream) he began calling over and over, "'Athair 'Athair, please come! Oh, please come find me!" he became aware of someone pedaling a bicycle in the street, close to the curb, slowly, keeping even with him. And just as he was turning his head to steal a frightened look, a cold, hard, angry, but oh, so welcome voice asked, "Going my way, chum?"

And there was Pat.

He wanted to shout and sing, to laugh, to say a thousand prayers, to let Pat know how glad he was to see him, how much he loved him, but all he could do was cry harder.

"Pat, oh, Pat . . . !"

Pat said, "Don't tell me how it happened, I might believe you! Climb on the carrier, you little louse, and keep your mouth shut, and hang on. And just you wait till I get you home!"

But when they reached home, nothing was quite as he expected it to be.

It was not quite as late as he had thought, no one was quite as worried as he had thought, perhaps he had not been quite as lost as he had thought.

But the disturbing thing was that his mother wasn't there to comfort him even while she scolded him. Aunt Nora was there instead, getting supper. Aunt Nora scolded, but, unlike his mother, she didn't put her arms around him; he had no opportunity to let all the fear and the remorse and the relief and the joy of Pat's coming spill out against her in a renewed flood of tears. She seemed to reproach him not so much for getting himself lost, as for choosing this particular afternoon to do it, as if it were a special bit of thoughtlessness directed personally at her. He didn't know what to say, except to whisper that he was sorry, *"Tá brón orm, Áintín Nóra."* He couldn't tell her about the banshee.

It hurt him that his mother wasn't there. He had been so frightened; his bare hands had been nearly frozen from clutching the bicycle carrier and the tears had frozen on his face. He wanted his mother. He needed her.

She had left a note on the kitchen table. "Darlings," the note read, "take care of one another for me." It seemed strange that his mother would write them a note. She had never done such a thing before; because, of course, she was always there, she had no need to write notes. He remembered very clearly the last time she had gone to the hospital, when John was born. She had told them all sorts of things they must be sure to do or not to do, and she had said they could each take twenty-five cents on Saturday out of the little change purse that she kept in the drawer of the kitchen cabinet, and that there was a fresh baking of sand tarts in the white can, but they must finish up the chocolate chip in the red can first; and last of all she had given each of them a big hug and kiss, and they had all stood at the gate waving good-by until Aunt Nora's car was out of sight. But that had been in the summertime. The sun was shining when she left, and there were a dozen delightful things to do to take his mind off her departure.

This time there was nothing, and he didn't like the note.

It made her seem so far away. So *gone*. And even the instruction—"Take care of one another for me." Who could he take care of? Everyone knew he couldn't even take care of himself. The bitter sense of his inability to take care of anyone filled him with grief, as if he must fail his mother in her *last* request? Wasn't she coming back? Of course she was coming back. But then why did she say, "Take care . . . *for me,*" as if she wouldn't be able to do it any more herself, wouldn't be there to do it any more.

He tried to take care of Rose and John by telling them about the yellow cat he had seen. He made it even bigger than it had been, as big as a dog, bigger than a dog; with hair a foot long all over, and little orange flames coming out from the ends of its hair. It was a cat of the *Sluagh Sí,* he told them, the fairy people, and it could change from being a cat to being a very very old woman, and back again, any time it wanted, and its eyes——

But here Aunt Nora interrupted to tell him sharply that she wouldn't have him filling up the heads of his little sister and brother with such wicked nonsense, and he ought to be ashamed to tell lies. When he protested that it wasn't a lie, it wasn't, he had so seen the cat, she said if he had seen a cat, it was just a perfectly ordinary cat like any other cat, and he shouldn't make things up to frighten those poor innocent children. Besides, she wanted to know, hadn't he already caused trouble enough, worrying everybody and making his brother go out looking for him instead of taking care of the furnace and doing the other things he was supposed to do when he came home from school? Now if the fire wouldn't come up, and went out during the night, they'd all have colds as a result of his running off.

"You just sit down and keep still, young man, until supper's ready."

He crept away from the kitchen and into the living room to watch out the front window for his father. Everything would be all right when his father came. He would get warm again, he would know he was safe, he would know he was loved. The uneasy thought came that Peggy and Paul would tell right away about his running off, and Pat would tell about having to go looking for him and how far away he had been. But no thought was uneasy enough to tarnish the soon-to-be joy of his father's coming. Even if, even if . . . well, no matter what, he would be safe. And he was sure his father would understand about everything: about the banshee, even if perhaps it wasn't really and truly a banshee at all; about his terror; about his running off like that and getting lost.

Deep in a corner of his mind lay the hope, the sweet hope—the hope so exquisitely but so fragilely beautiful that he dared not really think it out in words—the hope that he might, he just might, be allowed to sleep in his father's bed tonight.

He pressed against the window, peering into the early winter dark, watching for his father.

The telephone rang. He heard it with alarm. Once in a while, at this hour, just before supper, his father would call to say that he was delayed, something was keeping him, he would be a little late getting home. When that happened they sat down to supper without him, but seeing his father's chair empty was always upsetting; he never wanted his supper, those times when his father wasn't there.

He prayed that it would be just his Uncle Paul or one of his cousins calling Aunt Nora. It couldn't, it couldn't be his father calling to say he wouldn't be home. Aunt Nora was expecting his father home. He had heard Katie ask while she was setting the table, and Aunt Nora had said yes, most likely the baby had come as much as an hour or two ago, and she had no reason to think he wouldn't be home for supper.

Pat answered the telephone.

He held his breath while Pat stood listening.

"Yes," said Pat. "Okay. . . . Sure I will. . . . Right, Pop."

Pat replaced the receiver and went out to the kitchen.

"He's still at the hospital. The baby hasn't come yet. He said he doesn't know when he'll be home, but I'm to look out for the kids and you shouldn't wait. He said if he isn't home by ten o'clock, we're just to lock up everywhere and go to bed."

"Ten o'clock!" There was surprise and something else—a note of alarm—in Aunt Nora's voice. "Why in the world would he think he might not be home by ten o'clock?"

"He didn't say."

It seemed to Brendan that Aunt Nora stared at Pat for a moment in a very strange way, then he could almost see her give herself a little shake before she said briskly, "Well, all right, then. You might as well all come have your supper. Bring in the highchair, Paul. Peggy, fill the glasses."

They had their supper. Brendan played with his food, and Aunt Nora was sharp with him.

"No dessert for you, young man, and you don't leave this table until you've cleared your plate. All that good food! There's many a little boy would be glad to have it, you know."

There was many a little boy Brendan would be only too glad to give it to, but he didn't dare say this; Aunt Nora would call it being impudent.

He couldn't clear his plate. After everyone else was finished, even their dessert, he still sat looking at a nauseating little mountain of cold noodles, ringed by foothills of still colder peas. He had eaten a small piece of chicken and had nibbled the edges of a slice of bread. The others looked at him impatiently, because they wanted to clear the dining-room table and get started on their homework.

Katie rescued him.

"If he's made to eat when he's upset, Aunt Nora, he'll be sick at his stomach."

"On purpose," Peggy said.

"*No* one," said Katie, "would do anything so unpleasant as to vomit on purpose."

94

"*He* would."

"He would not! Father watched him one time to make sure. And he didn't do anything at all but just sit there. I heard Father tell Mother he could see him start to turn green, and then——"

"Then he just opened his mouth," Paul contributed, "and put it all right back on his plate!"

"Children! Please! Such talk at the table!"

But Aunt Nora's resolve was shaken. Her voice-of-authority changed to her voice-of-entreaty.

"Brendan, dear, won't you please eat your supper?"

He whispered, "*Tá sé fuar.*"

"What?"

"It's cold, Aunt Nora."

"If you had eaten when everyone else did," she pointed out uselessly, "it wouldn't have been cold."

But her heart melted when she saw his blue eyes swimming in tears, and anyway *she* didn't want to test the results of making him eat.

"Oh, very well. You needn't eat it, then. But I'm sure I don't know what you live on, and I'm sure your poor dear mother would worry if she knew you didn't eat your supper."

All the time he was doing his homework, Brendan kept listening for the sound of the car door closing and his father's footsteps on the front porch. He didn't have much homework, only six problems in arithmetic and it required a good deal of ingenuity to make them last any time at all. He carefully and neatly wrote his name at the top of his paper and set the problems down very painstakingly and prettily, with special little flourishes and curlicues, and perfectly round 0's, and all his eights made up also of perfectly round 0's, a smaller one set on top of a larger one. But the problems were easy, and at most could consume only half an hour of the long, anxious evening.

When he had finished them, he slipped away from the table and went into the living room, where he would be closer to the car door and the footsteps. He turned on his father's reading lamp and sat in his father's chair and labored alone through a whole page of the *Táin Bó Cualnge,* studiously looking up in Dinneen's dictionary the English translation of any words he didn't know.

At nine o'clock, because tomorrow was a school day, Pat

sent him and Paul to bed. Their room was the third-floor back, and even with a window open he was afraid he might not hear the car door close, even if he made himself stay wide-awake, as he intended. Paul said it was too cold (on account of the furnace fire having almost gone out) to have the window open, and closed it again, not leaving even a crack. Brendan intended to stay awake anyhow, and ordinarily he would have been able to, for just thinking about any strange thing like the cat named Horace, or any terrible thing like being lost, would keep him awake; but all that running up and down the streets had made him very tired, and the long time out in the cold had made him very sleepy, and against his will sleep came, like one of the long, slow, curling rollers of the surf as his father described it breaking over the gray limestone shore of Inishmaan. He watched it come. It crested in a long line of green shadow and white foam, over the bed. When it receded it sucked him along, down and down, into the deepest valleys of the sea.

Some time late in the night a sound awakened him. He knew there had been a sound, although at first, while he lay there rigid and unbreathing with fear, he did not know what it had been like, nor whence it had come, nor how long he had been hearing it through the slowly dissolving wall of sleep.

All he heard now was Paul's breathing there in the bed beside him, and outside the December wind sweeping the streets.

He listened, and to his ear came the faint beginning of the sound, a soft keening. It rose and fell. It grew louder. It mounted to a scream. It dwindled to a low wail. The wind hammered at the window like someone pounding with a fist, and the sound abruptly changed, first to a wild sobbing, then to the beating by unseen hands of a rapid, long-drawn-out tattoo on an unseen drum.

The sound stopped.

Brendan was paralyzed with terror. He could not move. He could do nothing at all but lie there waiting for the fearful sound to begin anew.

Three times he heard it begin, rise to a shriek, and die away in the drumming.

And he knew what it was. He knew, he knew! Everything that had been so strange, so wrong, since that fateful moment on the way home from school—his getting lost, his mother not being there, his father staying so long at the hospital—everything became clear.

She was telling him. It was not the sound itself that was to be feared, but what the sound told of. . . .

When it stops—his mind groped through its terror to fix on what he must do—this time when it stops, I'll get up right away and run downstairs. If Father isn't home, then Pat. I'll go to Pat.

The wild keening rose to its peak, hung there, sank to a low sobbing, dwindled away.

He slipped out of bed and ran.

Never had he gone down the third-floor stairs so fast, swift as a fleeing shadow. His parents' room was the second-floor front, at the foot of the stairs, and the door stood open. The street light outside shone through the front windows, and he did not need even to hesitate in his flight to see that the bed was empty; the smooth white bedspread lay like a patch of the desert that haunted his dreams.

He raced along the hall to his brother's room, at the back. Below the banister the cavernous depth of the stairwell fell away to the lower floor, where only the dimmest of night-lights burned. Middle-of-the-night stillness wrapped the house, except for the sound of his running feet.

The door of Pat's room was ajar, and through it shone a saving, welcoming light to tell him Pat was there and still awake. Pat was there, was there. . . .

"Pat! Pat!"

There was no rule strict enough to make him remember to knock and wait, when terror was at his heels. He ran full into the door with his hands out to push it wide. He slammed it shut behind him. He stood against it, shaking. He made two attempts to speak before he could say, "Pat, there's a noise. . . ."

Pat, with a sweater on over his pajamas, was sitting at his desk working on his radio. He had an electric soldering iron in his hand; the hot smell of it was in the room. He had already paused in his work, holding the soldering tip poised above the connection he had been making, and was looking expectantly toward the door when it burst open, for he had heard the racing feet and knew all about the dreams.

He said at once, very calmly, very unimpressed, "You're having a nightmare. There isn't any noise."

"Yes, there is. Yes! I've been awake for a long while, listening. I . . . it's a banshee, Pat! On the roof!"

Pat laid his soldering iron down carefully on a brick that he kept on his desk for that purpose. He got up, pulled the top blanket off his bed and wrapped it around his shivering and shaking little brother.

"Come, sit down. You're having a chill. How often have you been told not to run around in your bare feet?"

"I . . . forgot . . . to put my slippers on, Pat."

"The floor's cold," Pat said. "Put your feet upon the rung of the chair. Here." He tucked the ends of the blanket under the icy feet. "Okay, now, let's have it. You heard a noise on the roof. What kind of noise?"

"A banshee. Wailing and crying."

"You didn't hear a banshee, because there's no such thing as a banshee."

"Yes, there is, Pat. They wail when someone's going to die. They wail and comb their hair. Mother——"

"They don't wail any time at all," Pat said flatly, "for any reason at all, because they don't exist at all. And Mother isn't dying."

Tears started streaming now.

"She's in the hospital. . . ."

"She's only in the hospital having another baby."

"But then why hasn't Father come home? When John was born, Father only stayed a little while. I remember. But he's been there now for hours and hours!"

"Some babies take longer than others," Pat said. "Mother's all right. But if you want to know—and I guess—although you certainly don't act it—you're old enough to hear some of the facts of life—Mother had trouble. The baby was a long time coming, and then after it did come, she had a hemorrhage."

Fearfully: "What exactly is a hemorrhage, Pat?"

"It means she lost a lot of blood. She had to have a transfusion. Pop called about ten o'clock. He said he'd be a while yet because they were going to use his blood."

"Use . . . his . . . blood?" Brendan whispered, as the last of his own drained out of his face.

"Sure. He's got the same type, so they were going to take some right out of him and put it in Mother."

"Won't it . . . won't it hurt him, Pat?"

"Of course not."

"But if they . . . if . . . do they cut him open, to get his blood?"

"They don't cut him *open,* for Pete's sake! They only make a little incision, here in his arm, and then his blood runs through a tube and right in a vein in Mother's arm."

"How . . . how much of his blood, Pat?"

"That depends. A pint, maybe. Don't worry, he's got plenty to spare. Which is more than I can say of you. You're white as a ghost. Now quit worrying. Mother's all right. Pop said so, and you know darn well he'd never say it if it wasn't so. And he's all right. And we've got another brother, and *he's* all right. Now you hike back upstairs to bed. It's past midnight."

"Pat . . ."

"All right," Pat said with weary resignation. "Tell me about the noise. But if you say 'banshee' again, I'll smack you one! What was it like?"

"Like wailing. Like a . . . like what I said. First scream-ing, then sobbing."

"Sobbing?"

"Well, something like sobbing. Something like . . . like drumming. Like chattering."

"That was your teeth."

This made Brendan laugh; but the untrustworthiness of laughter, when it comes mixed with tears, made the tears come faster.

"Pat, it was . . . I saw it . . . her . . . this afternoon."

"You saw *who* this afternoon?"

"A . . . one of *them.* On the way home from school."

"When are you going to grow up? You didn't see 'one of *them,'* because there *aren't* any of *them.* Any kid nearly nine years old that believes in fairies ought to have his head examined. But go ahead." Pat sat down on the edge of the bed and folded his arms as if steeling himself for a long and trying ordeal. "Give me the works. Out with it!"

The story came spilling out. All the terror, all the tor-ment, the lonely streets, the cold, the coming dark, the old lady with the cat named Horace, the joy of Pat's coming, but then his mother being gone, the note, the long evening of waiting for his father, who never came, the noise on the roof . . .

Pat heard it out. When the story had trailed off into

silence punctuated by hiccups, he said, "Hold your breath and count to nine."

Brendan held his breath and counted to nine. The hiccups stopped.

"That was Angie Stevens," Pat said.

"What was, Pat?"

"Your banshee in the green coat. She's always combing her hair all over the place. She thinks she looks like a movie star. Wait till I tell her she looks like a banshee!"

"Pat, you won't tell her *I* thought she was a banshee?"

"You think I want anyone knowing what a nut I have for a brother? And the noise on the roof," Pat said, "was the wind."

"Pat, I've often heard the wind. It never——"

"You never heard it before in my new short-wave antenna. You know those eight-foot-long aluminum tubes? When the wind goes through those tubes, it makes the wailing noise you heard. Then when it shifts, it sets up a vibration, and that's the drumming you heard. I heard it, too. That's all it is. Satisfied?"

"Yes, Pat."

"Then beat it. Back you go to bed now, on the double. And if I hear another squawk out of you tonight, boy, you'll have reason to squawk!"

"Pat"—a pleading whisper—"I believe you. If you say that's all it is, I do believe you, truly I do. But if I go upstairs, it will still *sound* like . . . like what I thought, and . . . Pat, if I could just not have to go upstairs again tonight, I promise I won't ever pay any attention to it again."

"You're a liar. You'll put on an act any time and every time you think you can get away with it. Well, you won't get away with it with *me,* so don't go thinking you can. But, all right, this once. This *once,* mind you!"

Safe in Pat's bed. Warm and safe under Pat's blankets. Well, soon to be warm, if he could just stop shivering.

"Are you coming to bed, Pat?"

"When it suits me."

Pat busied himself for a few minutes with his radio. He plugged it in and tried it, but the stations wouldn't come clear. He turned it off again. He went over and opened his door and stood listening for a moment to the stillness of the house, and then, leaving the door open, came back and took off his sweater and got into bed.

100

His desk light still burned.

"Are you going to stay awake, Pat, till Father comes home?"

"Maybe. You keep over on that side, now, you hear?"

The answer was given humbly, "I'll keep way over here on the edge, Pat."

"Yeah, for about two minutes. Then you'll start jabbing me with your knees and elbows. I must be soft in the head, letting you get away with this!"

"Pat."

"What?"

"You won't tell Paul and Peggy, will you?"

"Any time I waste my breath telling those bird-brains anything, you'll know it. Now shut up and go to sleep. And for Pete's sake, stop shivering! You're shaking the bed!"

Brendan tried his best to stop shivering. He tried holding himself very stiff, but that only seemed to make it worse. He tried pulling himself into a ball, but then he didn't know what to do with his feet; they were so cold he couldn't bear to have them touch each other. For himself he didn't mind shivering; it was heaven to be here, shivering or not, but he didn't want to annoy Pat. He lay on the very edge of the bed, as he had promised, leaving a good twelve-inch clearance; but the very edge of a bed is always a little chilly, with cold air finding its way in under the covers when they aren't tucked in. Fear that Pat would lose patience and send him upstairs after all did nothing to help.

"Aw, nuts!"

Pat's arm slipped around his waist, roughly and unexpectedly pulling him close.

And there he was. There he was, with his back to that warm, solid, comforting wall, the curve of his body fitting blissfully against the curve of his brother's, and warmth and joy flowing all through him, all over him, all around him.

"Now, damn it, *get warm,* will you!"

Their father, coming home, twice looked in the room on the second-floor back, the first time merely glancing in from the doorway before making the rest of his rounds.

He moved very quietly, for a man his size. There still remained in his step a trace of the same primitive lightness that permitted the third of his five sons to move from place to place as soundlessly as a cat. No one heard him in the

101

hall or on the stairs, and when his tour of inspection revealed only six where seven should be, and he came back again to his starting-point, everyone still slept on.

He went into Pat's room the second time, close to the bed, and he stood above it for a long while looking down.

It seemed to him, then, a fitting place for a man to say his prayers, and he knelt beside his son's bed and offered thanks to God for more mercies than he could count.

Pat woke to a light touch on his shoulder. Waking, a full sense of his guardianship was still upon him, and he did not move his body, but only his head, and spoke very low.

"Hi, Pop. How's everything?"

"*Tá Dia maith*," his father answered in the same low tone. "God is kind. It is well with your mother, and with your new brother, James, and with this one also, I see."

Pat grinned. "He had a scare, Pop, and a bad chill."

"Not least is it to me, Pádraig," his father said, "at the end of this day, in which a new son has been given me and her also spared who is the beloved of my heart, not least is it to find that in this room has God a dwelling place, for such is the heart of one who with compassion sees his brother's need. Do you not disturb yourself now, but sleep again, for the new day is already two hours spent, and soon enough must we all be up. Then will we talk. A good night to you now, my son . . . *go dtugaidh Dia oíche mhaith dhuit. . . .*"

"*Gurab amhlaidh dhuit* . . . the same to you, Father," answered Brendan in his sleep, smiling the smile of heaven.

6

BRENDAN O'NOLAN sat at the kitchen table dawdling over his lunch.

With half his mind he listened to his mother saying to his sister Peggy that she thought the bread man must have shortchanged her that morning. With the other half he was thinking up charms that might cause the food on his plate to disappear so that he could go outside and climb the cherry tree to the platform Pat had made for him, and read his new library book.

None of the charms worked. The food remained: cold scrambled eggs and a piece of toast covered with creamed dried beef which had congealed to a thick paste. He didn't have to eat it, but until his plate was cleared he couldn't leave the table. That was what his mother had said.

The scrambled eggs were by this time dry and leathery. He watched his chance, and whenever his mother and Peggy both had their backs turned, he deftly slipped two or three of the yellow lumps off his plate into a pocket of his jeans. This was easy, but he hadn't yet figured out a way to clear his plate of the creamed beef.

The bill had been two dollars and sixty cents, his mother was saying, she had given the bread man three one-dollar bills and he had given her three coins in change, presumably a quarter, a dime, and a nickel, as no other combination of three would make up forty cents. She had put the change in the little purse that she kept in the drawer of the kitchen cupboard, and there had been four coins in the purse at the time, one of them a quarter, she was certain of that, because it was a shiny new quarter that she had been saving for Rose's birthday. There were seven coins in the purse now, but only the one quarter.

"But Mother," Peggy asked, "didn't you *count* the change when he gave it to you?"

"No, only to notice that he handed me three coins. I suppose I just assumed——"

"For heaven's sake!" said Peggy. "If he knows that you only notice how many *coins* he gives you, instead of how much *money,* he's probably been cheating you right and left for ages!"

"Oh, no, I don't think so. He's a very nice young man. I'm quite sure he's completely honest. It would be very easy to make a mistake, a five-cent piece for a quarter."

"You're really terribly naïve, Mother."

Peggy sounded very pitying, but when Peggy sounded that way it nearly always meant that she wasn't really sorry for you at all, quite the opposite, really.

"Anybody who makes change all the time knows perfectly well what they're doing," Peggy said, "and certainly would never mistake a nickel for a quarter. Of course," said Peggy, who was fourteen now and had a very superior way of talking, "if you make it so ridiculously easy for people to cheat you, by only counting the *number* of coins they give you in change, I really don't see how you can blame anyone if they take advantage of you."

"I'm not blaming anyone but myself, Peggy. I've always done it that way. It used to provoke your grandmother, too. . . . Darling"—his mother turned to him, offering encouragement, "you've done very well with the eggs. Now can't you eat the creamed beef? At least, some of it?"

Brendan gave her a gentle smile. They both looked at the cold, sad remains of his lunch. He could feel his mother wavering. For just a minute he was almost certain she was going to relent, but then she sighed and reaffirmed her position.

"Well, I'm sorry, you will just have to sit there, then."

"Until suppertime," Peggy said. "And if *I* had anything to say about it, *that* would be your supper. And your breakfast and your tomorrow's lunch, too!"

Brendan gave Peggy a gentle smile also, and with his fork began scraping the creamed dried beef off the toast. If he scraped the toast clean enough, he could fold it over and put it in his pocket with the eggs.

Purely as something with which to occupy his mind, he thought about the bread man and the change. He was struck by the peculiarity of his mother's way of keeping a tally of her small change, not because he was critical of her, as Peggy was, but simply because it was such a very different way from his own. He saw that Peggy was right—it would be very easy to take advantage of someone who counted only the number of coins they had, and not what the coins totaled. He saw how easy it would be for anyone to help himself to a bit of change from the kitchen purse, if he wanted to. He had, of course, no idea that anyone ever would.

He always knew exactly how much money he had; how much he would have left if he spent ten cents, or five, or two; how much he would have to beg, borrow, or earn before he could buy some special item that he specially desired.

Money had become a burning need. Unfortunately, just about the time he came to a realization of its prime importance, it became much harder to get.

The financial affairs of the O'Nolan household had been under severe strain for several months, ever since his mother had been such a long time in the hospital when Mary was born in January. It was a much longer time (as he knew from listening to conversations that he wasn't supposed to hear) than the insurance covered. His father had to borrow money to pay the hospital and doctors' bills, and then for a month after she had come home his mother had to have a nurse with her while his father was at work. The effects of all this extra expense were manifest in many ways, one of them being that throughout the spring, at a time when everybody Brendan knew at school received at least one dollar a week spending money, and most received two, his weekly allowance had been cut from a meager fifty cents to an incredibly meager twenty-five.

And then, while his mother was so sick, his grandfather had died. This was a loss over which he grieved for reasons having nothing to do with the cessation of the easy flow of nickels and dimes and quarters, even on occasion of dollar bills, that used to come to him from his grandfather. He liked having the money, but money hadn't been so important when he was younger. He had always shared what his grandfather gave him, usually in the candy store or the pastry shop on the way home from school, when he turned the money over to Pat, or, after Pat started high school, to Katie, letting them decide what to spend it for, because in the midst of all that deliciousness, with everybody wanting something different, he never knew what to get or even how much the money would buy.

It had been fun to have the money to spend on the way home from school, but it had been more fun to sing the Irish songs his grandfather was always asking to hear. (The money was specifically for the songs, not the prayers, which his grandfather had also liked to hear; but his father said not must he take money from his grandfather for saying the Irish prayers.)

Now his grandfather was gone. He had been gone for a long while, several months, but it was still a hard thing to bear. Brendan had not been able to understand how his mother could bear it at all. The terrifying thought would come to him—what if it were *my* father!—and he had marveled that she could accept her father's death, and herself go on living, go on loving all of them and fretting because she wanted to be up and around and doing for them. He could not have borne it. He would have died too.

God had taken away his grandfather, whom he loved. On that account he grieved; but so many were left to him, he was so bountifully supplied with people to love, he could not, on that account, without seeming greedy and ungrateful, lodge any protest with God. But God had taken away his grandfather who loved *him,* and there were not so many of those that one could be spared. Now in all the world he could be sure—absolutely sure—of the love of only two people: his father and mother. The total of People Who Truly Loved Him had been reduced, when his grandfather died, by one third. It seemed to him a very drastic cut.

Sitting there looking at the depressing food on his plate, and thinking about his grandfather, he felt tears come to his eyes and start sliding down his cheeks. He kept his head down and busied himself scraping the piece of toast, but Peggy happened to look his way, and Peggy had sharp eyes.

"For goodness sake! Look at him now, Mother. What a baby! He's *crying!*"

He didn't raise his head, but he could feel his mother

looking at him. He knew she would think he was crying because she was making him sit at the table until he cleared his plate.

She said, not sharply, but with patient resolve, "Brendan, there's no use crying. You *must* learn to eat what's put on your plate, while it's hot and while the rest of us are eating. You are very wasteful of food, and we can't afford to be wasteful. You must learn," she repeated, and went out of the kitchen and upstairs to see if Mary was awake.

Peggy laughed at him.

"It didn't work, did it?"

Feebly, he said, "I'm not crying about that."

"Oh, of course not. I suppose you have a pain. Or you feel sick at your stomach. Or you just remembered a very sad, sad story."

He whispered, "I was thinking about Grandfather."

"You pious little hypocrite!" Peggy said scornfully. *"Grandfather.* Who do you think you're kidding? And even if you were thinking about Grandfather, it isn't him you're crying for, it's the money he used to give you!"

When his mother came back the toast was gone. He was certain that no one, *no one,* would insist that he eat that horrible cold paste, all that now remained on his plate of his lunch. Certainly not his mother, who was so kind, so loving, so merciful.

"All right, dear," his mother said. "You may go."

Before he left the kitchen he threw his arms around her waist in a tight hug. It was nine tenths because he loved her so much. The other one tenth was atonement for his deceit.

Now he had the rest of the afternoon in which to figure out a way to dispose of the toast and the scrambled eggs in his pocket. It might require considerable ingenuity, for the one thing he could *not* do was flush them down the toilet.

That had always been such a wonderfully convenient method of disposal—until the day last winter when he had tried to flush away two hard-boiled eggs. The perfect clarity with which he remembered every detail of the incident effectively prohibited his use of that method ever again.

It had happened while his mother was in the hospital with Mary.

Aunt Nora didn't come that time to take care of them, but took John and Jimmy to stay at her house; the rest of them were old enough to shift for themselves. Pat was in supreme command throughout the day while his father wasn't there. Katie and Peggy got the meals and took care of the house.

It was the matter of lunches that brought the well-remembered incident to pass.

Pat and Katie and Peggy bought their lunches; he and Paul and Rosie carried theirs from home. By division of labor, Katie got breakfast and Peggy fixed the lunches. But Peggy wasn't feeling well that morning, she was late coming downstairs, and there wasn't anything to make sandwiches of. She boiled three eggs, and put two buttered slices of bread, one egg—even though she knew neither Brendan nor Rosie liked hard-boiled eggs—and two cookies in each of their bags for their lunch.

He ate the bread and the cookies at lunchtime, and put the egg in his pocket.

On the way home from school, when Paul stopped to look in the window of a hardware store, Rosie edged up close and asked, "Did you eat your egg?"

He never had to lie to Rosie. She was not yet seven, but she never betrayed a confidence.

"No."

"Neither did I. Will we have to eat them for supper?"

"Not if we don't tell we didn't eat them for lunch."

"But what will we do with them? Peggy will see if we put them in the garbage. And Dinty won't eat them; *he* has better sense. I *hate* hard-boiled eggs," Rosie said bitterly. "Mother *never* makes me eat hard-boiled eggs!"

He asked, "Where is yours?"

"In my pocket."

"Give it to me," he said on a noble impulse. "I'll get rid of it for you."

The first thing he did when he reached home was to go upstairs to the bathroom and flush the eggs down the toilet.

Half an hour later, when the others came home, the dreadful thing happened.

He was on the third floor, in his room, but he heard Peggy in the second-floor hall screaming for Pat, and he ran down to see what was wrong.

The toilet bowl had overflowed.

"It *isn't* my fault!" Peggy was protesting hysterically when he got there. "All I did was flush it! But instead of
108

going down, the water just kept coming up and up until it ran over. And look at the floor, look at the *floor* . . . !"

Pat got the big red rubber plunger that his father used to open the washtub drains when they got clogged and worked it up and down in the bowl. It made loud sucking and whooshing noises, which were fascinating in their own right. In conjunction with the already present, deadly fascination of the fear and foreboding born of his consciousness of guilt, they drew Brendan as close as he dared come to peer into the toilet bowl.

Suddenly there was an extra loud *whoosh,* the plunger came up, and also up came the eggs!

They went right down again. Brendan hastily slipped away and returned to the third floor, hoping that Pat hadn't been able to tell, so quick, what they were.

There was little basis, as he found out, for his hope.

Pat had seen, and Pat didn't even need to ask how the eggs got there. Pat turned the job of cleaning up the bathroom over to the girls, and came upstairs, straight upstairs, and straight into the room, and closed the door.

"The next time," Pat said, in a very misleading tone, as if he were seriously offering instruction and advice that might be helpful, "put them down one at a time and flush each one separately. That way you've got a chance. But when those things travel in pairs they get chummy, and want to cuddle up in the gooseneck. Only I don't think" —and here Pat's tone underwent a grim change and was no longer misleading at all—"I don't think, when I get through warming your tail, there's ever going to be a next time!"

So Brendan had to think up something different to do with the toast and the scrambled eggs.

He took his book and climbed the cherry tree to his platform. No one else would come up there, and no one would see from the second-story windows—the leaves screened him. It was safe to empty his pocket. He drew out the toast, limp but still in one piece, and laid it on the boards in a spot of sunlight. He arranged the yellow lumps of egg in a neat circle around it. His pocket felt rather nasty, so he pulled it inside out to dry. In a little while, he thought, the sun might dry the toast and the eggs enough that they could be crumbled very fine and scattered. Sparrows and starlings would then consume the evidence.

Birds were his friends. If he couldn't do that, he'd think up something else. In the meantime he would read a few chapters of his book.

The book was absorbing and the birds were not his friends. Behind his back the sparrows came to investigate the yellow lumps, pecking at one or two of them and dislodging several that were near the edge of the board. A starling flew off with the piece of toast, but finding it too heavy to carry, came to earth with it just outside the kitchen shed. Starling and toast were both there when his mother came out the back door a few minutes later. The starling flew away. The toast remained, mute evidence of her son's duplicity, there in plain sight at her feet.

His mother called him down out of the tree. She took his book away. He returned to sit, for the rest of that bright summer afternoon, at the kitchen table, meditating on his sins.

Barring an occasional mischance such as this, the summer of 1948 was a pleasant time for Brendan. There were fewer problems, fewer crises, than had to be met during the school year. Partly it was the wonderful freedom, the long days of not having to do anything at all except just what he felt like doing. He had no stated chores. The girls helped with the housework and Paul did any yard work that needed to be done, and though Brendan sometimes almost ran his legs off fetching this and that for them, neither the girls nor Paul ever wanted him to do any of the actual work. Not that they wanted to spare him. It was simply that he couldn't be counted on to do it right. He was always sure to drop a dish or trip over the scrub bucket or get more paint on his clothes than he'd ever manage to get on the back fence. They wanted him handy to wait on them, but they wanted him at a discreet distance, well out of the way.

Another factor contributing to the peace and pleasure of the summer was that money, during vacation time, was not the serious problem that it had become in the last few months of school. He had little opportunity to spend it, so there was little need to worry about not having it. He wasn't allowed to go anywhere alone, for he couldn't be trusted not to lose himself. It had been tried, and he always took the wrong bus or trolley car; or, if he happened to take the right one, then he walked in the wrong direction when he got off. The trouble was that he daydreamed. He could ride right past his own street, and clear on out to the end of the line, without being aware of it. He was allowed to go alone as far as the drugstore, two blocks down, for an ice-cream cone or a candy bar; and this he did five days a week, unless he recklessly spent his whole allowance the first trip out. Every other Saturday he went to the library with Katie, and usually Katie treated him to an ice-cream soda, or at least to a five-cent root beer or lemonade. At the library he could take out four books on his own card and four on Paul's, if he wanted to. The rest of the time he just stayed home and read.

He did not look forward to the start of school with joy. He liked school, in the classroom. Outside the classroom it brought him face to face with many problems that he would be happy to avoid.

The problem of money loomed large, because money made up for a lot of other things; when you had it, nothing else ever seemed quite so bad.

There would be no use asking for an increase in his weekly allowance. That had been made very clear.

Borrowing from his brothers and sisters was next to impossible. He was, with justice, considered a poor risk.

Begging from them was equally unfruitful. The girls' allowances, although considerably more than his (because they were so much older, and girls needed so many more things) were as insufficient for their needs as a quarter-dollar was for his. Katie would sometimes give him something. Peggy, never.

Paul had a paper route and, besides, worked on Saturdays for Mr. Fletcher, the grocer. He had money of his own and needed no allowance. But he absolutely would not spend any of his money, even on himself, much less give any of it away. He put it all in the bank. With what he could earn and save, plus interest, he had it all figured out that in three years, when he would be sixteen and able to get his driver's license, he'd have enough money in the bank to buy a secondhand delivery truck, and then he'd go in business for himself.

Pat, of course, had been working after school and on Saturdays and all through the summers for years. Pat, at seventeen, had more than a thousand dollars saved, and his own car, and he bought all his own clothes, and even paid board. But Pat wouldn't give him anything either, although it wasn't that Pat hadn't a generous and compassionate nature. It was a matter of principle.

"It doesn't come easy, kid," Pat told him, "and now's the time to find that out. If you want money, buckle down and earn it."

Once in a while Pat would pay him for rendering some small service. Yet, much as he wanted the money, he never wanted to be paid for doing things for Pat. It was enough just to be *allowed* to do something for Pat, just to be near, just to be noticed. He would have served Pat on his knees. He delighted in serving Pat, out of love. To be paid for the service seemed to put a price on his love, to cheapen it, even in a sense to deny it.

Besides, he was always doing things for the others, countless little things, and no one else ever paid him. He never thought of asking to be paid, or of refusing to do the countless little things unless he was.

"Bren, run upstairs and get my sweater, will you?"

"Give me a hand with these ash cans, Bren. You're big enough to do some work."

"Go get the paper."

"Go get me a glass of water."

"Bring me my spelling book."

"Hey, it's raining! Go bring my bike up on the porch."

He was everybody's errand boy, everybody's helper to hand-me-this, hand-me-that, everybody's gun-bearer. He had always been perfectly willing, even eager, to assume this role, so willing and eager that it was considered sport for someone to ask him to do some ridiculous or bizarre or totally impossible thing, and watch him set off blithely and unquestioningly to do it. "What a fall guy!" Paul and Peggy said, and they thought it uproariously funny that Brendan —the silly!—never had sense enough to know when something was intended as a joke.

But nobody ever paid him, except Pat.

Last spring, acting on Pat's dictum that if he wanted money he must earn it, he made an ill-starred (but wonderfully lucrative while it lasted) venture into the literary profession: he set himself up as a ghostwriter, at the modest rate of ten words for one cent.

Sister Mary George was first surprised and then delighted when, near the end of the school year, a number of her fourth graders showed sudden and marked improvement in English Composition. Even those boys who did very poorly in class began turning in homework that fairly bloomed. She wasn't without suspicion, at first: she asked if they were being helped at home by older members of their families. They assured her earnestly and with the ring of truth that such was not the case. They said it was simply that they hadn't enough time, in class, to write well; at home, of course, they had all the time they needed. Still suspicious, she made a spot check among their parents, and the same assurances were as earnestly given: they were not being helped at home.

So Sister Mary George ceased to question and came to believe. She told them how pleased she was, after months of the most discouraging results from the main body of the class (there were, of course, a few brilliant exceptions, she said, some of the girls, and Brendan O'Nolan), to find her fourth grade blossoming out in this way with a remarkable number of students who were at last responding in a most gratifying manner to her unflagging efforts to drill proper English usage into their heads and a spark of creative fire into their hearts. She said she was proud of them. She told them that things like this repaid a teacher for all her years and years of hard work.

She gave Brendan a bad fright one day by telling him that she wanted to see him after school; but the reason turned out to be only that she had noticed how, after having been rather solitary all year, either consistently ignored or consistently tormented by the other boys, he had recently become quite popular and was usually at the center of a little group. She only wanted to compliment him upon the belated, but successful, adjustment he was making, and to remind him that she had always said he could do it if he just corrected his attitudes.

It was quite apparent that Sister Mary George did not know *what* attitudes he had corrected. There was nothing in anything she said to indicate even the barest suspicion of any connections between his new popularity and the improved ability of some of her less literate fourth graders to use their day's spelling words intelligently in sentences, or to write really creditable fifty- to one-hundred-word compositions on such subjects as How I Plan to Spend My Vacation, or What It Means to Me To Be a Catholic.

Her complimentary and encouraging remarks pleased him greatly, first, because his sins had not, as he had feared, yet found him out. He was not in danger—at least not in imminent danger—of losing his new-found income, which sometimes amounted to an incredible dollar and a half a week. He had not given himself away by any maladroitness, but was, indeed, being uncommonly clever. He was very careful to guard against making the sentences *too* good. He never, for example, made them intricate and ingenious, as he made his own, by contriving to use two or three of the words, or once in a while all five of them, in one artful sentence. And when he wrote a composition for, say, Anthony Rimado, whom he considered a rather brutish person with absolutely no finer sensibilities at all, he was extremely careful to fit the content of the composition to Anthony's spiritual character, or lack of it.

Also, Sister Mary George's remarks went a long way toward easing his conscience. He knew, of course, that he was guilty of wrongdoing in helping the other boys to cheat, but he found all manner of justification for it. It was done in a good cause. You were *supposed* to help other people. He was showing the other boys how the work should be done, how to form grammatical sentences, how to write good compositions. Surely, with all the beautiful examples he was supplying, they would soon learn to do it themselves. Would he not then have taught them something very useful, something that would be a help to them all the rest of their lives? And now here was Sister Mary George pointing out to him another beneficial effect that he hadn't thought of, the matter of his own social adjustment. That would please his mother, who worried because he didn't make any close friends at school. It was all very comforting.

But he had a second bad fright, an even worse one, when he committed the nearly fatal blunder of spending his money too freely, thus exciting comment at home. He told his mother that it was money his grandfather had given him a long time ago, but his mother knew that he had always spent the money his grandfather had given him, almost at once. He then had to make up on the spur of the moment a long and involved account of how it had slipped down in back of one of the little drawers of his desk, and how he just happened to find it because the drawer got stuck, and when he finally got it open and looked to see what had been holding it—why there was the two-dollar bill that Grandfather had given him one time when he happened to mention that he had never seen a two-dollar bill.

"And don't you remember, Mother, that I never could find it, and I thought I must have spent it for a one?"

His mother remembered.

"But you never mentioned finding it," she said.

Now he had to look ashamed, which was very easy because he *was* ashamed; and though what he was ashamed of was lying to his mother, the look was equally appropriate to the fault which he confessed.

"I was afraid you wouldn't let me spend it. It was very wrong of me, Mother," he said, ready to cry.

"Well, not *very* wrong," his mother answered, offering quick comfort, "but a little wrong, I think. It was your own money. The thing is—you aren't very careful about how you spend money. And two dollars is a great deal just to let run through your fingers."

He hoped the matter would be allowed to rest there. But no, his mother passed the story along to his father, and that same evening he was called to explain all over again about the stuck drawer and the lost-and-found two-dollar bill. Ordinarily this would have been much more difficult, because lying to his father wasn't the easy matter that lying to his mother was. His father wasn't nearly so trusting; he asked more pointed questions and his eyes looked right into you, right down into the very place in your mind where you were making up the lie. But having already told the story once, on the second telling he so nearly believed, himself, that it had happened exactly that way, that he breezed glibly through it in what he felt must surely be an entirely convincing manner.

Yet his father didn't believe him. He knew very well that his father didn't believe him. Not that he accused him of lying. Not that he became angry, or coldly suspicious, or even raised any question. He didn't do or say anything at all, just sat and looked at him, listening to the story.

Brendan heard his own voice begin to falter, to tremble. He ended on a very uncertain note. His father looked at him and he looked at his father.

He asked tremulously, "Don't you believe me, Father?"

"Remember you any time," his father answered, "that I have not believed you, Brendan, when you have spoken truth?"

"No."

"Then what makes you ask if I do not believe you now?"

"The way you look at me, Father."

"Now it may be," his father said, "that we look at each other in a way which neither the one nor the other of us quite understands. You have told me of finding the two-dollar bill given you by your grandfather. Not have I questioned either your finding or your spending of it. But if you should háve such good fortune again, my son, then I think I might question. . . ."

After that, the money he took in from his ghostwriting did him little good, for he dared not spend it openly, and opportunities to spend it secretly were rare. The wages of sin, accumulating, became difficult of concealment. The money was all in small change, he had no idea how much it amounted to, he could not even have the pleasure of counting it—he had not that much privacy. He lined a box with cotton to keep the coins from jingling, and kept the box hidden at the back of the bottom drawer of his desk, with a lot of school notebooks and papers stacked carefully in front of it. His mother respected personal belongings if they were kept orderly, and it wasn't likely that she would disturb the contents of his desk; nevertheless he lived in fear that while cleaning his room she might pull open the desk drawers to dust them, and take out the box, and wonder at its being so heavy, and open it to see . . .

He would have terminated the whole enterprise had it not been for that matter of social adjustment of which Sister Mary George had spoken. The boys wouldn't like it if he stopped; they were counting on a continuance of their excellent homework to pull up the inferior grades they otherwise expected. He put out a feeler—he said he was going to be awfully busy from now on until the end of school; he didn't know how much time he'd have for helping them. But Anthony Rimado put out a fist—right under his nose—and said, "You ain't quittin' now, boy!" And he said, oh, no, he hadn't meant he was quitting, he just meant he might not have time to do quite as much.

Ironically, it was Anthony Rimado who brought everything to ruin.

Usually when Brendan did anything wrong, his own carelessness, or ignorance, or recklessness, or forgetfulness proved his undoing. Pat said he definitely wasn't the successful criminal type; he was too dumb about covering up his tracks. He always gave himself away, somehow. But this time it was someone else's carelessness, someone else's stupidity, that gave everything away.

Anthony Rimado's.

Anthony Rimado, one fateful day during the very next to last week of school, hadn't time, or was simply too lazy, to copy his five sentences in his own hand. His penmanship was probably the worst in the room, but he turned in, that day, a paper written in a fine neat hand. He put his own name at the top of the paper, printing it, so that the contrast would not (he imagined) be too glaringly apparent. But Sister Mary George took one look at the paper and knew that that exquisite handwriting could belong to one and only one boy in the room, or, for that matter, in the whole school. The cat was out of the bag, and Brendan O'Nolan was out of business and into hot water up to his neck.

His whole world was shaken by the subsequent developments. He was charged with being not merely *as* guilty as any of the boys who had turned in his work as their own, but *five times as guilty,* because they had committed only their own individual crimes, but he had aided and abetted all of them. It was further charged that he was the instigator. The whole thing had been at his suggestion, he had offered his services, he had led the other boys into dishonesty; and he had to admit that this was so. Worse than anything, he had taken pay for it, he had done it for profit. In the eyes of Sister Mary George and—alas!—of his father, this took his offense out of the category of a misdemeanor and put it into that of a felony.

There was some talk of expelling him. All that saved him was the utter blamelessness of his past record. And his father. His father had to arrange to be an hour late reporting for duty at the Station, in order personally to escort him back to school and to have a talk with Mother Aloysius, the principal, because until he did so Brendan would not be permitted to return to class. Mother Aloysius had never met his father before, but when he assured her in a very firm way that it would never happen again, she appeared completely satisfied.

The story went over the whole school. Everybody sympathized with the other boys, who had to make up all the work they hadn't done, before they could be promoted. Brendan became notorious. Everybody pointed him out to everybody else, but nobody seemed to feel he needed to be sympathized with. His social adjustment reached a new low.

At home, Paul and Peggy seized every opportunity to treat it as a great joke.

"Our house is just like one of those old castles now—we've got a ghost!"

"Get Bren to tell you a ghost story, Johnny; he's awfully good at it."

"Bren was doing fine till he got his wires crossed and wrote Tony Rimado's composition in Irish!"

"He turned green when Sister Mary George caught him. That's how she knew it was an Irish ghost!"

Pat told them to shut up. When Pat first heard the story he said, "Holy Moses! And I'm the one who told him to get busy and earn some money!" And this had been comforting, somehow, just a little comforting, as if Pat was taking a little, just a little, of the blame. The closest Pat came to making a joke of it was to call him Public Enemy Number One-half, but not in front of the others.

And he couldn't keep the money. His father made him turn it all over to Mother Aloysius for the school. He never even got to count it. But he was glad to be rid of the money. It had brought him no joy.

After this shattering experience he was absolutely certain that he would never do another dishonest thing in his life.

That was why he had no idea, absolutely no idea at all, that day during the summer, that he, Brendan O'Nolan, would ever dream of taking advantage of his mother's curious method of counting her change.

It was with great reluctance that he approached the start of the new school year; yet, once under way, nothing was quite as bad as he had feared it would be. Everybody seemed to have forgotten all about that episode of the previous spring. No one paid any particular attention to him, except a few of the girls, who almost seemed to like him. And the fifth grade had a new teacher, Sister Cecilia, who had just come that year and didn't know anything about anybody.

Sister Cecilia was young and pleasant. If she had been warned to keep a sharp eye on Brendan O'Nolan, who wasn't to be trusted, she disregarded the warning. True, she kept an eye on Brendan, but it was an eye that lighted with warm friendliness and his responded in the same way. He loved her from the first minute he walked into the room, and he knew right then that it was going to be a wonderful year.

And it would have been, if there hadn't been the ever-present, spectral problem of having no money.

There were so many things he needed. Or wanted. It was hard to tell the difference, because if you wanted a thing badly enough, if not having it left an empty place in your life (or in your pocket, or in your stomach), then certainly you needed it. Cravings were needs. They took possession of you. They were stronger than you were. You couldn't fight them. If you tried to suppress them, you only made them worse.

To walk past the bake-shop, for instance, and see a whole tray of cinnamon swirls in the window and know that for five cents you could have one, if you had the five cents . . .

Or to be the only boy in your room who didn't have a yo-yo.

He had to have a yo-yo. He couldn't work one very well —somehow he couldn't quite get the knack of it—but that didn't matter. The important thing was to have one. To be able to put his hand in his pocket and feel the smooth roundness of it under his fingers. To bring it out of his pocket and hold it in his hand, the way the others did, during recess in the schoolyard, even if he couldn't make it come back up again when he dropped it. If he had one, he could learn. He could practice at home. Pat would show him how to do it.

A yo-yo cost ten cents and he had managed to save only six. He couldn't get it out of his allowance, which he received on Saturday, because on Monday there was the collection for the Missions, and everyone was expected to contribute a quarter unless it was someone whose family was absolutely too poor.

Sister Cecilia said it ought to be their own money. She said that anyone who had an allowance—and she was looking directly at him when she said it—ought to be glad to contribute twenty-five cents to help other children who had nothing at all, not enough to eat, or clothes to wear, or medicine to help them when they were sick. It pleased God best, Sister Cecilia said, when a gift was a personal sacrifice, and she knew they all wanted to please God.

Brendan wanted to please God. He also wanted to please Sister Cecilia. She didn't know, of course, that twenty-five cents was his *whole* allowance, but if she had known she would have said that that gave him the opportunity to make an even greater sacrifice, and thereby to make himself even more pleasing to God.

So he had to give all of that week's allowance to the Missions, and he couldn't ask for anything extra. Not even four cents.

He wasn't allowed to ask his mother for money any more. She always used to understand how desperately he needed it, and she never had the heart to refuse him a tiny little bit. Like five cents. Or four.

If he really needed extra money, if he needed a new pencil or a new notebook (unless he had lost the old one through his own carelessness, in which case he had to pay for the new one himself), he could get it, but he had to get it from his father. First he had to tell what it was for, and show the old pencil stub or the used-up notebook; then, because there had been times in the past when he hadn't been exactly truthful, he had to show the new pencil or the new notebook. Unless his father forgot to ask to see them, which wasn't likely. Anyway, it was too soon after the start of school to pretend that he needed anything new. And there would be no use asking his father for an extra four cents to buy a yo-yo. He knew very well that his father would say not was a boy suffering privation for lack of a yo-yo.

Pat might be counted on to pay him ten cents Saturday evening for brushing out his car, but Pat never paid in advance, and if he didn't get the yo-yo Saturday afternoon he would be without it for another whole week because the neighborhood five-and-ten wasn't there any more; he would have to go all the way up to the avenue, and he knew he wouldn't be allowed.

Katie had given him five cents last week. It was too soon to ask Katie again.

There was no use asking Peggy or Paul.

Rosie would lend it to him if she had it, but Rosie had to give her whole week's allowance to the Missions, too.

This exhausted all sources previously drawn upon. It was at this point that out of a memory now two months old came the thought of how easy it would be to take a nickel out of his mother's purse and put a penny in. She would never miss it, because there would still be the same number of coins, and she only counted the coins.

It wouldn't actually be stealing, because if he were allowed to ask his mother for the four cents, she would give it to him. Looking at it that way, he would really only be taking what was, in a sense, already his own. Or the same as his own. It would, at its worst, simply be a way of by-passing his father's strict order that he must not ask his mother for extra money. He wouldn't be disobeying his father, because he had never been told that he must not help himself.

And there was virtually no risk. No one, not even Pat, who had a sixth sense for knowing when he was doing anything on the sly, or even just planning anything, would ever dream he'd have nerve enough to help himself to money out of his mother's purse. Even if his mother had become more careful about counting her money, since the bread man short-changed her that day, she wouldn't suspect him. No one would. They all knew what a coward he was, and it wasn't a thing you would expect a coward to do.

He thought about it for a long while, all day Friday and all Saturday morning.

After lunch his mother took Mary to the doctor for shots. His father was on duty that weekend. Pat got dressed in his best clothes and went away somewhere; he didn't have to tell anybody where. Paul was working. Peggy had gone to the library. Rosie and John were out in the yard, playing. Katie was upstairs, putting Jimmy to bed for his nap.

Brendan was alone in the kitchen.

He didn't really intend to take the nickel; he really only intended to look and see if his mother had one.

She had.

If he hadn't happened to have his six cents right there in his pocket, if he had left it upstairs in the little Japanese lacquered box he kept his religious medals and his money in (when he had any money), he probably never would have done what he did, because in the time it would have taken to go upstairs and get the penny, conscience would have asserted itself. If not conscience, then cowardice.

But there was the nickel, and there, too, was the penny, and somehow—almost against his will—they had changed places, and he had put the purse back in the drawer, closed the drawer, and slipped out of the kitchen.

It had taken a great deal of courage. But the next time was easier.

Then one time he had a white penny. It would have been completely illogical not to have traded that one for a dime.

He became quite callous about it. At first he was surprised and somewhat puzzled at finding how little his conscience troubled him, but then he realized that this was proof—all the proof he needed—that the arguments he had used in the beginning to justify his action to himself were entirely valid. This was very pleasing to know.

It was much less pleasing to discover that his conscience was equipped with a delayed-action mechanism which went into operation suddenly and without advance warning, catching him wholly off guard.

The mechanism was triggered just before the Christmas holidays by his gift to Sister Cecilia. A great deal of love went with the gift, and a great deal of care to the selection of two nearly plain but very beautiful fine white linen handkerchiefs, one with an embroidered "C" in the corner and the other with a rose. But into the gift had gone, also, twenty cents stolen from his mother.

The class had taken up a collection of ten cents from each person, a total of three dollars and sixty cents, to buy Sister Cecilia a Christmas present. Decided upon was a big box of writing paper, which he thought very nice indeed, but a ten-cent share in a joint gift did not seem to him anything like enough to show his devotion to Sister Cecilia. He longed to give her something personal, something from himself alone, something that would tell her how he felt about her.

His father gave him a dollar to buy a Christmas gift for Sister Cecilia. To this he was prepared to add his week's allowance; but when he came to make his selection, after Katie had pointed out to him in the window of The Linen Shop the kind of handkerchief she thought would be nice enough and in proper taste for Sister Cecilia, he found that the ones he wanted were seventy-five cents each. And one wouldn't be enough. Sister Cecilia's name was really Cecilia Rose, the loveliest name he had ever heard, and he found it impossible to decide between the embroidered "C" and the embroidered rose. It was imperative that he buy both. He paid the dollar and asked to have the handkerchiefs put aside until he could bring the rest of the money.

That was the first time he took a quarter out of his mother's purse and put a nickel in.

He was still five cents short, but the lady at The Linen Shop very kindly said that he could owe her the other five cents until after Christmas.

She let him select, without charge, a small card to put in with the handkerchiefs. The cards contained no greeting, nothing but a holly wreath or a candle or some other picture of Christmas significance in one corner.

He selected a card with three little angels singing, and the lady lent him a ball-point pen and went to wait on another customer.

Painstakingly, delicately, he printed on the card in Gaelic letters:

Nollaig Sona Duit
a Siúr Cecilia Róir
ó do buan-cara, Breandán
le grá

The other customer left, and the lady who owned the shop came back to him just as he finished.

"My!" she said, sounding surprised. "What nice printing. You're quite an artist, aren't you?"

She was looking at the card upside down. When she turned it around she sounded even more surprised.

"Why, it's foreign! Aren't you an American boy?"

"Oh, yes," Brendan said. "It isn't foreign, exactly. It's

123

Irish. I just like Irish better than English," he explained. "I'm like my father."

He tried to say this modestly, but to be able to say that he was like his father, even if only in this one way, was the proudest thing he could lay claim to, and he couldn't help saying it proudly.

"Of course," he admitted, "I don't really know much Irish, compared with my father. He lived on the Arran Islands when he was a boy. He's a really native Irish speaker. I only know what he taught me."

He thought the lady who owned the shop looked at him curiously now.

"Oh," she said, *that's* who you are. I know about your father."

This didn't surprise him—he assumed that a great many people must know his father—but when she added, "He's a very fine man," pleasure fairly blazed up in him.

She wrapped the handkerchief box in gold and white striped paper and tied it with shining gold ribbon in a fancy bow, all so beautiful that the package alone seemed to him a wonderful gift, just of itself, even if there hadn't been anything in it. He scarcely knew how to thank her— the politest words he could think of didn't half express his appreciation—but she seemed to understand. She said, "Good-by now, and Merry Christmas," and because she had become his good friend he answered, *"Gurab amhlaidh dhuit,"* and then had to explain that it meant "The same to you."

On the last day before Christmas vacation, he made a point of getting to school very early, the first one in the room, so that he could put his present on Sister Cecilia's desk without anyone else seeing, and right after lunch she stopped beside his desk to say she would like to see him after school, and would he please wait.

Then the class presented her with the big box of writing paper. She was very pleased, and told them how happy she was to be teaching them, and that she had never been at any school before where everybody was so nice, so well-behaved, so intelligent, and so altogether charming. She wrote "Merry Christmas" in great sweeping letters on the blackboard, and then she handed out the little boxes of hard candies that were the school's gift to everybody. She asked them if they wanted to sing a few carols, and she called for the person with the best voice to come to the front of the room to lead the singing. Everybody modestly refrained from coming forward, but two or three of the girls said, "Brendan O'Nolan!" So Brendan led the singing.

School was dismissed an hour early. Brendan remained seated while everyone else filed out of the room and into the hall and down the stairs. Presently Sister Cecilia returned from her post at the head of the stairs, and beckoned him to her desk.

"I opened your gift at lunchtime, Brendan," she told him. "The handkerchiefs are lovely. They are the loveliest I have ever had in all my life. It was so very thoughtful of you, and I think you picked them out yourself, didn't you?"

"Yes, Sister."

"I was sure you had, I think it was the rose that told me. I do thank you so very much, Brendan. For everything. For the beautiful gift, and your thoughtfulness, and your loving heart, and for just being here. And for the card. Oh, very, very much for the card!"

The card was lying on her desk. She picked it up.

"I'm going to ask you to read it to me," she said, "because I don't at all know how to pronounce some of the words. Will you read it, please?"

"*Nullig hunnah ghuit,*" Brendan read, "*a Hyioor Sheeleh Rowish, oad voon-khorra, Brandawn, le graw.*"

"How wonderful!" Sister Cecilia exclaimed in delight. "How very wonderful that you have command of two languages, and you so young! It's all a little puzzling, though, because when you say the words they don't sound at all as one would expect them to. Apparently some of the consonants are pronounced another way entirely. Now I'm going to ask you to read it again, slowly, while I write it phonetically, as it sounds to me. And then I'm going to ask you to explain."

Ten wonderful minutes were spent in reversed roles, he the teacher and Sister Cecilia the pupil. He explained the vowel sounds, and the aspiration of certain consonants, whereby in what he had written *s* was changed to *h*, *b* to *v*, and *d* at the beginning of a word to *g*. He explained further about the position of the verb at the beginning of a sentence, preceded by the negative, if it was a negative statement, and told her how his father, even when speaking English, always used this form; never said, for example,

125

"It is not," or "I will not," but always, "Not is it," or "Not will I." He told her apologetically that his card wasn't quite correct, because he hadn't been sure of the Irish form of the name Cecilia, he thought it was *Síle*, but anyway . . .

Here he hesitated.

"But anyway," Sister Cecilia said, "you wanted to be sure that I would know you meant me!"

This was exactly what he had been going to say, but it hadn't seemed polite to indicate that he had been aware of Sister Cecilia's ignorance of anything, even of something that she really couldn't be expected to know, but when she took the words out of his mouth they didn't sound impolite, only funny, and they both laughed.

"Well," Sister Cecilia said then, "I mustn't keep you too long. I know your little sister is waiting for you to walk home with her. But there's just one more thing. Will you read your card to me now, please, in English?"

"Merry Christmas," Brendan translated, pointing to these two words, because they were reversed, *"to you, Sister Cecilia Rose, from your sincere friend, Brendan"*—he paused before adding the last two words almost in a whisper—*"with love."*

He thought he wouldn't be able to contain the joy that welled up in him when her smile showed him how much these last two words meant to her.

"You are a very dear boy," she said. "A very good boy. God must love you very much to have made you as you are, to have put so much of His own love in your heart. God must love *me* very much," Sister Cecilia said, "to have given me the special privilege of being sent here to your school, so that I might have the great joy of knowing you."

Sister Cecilia liked him. She liked his gift. She thought he was good. She thought God loved him. She thought . . .

Oh, she didn't know, she didn't know . . . !

What would she think of him if she knew that to buy the gift he had stolen money from his mother?

The upsweep of joy in him a moment before had brought him close to tears; now the joy in an instant was swamped by a tidal wave of shame and grief, and there were the tears, spilling over and out of control.

He started to say, "No, Sister, no . . . ," but he couldn't

126

tell her. Never, never could he tell so shameful a thing. The broken-off words hung there between them, hurting.

Bewildered and distressed, she asked, "Brendan, what is wrong?"

He couldn't answer. He could only put his head down, as he always did when he cried, and let the tears flow silently, forced out under the terrible pressure of his terrible guilt.

"Brendan, dear, I haven't hurt you in some way? Surely I haven't?"

He whispered, "No, Sister, oh, no! It's just . . . that you think I'm good. And I'm not. You don't know how wicked I really am, you don't know——"

"My dear child! You could not possibly be wicked. If you have done something wrong," Sister Cecilia said gently, putting her arm around him, "you must confess, and you will be forgiven. God doesn't want you to torment yourself. Whatever wrong you have done, God will forgive you. You are His Child."

God forgave him.

He had thought, in his agony of remorse, that the whole Christmas season would be spoiled; but he went to Confession, and poured out his sins to the priest, and did penance for them, promising to put ten cents in the poor box each week until he had made restitution, and by the goodness and infinite mercy of God, the burden of guilt was lifted.

Only one shadow remained. He longed to pour out his sins to his father also, for unless he had his father's forgiveness as well as God's, he thought his heart could never be wholly given over to joy. But he couldn't bring himself to tell his father. Not before Christmas. After Christmas would be time enough. He knew with absolute certainty that he would never again, as long as he lived, take another cent from his mother's purse. All that was past. But the telling would be easier, he thought, when it was all just a little bit more past.

One blissful moment followed another, during the holidays.

To begin with, Pat took him Christmas shopping, downtown, to the big department stores. Nothing could have more surely convinced him that in spite of everything he was in a state of grace than this unexpected, undreamed of delight. It would have been an excursion into heaven just to go with Pat, anywhere at all. Just to go. With no motives of his own. With no money to spend. With nothing but the wonderful closeness, the sharing of the same seat on the bus, the firm hold of Pat's hand on his arm to make sure they didn't become separated in a crowd.

This would have been joy enough. But Pat gave him ten dollars to spend. Ten dollars, all his own. Gave it to him, actually into his keeping, which was very different from just paying for everything and then letting him put his name on the tags, as giver.

Ten one-dollar bills. Pat made him distribute them among his pockets, as insurance against loss. And Pat helped him budget it, for this was the first time he had ever bought gifts for everyone, and there was the problem of suitably allocating his funds. They disagreed on only one thing; he wanted to reserve the same amount for Pat as for his father and mother, but Pat said Nuts, put him at the bottom of the list with two-year-old Jimmy and ten-month-old Mary. But the final say was his, because it was his money, and when they had finished all their shopping for everybody else, and separated to buy surprise gifts for each other, Brendan still had two dollars. Pat left him in the men's department with a hint that he didn't like loud neckties and was partial to blue, and with stringent orders not to set foot beyond the limits of that department, because if he had to go chasing over the whole store looking for him he'd you-know-what right in front of everybody when he found him. He bought a beautiful tie for Pat, narrow stripes in half a dozen different shades of soft blue. It cost the whole two dollars.

Then there was Christmas Day itself, which began as usual with attendance at six o'clock High Mass.

At this Mass it had long been the custom for the girls' choir to file into the church, singing, walking slowly two by two down the center aisle, each holding a small book of Christmas Carols in one hand and in the other a lighted candle. He had always loved to see them, the candleflame lighting their faces, giving a curious, unfamiliar, heavenly beauty even to those who weren't, when you saw them every day, especially pretty.

This year there was an innovation. One of the altar boys led the procession down the aisle. He also carried a book and a candle, and he also was singing.

When they filed into their places in a double row before

128

the altar rail, turning to face the crowded nave, still singing, the altar boy's place was front center; and when they
finished the second verse of "Silent Night," all the girls'
voices were hushed, and the organ was hushed, and all
alone (clear and pure as the voice of an angel, his mother
said) the altar boy sang the third verse:

"Son of God," he sang, "love's pure light . . ."

(And the light was there, his mother said, such a light as
could only shine in the presence of God.)

Again, in each of the other carols, he sang a portion
alone.

"How silently, how silently . . ."

he sang, and the whole church was silent, with only the
sound of his voice spinning a golden thread across the
stillness;

"The wondrous gift is given . . ."

The girls moved away again in double file while singing
the last carol, to take their places in the choir loft. The
altar boy stood waiting. When the last two started up the
aisle, he turned and took down the velvet rope and let
himself into the sanctuary, where he genuflected before the
altar, and then went through the door on the left, into the
sacristy.

The altar boy was himself, Brendan O'Nolan.

It had been Sister Cecilia's idea.

He was happy through the Christmas holidays with a
happiness that was like . . . oh, how could he say it? . . .
like a ringing of bells, like a sounding of trumpets. He
shared his happiness with all comers; they needed only to
come close and they were automatically showered with it,
as by spray from a fountain. Or, if they wished, he was
ready to slice off portions of his happiness and hand it
around like helpings of a wonderful cake, mountainous with
frosting and decorations, and undiminishing, for the more
that was sliced off and served, the more remained. He kept
his little brothers entertained by the hour with stories. He

taught Rosie to play the song-flute that Aunt Nora gave her for Christmas. He ran up and down stairs fifty times a day waiting on his mother, and when Katie or Peggy or Paul said, "Do this, Bren; do that," he served them with joy, because when they asked him to do things it meant that he was important to them, that they liked having him around.

The happiest part of each day came at its close: the long evening, when his father was there. He would, if he followed his own inclination, have established himself on the hassock close beside his father's chair, as he had always done when he was very small, but he had been mocked and teased into giving up that practice. It looked so babyish, Peggy said. Whenever he sat there, she or Paul would begin reciting "Little Miss Muffet sat on a tuffet." But he contrived to be close, always close, even if he didn't sit on the hassock. Almost every evening he sang for them: in Irish for his father, in English for his mother. Sometimes he just sat there while his father and mother talked, not always listening to what they said, but to the sound of their voices, which he loved. His father's voice with its strong brogue, its careful but curious diction, its beautiful expressiveness—sometimes almost like something you would only expect to read in a book or a poem—was a part of his whole childhood, from the earliest time he could remember, and would be part, he knew, of his whole life, for there never was an hour of the day or night, whether his father was there or not, that he didn't hear the beloved voice, in his thoughts or in his dreams.

When school started again, he felt so at peace with the world, so filled with the grace of God and love of his fellows, that he innocently assumed all this would at once be recognized and reciprocated, that others must surely feel toward him as he toward them.

The harsh realities of life overtook him almost at once, in the unexpected hostility of the other boys, who took to calling him Brenda the Choir Girl. He would not have minded being teased about having been the only boy among thirty girl singers on Christmas morning. He was used to being teased. Even when teasing hurt, he knew how to smile in a certain way that indicated he had meant to do or say something ridiculous, that it had been his intention to make them laugh, that he was secretly clowning and they had fallen for it. This special, rather impish way of smiling

130

served the dual purpose of accepting the teasing and covering the hurt. But this was no ordinary teasing, basically good-natured and, if cruel, unintentionally so. This was different. At every opportunity the boys closed around him in a tight circle from which he could not escape, jeering and mocking and calling him names. It terrified him to be surrounded in this way, and he could do nothing but stand there, with no idea in the world how to meet such ugliness, or how to fend it off, or how to escape from it.

Then one day one of the boys pushed him down the outside steps, and he fell, skinning both knees badly, for the rough concrete tore holes right through the knees of his pants. There were a dozen witnesses, but when Sister Mary Clare came to investigate, no one told her that he had been pushed. They said he fell. He cried a little, in his silent way, not because of his hurt knees but because of his hurt feelings, because the boys had wanted to make him fall down the steps, had wanted to hurt him. Sister Mary Clare sent him to the office to have iodine put on the abrasions, and Mother Aloysius questioned him sharply. He admitted, under her questioning, that he had been pushed, but he said he didn't know by whom. She made him tell the names of all the boys who were on the steps at the time, and she sent for them to come to her office, but none would admit having pushed him and none would name any other. They knew they were safe, they knew that either he really didn't know who had pushed him, as he said, or, as was indeed the case, that he was afraid to say it was Anthony Rimado. (Anthony and two of his friends had waylaid a boy going home from school not long ago, and dragged him into an alley, and beaten him for telling tales. The boy wouldn't tell who did it, because they said they'd do it again, and worse, if he told. But everybody at school knew.)

At home, reactions to the incident were varied.

His mother was angry. She thought it a terrible thing that he should be hurt and his clothes ruined and that bullying Rimado boy not brought to time for it, but she put no blame on him for not having told, for she no more wanted to risk his being set upon on the way home from school than he did.

His brother Patrick was disgusted.

"When are you going to learn to stand up for yourself?" Pat wanted to know. "Are you going to go through your whole life letting yourself be pushed around by any ugly little customer who figures he can get away with it? You're as big as that Rimado kid. And I know his kind; he's as yellow as they come. If you took one good swing at him and bloodied his nose, he'd never come near you again the rest of his natural life!"

"That's what *I* told him," Rosie said belligerently. "I'd just like to see anybody push *me* down the steps! And I'd just like to see that Tony Rimado start anything on the way home from school, too! I'd scratch his eyes out!"

And no one had any doubts about it. Rosie would. Rosie had behind her a whole long line of Fighting Irish. Effectively disguised her heritage might be, by blonde and blue-eyed, fragile-seeming, little-girl prettiness; but impaired, never. Rosie could take care of herself. (And, if need be, of her fainthearted older brother, also, a circumstance which provided Peggy and Paul with long-lasting amusement.)

His father listened to the story with judicial lack of emotional bias, and it drew from him neither pity nor blame.

"Not is it a thing," he said when he had heard the story and the varying opinions, "that one person may say for another, this you should have done, or that. No problem is the same for any two, and each must meet it in his own way as it comes. If there is a better way, then is that way learned in time, for a problem not well met will keep recurring, and many will be the opportunities to try other ways of meeting it. Not do I see fault in you, my son, for that you deem bloody knees enough, without adding bloody noses. For well may it be that the nose you spared was your own."

At this they all laughed, and his father's arm around his shoulders offered understanding and comfort and love, and filled him with a courageous resolve to meet the problem in a better way, if Tony Rimado ever picked on him again.

He was very lighthearted the rest of the evening, but some time in the night he woke from a dream, and knew that in the dream he had been crying. The dream itself was gone, only the broken memory and the shadowy grief of it remained. But he couldn't sleep again. He lay there thinking that his father had only spoken as he did because he was so kind, and that in his heart he must be ashamed of having so cowardly a son and must wonder how it could be that after Pat, who was in every way so splendid, and

Paul, who was so capable, so self-reliant, and both of them so to-be-proud-of, there could have come a son like himself, so weak, so worthless, so without every quality that a father would want a son to have.

He lay cold and alone in the bed beside Paul, who hadn't wakened even though Brendan was almost certain he had cried out in his sleep. He was still awake when the alarm clock in his parents' room went off at six-thirty, and when he came down to breakfast his mother looked at him anxiously and asked if he felt all right. She could always tell when he hadn't slept. She said he looked tired and pale, and had shadows under his eyes.

He didn't tell at home about the taunting over his having sung with the girls, and he got Rosie to promise that she wouldn't tell either. There wasn't anything anybody could do about it that wouldn't make it worse, and it would only make his mother feel bad—she had loved the singing and had been so proud of him. He pretended to Rosie and to Sister Cecilia that he didn't mind the teasing, that the boys were all his friends, they only meant to be funny, not to be mean. Rosie and Sister Cecilia both knew that the boys weren't his friends and did mean to be mean, but they saw, too, that to try to make them stop might only make them meaner.

And then he lost his allowance. Saturday had been a day of freezing rain, he hadn't gone anywhere, he still had his whole quarter, untouched, on Monday morning when he arrived at school. Now it was gone. Actually he knew he hadn't lost it, but that it had been stolen. If he told at home that it had been stolen, his father would without doubt make it up to him; but his father would also make him report the theft to Mother Aloysius, and name whoever he thought had stolen it, and tell his reasons for thinking so. It hadn't been Tony Rimado, but it had been one of his friends, which amounted to the same thing. Brendan wasn't ready, just yet, to meet the problem of Tony Rimado in some other way, some better way, than letting himself be pushed around, and made fun of, and stolen from. Later, perhaps, but not just yet. So it was better to say nothing about it at all.

But life had, unaccountably, become a succession of little cruelties that were increasingly hard to bear.

He was able to borrow five cents from Rosie, on Tuesday. They stopped in the bake-shop on the way home from school, where something in the nature of consolation for his various misfortunes could be found. Rosie bought a caramel bun and he bought a cinnamon swirl, the last one Mrs. Santucci had. It wasn't quite as large as it should have been, so she let him have it for four cents. It was simpler to keep a debt in round figures, so he put the leftover penny in his own pocket, and continued to owe Rosie five cents.

Strange that something so trivial as a cinnamon swirl costing only four cents instead of five should have such great and grave consequences. Because if he hadn't had that penny . . .

That night, before he fell asleep, he got to thinking about how little use one penny was going to be to him, with three more days left until Saturday. If he spent it, it would buy only one piece of candy. But if the penny could be turned into a nickel . . .

After all his stout resolves at Christmas time, and all the relief it had given him to put his wickedness behind him and to know that never again would he do so shameful a thing as to steal money from his mother's purse, it surprised him to find how easily the thought could slip into his mind, and how it could remain there, taking root.

He had no intention, when he came down to the kitchen the next morning, of touching his mother's purse. It just happened that he was the first one down; he was sure he had made no special effort to be ahead of everyone else, but there he was, and since another opportunity might not come again for a long while . . .

And as long as he was doing it anyway, why not a dime?

Strangely, having done it, he again found that it did not rest with any oppressive weight upon his conscience. He felt almost resigned to the fact that he was powerless to resist temptation. If powerless, then why blame himself? He couldn't help being powerless, that was the way God had made him. The consuming need for money was stronger, much stronger, than his own will. He was a victim of his own weakness. He could not help himself.

Still, it frightened him to find that each time he went to the purse he was making less effort to resist the temptation. No effort, really. Even if he knew that he would yield in the end, he ought to set himself against it, to hold back as long as he could. If he made no effort at all, might there

134

come a day when he would steal from someone else? Might he, sometime, see something he wanted in a store, and be powerless to resist the temptation to slip it off the counter and into his pocket, the same way he slipped a piece of silver out of his mother's purse? If he did, and was caught, they would have him arrested. They would take him before the Juvenile Court, and the judge would send him to a reformatory. His whole family would be disgraced, all his brothers and sisters, his mother, his father. His father would be pointed out as a policeman who hadn't taught his own son to obey the law.

For two weeks this chilling prospect served as a deterrent, but at the end of that time some pressing need arose and he slipped back again, almost without a struggle, into repetition of his sinful acts. He realized, then, sometimes with fatalistic calm, sometimes with cold fear, that he was on the road to ruin.

Late in February he caught a bad cold which kept him home from school for several days. Toward the end of his brief illness, there came an unseasonably warm day; he was not well enough to return to school nor sick enough to be housebound. It was his father's day off, and they went for a drive in the country. Not to go anywhere in particular, but just to get out into the fresh air and sunshine. They went alone, the two of them, himself and his father.

Like the days of Christmas, this seemed to Brendan reassurance, proof that he had not, after all, renounced his own salvation. It was an interlude, a day like a page torn out of a book, separated from anything that went before or anything that would come after. A day of pure delight. Of sun without shadow. Of time without beginning or end. He sang while they drove, and the day was like his song. They crossed a bridge just below the spillway of a dam, and the day was like the cascading of the bright water. They were late coming home, and the day was like the sunset that rimmed every cloud with golden fire.

There was only one moment touched with a strange grief.

It occurred after they had parked their car on the shoulder of the highway and were walking along a narrow intersecting road. Something seemed familiar to him about the road; he felt that he knew what lay beyond every bend and on the other side of every little rise. When they came to a small stream bridged by wooden planks, with no guardrails and the planks laid so loosely that you could look down between them into the dark running water, he knew he had been there before. They walked a little farther, and there were high banks on both sides of the road, covered with some kind of lowgrowing shrub, bare and brown now in February.

Puzzled, he looked at his father, and he thought his father was looking at him with a question in his eyes.

He asked, "Are those huckleberry bushes?"

"They are that. Not would everyone guess it as readily," his father said, "so early in the year, and bare of leaves and fruit as they are."

Now he asked, "Have I ever been here before?"

His father was pleased by the question.

"Well does memory serve you, my son. A long time ago it was, six years and more, and yourself but four years old."

The February sun lay bright on the bank; but he remembered a brighter sun and a bluer sky, and wind-blown leaves of burning red and gold, and . . . a purer joy?

There swept over him, the way a cloud shadow races over the land, a terrible longing to recapture the joy of that earlier day. The joy of a day before ever he had done any wrong. Before he had lied to his father, or stolen money from his mother, or cheated at school. Before anyone had disliked him, or jeered at him, or wanted to hurt him. Oh, to go back to that day when he was only four years old. . . .

The racing shadow passed over his face, swiftly, but when it had passed his eyes were hot with tears. His father may have seen the shadow; there was no need to wonder if he had seen the tears.

"Does something trouble you, Brendan?"

Here was his chance, and he rejected it. So ready had he learned to be with a lie, that a lie came quickly and automatically, even when he didn't want it, even when there was nothing in the world he wanted so much as to tell his father the truth.

"*Níl*," he said at once, summoning a smile. "*Níl buairt orm, 'Athair.* I am not troubled, I am just so happy. I'm so very happy, Father."

So the day provided respite but not salvation. And the chance might never come again.

That night he had his old dream of the desert, the empty place, the first time in more than a year.

136

After that day his conscience reasserted itself and he lived in torment, desperately wanting to stop stealing but unable to. It had become too easy. He had done it too many times. He had gone too far.

In April, when the weather turned fine after a cold and rainy beginning, the boys at school began playing ball at recess. They weren't permitted to play baseball, because of the windows, but softball was permitted. The only ball they had wasn't much good; it had seen hard use and was no longer completely spherical, but they made it do, because no one had the price of a new one.

Brendan didn't want to play softball, but he thought if he owned a ball and lent it to the other boys they would be grateful to him, and being grateful would be friendly. They would have the pleasure of playing with his ball, and he would have the pleasure of watching them. They might even start to like him. They might stop calling him Brenda and start calling him Bren. Everything would be so different . . . if the boys liked him.

It was to buy a softball that he took the second quarter out of his mother's purse.

He had an uneasy feeling, that evening at the supper table, that his mother avoided looking at him and that his father looked at him too long.

When supper was over, his father told him to come upstairs.

They went into the second-floor front room, his father's and mother's room, where no one would interrupt. It was in this room that offenders against domestic tranquillity were brought to trial; and in this room, if convicted, sentence of a certain nature was summarily carried out.

His father closed the door.

Fearfully, with the blood congealed in his veins, Brendan waited.

"Known to you, I think," his father said—and he spoke in English, a very bad sign—"known to you is the small purse in which your mother keeps handy to her in the kitchen a bit of change for her household needs?"

The answer was given in a frozen whisper.

"Tá eolas agam air, 'Athair."

This failed of its purpose, as he had been almost sure it would. For lesser crimes, speaking in Irish could be depended upon nineteen times out of twenty. Pleas and promises made in his father's language were incalculably more effective than the very same pleas, the very same promises, in English. He had long known this, and had long put the knowledge to use when the need arose to extricate himself from the web of his own misdeeds. Long, too, had his father known it. But once in a while, once in a very great while . . .

"Tonight we speak in English," his father said. "You say, then, that you know the purse. Have you ever touched it?"

Now the frozen whisper, obediently, came in English.

"Touched it, Father?"

"Less than an honest answer," his father warned, "will not serve you well, Brendan, and may serve you ill. Not is it evasion I wish from you, but truth. Did you, this morning before you left for school, take money from your mother's purse?"

"I took money, Father."

"How much?"

"Twenty cents."

"Your mother misses a quarter-dollar."

"I took a quarter, Father, but I put five cents back."

His father appeared to consider this answer, as if finding it a curious thing.

"That was to ease your conscience, it may be?"

"No, Father. That was—so Mother wouldn't miss—the quarter."

This was as long as the whispered answers remained frozen. At this point the freeze melted away into tears, and with the flood of tears the whole shameful story came in a flood also—of words, of remorse, of fear.

He didn't know how many times he had taken money. He didn't know how much money he had taken. He had been doing it for a long while. Six months or more. . . . Yes, he had, he had. He was a thief. He should be sent to prison. He wasn't fit to live any longer in the same house with the rest of them. He wasn't fit even to look at the rest of them, or be seen by them. He was a thief who stole from his own mother, from his mother who trusted him, who was so good to him, so good to everybody. And even though he was sorry and would never do it again, never never do it again, it was too wicked a thing ever to be forgiven for. He knew that as long as he lived they would never forgive him. God would never forgive him either. . . .

138

Everything came pouring out in a welter of confused detail. Even to his own ear as he told it, it had a fantastic sound: the enormity of his crimes, the hopeless battle against inexorable temptation, the terrible anguish of remorse that struck even into his dreams yet did not deter him—all this grandscale sinning and suffering inextricably and absurdly mixed with such factors as being the only boy who didn't have a yo-yo, with Sister Cecilia's name really being Cecilia Rose, and with the matter of a penny discount on an undersized cinnamon swirl.

How could he expect his father to understand? How could he ask his father to forgive him? To go on loving him?

But he could not check the story until it had all been told and the flood had run dry. His father made no attempt to check it, nor even to interrupt with questions. His father listened.

This was the confession Brendan had longed to make and had feared to make. Now it was made, and his fear was an icy coldness and a violent trembling, and in his mind was confusion as to why he had told.

Would it not serve only to make things worse for him? Would it not have been enough to face punishment for one crime, without confessing twenty?

This fearful question came into his mind only at the very end, when, exhausted of words and tears, he at last stood silent, waiting for what his father would say or do.

Brendan could not supply the answer to the question; it was too clouded, too complex. There seemed indeed to be two answers, but they contradicted each other and he could not understand how both could be true.

It seemed, on the one hand, that in spite of his fear of punishment he wanted to be punished, that only by being punished for his crimes could he hope to escape from his bondage to them. Only so could he be released, purified, restored.

But, on the other hand, he seemed to entertain a feeble hope that by confession of the full and hideous extent of his wrongdoing, he would have made it plain that he could not possibly survive being punished as he deserved, and that it might, therefore, appear rather purposeless to punish him at all.

If he had this hope, he read in his father's face that it was vain, and in a piteous voice he confirmed his own doom.

"You will have to punish me, Father."

"I will have to punish you, Brendan," his father said; and surely he said it sadly?

The piteous voice might ensure, at least, that justice be tempered with mercy.

"Will you beat me with a strap, Father?"

"Not will I 'beat' you, Brendan, with aught but the flat of my hand."

Now the piteous voice sank again to a whisper.

"For all the times?"

"For but this time," his father said. "Must the rest lie then between yourself and your mother, that you decide between the two of you what total sum you have taken, and that you make arrangements with her as to the manner in which you must pay it back. Something of your allowance must you give her each week, I think, until the matter has been fully rectified."

"I will give her all of it, Father. I never want any money again," he declared passionately. "I could never bear to touch money again! Never!"

"Not will she wish to make the terms too hard," his father said. "But that is between the two of you. Beyond that, Brendan, must the rest be also between yourself and God. Not can I think but that you have already in the Confessional asked for and been granted forgiveness for the rest, from God; that is now past, and out of my hands. But not could *I* go before God and ask forgiveness were I to ignore the duty which is upon me not to let son of mine grow up a thief. Were my duty less or did I love you less, then might I depend this time, as other times, on your repentance and your promises. But not are these always to be depended upon, as we know. Plain is it by your telling, dependence on your own intentions has produced none but most unsatisfactory results. Help you need, as I can see. Not have I choice, then, but to depend this time on that which you will remember a little longer, I think, than you remember most of your promises."

"Father . . . Father, please——"

His father cut him off.

"Not can you beg out of it, Brendan."

"No," he said, weeping. "No, I didn't mean . . . I only meant . . . I wanted you to tell me . . . Father, do you love me? Do you love me?"

140

There was little change in his father's face. If anything, it cemented itself in even harder lines. But in his eyes . . . oh, surely there was nothing but tenderness, nothing but love in his father's eyes?

"*Bheirim grá mór duit*—I bear great love for you, my son," his father said.

Brendan O'Nolan's career in crime ended on that April evening, when he was exactly eleven years, two months, and nine days old.

The evening turned out to be the happiest he had known since the Christmas holidays. It was on that evening that his father taught him to play chess.

Beyond that, the incident had a curious aftermath.

He had stated, in his passion of remorse, that he never wanted to touch money again, that he could never bear to touch money again.

He had no occasion to touch it for several weeks. He estimated, in conference with his mother, that he may have taken in all as much as one dollar and thirty-five cents (twenty-five cents twice, nine cents five times, four cents perhaps as many as eight or ten times). They agreed on the sum of one dollar and a quarter in restitution, and he begged his father not to give him his weekly allowance at all but to turn it directly over to his mother until the full sum had been paid.

By the end of these five weeks there had been significant improvement in the general affairs of the household. The debt incurred more than a year earlier, at the time of Mary's birth and his mother's long illness, had by then been fully discharged. Much more than that: the debt incurred nineteen years earlier, the mortgage on their house, had been finally and fully lifted. The last payment had been made, the mortgage had been satisfied. There was the paper itself, in proof, spread open on the dining-room table, beginning with the awesome words THIS INDENTURE in half-inch-high letters which, to his surprise, were in the Gaelic form. (He amused everybody by asking if that was because they were Irish, but his father explained that legal documents made use of much that was left over from the Middle Ages, and this but an example of it.) The document bore his parents' signatures, written long ago, before even Pat was born; and various other signatures and seals, most important of them

141

the official stamp on the back which proved it had been satisfied of record, and the date, May 21, 1949.

True, though these debts had been paid, the cost of living kept going up all the time, but the effects of this were not so stringently felt, chiefly because Pat, to make up for rising costs, increased the amount of money he insisted upon paying out of his savings, for his weekly board. It was this increase which made it possible for Katie and Peggy to have their allowances increased fifty percent, and for Brendan and Rosie to have theirs doubled.

Their father explained this to the younger ones early one Saturday morning before he left for work, and drew out of his pocket two new half-dollars. They put out their hands, and on each extended palm he placed one of the shiny coins.

Rosie's fingers closed over hers instantly and eagerly, and she at once threw herself into her father's arms, thanking him in the way the girls always thanked him for anything, with an extravagance of hugs and kisses.

But Brendan stood looking at the fifty-cent piece lying there on his open palm, and as he looked a cold feeling went all over him, excepting only his palm, which felt hot under the weight of the silver. It was a feeling of revulsion, almost of horror. Involuntarily he turned his hand sideways, and the coin slid off and fell to the ground.

"For goodness sake!" exclaimed Rosie, stooping to pick it up. "You dropped it! Here, butterfingers!"

But he didn't take the coin from Rosie. He put his hands behind him, and in anguish raised his eyes to his father's face.

"'*Athair*, please don't make me take it."

"Are you crazy?" Rosie demanded in amazement. "Here!"

But his father took the half-dollar from her and returned it to his pocket.

"Later will we talk of it," he said, and added, to Rosie, "A private matter it is, touching only your brother. That is a thing you understand, Róisín?"

"Oh," said Rosie, "I never tell *anything*, Father!" And this made them laugh, because it was sometimes thought that Rosie kept more secrets than she should.

When their father had gone, Rosie asked, "Bren, why didn't you take the money?"

He looked at her, and then looked around to make sure they were alone. In a voice of deep mystery he answered:

"I read a story. It was called"—he hesitated just long enough to gather himself for a running leap into the wonderful fields of fantasy—"it was called *Silver-Dollar Death.* Do you want to hear it?"

"Is it real scary?"

Knowing Rosie, he knew that her reason for asking was not that she didn't want to hear it if it was, but that she definitely did.

"Scary as anything! Come on, let's go up in the tree, and I'll tell you."

Rosie wanted just a little more guarantee that the story was down her alley.

"Is it fairies? Because," she said flatly, "I don't believe in fairies."

"It's thieves and murderers and witches," he told her. "It has a cave full of hidden treasure, and a head without a body, and a——"

"And a body without a head!" Rosie supplied with enthusiam. "You'll have to give me a boost."

When they were settled on his platform, he told her the story.

It was a wonderful story. It had everything in it anyone could want, including an electronically controlled silver dollar—an Instrument of Death. It traveled by rolling on its edge, and it could roll upstairs as easily as down. There it came, eerily shining, up the stairs to the second floor, along the hall, up the stairs to the third floor to the room at the back. Here it turned itself flat to slip under the door. It rolled slowly up the bedspread and along the edge of the bed. A girl, the heroine of the story, was asleep in the bed. She woke up at that moment and saw the Thing coming toward her, weirdly gleaming in the pitch blackness. She . . .

It wasn't enough just to *say* she screamed. Brendan liked to supply sound effects with his stories, so here he screamed, a good, loud, blood-chilling scream in the higher frequencies. It nearly caused Rosie to fall off the platform, and it brought his mother and Pat running out the back door, Mrs. Moran running out her front door; and it stopped a number of passers-by in their tracks, out on the front pavement.

Rosie, recovering her aplomb (both literal and figurative), called down cheerful reassurance.

"It's nothing, Mother! Bren's just telling me a story!"

Their mother closed her eyes and put a hand on Pat's arm to steady herself.

Pat shouted, "You cussed little clown! When I get my hands on you . . . !" and reached for the first branch of the cherry tree.

Brendan went up the tree with agility. All the way up, to the topmost branches that swayed even under his not-too-considerable weight.

"Pat, no!" their mother said sharply. "Don't you dare go after him; one of you will fall and be hurt. He didn't mean to frighten us. It's just . . . it was so very realistic. Rose, come down. Brendan, dear, please be careful, you're much too high."

"I'll show him who's realistic!" Pat promised, and called into the tree, "You wait! I'll take care of you tonight, and you can do some yelling for real, boy!"

They went back into the house, Rosie trailing along. Her bitter protest came up to him: "But, Mother, we were just at the very *best* part of the story!"

Brendan rested his weight on two light branches that forked out only a few inches apart, neither more than two inches in diameter, but the two strong enough to support him. They were at an angle of about forty-five degrees. He folded his arms across them and rested his head on his arms, half reclining, there in the very top of the tree. There was a light wind; down in the yard you would scarcely feel it at all, but up here the branches were swaying. It was a wonderful feeling.

It was a wonderful world.

Pat was only talking. He could tell the difference. He didn't have to worry about Pat.

He didn't have to worry about anything.

He could look across the tops of the houses. There was no end to how far he could see, a whole ocean of rooftops stretched away.

He imagined himself in the rigging of an old sailing vessel. The sea was calm, but there was a storm brewing. The boat would ride out the storm, and he would lash himself to the rigging, keeping watch. The waves would rise fifty feet high, and the ship would roll and pitch fearfully, the waters

144

washing over her decks, but he would keep watching and watching for the lights that warned the reef was near.

Someday perhaps he'd join the navy.

Someday he'd go to the Arran Islands, where his grandmother lived, and cross from Inishmore to Inishmaan in a curragh. His father had often crossed the strait in a curragh.

His father knew how he felt about the money. There was no one who knew things the way his father knew them.

God knew everything, but then God was in a position of advantage. God was where He could look down on everything all at one time, and see everything that was going on, everywhere in the whole world, everywhere in the whole universe. The way you could see all the houses, from up here in the tree. The way a sailor could see from the rigging.

His father wasn't away up somewhere, looking down. His father was just here in one place; but no matter what you did, or what you thought, or how you felt, his father always knew. Usually right away. The way he knew about the money.

His father was the most wonderful man in the world.

Because he was so wonderful, people naturally expected his children to be wonderful, too. Like Pat and Katie. Pat was going to be a policeman. Katie was going to be a nun.

Someday *he* would do something to make his father proud of him. Something splendid. He'd have to start thinking about what it would be, before so very long—in a few years, after he got to high school.

Right now he didn't have to think about anything, except how blue the sky was with the cottony clouds floating across it, and how comfortingly the wind rocked the high branches of the cherry tree.

The tree was a cradle and the wind was a woman in a blue gown, rocking it with her foot and crooning a lullaby. Softly, he sang along with her:

> "*Dilín ó dí, dilín ó dé,*
> *Is láidir í an ghaoth.*
> *Dilín ó dí, dilín ó dé,*
> *Tá sí ag séideadh imeasc duilliúr na gcrann,*
> *Beidh sí ag bogadh an chliabháin go luath. . . .*"

From the window of the room he and Paul shared, the

third-floor back, his brother's voice came through the leaves to him, loud and laughing:

"Rock-a-bye, baby," Paul sang lustily, "in the tree-top. . . ."

He kept very still.

"I know you're there, baby," Paul called, but the leaves hid him and he didn't answer, and presently with a parting, "Watch out the squirrels don't get you—nut!" Paul gave up and left the window.

When Brendan felt sure Paul had gone downstairs, he sang his lullaby again, this time fitting the English words to the Irish "sleep-music," so that he could later teach it to his mother:

> *"Dileen o dee, dileen o dae,*
> *Strong is the wind.*
> *Dileen o dee, dileen o dae,*
> *It is blowing among the leaves of the trees,*
> *Soon it will be rocking the cradle. . . ."*

High in the tree he was sheltered and safe. He felt sorry for everyone who didn't have a tree, a big old oxheart cherry tree, eighty years growing. As soon as the cherries were ripe he would pick a whole bushel of them for his mother. No one could get around in a tree the way he could. His father called him *iora rua*, a red squirrel.

The beautiful day was just starting. Hours and hours of it lay ahead.

And his father loved him. His mother loved him. His little sister Rose loved him. Once in a while (but not today) his brother Patrick *almost* loved him. Sister Cecilia loved him.

And he loved everybody in the whole wide world.

He was Brendan O'Nolan, child of God.

7

No one knew just what the words had been that started it. Some bit of teasing, for Paul and Peggy must always tease, but days had intervened, and words perhaps unkindly spoken yet not truly meant had passed quickly from their minds; words of no consequence, they thought; idle and harmless.

It was never to be expected, certainly, that Brendan would brood upon such words. Brooding was as unlike him as the dark of the moon is unlike the sun of morning. It was suggested that he may have dreamed, and that in the dream the words—whatever they had been—had come back to him, distorted and discolored and wholly out of proportion. Or perhaps it was all because he had just turned fourteen, an unpredictable, incomprehensible, changing, difficult age. Whatever the reason, the trifling words somehow became mountainous, threatening to crush him.

Brendan had always burned like a candle in the wind. There had never been another with so many ups and downs, with such extremes of joy and grief, such springing of fire out of ashes, such excessive remorse for such small sins, such profuse bleeding from such slight wounds, such exhaustive outpourings of love, such replenishing from the God-given springs within him. But in the past the problem had been how to keep up with these changes, which occurred with the swiftness of light passing from star to star. This was different. This was a slow, spreading darkness.

They were at breakfast the morning they received the first intimation of it.

It was a dull gray Monday, a day of freezing rain and

sleet. This in itself was dispiriting. Some had to go out in it, within the next twenty minutes: Pat, who did not look forward with pleasure to a day of cruising icy streets in a patrol car; Peggy, who must be ready to leave with Pat if she did not want to walk the eight blocks to the branch bank where she was now working; Paul and Brendan, Rose and John, who must go to school. It was no less dispiriting for those who would remain indoors: Jimmy, who was just getting over chickenpox; Mary, who almost certainly was on the verge—was that not a small vesicle, there, on her forehead?—of coming down with chickenpox; Anne, who must do her housework, contrive to dry her Monday wash in the cellar, and along with everything keep two young children warm, fed, amused, doctored, and comforted; and Police Sergeant Tadhg O'Nolan, until mid-afternoon, for he was now assigned to the four-to-midnight shift, including Saturdays and Sundays.

Brendan was late coming down to breakfast. When the others were assembled and he had been called twice, they sat down without him. Rosie said Grace. He came hurriedly, a moment later, slipping into his place with his eyes down, not looking at anyone, not speaking. His father said, *"Dia's Muire dhuit, a Bhreandáin,"* and without raising his eyes from his plate he answered, "Good morning, Father."

A little shock went around the table, rather as if the cold winter rain had penetrated the room somehow and drenched them all in an icy shower. His father and mother looked first at him and then at each other. Paul and Peggy did the same. Pat checked himself in the act of sprinkling his oatmeal with sugar. Rose and John, whether noticing the strangeness of his answer, or simply noticing that everyone else was staring, stared too.

It was probably the first time in his life that he had ever said those words.

"An bhfuilir go maith, a mhic?" his father asked.

"Yes, I'm quite all right, Father," he answered, and raised his eyes for one agonized moment to his father's face.

There was no time, then, to go into the matter; the day's activities could not be postponed. Pat's arrested sugaring of his oatmeal was resumed. Peggy and Paul, in whom memory had stirred, disengaged their questioning and faintly guilty looks from each other's faces. Brendan buttered a
148

slice of toast. He was a long while eating it; he appeared to find it difficult to swallow.

That was the beginning. Without explanation. Without warning.

The earliest opportunity his father had to seek an explanation was the following morning, for under the new work schedule it was well after midnight when he reached home. In the morning, when he heard Paul leave the third-floor-front room—he no longer shared the back room with his younger brother—and go downstairs, he went up to Brendan's room. He hoped to discover that the curious conduct which had worried and grieved him through the whole of the day before had been a passing thing, and that Brendan would automatically and with his usual good cheer return his "God and Mary to you," with the "God and Mary to you, and St. Patrick," that was standard between them. But the first glimpse of his son's face told him it had not been a passing thing.

"I'll be right down," Brendan said, pretending to think it was to hurry him along that his father had come upstairs. "I didn't realize it was late."

"Not is it late." His father closed the door of the room. "Rather, it is yet early. Time have we for a word or two between us."

It came out, under questioning, that something Peggy and Paul had said—he couldn't remember just what, it had been nothing at all, really, and they had only been teasing—but something they said had made him realize that all through the years he had made wrong and unworthy use of his ability to speak Irish. Knowingly, purposely, artfully, shamelessly, he had used it to his own advantage, to serve his own ends. Used it to get around his father. Used it to gain special favor. Used it to escape punishment. Used it to make himself necessary and indispensable to his father, and thereby a person of importance. Used it to draw to himself, to bring to focus upon himself, his father's attention, his pleasure, his appreciation, his gratefulness, and his love.

Why he had suddenly come to see this as a terrible wrong was not clear. He was as unable to offer any satisfactory explanation of the obsession as he was to rid himself of it. Somehow the bit of teasing—unintentionally, unexpectedly —had gone too deep. It had caught cruelly in his heart, the way a fishhook catches cruelly in the flesh. He could not dislodge it.

"It's dishonest," he tried to explain. "Everybody knows I just do it to—to take advantage. Because I know that if I please you in that way, you will not be so—so displeased with me in other ways. It's unfair to everyone else. It puts me in a preferred position, where I have no real right to be. And you've always known." This seemed obscurely to be the cruelest part. "You've always known why I've done it. You've always known it wasn't really to—to share something with you, or to please you just for the sake of pleasing you, but only to please you in order to serve myself. You've always known."

"Now of what you say, Brendan, it is true that we have known, each of us, how greatly it pleases me to have you speak Irish. Not has it ever seemed wrong to me that you would take this way, or any way, of pleasing me. Wrong would it seem to me did you not."

"You've always known I've done it just to gain favor."

"Not is that a thing I have always known, and not is it a thing that I know now. Always have I thought you did it because it was a natural thing and a pleasure to both of us. If you have won favor, not have you won more than you have earned. Those who accuse you could have taken the same way of pleasing, had they wished. Always has the way been open, but the trouble was great, to all except yourself."

"It is spoiled," Brendan whispered, and stood with his head down, weeping in the silent, heartbreaking way he used to weep when he was very small. "It is all spoiled."

In this way ended every attempt his father made to reason with him; and because to talk of it caused him such anguish, there seemed little to do except wait in the hope that it would pass.

But one day slipped into another, and it did not pass.

He had always been full of light talk and laughter, always ready with a story for the younger children, always ready with a song. Now he grew quiet. He talked little and laughed not at all. He told Mary he couldn't think of any stories, and when she begged for one of the old ones, he said he couldn't remember. He told his mother his throat was a little sore, he thought he was getting a cold, he didn't think he could sing.

All his life he had feared being alone. The terrible, recurring dream that had tormented him through most of his ninth and tenth years had been a dream of an empty place in which he was alone and lost. He had no instinct to be solitary. Always he had needed to be close to those he loved: within sound of the voice, within touch of the hand. Now he began to keep more and more to himself. He did not stay downstairs in the early evening to do his homework at the big dining-room table with the younger children, as he had always done before. He pleaded that they distracted him, and he went upstairs to his room and closed himself in, and that was the last anyone would see of him till morning.

He was at an age when he was growing fast, and the growth together with the brooding began to tell upon his health. He had no appetite. He became listless and pale. He acquired a look not quite of this earth.

"I wish I had your looks, Bren," Peggy told him, trying with affectionate teasing to undo what past and less affectionate teasing had done. "You should have been a girl. You're too beautiful to be a boy."

He developed a way of slipping into the house so quietly, slipping through a room so unobtrusively, that it seemed to his father he no longer saw Brendan at all except disappearing. There would be some small sound—a doorknob turning, a light step—and he would turn or look up, but never to see Brendan coming into a room, only to see him going out.

When those who had hurt him assured him again and again that they had not meant a word of it, he answered, yes, he knew, but neither their assurances nor his knowing wiped out the damage.

Peggy pleaded, "Please don't keep on feeling hurt, Bren. You know we were only trying to be funny. It wasn't funny, not in the least funny, only mean. But it isn't the first time we've been mean," she said, deeply ashamed, "and you never refused to forgive us before."

Paul became angry.

"You're only trying to get even by going on like this! It's only a sneaky way of trying to make everybody sorry for you!"

But then Paul's conscience would be additionally burdened by these bursts of anger, and he would try to make amends in various ways: taking Brendan to a high school

151

basketball game, or on an all-day trip one Saturday when he had a long-distance delivery to make in his new truck.

His mother, with pain in her heart for both of them, reproached him for the hurt to his father.

"Surely you know how much it has always meant to him," his mother said. "And right now, of all times. . . ."

He understood that she referred to his father's recent transfer to a new district, a river-front district, at the same time that his hours had been changed. He had heard them talking, and knew that his father had been coldly angry, although little had been said.

His mother's gentle reproach and the knowledge that he was hurting his father (and to hurt him at any time would be bad enough, but to hurt him at a time when someone or something else had already hurt him was immeasurably worse) filled him with a passionate extravagance of grief. After that he resumed the exchange of greetings in Irish, and even compelled himself, on the evening when his father was home, to entertain with a song or two. On the surface the song was gay or tender or sad; but underneath, it was without any feeling at all, for he did not sing it from his heart.

This was Brendan with the light gone out of him. It was worry and grief to his father, and in varying ways and to varying degrees it became a matter of personal concern to everyone, all the way down to little Mary, who glimpsed deep tragedy in whatever it was that had caused her brother suddenly and unaccountably to forget all his stories.

In the end, it was Patrick who rekindled the flame.

Pat's efforts in the beginning had met with the same results as his father's, and Pat had reacted to these results in much the same way.

"Let him alone," Pat had said. "He'll snap out of it quicker if we don't keep the heat on."

Pat had endured, thereafter, patiently and forbearingly, through three weeks going on four. By that time he had had enough, and when Pat had had enough of anything, there must come a quick, complete, and final end.

This saturation- and turning-point was reached one Friday evening, the only evening of the seven that their father could spend at home. On that evening, when they had finished supper, and Brendan, saying that he didn't want dessert and could he be excused, please, slipped away from the

152

table, heading for the stairs, Pat saw the look on his father's face and knew that the moment had arrived.

"Okay. I've *had* it!" Pat shouted, and crashed his chair against the sideboard behind him as he jumped up.

Three strides took him out of the dining room and another across the hall, to intercept his brother at the foot of the stairs.

Pat had, it may be, a tendency to oversimplify. His methods were frequently along the lines of shock treatment. That they were effective no one would deny, because there had been occasions in the past when other more circumspect, more cautious, or more kindly methods failing to produce results, Pat had stepped in and set things straight in his own extremely forthright style.

Pat did not, on this occasion, request his young brother to come into the living room instead of going upstairs alone to crawl into his hole. He simply took a firm grip on his collar and propelled him there. He wasted no breath in gentle words. He said, "Now, damn it, I'm fed up with having a death's head at the feast! You're going to start from scratch and tell me what this is all about, or I'm going to whale the tar out of you! What in hell's the matter!"

"Nothing's the matter, Pat."

"That's lie number one. Lie number two gets you one across the mouth! Now talk, damn you!"

"Let me go, Pat. Please let me go."

"When I let you go," Pat said, "you won't even be able to crawl upstairs on your hands and knees, unless you come clean. First, we're going to drag this thing out in the open, and then we're going to bury it—deep. Now, I want to know what's eating you. And if you say 'Nothing' again, I'll belt you!"

In the dining room Anne made an anxious move to rise.

"Tadhg, you won't let Pat . . . ?"

"Not will he do the lad harm, and he might do good. Let them be."

Brendan's voice reached them faintly.

"They said——"

"*Who* said?"

"Peggy and Paul."

"A pair of Grade-A loudmouths," said Pat. "The two of them together talking both at once never said anything yet that was worth anyone's time listening to. But go ahead, spill it. All of it! What did they say?"

"They said I only learned to speak Irish because I'm a . . . a fraud and a sneak, and I saw how . . . how my father would be a . . . a sucker for it and how I'd be able to . . . to use it to get away with anything, and to put myself in right and . . . and everybody else in wrong, just so I'd be a special pet and . . . and be pampered and babied and spoiled and always get the best of everything. They said I figured it all out, in the very beginning, and that my father . . . my father has always known that's what I did, and why."

"Holy Moses!" Pat exclaimed, when this tragic recital was finally choked off. "And didn't you like the compliment?"

"C—compliment, Pat?"

"The first word you ever spoke was Irish. And any year-old baby who figured all that out was sure as hell one smart little wheeler-dealer," Pat said, "if you ask me!"

Those in the dining room listened now to silence, a long, suffering moment of silence, before Brendan's voice was heard again. A faint change was in it: a lift of hope, a quick little flame springing up, as a flame would come from the touch of Pat's thumb on a cigarette lighter.

"Pat—Pat, do you mean you think, you truly think, that never was the reason?"

"What I think," Pat said roughly, "is you're a clown. I think you ought to have a good kick in the pants for not having any more sense than to pay attention to what somebody says who doesn't even know what day of the week comes on Monday! How the hell do I know why you talk Irish? Maybe for the same reason you climb trees—you're a reversion to ancestral type, or something. Or maybe you just want to be able to call people names you wouldn't have the guts to call them in English. Anyway, the only thing I can see wrong with it is that the rest of us have to listen to the damned gibberish, or else say the hell with it and go out and get drunk! But I'll tell you this: If I hear anything *but* Irish out of you for the next hour—while you and Pop catch up on your gassing—I'll stand you on your head in a bucket of water for a long slow count, so help me God!"

Brendan was quicksilver that night.

The wounds healed without scars. Brendan returned to the family stage: to entertain with songs and with his own special brand of humor; to tell stories, endlessly weaving for Mary the glittering fabric of dreams, through which a beautiful King's Daughter rode forever on a beautiful snow-white mare; to help Rosie and John with their homework, sometimes at the expense of his own; to be laughed at by Peggy and Paul (and roundly berated by Pat), for once more absent-mindedly riding the bus to the end of the line and then being stranded there, three miles from home, because he had no money to pay his fare back; and to persuade his father (in Irish) that he truly hadn't done it on purpose, that he had just happened, purely by chance, when Pat found him, to be not walking in a homeward direction at all, but watching an ice hockey game on a lake in the park.

But the terrible, self-imposed isolation of those three or four weeks left in him a little residue of loneliness that was never completely absorbed.

It was not quite like the loneliness of younger days, when he had been able to people his world plentifully with friends of his own creation. Now he was too old; those good companions were lost to him.

Now, when he went anywhere for the first time—into a new classroom or to an after-school meeting or an occasional party—he looked carefully into every face, because somewhere, he knew surely, somewhere in the world there was someone God had designated to be his special friend. Someone he must keep looking for, because if they missed each other, in the dark, in the vastness of the world, their paths might never cross again.

Other factors contributed to the loneliness.

The new working hours meant that he saw much less of his father. Sometimes when he had lain wakeful and waiting to hear the familiar sound of the car door closing that would tell him his father had come home, he would slip downstairs, but this could only be done once in a while or it would be forbidden. Other times, if when he heard his parents come upstairs to bed, he coughed or in some other way let them know he was awake, his father would come up to his room to make sure he was covered or that his window was not too wide open. They would talk for a few minutes, keeping their voices low so as not to wake Paul in the next room, and all the loneliness of the night would be pushed away, like a dark curtain, by his father's hand, and the shadow-haunted stillness would be made warm and bright by the sound of the loved voice. But his father didn't come every night. He said it would encourage him to lie awake waiting, and not was it good for him to lie awake so late.

And he missed going to and from school with Rose, now that he was in first year high and Rosie only in fifth grade. Rosie was much younger than he, but she had acquired a deep sense of responsibility at an early age, and this, contrasting as it did with his own irresponsibility (Peggy and Paul said he would never grow up), made them seem a great deal closer. Rose was good company. She took him as he was; she didn't seem to think the things he did were any crazier than the things most people did (she was intensely practical herself). Last year she had even been boastfully proud of being his sister, because he cleaned up all the prizes in everything at St. Andrew's: the Essay Contest sponsored by the American Legion; the Poetry Contest sponsored by the Woman's Club; the General Excellence Award at graduation exercises; and even the silver dollar that the new parish priest, Father Morissey, offered as prize to the first person who could tell him who were called Saints in the early days of the church. (Father Morissey hadn't expected that anyone could tell him without looking it up or at least asking at home. He had been greatly surprised when Brendan raised his hand and gave the answer. He had also been surprised when Brendan didn't come to the front of the Assembly Hall to get the silver dollar, but asked him to give it to Mother Aloysius for the school, instead.)

Now Brendan traveled to school with Paul instead of with Rose, but the strait was wider and deeper on that side of his island. Paul had his own friends who regularly rode the same bus, and he accorded only a minimum amount of time and attention to a young brother, only enough to make sure that he got off the bus when they reached the school and to stay beside him until he was safely within the building, because there were a few rowdies who hung around on the steps until the last bell rang, looking for someone to pick on.

He was lonely at school. He had skipped seventh grade,

156

which meant that he entered high school ahead of most of the boys he had known in earlier years. New classmates looked at him and said, "Ain't he purty!" and dubbed him Mamma's Little Angel. It was no help to him, in the matter of being accepted—or not accepted—by them, that he consistently got good marks, that he was quiet and well-behaved in the classroom, and that the priests liked him.

He joined the Glee Club and the Language Society, but first year boys sang with the chorus only in practice sessions, not in public appearances; and they only listened to the discussions or to the speakers at the Language meetings; they weren't expected to contribute anything. His voice had undergone a gradual but not radical change, it was still very clear and true, and he still sang once in a while at church, but he didn't tell the director of the Glee Club that he had experience as a soloist and he didn't tell anyone that he spoke Irish.

He rode home by himself. Paul, by reason of his trucking business, had obtained special permission to skip his last period, which was study-hall, and thus to leave school fifty minutes ahead of everyone else. Brendan, on the contrary, usually stayed an hour overtime, either for Glee Club practice or reference work in the library. By the time he left, those who loitered on the steps had left also; if he saw they hadn't, he remembered something he had neglected to look up in the library and went back inside.

On Saturday afternoons he went to the branch Public Library, which was on the avenue, about six blocks from home. He could, of course, have stocked himself for a month on one trip, with as many books as he could carry, for he had the use of Katie's card now as well as his own; but it was something to look forward to at the end of each week, riding up with his father, who dropped him off at the library on his way to report for duty on the late afternoon shift.

It was at the Public Library, one Saturday afternoon in March, that Brendan met Bill.

He had an armload of books that day, returning some for other members of the family, and was just about to open the door when the door was suddenly opened from within, smack against him. It nearly knocked him off his feet, and it sent two or three books spinning down the steps.

The young man coming out, also with a load of books,

157

said, "Oops! I'm sorry!" and made a quick grab to keep Brendan from falling, whereupon two or three more books went down the steps.

"Why don't I watch where I'm going?" the young man asked. "Did I hurt you?"

"Oh, no," Brendan denied, wondering if he was going to have a lump on his forehead where the door had caught him. "I'm all right. The door hit the books, mostly. Anyway it was my fault, I was standing too close."

"Someday when I've made my first million," the young man said, "I'm going to present the city with a glass panel for that door."

Together they picked up the scattered books.

"Well, I'll be darned!" the young man said, looking at the title of one he had retrieved. *"Social History of Ancient Ireland, Volume I.* So that's why it wasn't on the shelf."

"I've been working on a paper for history," Brendan said.

"That makes two of us. I'm working on a history thesis, too. Mine's on codes of law among various ancient peoples. What's yours?"

"Pagan Ireland."

"Ah. That's it. Right there's where we coincide."

"I'm returning the *Social History,*" Brendan said, "if you want it."

"I do, but I've got one over the legal limit now. Let's see. I could trade . . ."

"I can renew it," Brendan offered, "and then you can have it."

"No, because I left a holding order. But I can go in and lift that, and then . . . look," the young man said suddenly, "don't I know you?"

"I hardly think so," Brendan answered, with the added explanation, "I'm not very well known."

This came out sounding very modest but also rather funny, and it made them laugh.

"Well, I've an idea you're better known than you think, because I do know you. I see you nearly every Sunday at eight-o'clock Mass. You're one of the altar boys over at St. Andrew's. Frankly," the young man said, "in church I've always been pretty sure you were an optical illusion. But now I see you're for real. What's your name?"

"Brendan O'Nolan."

"It fits beautifully. Mine's Bill MacCarthy."

Brendan searched the face of his new acquaintance. It was a pleasant face, the mouth was smiling, the eyes were dark and friendly. Was it—?

"You look as if you're trying to decide where you've seen *me* before," Bill said.

"No. No, I've never seen you before. Not that I know of, anyway. I was just wondering . . ."

But it wasn't a thing he could say. He could search this new face and wonder: Are you to be my friend? But he couldn't ask it. Not of someone who must be almost as old as Pat. No one that old would want to waste time being friends with anyone like him.

"I was just wondering," he said again. "Your name's MacCarthy, but you don't look Irish."

"I'm the Mediterranean type," Bill said. "A lot of us Phoenicians went up to that island from time to time. Some on trading vessels, as far back as a thousand years or so B.C. More recently, of course, some of us swam ashore, with Sir Francis Drake taking potshots at us from the deck of Her Majesty's flagship. You, now," Bill said, "you're a Celt. You were there ahead of us, but I've never found anybody who can tell me to my satisfaction just how you got there, or when. That's because you're older than history. How does it feel, being older than history?"

"My father could probably tell you," Brendan said eagerly. "He's read just about all the books that ever were written about the Celts. And he knows the names of our ancestors back a thousand years."

"You wouldn't kid me, would you?"

"No, Bill. Honest."

"Well, a fellow once said 'old families last not three oaks,' but I don't remember that he mentioned how long the oaks last. A tree like that, though," Bill said, "generally has a coat of arms hanging on it somewhere. You know, with motto and stuff."

"Seasaim," said Brendan.

"What?"

"Seasaim. It means 'I stand.' "

His new friend stared at him, looked questioning, looked doubtful, laughed, and clapped a hand on his shoulder.

"Quick on the draw, aren't you, partner? If I hadn't remembered that history paper you're writing, I might have bought that one."

After they had gone into the library to renew the *Social History of Ancient Ireland*, they sat outside on a low wall that separated the library from the adjoining property. Their talk jumped easily around from one thing to another, the light, informal conversation of friends. Brendan learned that Bill was a university student in his junior year; that after he got his A.B. he was planning to study law; that to pay his college expenses he worked six nights a week, waiting on tables in the main dining room of the Lanchester-Warren Hotel; that his father was dead, and that he and his mother and sister lived in a second-floor apartment in the big old place next door, to which the wall on which they were sitting belonged. Bill learned that Brendan's father and oldest brother were both policemen; that his sister Katie was making her novitiate; that last spring, when he assisted at Confirmation, he stepped on the Archbishop's robe; and that ever since he read "A Cask of Amontillado" he got cold chills any time he had to go down to the cellar.

It was a wonderful half hour. But the sun went out of sight behind banked clouds, the wind got a fresh bite to it, and the stone wall began to give Brendan a worse chill than he ever could get from remembering the "Amontillado."

Bill saw that he was shivering.

"You'd better hike for home, fella. I'd be glad to drive you over," Bill said, "but we're a one-car family, and Mother's got it."

"Oh, I'll get warm," Brendan said. "I'll run. Bill"—he tried to sound casual—"will you be here next Saturday?"

He thought a very slight hesitation preceded the answer.

"Could be," Bill said. "Take a look around. I'll probably be at one of the tables with my nose to the grindstone, as usual."

Brendan didn't tell at home about this meeting. He meant to, but there didn't seem to be just the right opportunity, and then, because he hadn't told right away, it became increasingly awkward to tell at all. He thought up several ways of mentioning it, as if it had slipped his mind and he had only at that moment remembered, but when he re-heared these approaches in his mind, they all seem unconvincing and he discarded them. He postponed the telling.

The following Saturday Bill was at one of the library

tables, as he had said he might be, reading and making notes. Brendan took an encyclopedia from the reference shelf, and sat down at the same table. They traded smiles and a few whispered words of greeting, and spent the next three quarters of an hour in companionable silence, enlivened by an exchange of written questions and answers.

On a page of his notebook Bill wrote: *How's the history of pagan Ireland coming along?*

Brendan wrote under it: *Finished.*

Bill wrote: *Have you ever read the Cuchulain legends? Yes,* Brendan answered. *In Irish.*

Bill grinned and wrote: *Wise guy!* And then, a little later: *Who was that lady I saw you with outside church last Sunday?*

And Brendan, picking up the cue, wrote: *That was no lady, that was my sister.*

Saturday afternoon became more than ever the highlight of the week. On good days, after they finished inside, they sat on the wall for a while and talked before Brendan set out for home. Once, when it was raining hard, and Bill saw his mother's car parked under the big porte-cochère of the house next door, he said to wait a minute and he'd bring the car around and run him home. Brendan planned to say Bill was a brother of some boy he knew at school, if anyone asked, but no one saw the car stop, so no one asked.

Several times Bill asked questions about Peggy.

"How old is your sister?"

"Peggy's eighteen, Bill."

"Still in school?"

"No, she finished in January. She's working now, in a bank."

"What bank?"

"This one. Right over here."

"The Security Trust branch? H-m-m-m," said Bill. "I've been thinking of transferring my account to the Security, all twenty-six dollars and forty-five cents of it."

On Easter Sunday, Bill sat directly behind the O'Nolans —nine of them—at eight o'clock Mass. The following Saturday he told Brendan of this experience. It was almost more than any man could take, Bill said; all in one dose, they took his breath away. He said he hadn't been altogether able to believe it; he said he kept closing his eyes and then opening them again, feeling certain each time that it was all a vision and would have disappeared when next he looked. But no, there they stayed, one whole bench completely filled with them. The two handsomest men he had ever seen, Bill said (who could, of course, be none but Brendan's father and brother Patrick), had occupied the extreme ends of the pew, with the rest of the family well guarded between them; and among the rest, Bill couldn't conceive of anyone disputing it, were the world's two most beautiful women.

And again he asked questions about Peggy.

"Your sister hasn't made any irrevocable decisions, has she, concerning her future?"

"Irrevocable decisions, Bill?"

"Okay," Bill said, "in plain words: is she engaged?"

"Oh, I don't think so."

"But I suppose her opportunities are legion? I mean, aren't the rest of you always tripping over the multitudes who keep coming to lay their hearts and hopes—and their twenty-six dollars and forty-five cents—at her feet?"

"Well, she goes with Jerry Kennedy, mostly. He lives down the street from us."

"Steady?"

"Well, pretty steady, I guess."

Bill said, "Just my luck." And then: "Old friend, childhood sweetheart; who are you, MacCarthy, to think you might horn in?"

This last remark, being self-addressed, seemed not to require an answer, so Brendan offered none.

As he walked home that afternoon he was deeply troubled. He had laid no groundwork for such a contingency as this. He had not told anyone about Bill. Not anyone at all. Not a word. It would be very awkward, not to say extremely uncomfortable, to let it be known at home, now, that he had been meeting somebody at the library for six weeks without ever mentioning it. It would be very hard to explain. He wouldn't be able to deny that he had been sneaky. He would only be able to say that he hadn't really meant to be. He had meant to tell about Bill. Actually he had wanted to. But for some reason (a reason that had never become clearly defined in his mind) he had kept putting it off.

But suppose Bill met Peggy some other way. At the bank, for instance. Wouldn't it be even harder to explain then?

How would he explain that, although he knew Bill liked
Peggy, he had never mentioned it? Had never looked
around for Bill outside the church, but had, in fact, lingered
in the sacristy so that by the time he joined the others, Bill
had gone? Why had he not this afternoon, said right away
that he was almost sure Peggy was home, and why didn't
Bill come along over, and stop in to see his father's Irish-
language collection, as he had said he would like to do
someday when he had time?

Why hadn't he?

Was it because he didn't want to share Bill?

He knew what would happen. Bill would be Peggy's
friend then. Not his. Not ever really his again. The specialness would be gone.

But wouldn't the specialness be gone anyway, if he didn't
do what was right for a brother to do? For a friend to do?

Next Saturday he would do it.

The opportunity came before Saturday.

It was on Friday afternoon, late, that Peggy received a
telephone call. There was nothing to indicate, in her cool
and polite answers, that it was a call destined to change the
whole course of her life. When she replaced the receiver,
she did so with a restrained violence that did credit to her
upbringing; for Brendan, who chanced to encounter the
fury of her blazing blue glance, felt quite certain that had
she followed her instincts she would have torn the offensive
instrument out by its roots, smashed it into a thousand
pieces, reduced to kindling the table on which it had rested.

"The stinker!" she said. "The complete stinker!"

"Is something wrong, Peggy?"

"*Is something wrong!* You'd like to know, wouldn't you?
You'd always like to know! Always sneaking around sticking your nose in other people's business! Well, if anything
was wrong, I wouldn't give a sneak like you the satisfaction
of knowing it!"

"Peggy"—the protest was in bewilderment—"I didn't
sneak in. I was here all the time. I called you to the telephone. Don't you remember?"

"No matter what you did or where you were," Peggy re-
torted viciously, "you're a sneak! A pussyfooting, crawling
little sneak! You always have been! You always will be!
You . . ."

Peggy put her hands to her face and started to cry.

"Oh, I'm sorry, Bren, I'm sorry. I don't mean what I'm saying. I don't even know what I'm saying. I'm just so spitting mad!"

Later, helping her mother with the final preparations for the evening meal, Peggy was wrapped in a mantle of cold dignity, and to the anxious "Is anything wrong, dear?" she answered calmly, "Not a thing. Father just came in, I believe. Shall I start putting things on the table, Mother?"

They sat down to supper. There was a slight feeling of strain—there was always a feeling of strain when something was amiss, for the family intercommunications system was acutely sensitive—but it was not until the meal was two-thirds over that Peggy put her composure to the ultimate test with a superbly casual: "If you want to go to that meeting of the Altar and Rosary Society tomorrow evening, Mother, I'll be here to take care of the children."

"Tomorrow evening, darling? Not tomorrow, surely?"

"Oh, I guess I didn't tell you. I won't be going to the dance. Jerry's leaving for California early tomorrow morning, with the Fletchers."

"California?" Anne was stunned.

Patiently, Peggy explained, "It's a state on the West Coast."

"But you can't mean——"

"She means she's been stood up," Paul said. "That's what you mean, don't you, Sis?"

Peggy permitted a frigid, supercilious glance to brush him lightly.

"If you wish to call it so."

"So the guy's a heel. I could have told you that."

"My dear brother, you couldn't tell me anything, for the reason that your childish opinions are of not the slightest interest to me. I'm sure no intelligent person would expect Jerry to pass up a trip to California just to go to a stupid little high school alumni dance. After all, it's a matter of values."

Values? Anne thought of the beautiful new formal hanging upstairs in her daughter's closet. She thought of the weeks of looking forward to tomorrow night. It was no ordinary dance. Not like the monthly parish dances. Not like last year's senior dance in the gymnasium at the school. It was altogether different. . . . It was the annual benefit

164

dance for the school, held in the main ballroom of one of the big downtown hotels, with a name orchestra and dancing until three in the morning.

"Darling, isn't there someone else you—?"

"At this hour? Don't be fantastic, Mother. And even if it weren't the eleventh hour," Peggy said on a strongly acid note, "it isn't as if I *know* anybody else. How would I? I've never *gone* anywhere, to meet anybody. You don't meet very many boys at an all-girls' school. And there's nobody at the bank who isn't ninety years old, or married, or else the kind of person I wouldn't be seen dead with. And when you remember that I was never even allowed to have any real dates until I was seventeen, I really don't see how you could expect that I'd have any friends."

This barb was addressed to but not aimed at her mother. It found its target at the other end of the table, but produced no response—from the target—except an unreadable stare. The response from the rest of the company was a somewhat prolonged silence, eventually broken by Pat.

"Don't everybody, for Pete's sake, look at me!" Pat said. "I've got my own troubles lined up for Saturday night."

"And don't look at me," Paul echoed promptly. "She roped me into dragging her dear, darling, palsy-walsy little friend Winnie to this shindig."

Pat said, "Next!"

And Paul turned with a grin to say, "Looks like you're elected, Bren."

Anger flashed through Peggy's composure like lightning seen at a distance, with the promise of what it would be like if it came near.

"Very funny. You're really a card, aren't you, dear brother?"

"What's funny about it?" Paul contrived to sound very logical and sincere. "Bren's always ready to do anyone a favor. Sure, he's a little young, but he's as tall as you are, Peg, and you taught him all that fancy dance stuff so you'd have someone to practice with. Here's your chance to make it pay off. Get him in a tux and you won't know him. You'd be glad to squire Peg to the Saint Elizabeth Alumni Benefit Dance, wouldn't you, Bren?"

Indeed, Brendan would, and almost said so at once. He had a shining glimpse of a whole evening of music and dancing and personal delight, plus the rare and distinctive

165

privilege of being helpful to Peggy in a moment of crisis. But he had acquired, through the years, some rudiments of caution, and he was warned that Paul was only joking. Taking refuge behind the special little smile that he had learned made it almost as hard for anyone to know whether or not he was being serious, as it was for him to know whether or not they were, he said, "Yes, I would be glad to, but I don't believe Peggy would want me."

"You're so right!" Peggy said.

At that instant Brendan remembered the obligations of friendship, and forgot everything else. Forgot to guard against Peggy's anger or Paul's ridicule. Forgot the awkward explanations he would be called on to make. Impetuously and eagerly he brought out, "But I have a friend——"

Paul's laughter stopped him. Whether Brendan had spoken in sincerity or jest made no difference; it was hilarious either way. But, as Brendan's look changed from eagerness to apology, Paul knew that the offer had indeed been made in good faith, with no idea in the world how ludicrous it was that a friend of his might be considered a suitable escort for Peggy, especially as his "friends" in the not far distant past had often had more than a little of the supernatural in their make-up.

"Where does he live?" Paul asked, when he could control his laughter. "In the tool shed?" And this set him off again.

Brendan carefully put his smile in place again, the puckish little smile designed to make them all think he had meant to be funny.

Peggy saw it and was fooled. She lashed out at them:

"It's very amusing, isn't it? Well, enjoy yourselves, both of you, and I hope you choke!"

His mother saw it and was doubtful. It was so unlike Brendan to jest at another's expense, and yet—what could he have been thinking of?

His father saw it, and saw beneath it. Because he was looking carefully beneath it, his eyes rested longer on his third son than on his second, giving the impression that it was Brendan's remark rather than Paul's laughter to which he alluded when he said, "Not is it seemly for a brother to make sport of a sister's disappointment."

Brendan lost his smile. Thoroughly abashed, he bent over his plate and gave all his attention to eating peas, one at a time, speared on a prong of his fork.

One other who had seen and analyzed the smile was Patrick. Patrick was neither deceived nor doubtful, but he finished his supper and waited to be served his dessert before he asked, "Who's your friend, kid?"

This delayed, casual-sounding question produced a variety of reactions around the table. His mother gave him a surprised and rather anxious glance. Peggy said, "Oh, for heaven's sake!" and got up and started clearing the table. Paul snickered, but a look from his father warned him this time to keep his amusement within bonds. And Brendan raised his head with a quick and grateful smile.

"It's someone I've been meeting at the library, Pat."

"What do you mean, you've 'been meeting' at the library?" Instant suspicion was in Pat's voice. "On the sly?"

"Oh, no Pat. I mean, all I mean is, I go every Saturday afternoon and he goes every Saturday afternoon, and we just happen to be there at the same time."

"And they converse by wigwagging," Paul said.

This sent a ripple of laughter from one to another of the younger children. Rosie and John both saw the humor of it. Jimmy laughed because they did. Mary laughed because the word "wigwagging" had such a funny sound.

"All right," said Pat, "start at the beginning and give with the story of this burgeoning friendship. After that, you can start on the reason why tonight's the first we hear of it. And"—to Paul—"any more out of you, I'll put one on you that will lift you out of that chair and land you on your backside in the middle of next week!"

Anne said, "Pat, please. The children . . ."

Brendan told the story. Peggy stood listening contemptuously for a moment to the curious coincidence of the overlapping history papers, and then went upstairs. Rosie finished clearing the table and set about washing the dishes. John and Jimmy went outside. In was a fairly long story and Brendan told it in detail, for he knew that what he didn't tell, Pat would get out of him sooner or later anyway.

And Pat wasted no time.

"You say he drove you home. What are your orders," Pat asked, "about riding with these hare-brained kids who've just got their driver's cards?"

"I don't think Bill just got his driver's card, Pat."

"You said he's a junior. Any high-school kid writing

167

about codes of law among the ancients sure as hell doesn't sound retarded, so I figure him about sixteen."

"No, he's older, Pat." Brendan felt an uneasiness, something having to do with the undefined reason why he had not told about Bill before. "He's a junior at the university."

"The university!"

"Yes." The uneasiness mounted. "He's going to study law, after he gets his A.B."

"If he can spare the time," Pat said in a hard voice.

"Spare the time, Pat?"

"Between his other intellectual pursuits," Pat said, "such as striking up friendships with fourteen-year-old kids at the public library."

With a shock, Brendan realized the inference Pat had drawn. Wondering if subconsciously he had known this all along, he protested in anguish, "Pat, Bill isn't the way you're thinking."

"Who rides herd on this kid," Pat asked his father, "since I was relieved of the assignment? Or have you got the balmy idea that he knows the ropes now and can look out for himself?"

Hard looks were exchanged, but the answer was given mildly.

"Not is it a matter of knowledge to me that you ever were relieved of the assignment. Unless it is so that you yourself disclaim it."

"I never put *my* okay on him running around loose!"

"Fourteen he is. A great deal more freedom you had when you were but twelve."

"I hope you don't imagine you're drawing a parallel!"

"Parallel there may not be. But not does it seem to me that a public library offers significant danger."

"Don't kid yourself. The intellectuals aren't in the clear by a damned sight. I should think you'd at least make a routine investigation of any friends he picks up."

"Do you proceed with your investigation," his father replied equably, "and I will accept your findings."

"Oh, sure, you think I'm jumping to conclusions. Well, it's a hell of a lot safer to jump to a conclusion than to have one sneak up and knife you in the back. If there's any likelier reason why some joker half again this kid's age would cotton up to him, you tell me what it is!"

"Pat," Brendan pleaded, "it was just because he's so nice.

168

It was because he knew that *I* wanted to be friends with *him*. I don't think he meant to be at the library the second time, but I think he saw how much I hoped he would be."

"I've got an open mind," Pat said. "Go ahead and convince me. Tell me what you talk about besides the legal codes of the ancient Celts."

"Oh, everything! Books, and things we like to do, and our families. His father was a foreign correspondent. They used to travel to all sorts of places all over the world, Japan and Korea and India and everywhere. But when his father died, they came back here. And, of course, I told him about my father. And about you, too, Pat. And he was always asking questions about Peggy. That's why I thought——"

"Whoa, now wait a minute. Did you tell him Pop's a policeman?"

"Yes, Pat."

"And I'm a policeman?"

"Yes, Pat."

"And he didn't take a powder, pronto?"

"Didn't . . . ?"

"Scram. Vamoose. Evaporate."

"Oh, no."

"Well," Pat said generously, "I could have the guy wrong. MacCarthy? MacCarthys are a dime a dozen, but I don't quite place. . . . Did he ask you questions about Peg the first day?"

"No, the second day. After he saw Peggy with me outside church."

Paul laughed and said, "Elementary, my dear Officer Watson."

"Were you requested to comment?" Pat asked coldly.

"I'm not shy," Paul said. "And if you could ever look at anything normally, instead of always having to make like a cop, you'd get the picture without having to be hit in the eye with it. It's Peg this character has a yen for. He's only been using our champion fall guy here as a way of getting his foot in the door."

No one did more than glance at Brendan. No one, not even Paul, could bear to. Paul pushed his chair away from the table and stood up.

"Me and my big mouth. Okay, I know when I've overstayed my welcome. But you're all on the wrong foot.

169

Who's going to cushion the knocks for him when he gets out on his own? If he ever does. It's a hard, cruel world," Paul said, and turned to leave the table.

His father stopped him with a gesture and a stony rebuke.

"Great is the difference between a hasty conclusion born of an instinct to protect, and one born of an instinct to wound. Hard and cruel is the world, as you say. Better would it be, then, did cruelty not start at home."

"Sorry," Paul said, and went on out of the room.

Brendan succeeded in putting his little smile in place. As cover for the sudden bitter desolation of the truth, it was thin and poor, but he made it tell them that he saw, now, how ridiculous it had been to think Bill had made friends with him just for his own sake; that he should have realized the second Saturday's meeting was due to Bill's having seen him with Peggy in the meantime; that this was just the sort of silly mistake that could be expected of him; that they should go ahead and laugh, he wouldn't mind, because, as they could see, he was already laughing at himself.

No one laughed.

His father said, "Some fault might I find with your secrecy, my son, but not with your judgment of your friend. Not is he less friend to you for that he might wish to be friend to your sister also."

His mother said, "It's perfectly plain, dear, that he hadn't made any connection between you and Peggy in the beginning. He was friends with you first. It's also perfectly plain," Anne said, aching with pity, "that your Bill Mac-Carthy is a thoroughly nice person, and I should very much like to meet him."

Pat said, "I'll buy that, too. The only thing that puzzles me, I can't tie him to any MacCarthys I know. I even draw a blank on an apartment house up there by the library. Which side of the street is it?"

Brendan turned gratefully to the reintroduction of this purely impersonal detail, which could be discussed without pain.

"The same side, Pat. Right next door."

"You've got me, kid. There *is* no apartment house next door to the library."

"Yes, there is. It's that big old place with the wall around it."

"Oh, that place. But that's not apartments. That's——"
Pat broke off, stared for a moment, said, *"Holy Michael and all the Saints!"* and looked at his father. "That's the old Kane mansion. The MacCarthy he's talking about must be——"

"Grandson to Mr. Clement Kane," his father said.

"That's who it is, all right. The old guy disowned one of his daughters when she married a Catholic. But then after she was widowed they patched it up and she went back there to live. There's no money—she works for the family law firm. One of those mile-long ones—Lippincott, Spencer, Kennard, and Kane—give or take a few. Somebody told me it takes every cent the old man can squeeze out of his clients just to keep that ancient ruin shored up, and pay the taxes."

Anne said, "That house predates the Civil War, Pat."

"Which makes it ultramodern," said Pat, "when you figure that the family predates the Revolution. Yep, old Georgie Three and the Kanes were just like that, so they tell me. Holy Moses! What have we got here? Poor but proud scion of one of the oldest families in town, worshiping our Lady Margaret from afar! Well, it figures. Peg's quite a dish when her hair's combed and she keeps her claws in." Pat wore a rather wicked smile. "And something tells me she might not be averse to meeting Brother Brendan's little friend after all. This could be good," Pat said. "This could really be good."

"I was going to ask Bill to come home with me tomorrow afternoon," Brendan said, "if Peggy was going to be here, so he could meet her."

Pat asked, "Why?"

"*Why*, Pat?"

"That was the question. Why? You wouldn't want to say you honestly think you'd be doing your friend a favor, would you?"

"You're joking, aren't you, Pat?"

"Half. But the other half is this: You don't owe Peg anything, kid. Not a damned thing. Unless there's something you'd like to pay back to her in her own coin."

Anne began to protest, "Pat, you shouldn't——"

But Pat laughed and said, "Don't worry. We have here the original model of the turner of the other cheek. Haven't we, Little Brother of All the World?"

171

Brendan looked from one to another of the three, who seemed to be waiting expectantly to hear what he would say.

"Once you make the introductions," Pat said, "you'll be invited to get lost. Wouldn't it be smarter to keep your friend and your Saturday afternoons to yourself, and let Peg flush her own game?"

Pat was teasing, but Pat's teasing never laid a trap. Pat wasn't waiting to laugh at him. He didn't have to guard his answer.

"Bill's my friend, Pat. Peggy's my sister."

As an entertainer, Brendan outshone himself that evening.

Mary had never been told such a bedtime story before. It concerned not one King's Daughter, but six. There was not one milk-white palfrey, but a coach-and-four—a glittering glass coach trimmed with gold, and four white ponies to draw it—one coach for each Fair Princess; and as the six Fair Princesses went everywhere together, there went the twenty-four white ponies also, prancing endlessly down the shining streets of a beautiful city somewhere in the Isles of the Silver Seas.

Peggy had never heard so provocative an account of an unknown admirer: with what rapture he had beheld her on Easter morning, how indelibly the picture of her in her new green suit with the little hat that was no more than a chaplet of daisies had stamped itself upon his memory; how he had called her one of the world's two most beautiful women; how courageously he had borne the blow when informed that she went steady (almost) with Jerry Kennedy, and, finally, how good-looking Bill was, how clever, how learned, how traveled, how ambitious, and how nice.

John and Jimmy had never been entertained with such a sidesplitting variety of Pat-and-Mike stories, or with such a riotous impersonation of the cheerleader who put his megaphone over his head every time the opposing team scored, and one time couldn't get it off again.

When he sang, his voice had never been sweeter or purer . . . or sadder. His mother asked for the *Ave Maria,* its beauty almost breaking her heart. His father asked for a song of his homeland, and heard the song of the thrush and the sigh of the wind over the green hills of his childhood mingling with the keening note of a timeless grief.

And never had there been such a game of chess before, never so boldly and brilliantly played, in a rapid succession of aggressive moves that trapped and checkmated his father's black king while the black queen was helplessly hemmed in by her own bishops.

That incredible game was, in a way, the climax of the evening. Because it was so short they played another, and the second one ran to great length. When it had ended, the hour was late and Brendan was very tired.

Leaning back in his chair he closed his eyes—only for seconds, yet in those seconds the tiredness seemed to spread out all around him in a dreary barrenness. As in sleep a dream comes, seeming to cover hours, days, even years, yet in truth occupying only the space of a thought as it comes and goes, so in that moment of closing his eyes he had a dream-vision, in which he saw himself standing on the center section of a bridge, of which the part that he had just come over, and the part that he had yet to cross, had been swept away, leaving him stranded, cut off from all the rest of the living world; and all around, as far as the eye could see, was nothing but a desolate gray waste, like the sand-flats and salt-water marshes over which he had driven with Paul one day last winter, on a trip to a coastal town.

His father, from across the table, looked into his face, and saw the tiredness and the shadow that he had long ago learned to recognize as the shadow of fear. To his father, what had happened in these past hours was plain: Brendan had expended all his energies, had consumed himself in his own fires, had extravagantly poured out the libation of his spirit until every other cup was filled and his own empty.

"*Tá tuirse ort*," his father said. "*Tá sé deireannach*."

"*Tá*."

There was no denying, he was tired and it was very late.

He opened his eyes and smiled at his father, a smile of such sweetness that it was like the lighting of the candles of Heaven.

"*Raghad 'mo luighe, 'Athair*. I will go to bed. I am tired, though I am not sleepy."

He didn't want to go to bed. He would have to, but he didn't want to. Sleep was so treacherous; there was no way of knowing how deep you would go, or how far, once you had slipped over the edge of the world into that dark stream.

He didn't know that his father could see the shadow of fear.

"You have given too much," his father said.

"Given . . . ?"

"Of yourself. There is great weariness on you now, because you have kept no reserve of strength and joy within yourself, but have let it all flow out to us. The more generously," his father said, "because you have not yourself been happy tonight."

"*Tá áthas orm,*" Brendan protested at once. "*Tá áthas mór orm, 'Athair.*"

"Not so," his father said. "Not are you glad. Yet you have given nothing but gladness to the rest of us."

"Oh, that's just because I'm such a clown. It comes so naturally, you see, that I can't help it. Even when I'm——"

He caught back the word "unhappy," but there was no other word to finish with and the little empty space at the end of what he had said hung there between them.

He thought of pouring out to his father the longing, the need, the hope, the search of faces, the unspoken question, "Are you to be my friend? Are you the one?" And of how he had thought that Bill was the one. Had been almost certain Bill was the one. . . . No, he couldn't trust himself to tell about that. He would give way to self-pity, the telling would bring tears.

Neatly and carefully, white on one side, black on the other, he finished putting the chessmen away in their box.

"I will go to bed now, I think."

"*Tá go maith,*" his father said. "That is good, for plain it is that you are very tired, and not would I keep you longer. Tomorrow will be time enough to tell you of the great pride I take in your courage and your goodness, my son, and of the love I bear you which has never been greater than at this moment."

Brendan whispered, "'Athair . . ."

"But do you not wait, now, to hear of these things," his father went on. "Go you to bed. And in but a while I will come to make sure that you are sleeping, for well do I know your way of lying long awake in disobedience and defiance of your father's command."

When sleep came, it did not come as a slipping away into

darkness. The dream shadows loomed around him, towering and fantastic, arching over, closing in, but never obscuring the circle of light in which he moved.

He walked the dark caves of sleep holding aloft a lighted taper. Where a cold draft caught it, or the fog pressed black and thick, his father's hand reached out to shelter the flame.

8

Peggy O'Nolan knew, as soon as she started going with Bill MacCarthy, that she had never been so happy in her life.

Or so unhappy.

Only this was happiness: the diminishing moments that separated them when the appointed time of being with him again drew near; and then the joy of being together, which was like no other joy she had ever known.

Paradoxically, increased happiness was the wellspring of increased unhappiness, which clouded all existence in between.

One night a week and Sunday afternoons they were together. The rest of the time he attended classes, or studied, or worked.

At first it had seemed to her wholly incongruous that he should wait on tables, but soon she realized that because he was William Kane MacCarthy, old Mr. Clement Kane's grandson, he could work at anything without lowering his social status. For every raised eyebrow there were a dozen expressions of approval. He was admired for his independence, his self-reliance, his determination. Eventually, after he had gone through law school and been admitted to the bar, he would become the junior member of the well-known, highly respected law firm from which, when that time came, his grandfather Kane planned to retire. The firm would then become Lippincott, Spencer, Kennard, and MacCarthy.

That time was still several years distant, but to Peggy the intervening years did not represent a long time—indeed, not as long a time as she could wish; for when the years of schooling were ended and he was ready to practice law, he would undoubtedly marry. And, again undoubtedly, he would marry someone in his own circle, his own class. Someone from one of the fine old families that, like the Kanes, had been here since before the Revolution. Someone who would be an asset to him in his profession. Perhaps even someone with money. But not, very certainly not, someone like Peggy O'Nolan—a girl without background, a girl with only a high-school education, a policeman's daughter.

She had never thought much about status before because there had never been reason to. The parents of her friends, of most of the people she knew, were all in pretty much the same position, socially and financially. Some had a little more money, some a little less. Some lived in row houses, some in single houses like their own. Some were shopworkers, some were office workers, some clerked in stores, some drove milk or bread routes, a few were schoolteachers, a few had small businesses of their own, a few were doctors or dentists. Even at St. Elizabeth's, a private school, there had been no daughters of the wealthy or of the socially prominent, but only other girls like herself, whose parents took upon themselves the added burden of tuition costs, not by reason of social pretensions, but purely for the superior quality of the schooling.

She had always been intensely proud of her parents. Her mother was so beautiful, so much more beautiful than anyone else's mother. Her mother had had only a high-school education, too, but that was because she had married so young. She could have gone to college had she wanted to. Her mother's brother, Uncle Paul, Aunt Nora's husband, was a college graduate in business administration, and held a very responsible position as personnel manager at one of the big industrial plants. Her mother's father had been locally a person of importance, a Democratic committeeman.

And her father . . .

Well, there was no one like her father. No one else's father compared with him in any way. She had always loved him more than she loved anybody else in the world, and had always known that no matter how dearly she loved him, he was worthy of being loved more than she had the capacity for. He was so strong and handsome, so proud-looking, so fine and good; and though he was very strict, he was also always very kind, and he loved them all so much. It had always seemed to her that his love put an impregnable ring of safety around their home, like a stockade around a fort.

Bill admired her father, and was impressed by the ease and eloquence with which he could discuss any subject that came up. She liked being able to say that he had been very well educated, in Ireland; and that for years after he and her mother were married, he had taken night courses at the University here, mainly in political science and law, and had needed only a few more credits to obtain a degree. "But frankly," she was also able to say, "he couldn't afford to complete the degree requirements, because of us."

It was possible to speak frankly about such matters as financial pressures, because Bill was getting by on a shoe-string himself, and to him lack of money was not only an old story but a standing joke. Bill, himself, was a living example of how you can be a person of quality and yet be downright poor at the same time.

And she didn't have to feel ashamed about having Bill come to the house. It was an old house, and a lot of the furniture had been secondhand when her mother bought it, but it had been chosen carefully, and there wasn't a table or a chair in the living room that you would call shoddy. Just old. When she was younger, she used to fret about all their things being old, because when she went to her friends' houses their living rooms and bedrooms looked like store windows—everything new and matched and shiny. Yet it had always given her a queer feeling, when she stopped at Winnie Ring's house after school, to see Winnie let herself in with her own key, and to find nobody else at home. Winnie's mother and father both worked. Her father even held down two jobs; Winnie hardly ever saw him. But they had loads of money for new furniture and wall-to-wall carpeting and things like three television sets. But even then, even when she was wishing that her family had just one half the lovely things the Rings had, somehow she always liked her own house better.

The third or fourth time she went out with Bill, one Sunday afternoon when they were on their way to a concert in the park, he stopped at the old Kane mansion to pick up his mother. From the outside, that enormous old house overwhelmed her; inside, it only amazed her. At the end of the last century, before the Kanes lost their money, it had been, so she had heard, one of the show places of the city. Now it was just a shell of dingy white stone enclosing the moldering remains of past glory.

To reach the MacCarthys' apartment they went through a huge reception hall with a twenty-foot high ceiling, from which hung six massive chandeliers. Bill cautioned her not to walk under them because they were so old that every now and then one of the prisms let go and landed on your head. The hall was lined around its vast perimeter with gilt chairs from which the gold leaf was peeling. Bill said that as far as he knew no one had sat on any of them in fifty years, and he suspected mice had made their nests under the faded gold brocade. They went up a curving white marble staircase so fantastic that Peggy was sure it must be just a stage setting, not really leading anywhere—just up; but no, it led to a hallway on the second floor. And there Bill opened a door and called in a loud voice, "Glenlyn Hill local leaving on Track Fifteen! All aboar-r-rd!"

The apartment was just like any other apartment, if you could forget what you had gone through to reach it.

"This is Peggy," Bill said. "You know, *the* Peggy whom you've been hearing so much about. Peg, my mother. She's mislaid her diamond-studded lorgnette, or she'd be peering at you through it. But don't mind her high and mighty ways. Just remember she's the gal who ran off with a guy named MacCarthy."

Bill's mother wasn't high and mighty at all; she was pleasant and congenial, and even a little shy. Still, Peggy knew she was under inspection that afternoon. And though Bill's mother had run off and married a newspaper reporter, a nobody, from her parents' point of view, that didn't mean she would take kindly to the idea of Bill's marrying a nobody.

"I have no doubt that she's a lovely girl," she could imagine Bill's mother saying, "but you must think of your future, dear. You can't start too early to make good contacts, and the right marriage is terribly important."

Marriage to a policeman's daughter would hardly be the "right" marriage.

She was glad Bill had known that her father was a policeman, because it obviated any need (which she might otherwise have felt) to make any pretenses or attempt any concealment. Perhaps she did, by speaking rather vaguely, give the impression that her father's "desk job" was in the administration offices and not just in a district station house. And she described Pat as a "career policeman." She said everybody fully expected that he would go very rapidly from one promotion to another; Pat was that way, there was no holding him down.

She knew, though only in a general way, that somehow, for some reason, their father had been held down. Or at any rate that was what Pat said. Pat had shown her a whole stack of old newspapers on a shelf of his closet, and told her to read them sometime. They had to do with some testimony their father had given to a special Grand Jury investigating the Police Department ten or twelve years ago. She didn't know exactly what, because she hadn't read the papers. She had never found time, and besides they were musty; she disliked handling them.

Bill had seen Pat in uniform, but not her father.

She wasn't ashamed of her father. *No.* But she was glad, just the same, that the times when Bill came to pick her up weren't times when he would be likely to encounter her father either just leaving for or just coming home from work. A uniform was so obvious. So leveling. It so exactly revealed your status. She preferred not to have Bill know that her father wore a uniform.

She felt that she was, on the whole, very fortunate in her family. It was a matter of pride that Katie was a nun. And everyone admired Paul—he had even had a write-up in a magazine—a seventeen-year-old "executive" they called him, with his own trucking business and three men in his employ. The younger children—well, it wasn't personal feeling; she could look at them objectively. They were all as nice as could be, their manners were good. John and Jimmy never made themselves obnoxious, the way small boys usually do; Rosie was *so* pretty, and little Mary—well, there really wasn't any word for Mary; you had to see her for yourself.

And then, of course, Brendan . . .

The first time Bill came to the house on a Sunday afternoon, Brendan wasn't home. The second time he stayed upstairs, and when Bill asked about him she said, "Oh, he's always hiding away somewhere with a book—in the top of

180

the cherry tree, most likely." But the third time Bill asked, "What gives with my young friend the altar boy, with the face of an angel, j.g.? Is he mad at me, or something?" And that time she called to Brendan to come downstairs.

He came with that curious mixture of eagerness and hesitancy so characteristic of him, his face lighting with pleasure in such a way as only Brendan's face could light.

"Here's your junior-grade angel," Peggy said.

Brendan, with that heaven-lighted smile, said, "Hi, Bill."

Bill said, "Why haven't I been seeing you around, fella?"

And: "Honestly, Mother, I could have *died*," Peggy complained bitterly that night. "Do you know what that horrible child said? And in that way he has of telling the most outlandish lies without even having to take time to think them up, so that anyone who doesn't know better might actually believe him? He said, 'Oh, they keep me chained in the attic, except when I'm between spells'!"

"And did Bill believe him?" Anne asked, unable to keep from laughing.

"Certainly not. But anyone less intelligent might have. I do think, Mother, that he was never properly corrected for that sort of thing."

And yet, on a following occasion, it was not of Brendan's facile use of untruth that she was ashamed, but of herself.

Bill's financial circumstances limited most of their dates to the fields of free entertainment: concerts in the park; visits to the art museum, the natural science museum, or even to the zoo, where admission charge was nominal; walks in the park or drives in the country; or an afternoon's swim in a private pool on the estate of a family friend, from whom he had a standing invitation to make himself at home. It was to the pool that Bill invited Brendan, one hot Sunday in July, to come along.

"Oh," Peggy said at once, "that's really nice of you, Bill, but Bren doesn't swim."

"So it's time he learns," said Bill. "I'll teach him."

The eyes of brother and sister had met, fleetingly but long enough for the plainest of messages to pass; and Brendan said immediately, his gratitude and his regret equally sincere, his excuse wholly false:

"Thanks, Bill, I wish I could. But I get earache and sinus

181

infection and anything you can think of when I go in the water, so I guess I'd better not."

And Peggy was ashamed. Because the thought came: How much nicer he is than I am. How much nicer they both are. And with the thought a little chill of fear went over her, and she prayed: Oh, don't let Bill know how selfish I am, how mean . . . !

"Brendan O'Nolan," she said severely, "you're lying. You're just making that up to get out of going with us, because you think I might not want you. You never had a sinus infection in your life!"

Under Brendan's meek reply she sensed the quick flash of joy.

"I did have an earache one time, Peggy."

"Yes. You also had the mumps. When you were four years old. You've never even been *in* a swimming pool. What in the world is Bill going to think of you, coming up with a whopper like that on a moment's notice? Why, he's never going to believe another word you say. Which may be just as well," Peggy conceded as an afterthought.

Bill laughed and said, "Latch on to a pair of trunks, Bren, and let's get started."

"Oh, dear," Peggy remembered, "he hasn't——"

"I'll swipe Paul's!" Brendan was already halfway upstairs. "They'll be safe," he called back, "they have a belt!"

Sitting on the edge of the swimming pool, resting, absorbing sunshine, Bill and Brendan talked across Peggy.

"Tell me something about this girl, Bren. What's she like when she first gets up in the morning?"

"Well, I usually try to keep out of her way, Bill."

"Does she come down to the breakfast table with her hair in pincurls?"

"Father would never allow it. But anyway, I *think* her hair is naturally curly. That is, *if* it's her own hair."

"Can she cook?"

"Just simple things. Like vichyssoise."

"And beef stroganoff?"

"Yes. And hard-boiled eggs."

"Which kind? The intentional or the unintentional?"

"Both."

"Except for that, is she fairly easy to get along with?"

"Well, she throws things when she gets mad. You don't know what a temper she has, Bill."

182

"The heck I don't. Didn't I sit behind her in church for an hour admiring that red hair?"

"One time she throw a book through one of the front windows. It was supposed to hit Paul, but he ducked. The window," Brendan added, "was closed."

"I'd call a performance like that a smash hit," Bill said.

"And another time——"

"Now see here," Peggy interrupted, laughing. "I suppose this is the price a girl must pay for letting her little brother pick her dates, but there ought to be a limit. Wasn't it bad enough to be introduced as an object of pity in the first place? 'Poor Peggy. Jerry Kennedy walked out on her, and she has no date for the Saint Elizabeth alumni dance. She doesn't know another soul to ask. Do me a favor, won't you, pal, and give her a whirl?' "

"That's not the way I heard it," Bill grinned. "What Bren told me was: 'Now's your chance, mister. Grab her while the grabbing's good. She's sitting beside the telephone this minute, doing eeny-meeny-miny-mo down a list of names that long. If you move but quick, you can beat her to the *mo*.' "

"I'm glad," Peggy said, and suddenly she felt the sting of tears, "I'm so very glad you didn't know then what a liar he is."

"Look, fella," said Bill, "how about letting us watch you do a dead man's float, all the way across the pool."

Young Jerry Kennedy came home from California and wasn't home a minute before he was calling to renew old ties, only to discover that the ties had been broken irreparably and forever.

Anne heard with misgivings the cool finality in her daughter's voice.

"No, I'm sorry, Jerry, I can't possibly. It's very nice of you to ask me. . . . Of course I'm not mad at you. Why should I be? . . . No, not next Saturday, either. . . ."

The voice lost its gently regretful note, became very cold.

"That is entirely my own affair, I think."

And now very sarcastic.

"Thank you. It touches me deeply that you feel such concern."

"I know exactly what you're thinking, Mother," Peggy said after she had put the telephone down. "You're thinking

I ought to keep Jerry on a string. As insurance. But I don't want Jerry, on a string or any other way. Now you're thinking, the day may come when I might, and then it will be too late. No. If I can't have Bill, I don't want anybody."

She spoke lightly, but she kept her face turned away.

"When Bill decides the time has come to select the future Mrs. Lippincott-Spencer-Kennard-and-MacCarthy, I'll select a career. I'll go into advertising, or designing, or politics, or something. Don't you worry for one minute about me."

She stopped behind her mother's chair and put a kiss on the top of her head.

"How beautiful your hair is, Mother. Absolutely unbelievable. Like gilded silver. Oh, why wasn't *I* lucky enough to be born with hair like that? I'd probably be a much nicer person. When you have red hair, you feel compelled to live up to your reputation. Just think, Mother, you were married when you were eighteen, no older than I am now. How lovely you must have been! Weren't there a dozen boys who died of broken hearts?"

"I never heard of any dying," Anne said. "I did hear of one who went a whole week before he asked another girl for a date."

"Jerry won't wait a week. He's on the phone right now, calling Winnie. I hope she turns him down. I'd like Winnie to marry Paul. I don't think it matters a bit that he's a year younger. She's rather a little-girlish thing, and Paul is so mature and aggressive. I think they'd complement each other perfectly, don't you?"

"I'm going to let all my children choose for themselves," Anne said, "without saying one word. Not one word, darling, even to those who try to read my mind."

But to her husband she said, "It breaks my heart. She's so deeply in love with him, and so sure nothing will come of it. She thinks he's just using her to fill in. He has no intention of marrying until he finishes law school, and when that time comes, she thinks he'll drop her and marry someone who, as she puts it, will be 'helpful' to him in his profession. But I can't believe that Bill would use her that way. He's too nice a boy. No one that self-centered would be as friendly and kind as Bill is. Why is Peggy so sure, Tadhg?"

He looked at her without speaking, and his look brought tears to her eyes.

184

"Tadhg . . ."

He said sadly, then, "Not can I think you really to answer that question, *Áine Ní Bhriain*."

"No," she said, "*no*. It isn't as you think."

"It is as I think," he answered. "In her mind is the ⟨viction that not would the grandson of Mr. Clement Ka⟩ care to marry the daughter of Police Sergeant Tadhg O'Nolan. But, if it may comfort you, the lad himself has not this conviction. He is one to depend upon himself, not upon others. When the time comes, he will marry the woman of his choice, to have for his wife, not to have for social advantage or professional patronage. God willing, our daughter may be that one. Pray for her happiness we may, but not is it in our hands to direct it, Anneen. Nor to alter that which she thinks may stand in the way of it. Many years too late it is to alter. This I did not foresee, when I chose the course that was to put an end to all advancement, but even had I, there could have been no difference."

Through the autumn it seemed to Anne that she could watch Peggy drawing away from them. From all of them, but particularly from her father.

She had always been warmly demonstrative toward her father. As a child she had wanted to be with him, to sit on his lap, to wait on him, to tell him the highlights of her day before she told anyone else, to seek first from him the answers to her questions. She had been lavish with her hugs and kisses and words of endearment, outwardly more affectionate than Katie, although Anne had suspected that Katie's love ran deeper.

The drawing away had not been so obvious while the summer lasted, nor even through the early weeks of fall, because then they were so little together, but in November her father was back on his old shift, and again he was home in the evenings. So, too, was Peggy, but there seemed always something to keep her busy in the kitchen or in her own room: she had letters to write, or she must press her suit, or wash her hair, or she must run over to the Rings for a while, there was something Winnie wanted to show her. If her father attempted to engage her in conversation, she was polite but uncommunicative. Anything that happened at the bank wasn't important enough to talk about, and about anything important she had nothing to say.

Anne saw the still, cold look come over his face, telling

plainly he understood. She couldn't bear it. She called daughter upstairs on a pretext and demanded to know why.

"Why, Peggy, why? Why are you hurting him? What reason have you? What need? What right?"

Coolly, as if she had anticipated and had prepared for these very questions, Peggy answered, "I'm sorry, Mother. I don't mean to hurt anyone. It's just—there's really nothing to talk about."

"Peggy, your father loves you. It's cruel to turn away from him. Cruel and unnecessary. Your new love is another love entirely. There's no need to take away from your father in order to give to Bill."

"I certainly don't feel that I'm taking anything away from Father."

"But you are. And worse than that," Anne said, "worse than that, you are refusing any longer to accept——"

"To accept . . . ?"

"His interest in you, his love for you. He has given you so much. All of you . . . so much . . . of everything that really counts."

"Have I ever seemed ungrateful?"

"Not until now."

"I'm not ungrateful now, Mother. Can't we say I'm simply—realistic?"

"No. Because I don't understand the word. Or your use of it."

"You seem to think I should go on acting like a child," Peggy said, "with a blind and worshipful devotion. But I'm not a child any more."

"What is it," Anne forced herself to ask, "that you were blind to, as a child?"

"To boundaries."

"Peggy . . ."

"When I was a child," Peggy said, "life was complete right here. I didn't see the boundaries because they didn't matter. Now I do see them because now they do matter. But there's nothing I can do about them. There's nothing anyone can do, except, I would think, let me alone, to meet my own problem in my own way."

"Not if your way is to blame your father," Anne said, trembling. "I won't have him blamed!"

"For heaven's sake, Mother, don't get so emotional. I'm

not blaming anyone. If I were silly enough to do that, I suppose I'd start out by blaming Brendan for having brought Bill around in the first place. Certainly I'm not blaming Father. It isn't a thing that anyone is to blame for. It's simply the way things are. If I had never met Bill, I suppose I would eventually have married Jerry Kennedy, or somebody like him, and everybody would have been happy. Including me. But I *did* meet Bill, and now all that is changed. I'm sorry I can't keep my feelings entirely under control. I suppose I should try harder to go around pretending that everything's wonderful, and that I'm perfectly happy, and nothing's any different."

"Your father is no different."

"Perhaps," Peggy answered with the heartless candor of the young, "that's where the trouble lies."

But when, inevitably, that meeting occurred which she had hoped to avoid, her reaction to it surprised no one as much as it surprised herself.

The time was five o'clock on Christmas Eve. Bill had stopped at the house for her, and they were just closing the gate behind them when her father stepped off the bus at the corner. They met beside Bill's car.

Perhaps she did, in the very first second, reveal her dismay. Perhaps her father, in the first meeting of their eyes, saw it. She didn't know. Nor did she know why she then responded as she did. Perhaps in remorse for having let him see. Perhaps in sheer resignation. Perhaps to impress Bill. Or perhaps the reason lay merely in something about the sight of her father, some reminder of how dearly she had always loved him, some recognition of how good he was, how strong and enduring, the rock on which their life as a family was built.

Whatever the reason, she felt something come alight within her, and suddenly there it was, full on the surface for him to see in her smile and to hear in the quick, bright warmth of her voice. The reticence of the past weeks, the coolness, the faint hostility, all vanished, and it was the Peggy of old whose arms went around him and whose cheek rubbed fondly against the rough blue cloth of his uniform overcoat.

"Father, guess what!" She drew away to look up at him, laughing. "Bill's taking me to dinner at the hotel. He's going to wait on me himself. Then he's getting off at nine, and

187

we're going to a late movie. And after that we're going to midnight Mass at the Cathedral. Won't that be lovely?"

"And then we're stopping at our place for a while," Bill said. "My sister's throwing a party; we're going to crash it. So don't worry when you see the hands of the clock whizzing around and around, sir. I'll take good care of her. Very good care," Bill added, with extra emphasis.

"Father"—Peggy hugged him again—"doesn't it all sound wonderful?"

"An evening of joy does it sound," her father answered.

There was no hidden reproach in his voice to speak to her of the way she had recently been hurting him. There was only the rich pleasure he took in her pleasure, and in his arm around her the generous assurance of his love.

"And do you have room for it in your heart, so full as it already is, take with you then your father's prayer that the joy of each moment as it passes be doubled in the next as it comes."

An evening of joy.

From beginning to end it was an evening of joy.

It seemed to Peggy that there was a special shine on every moment, a special significance in every word that passed between them.

"Your father's a great guy," Bill said as they drove away from the house, "and you're a great gal."

"Our song," Bill said, when for the third time on their walk from the theater to the Cathedral a loud-speaker outside some late-open store or restaurant poured into the street a chorus of voices singing "Joy to the World."

Driving home, when they spoke at all it was lightly of light things, for the deeper things—the memory of the splendor of the Cathedral, the beautiful Sacrifice of the Mass, the joy of the night—did not bear speaking of at all. And when, after they had pulled into the driveway that curved around the Kane mansion and had stopped behind half a dozen other cars, and yet continued to sit there, as if to join the party inside would be to break a spell that each longed to preserve forever, Bill unexpectedly asked a curious question.

"Do you like old things?"

With the lightness that they had been using as buffer and shield, Peggy answered at once, "Love them. Especially old

188

shoes. It breaks my heart to discard an old pair of shoes."

"How about old jewelry?" Bill asked.

"Oh, you never should have brought *that* up," Peggy protested. "You'll make me reveal the baser side of my nature. My grandmother—my father's mother—sent my sister Katie a gold necklace that's been in the family for ages. Katie's the oldest daughter, and Grandmother's namesake besides . . . well, some people just naturally have all the luck. Anyway, it's a heavy, twisted gold band, like a torque. Thou shalt not covet thy sister's torque. But I did. And when Katie went into the convent, oh, how I prayed she would give it to me. But she didn't. She gave it to Pat, for *his* oldest daughter, when he has one. I wept green tears. Bill, I *told* you you shouldn't have asked me that!"

Bill laughed.

"Well, I'm sorry I can't make it up to you, I'm fresh out of torques. But my mother gave me a piece of jewelry that's been in *our* family for quite a while, and it doesn't fit me, so I got to wondering if you might like to try it on for size."

No, Peggy said to herself in warning, closing her eyes against the thought. No, it isn't what you're thinking. Don't be a fool. Don't ride a cloud—it's so very, very far to fall.

Bill had taken a small box from his pocket. He put on the panel lights and held the box where she could see. It was very small, less than two inches square, covered with green velvet, old-looking, worn.

"There's no special tradition about it," he said apologetically. "No fixed line of succession or anything like that. It's just been kind of knocking around for a few generations, hit or miss, if you know what I mean. My mother acquired it on her sixteenth birthday. Today, of course, any girl would rather have a convertible on her sixteenth birthday. I can't remember ever having seen her wear it, but she hung on to it through some pretty rough times. She always said she was saving it for a special occasion. . . . There."

Bill pressed the little spring-latch, and the high-curved lid of the box lifted. Under the light a green stone flashed.

Peggy caught her breath.

"You're right," Bill admitted, "it's a little garish. Well, if you don't like it . . ."

"Bill . . ."

"It wouldn't hurt just to try it on," Bill said, "would it?

Let's try it on the third finger left hand, Peg, shall we? . . . Well, what do you know! Anybody would think that's the very finger it was meant for."

May the joy of each moment as it passes be doubled in the next as it comes.

"Bill . . . oh, Bill, darling . . ."

"Will you keep it, Peggy? Look . . . I know I'm going at this thing all wrong. I've got my gears in reverse. I should have asked you first if you'd marry me, and then, if you said yes, I should have given you the ring. But it takes a whale of a nerve to ask a girl to marry you, when you've got to ask her to wait three or four years. This way, kind of sneaking up on you, I guess I hoped it might be a *fait accompli* by the time I got around to asking. . . . Hey, what gives? You aren't supposed to be crying."

"Bill . . . dearest . . . I'd wait many more years than three or four. I'd wait forever. And without the ring. The ring is too beautiful, too priceless, too very much more than I deserve."

Bill slipped his arm around her and cut her protests short with a long kiss.

"The ring is a trinket," he said then. "A bauble. It's not even the right kind. A guy's supposed to bind the bargain with a diamond, not with a chunk of beryl just a little greener than the common garden variety. You deserve the best, Peg, because you *are* the best. You're everything that's sweet and warm and generous and loving and good. Everything I want. I've known it for a long time. You deserve better than I can give you, now and for a good many years to come, but once I get squared off, sweetheart, I aim to work twenty-four hours a day at the job of laying the world at your feet."

"I don't want the world, Bill. All I want is you. I love you so very much, darling, I don't know how I'm going to stand being this happy."

"You'll get used to it," Bill said. "And when you do, you can give me some pointers, because I'm kind of knocked off my moorings, too."

They sat for a few minutes in silence, very close, letting happiness close around them like a sheltering wall. But in Peggy's thoughts a worry lay, a shadow over paradise.

"Bill, are you sure your mother won't mind that you've given the ring to me?"

190

"Mind? What do you think her idea was when she gave it to me?"

"But she may have thought . . . someone else. . . ."

"The heck she did. Do you know what she said? She said, 'Wise up, William, my boy. Time's a-wasting. Any girl so nice that she doesn't mind sharing her dates with a fourteen-year-old brother is a girl you want to latch on to, but fast. Or you'll wake up some morning and find you've let her get away.' "

"Oh," Peggy said, rather faintly. And again, "Oh. How . . . how very kind of your mother."

Help me to be worthy of him, she prayed. Help me to be worthy of all of them. Help me to keep him from knowing how cruel I've been to Brendan, so many times. Help me never to be cruel again, to anyone. . . .

"Well, what do you say, Pegeen? That gang upstairs doesn't know yet that it's an engagement party they're whooping up. Shall we go tell them? Or would you rather keep it our own deep little, dark little secret for a while?"

"A secret?"

Peggy turned a radiant face to him, all the more radiant for the shine of tears on her cheeks. There was no telling about tears, whether of shame or of joy or of both.

"Oh, no, let's tell the world, darling! Let's hire a fleet of jet space-liners to write it in vapor trails all the way from here to the next galaxy!"

"I'll arrange for that tomorrow," said Bill.

9

It was Brendan who answered the telephone that afternoon.

The time was about four-thirty, always a significant time, for when the telephone rang at that hour it would be, nine times out of ten, his father calling to say that some matter was briefly delaying him and not would he be home quite at the supper hour, but fifteen or twenty minutes late, it might be; or was he that night filling in for someone else, and not would he be home until the end of the next shift.

The call today was from his father, but it was different. Different and extremely curious. His father would be late. Late enough that they were not to wait supper. But not so late that a bit of supper should not be kept back for him, was it convenient to do so.

For him, and for another.

Brendan sat looking at the telephone after he had put it down, and perplexity and a wild uprushing of delight filled him for the curious things his father had said.

Deartháir?

That was what his father had said.

Bead ag breith deartháir chughat. I will be bringing you a — —

"Will your father be late, Brendan?"

His failure to go at once to the kitchen to tell his mother had brought her to the living room to ask. When she saw him just sitting there staring at the telephone, she at once became alarmed.

"Is something wrong?"

"*Níl,*" he hastened to say. "No, Mother. No. I'm sorry

192

I was just . . . no. Father said he'll be late. Perhaps as late as seven o'clock. He said you should go ahead with supper, but keep something back for him. He said, for him and . . . someone else."

"Oh." His mother's voice indicated her relief, but also that some of his perplexity had reached her. "Is he still at the Station? Is that where he was calling from?"

"I don't think so, Mother. I think he must have been calling from the rectory. Saint Andrew's."

"The rectory?"

This was puzzling in itself. Not puzzling that he should stop at the rectory, but that he should expect to be delayed there until seven o'clock.

"He said Father Morissey is going with him somewhere. Downtown."

"Oh."

His mother sounded as if this made it all less puzzling, although of course it did nothing of the sort, as she appeared in a moment to realize.

"Back to the Station?"

She was thinking that someone may have asked for a priest. But Father Morissey? No, in such an event he would have summoned a priest from that parish, not from this.

"Is it Father Morissey he's bringing home with him, then?"

"No, Mother. It's . . ."

But the strange thing his father had said, the strange joy that filled him, raised an almost insurmountable barrier over which he must lift the word.

After a moment of patient waiting, his mother prompted: "Who then, dear?"

"*A brother.*"

"A Christian Brother?"

It wasn't because this was an illogical supposition on his mother's part, but because it was such a completely logical one, that Brendan's joy blazed up and over, finding release in laughter.

"No, Mother. Just a brother. A brother *for us.* To stay!"

"Overnight, did he mean?"

"To stay, always! He said he was almost sure—almost sure—it would be for always. He said his name is Barney. He's almost fourteen, only a year or so younger than I am.

He's . . . Mother, he'll have to come in my room, it's the only place."

Now the joy was transmuted into a fire of excitement.

"I'll go get things ready! We'll need another pillow, Mother! Is there an extra pillow? Oh, well, he can have mine, I don't use it half the time anyway."

Brendan took both flights of stairs at a run; but when he reached his room he did nothing at all. Standing in the middle of it, looking around, he was lost in picturing what it would be like not to be alone in that room any more. *Perhaps never to be alone again.*

It was a room meant to be shared. A room for two. Two closets. Two built-in desks with built-in bookshelves above them. A double bed. A chest of drawers on the one hand, a bureau on the other. Two bedside stands with matching lamps. Two chairs.

Paul had only shared it for three years, before moving into the third-floor front, which he had fixed up for himself, to suit himself, exactly as he wanted it. Paul liked privacy. He liked his own bed; he didn't like someone else in the way when he wanted to turn over or stretch out. He liked his own things; he didn't like other people touching them or even looking at them.

Barney.

It was funny. When Brendan said the name over to himself, it was like saying the name of someone he already knew. Had known for a long time. It was a very friendly-sounding name.

Barney what? His father hadn't said.

They would be here about seven. It was now almost five.

Brendan went to the bureau and swept everything out of the top right-hand drawer into the left. Then he swept everything out of the top big bureau drawer into the bottom one. He did the same with the chest, clearing two drawers. Then he went to the closet.

Only one of the closets was for his use. The other had been lined with cedar, and his mother used it for summer storage of their winter things. But there was plenty of room in the one closet, he had only two suits—his Sunday suit and the one he had worn to school last term. Besides these there was a jacket, and a suit that Paul had grown out of but that he had not yet grown into. He took his school suit off its wooden hanger and put it on a wire hanger, folding an old T-shirt under the pants so they wouldn't get a transverse crease from the wire. This left a good wooden hanger for Barney's Sunday suit.

Next he tackled the desks, a much more complex and difficult undertaking, for he had spread over both desks since Paul had moved out. He had a great many books. Even using both sets of shelves, there wasn't room for all of them. They spilled over onto everything, the window sills, the bedside stands, even the floor. There wasn't time to sort them carefully, but he gave them a quick going-over; those he deemed of interest only to himself he arranged on one set of shelves; the others, those he thought of general interest, especially to someone a year younger, he arranged on the other.

Clearing one desk of its accumulation of school papers and other collector's items also presented a challenge, which he met by appropriating space on the floor of the closet. Of such things as pencils, erasers, paper clips, rubber bands, unused tablets, notebooks and the like, he made equal division. While he was doing this, Rosie came in.

"Here," said Rosie. "Mother said to give you this pillow."

"Oh, thanks. Put it there on the bed, will you, Rosie? On the other side."

Rosie turned down the bedspread to arrange the pillows. When she had neatly smoothed it back, she came to the desk and stood looking over his shoulder.

"What in the world are you doing?"

"Just straightening up a little."

"You aren't throwing any of those things away, are you?"

"No."

"Well, then, what *are* you doing with them?"

"Dividing them."

"What for?"

"For Barney. But if there's anything you want," Brendan offered, "help yourself."

"Could I have a few of those index cards? I'd like to copy some recipes."

"Take as many as you want, Rosie."

Rosie took six.

"Bren, is this boy really going to *live* here?"

"Father said so."

"Here? In your room?"

"Where else would he?"

"But suppose you don't like him? I wouldn't want anybody coming into *my* room, unless I like them. And I'd have to like them an awful lot, too."

"I do like him."

"You don't even know him!"

"I don't have to. Father knows him. And he likes him, or he wouldn't be bringing him home."

"But that's not *you*. And it's *your* room!"

"No, it isn't."

"Isn't what?"

"My room."

"It most certainly is. It's been yours and no one else's for ever so long."

"It's ours now."

"Whose?"

"Barney's and mine."

"Honestly, Bren! The way you just jump into things! You have absolutely no . . . no *perspective*."

"I wouldn't know what to do with it," Brendan answered, laughing, "if I had."

"Well, what you'd do with it," said Rosie, "you'd see that you can't just all of a sudden have a brother, out of thin air. A brother is either someone you've known all your life, if he's older than you are, or else he's someone you've known all *his* life, if he's younger. Brothers don't just *materialize*. I know very well," Rosie said emphatically, "that *I'm* not going to think of him as a brother. He's just some boy. And probably, if he's from down there near Father's Station, he's one of those young toughs who roam the streets in gangs, beating each other up—and other people, too. But even if he's not," she added, willing to concede that this supposition might be unfair, "there are lots of boys, even nice boys, that I just plain can't stand anyway. Oh, of course, you're different. You're one of these love-thy-neighbor-as-thyself people. That's half your trouble."

"Trouble?"

"Well, I mean you're always leaving yourself wide open, Bren, for other people to take advantage of. You're so innocent and trusting. Just like now."

"Who's taking advantage of me now, Rosie?"

196

"This boy will," Rosie prophesied darkly. "Because **you'll** simply invite him to. You'll let him be like the camel that got its foot in the tent."

"Its head, wasn't it?"

"Well, its head. You just wait and see. Because there's no gratitude in the world. It never pays anybody to be nice. Because all anybody ever thinks about is just getting all they can out of everybody else. Especially out of you. Here. Take your index cards back!"

"Rosie, you're too young to be so cynical. I'll prove to you there *is* gratitude in the world. If you'll crawl under the bed and unplug that radio, and move it over to the other table, and then plug it in again, I'll not only give you six *more* index cards, but I'll say 'Thank you' in six languages."

Rosie moved the radio.

"Thank you, Rosie. *Buíochas, Róisín. Merci, Rosalie. Gracias, Rosita. . . .*"

"Oh, all *right*, that's enough. What did you want it moved for, anyway?"

"I thought Barney might like to have it," Brendan answered, "on his side of the bed."

At seven o'clock they came.

Supper was long over, the reserved portions being kept warm in the oven. There was nothing to do but wait and watch the street for the first sight of the car.

Not everyone waited. Peggy, saying that she had a great sufficiency of brothers as it was and could easily endure postponement of her meeting with a new one until later in the evening, went down the street to visit Winnie Ring. Paul, who had deliveries to make, hurriedly took off. Patrick remained home, but declined to serve on the welcoming committee.

"Whoever this kid is," Pat said, "it's a cinch he'd better be inducted gradually. All of us pile on top of him at once, he'll submerge."

John and Jimmy went out in the yard to play. Anne and five-year-old Mary sat on the front porch, enjoying the coolness of the summer evening. Rosie, before she joined them, went upstairs and put on a fresh blouse, and tied her yellow hair back from her face with a blue ribbon (because it was so hot, she said), and traded her old sneakers (which were wearing through at the toes) for her ballet slippers.

But Brendan didn't come out at all. Brendan stayed upstairs in his room until nearly seven, and then slipped down to wait in the living room, alone. He didn't watch from the windows. He didn't need to. He could tell the sound of his father's car half a block distant, and he knew, from years of listening, exactly how many heartbeats away it was from the house.

As the car drew up the two boys ran to the gate, and in another minute there they all were, coming up the front walk together, four abreast.

Anne had not tried to form any picture in her mind while she waited. Like Brendan, she was simply prepared to accept. It was with pleasure, then, but without surprise, that she saw a nice-looking Polish boy, with dark hair, light blue eyes, and a cheerful, friendly, open face—a face perhaps a little impudent, a little bold, but one that you couldn't help liking, and one that you would instinctively trust, although she knew he must have been in some kind of trouble. She watched him turn his head and look up into Tadhg's face as they approached. She read the look.

It is already consummated, the look told her. They are father and son.

Áine Ní Bhriain, . . ."

He stood, characteristically, with children pressing around him, each wanting to be closest. Mary, enjoying the prerogatives of the youngest, had been picked up and was riding on his arm. His other arm was around his new son's shoulders.

"Áine Ní Bhriain, the liberty have I taken to do with your heart as with this house, the liberty to assume that always can room be made in it to hold one more. Now, five fine sons you have, and much love for all of them, but did I think by fitting them together yet a little closer—sideways, it may be, to gain but the little space needed—you would find that six could then be made to fit where there had been but five a little earlier."

"Six, and six times six!" Anne assured them. "Welcome to my heart, Barney. Walk right in! It's very plain," she added, "that you belong here."

"Barney Taborszki is he," Tadhg said, "but son to us

and brother to our children, no less than if he were Barney O'Nolan. By his own mother's consent does he come to live with us and be as ours. Not is such consent given for that she loves him insufficiently and wants him not herself, but that she sees—as stated just now by yourself—that here with us he belongs. Elsewhere has he not a father, and suffers for that lack. By Divine plan must it be, then, that a lad who needs a father, and a father who counts another son ever a blessing, should come together this day and see at once that for each of them great gain must follow, do they but accord themselves to the will of God.

"But now does it seem to me,"—he glanced around—"that something less than a quorum is represented here, and from some who are here have I not yet heard any word of greeting."

He looked inquiringly at Rose, who, being of a disposition not to place blame where it didn't belong, and equally of a disposition not to accept it, said at once with that perfect candor which, coming from Rose, was never on any account to be confused with impudence: "Father, how could I? *You've* been talking."

"*A Róisín, a pháistín fhionn,*" he answered. "There is always sound reasoning in your words, my fair-haired child. But now you would wish, would you not, to welcome Barney to this house and into the circle of those whom you call brother?"

Rosie would wish to do only half of this. Politely and primly she followed the first part of her father's suggestion, while deftly sidestepping the second.

"I'm very glad you've come," Rosie said.

There was a light sound of the screen door opening, a light step on the porch, and Brendan was there. If Rose's greeting had (to her father's ear) left something to be desired, Brendan's filled in with such warmth, such eagerness, such gladness, that everything was suddenly edged with gold. The last of the day's sunlight, slanting through the street, was nothing to the light of Brendan's welcome.

The words he said were only, "I thought you'd never get here, Barney!" But his eyes said, "At last you are here, my brother, my friend! I've been waiting for you all my life! I've been looking for you everywhere! I've been waiting and looking and hoping and praying, and now at last you are here!"

The gold-edged moment was almost too beautiful to be endured. Barney, who had been able without great effort to say "Thank you" to Anne and "So am I" to Rosie, could only look at Brendan. It was Tadhg O'Nolan who spoke, restoring normalcy to the moment without sacrifice of its shining joy.

"Now as you must guess, Barney, this is your brother Brendan, of whom we have spoken. Closest will you two be, I think, for but something over a year lies between you, and much will you have of common interest. . . . Brendan, did it seem to me likely that you would wish your brother to share with you the third-floor room that now is yours, and did you suggest it, in my thought was I prepared to agree that it should be as you wish."

"Buíochas, a Athair," Brendan said, turning the radiance of his smile on his father. "Everything's ready! Are your things . . . ?"

He had started to say, "Are your things still in the car? I'll get them!" but then he saw the paper shopping bag that Barney carried, and it came to him that his clearing of all that drawer space had been done not only prematurely but on a mistaken assumption. In a breath he finished, "Are your things in here? I'll take them up!" And he took the bag from Barney and ran upstairs with it.

The empty drawers wouldn't do. With feverish haste he went through his own. Everything that he had in multiples of two—underwear, jerseys, socks—he divided equally, to stock these empty drawers. Single things, such as his new white shirt, he put in Barney's drawer. Things in odd numbers, such as his ties, went two in Barney's and one in his. He rushed downstairs again.

After the late arrivals had their supper, everyone, for hospitality's sake, joined them in having another round of dessert.

And then a totally unexpected and extremely disturbing thing occurred.

"Time it is now," his father said, in a friendly tone yet with an underlying meaning that sent through Brendan the cold tingle of an electric shock, "for you to come upstairs with me, Barney, that certain terms of our bargain may be met."

And Barney answered, with a good-natured, engaging, and, perhaps at that moment just discernibly anxious, grin, "Okay, Chief."

"Between us we have a little private matter requiring attention," his father explained to the rest of them. "But a few minutes of our time need it take, and then much pleasure would it be for us," he said, looking at Brendan, "could we have some music and song to lighten our hearts and make this such an evening as will be long remembered with great joy."

His father and Barney went upstairs. Brendan remained frozen at the dining-room table, praying that he had misunderstood.

But he hadn't. And it was wrong to pray—or certainly it was at least very foolish to pray—for something not to be so when you knew beyond any shadow of doubt that it was so, that it must be so, that it would be so . . . and presently that it had been so.

For Pat came downstairs, and Pat's surprised, amused, and puzzled question fully confirmed that which Brendan feared was so and prayed was not.

"What the heck goes on around here?" Pat asked. "I expected our newly acquired brother to get a warm reception, but I didn't think it would be that warm!"

He saw the expression on Brendan's face and laughed.

"What's eating you? Are you next?" He roughed his brother's hair as he passed on his way to the kitchen. "Cheer up, kid. He'll live."

At the end of the evening that would be "long remembered with great joy," when they went up to the third-floor room—the room that was meant to be shared—Brendan showed Barney which drawers were his, which bedside stand, which desk.

"Of course," he said, "you can have either one you'd rather. I just fixed them that way because—well, just to fix them."

Barney looked at the neat desk inviting his use, at the well-stocked bookshelves, at the radio, at the whole cheerful, welcoming room. He said. "You're a funny kid."

"Yes, I guess so," Brendan agreed.

"I mean, all this stuff is yours," Barney said. "What do you want to go divvying up for with somebody who just comes walking in on you like this? Some no-good alley-rat like me?"

"You aren't, Barney. You oughtn't to call yourself that. My father——"

"You want to know how I met your father? Old Dutchy Schmaltz hauled me over to the Station today for——"

"Don't tell me, Barney. Please, let's not tell each other anything about ourselves tonight. Let's just start right here, where we are. Because if you don't tell me any of *your* sordid past," Brendan said, smiling, "then I won't have to tell you any of mine."

Barney laughed.

"You've got a past, I'll bet." But he yielded to the plea. "Okay, I'm willing to skip it if you are. Say, that's a real neat radio. You get foreign stations and stuff?"

"Everything," Brendan said eagerly. "It was Pat's; he built it himself, he gave it to me when he got his new one. It has all the short-wave bands and the regular broadcast, too. You can get anything. Try it."

Barney experimented with the radio for a few minutes, but when a particularly loud blare of music sounded throughout the house, he switched it off quickly.

"Hey, I'd better watch that stuff. The Chief said we were to hit the sack."

"I like your calling my father that," Brendan said. "The Chief."

"It fits," Barney answered.

"That's what I mean."

Barney emptied his bag, transferring its meager contents to his bureau drawer beside the other things already arranged there.

Brendan said, "I'd been thinking your name was probably Bernard. But is it?"

"You can think again," Barney answered. "It's Barnabas. But nobody ever calls me that. Leastwise, not my friends."

"What year are you in school, Barney?"

"Eighth. Second time. I hooked so much last year I got left down."

"You won't hook this year," Brendan promised.

And Barney answered with a laugh, "I'll bet not."

They got into bed and turned out their lights, but they talked for a while, lying there in the warm dark.

Barney told about his own father, who had drunk himself to death. He was very casual about it.

"It sure wasn't any loss to anybody," he said. "He used to drink up every cent he earned, and as much as he could get hold of, of what my mother earned. It's been easier for her with him gone. She's had it plenty tough, though, with trying to keep herself and me and my three kid sisters. It would've been better if I could've gone to work, but they wouldn't let me. They said I got to stay in school two more years till I'm sixteen. So I had lots of time on my hands. Lots of time to knock around with the other guys that had lots of time, too . . ."

In the middle of what he was saying, Barney fell asleep. His breathing was slow and deep and peaceful. Brendan lay listening to it, and the sound was a good thing, a source of joy, for it told that he was there, truly there; not someone imagined, someone belonging to a dream.

But Brendan, himself, was far from sleep. He heard Paul come upstairs, move around in the front room for a while, and then click out his light. He heard Peggy in her room below him, and the sounds told him she was ready for bed. He kept listening, but his father and mother and Pat still stayed downstairs.

Presently he began to get thirsty. All the excitement, the singing, the talking, the hot middle-of-July night, had made him feel almost feverish. He started thinking about a tall, frosty glass of ice water. Lots of ice, so that after the water was gone there would still be three or four half melted ice cubes to enjoy. After about ten minutes, he slipped out of bed and went downstairs.

Barefoot and without a sound, he reached the first-floor hall. Pat's voice came from the living room.

"And what happens if the Dutchman doesn't keep his mouth shut? I'll tell you what happens," Pat said. "You're going to find yourself in one sweet mess. They'll throw the book at you. And I'm damned if I can see how you're going to duck it."

"Not am I a man who seeks to duck it," his father replied coldly.

203

"You thought it all out, I suppose? You took time to figure just where the ax would land if you stuck your neck out? The hell you did! You just waded right in there, slugging. And the fact that you're going to have to slug it out with the whole Juvenile Division, plus the Judge of Juvenile Court, plus the Welfare Department, never for one minute entered your head!"

"Not would it have stopped me, Pádraig, if it had."

"Oh, sure not. What's a little thing like odds of about six hundred to one? And what's a little thing," Pat asked, sounding angry, but in the way that showed he was only angry because he was so deeply concerned, "what's a little thing like giving whoever the stinker is that's got it in for you, the chance he's been waiting for to have you thrown out on your ear? Pop, you've let your guard down. They've got you dead to rights. You're a sitting duck."

"Not is there aught amiss in what I have done," his father said. "There was no charge made against the boy. No statement was sworn against him. Not was I derelict in my duty as a police officer, for that I did not hold him when none sought to have him taken into custody, but only to frighten him with threat."

"That's your story," Pat said. "When they get through working on your friend Schmaltz, you're going to discover that he brought the kid in to have him locked up, and you talked him out of it. You took the law and the administration of justice into your own hands. You said, 'Schmaltzie, old pal, there's no need to bother the juvenile authorities with a kid like this. All he needs is the seat of his pants warmed just one time, and he'll be right as rain. I'm the man who can do it, and it won't cost the taxpayers a cent.'

"Honest to God, Pop, who the hell do you think you are? That's not the way they work these things. That way, you knock a whole staff of bureaucrats right off their pins. Look. How old is this kid? Fourteen? Not quite fourteen? Four more good, busy years, then, to get the full treatment. Hell, you didn't even give the psychiatrists a crack at him. They're not going to like it, Pop. You cut the corners. You're not allowed to cut corners, it's unethical. Worse than that, it's old-fashioned. Here's a kid caught shoplifting. Not the first time, maybe the tenth. There's twenty different experts waiting around to find out what makes him tick.

Twenty more to get him readjusted, so he can become a good citizen. Twenty more to keep him that way. The problem of juvenile delinquency is one of our major national crises. They've got boards and commissions set up to handle it all the way along the line, from the neighborhood boys' club to the federal Department of Welfare. With all the investigating and analyzing and advising and re-educating and rehabilitating that's going on, where do you think you come in? Getting at the seat of the trouble doesn't mean you warm a kid's tail! How medieval can you get?"

"Not do I undertake to solve the problem," his father answered. "That will I leave to the experts and the boards and commissions. But not will I leave to them one who comes within the scope of the problem only by reason of such a lack as I am able to fill. There is none who can tell *O'Nolan* he must stand aside while a good lad sets foot on a bad road, merely for want of a father. Now must it be as plain to yourself as to me, Pádraig, that here is a boy with no fundamental wrongness in him of any kind. Honest is he at heart, and clean in his speech and in his thought, and good-natured, and kindly. A little overbold he may be, and ready with a quick word, but not is a bit of cheekiness serious fault, and sometimes it stands a young lad in good stead when he must make his own way with none to smooth the path for him. Not was either my first son or my second ever slow with a bold answer, as I recall; nor was I ever so myself. This boy is of our kind. That he is of another stock altogether makes no difference. He is yet one of us. You must see it yourself."

"I'm not arguing that with you," Pat said. "The kid's okay. What I'm telling you is, you've gone out on a limb. There's somebody who's been waiting twelve years for a chance like this, and it's a safe bet he's got his goons planted in every department. I know how that linkage operates. They'll be making lampshades of your hide before this week is out."

Brendan crept upstairs again, as silently as he had come down. He wasn't thirsty any more. He wasn't hot. In bed, beside Barney, he lay cold and frightened, filling the dark with pictures. Of his father in trouble. Of his father dismissed from the Police Department. Of Barney taken away from them . . .

He prayed that Pat wasn't right, but that was as useless, as senseless a prayer as his earlier one had been. Even his father knew that Pat was right. His father hadn't contradicted anything Pat said, hadn't said it wasn't so, hadn't said that nothing would come of it. He had said only that none of that made any difference; none of that would have prevented him from doing as he did.

Brendan didn't wish, he didn't for a minute wish, that his father hadn't brought Barney home. To be a son. To be a brother. No. He didn't wish that. But he prayed: Don't let anyone make trouble for my father. Don't let them take Barney.

He slipped out of bed and got his rosary. For a long while he knelt beside the bed, saying one decade, two, three. He knelt there so long that he almost fell asleep, with his forehead pressed against the edge of the mattress. When he got back into bed, he was still counting off the prayers. One: *Ár n-Athair atá ar Neamh.* . . . Ten: *Go mbeannuighthear duit, a Mhuire.* . . . One: *Glóir do'n Athair.* . . . One: *Ár n-Athair atá ar Neamh.* . . .

Somewhere about halfway around, he lost count. His fingers fumbled the beads. The prayers ran together. He let his eyes close. When he opened them again, Barney was already up and dressed, and Rosie was calling from the foot of the stairs that breakfast would be ready in five minutes.

When the trouble came, it was even worse than Pat had feared.

Nothing happened the first day. Their father left the house that morning as usual at seven-thirty, with no indication in his manner or in his voice that anything might happen. He gave Barney parting instructions: he was not to go outside the yard. The reason for the restriction was not explained, nor was any special emphasis placed upon it. Just: "Not are you to leave these premises, Barney."

When he returned at five there was still no indication of anything amiss. Brendan saw a question pass from his mother's eyes to his father's, and saw the unspoken reassurance. Later, at the supper table, Pat asked, "Anything said?" And their father answered, "Not to me," an answer which drew from Pat a long look but no further question.

But the next morning their father left for work at the usual time—and was home again within the hour. He talked for a few minutes alone with their mother before going upstairs to change from his uniform to his at-home clothes. When he came down, he told Brendan and Barney to come with him, and the three of them drove about the neighborhood, picking up such materials as they would need to continue work on the garage under construction at the rear of the yard.

He made no pretenses or evasions; he did not disregard their right to know the truth, even the worrisome truth. In plain words, as they drove away from the house, he told them, "A bit of trouble is there now, for it has been given around that not did I make a certain arrest the other day, as some say should have been done, but that I took upon myself to judge the merits of the case and to dispense justice in my own way. The charge is now made that this was an irregularity, an improper procedure, and that in so doing I failed in my duty and thereby became guilty of misconduct. Now must it all be looked into, and charges heard and charges answered, and in the meantime O'Nolan is relieved of his duties until such time as full investigation has been made and conclusions reached and suitable action taken.

"But not will we worry about it," he said firmly, "for these things happen as God wills, and had I the same thing to do again, would I do the same. Not does a man stop to weigh the cost to himself of doing what is right, nor have regrets for that he has acted according to his own best judgment. Therefore, my sons, do you clear your faces of these unbecoming expressions of dismay, that we may enjoy the hours for the good they hold, and not permit shadow to lie upon us. Will it all come right in the end, I think, for it is but a small thing which some try for their own purposes to make large."

They went home and worked on the garage.

But it was worse than Pat had feared, so also was it worse than any logical evaluation of the facts could indicate; made worse by unexpected, unwarranted, strongly prejudicial and highly inflammatory publicity.

The evening paper carried the story in headlines:

and there followed a long account which skillfully blended gross overstatement with supportable fact.

A thirteen-year-old boy had been caught by a shopkeeper in the petty theft of some ten-cent items. The shopkeeper had taken him to the nearest police station, to prefer charges. Police Sergeant T. P. O'Nolan, on duty at the Station, had talked the shopkeeper out of his intent, and had taken the boy to his own home instead, and allegedly had beaten him. Sergeant O'Nolan had been suspended, pending investigation of the charges. It was understood that the boy's mother, threatened with the alternative of having her son jailed, had consented to his being taken to the O'Nolan home, where the alleged brutality occurred. Steps were being taken to effect his immediate release. Sergeant O'Nolan had joined the police force in 1930, and had a long record of previous trouble within the Department, with a reputation for being contentious, uncooperative, and highhanded.

This was only the beginning. The next morning's paper carried the same story, embellished with pictures. There was a picture of Sergeant O'Nolan taken more than ten years earlier, grim and hostile, outside the Grand Jury room where he had been "called for questioning," the paper stated, in connection with the police scandal of that period. There was a picture of Barney, a good-looking boy with a friendly grin that instantly won the hearts and the militant compassion of every sob sister in the city. And there was a picture of the O'Nolan house, a perfectly respectable-appearing house made sinister by the caption under it: House Where Boy Is Held.

On the editorial page there was a long and impassioned cry from an outraged editor speaking for an outraged public, demanding to know how such a thing was possible in a Police Department which boasted of its well-screened personnel and its full cooperation with the various civic groups and agencies that were working day and night upon the distressing problem of juvenile delinquency. How, the editor asked, in a Civilized Society, within a Department dedicated to the Public Interest, could such a heinous offense occur?

By evening the civic groups had begun to get into the act —half a dozen of them—with loud demands upon the Commissioner of Police, upon the Mayor, upon the city Welfare Department, upon the Governor of the State, to take immediate remedial action which would not only punish the perpetrator of this sadistic deed, but would absolutely and forever ensure that such an atrocity could never again take place, even at the furthest imaginable time in the future of mankind.

At home, within the respectable-appearing but sinister "House Where Boy Is Held," reactions were individually varied, but all were one in shock.

Anne, pale and quiet, ministered to the needs of her family efficiently but automatically.

Pat said at the supper table: "So Mr. Somebody controls the press. They've got the town in a mood to lynch you, Pop. You'd better lay low."

Peggy did not come down to supper at all. She had come home from the bank with a sick headache, which with every passing moment (and every new bit of notoriety) became sicker. Even when Bill MacCarthy called, to express his sympathy and indignation, she was too sick to come to the telephone.

Paul came home with a bruise on his cheekbone and two split knuckles on his right hand. He said only, "You ought to see the other fellow," and no one asked him for details.

Brendan dared not look at anyone for fear of upsetting the precarious balance of his self-control. Barney dared not look at anyone because he was the cause of it all. No matter how staunchly they all might insist that it was in no way his fault, he didn't see how they could help blaming him and wishing him somewhere—anywhere—at the bottom of a very deep hole, where they never need lay eyes on him again.

Rosie looked pugnacious, but had not, as yet, any marks of battle to show for her dangerous mood.

Nine-year-old John, well able to read, was silent, sober, and apprehensive. The two youngest only knew that something was wrong.

Two more days passed before the matter was brought to

a head and, considering the buildup it had received, in short and summary fashion reduced to its appropriate level among the local happenings. The newspapers and the civic groups had kept it going under full steam during the two intervening days, but when it suddenly and unexpectedly ran off on a siding which obviously led nowhere, they lost interest in it. Perhaps the anticlimactic developments were faintly embarrassing to those who had joined in creating the furore; or perhaps other Causes, of greater moment, had come up in the meantime to divert the streams of righteous indignation into newer and wider channels.

Whatever the reason, interest that was still at white heat on the morning of the day when the infamous O'Nolan was to appear before the Commissioner of Police to answer charges brought against him by the Juvenile Division ebbed away during the afternoon, and had completely vanished by evening. An obscure paragraph in the evening paper mentioned the hearing, but said nothing of its findings or results: presumably the paper had gone to press before these were known. The next morning's editions carried nothing at all.

Yet the hearing room had been crowded that day, and everyone with anything to say was given fair and full opportunity to say it.

Assembled to hear and pass upon the testimony were the Police Commissioner, one of his Chief Inspectors, a Division Inspector, a District Captain, and two members of an impartial Board of Inquiry. In addition to these, there were the accusers, well represented by four members of the Juvenile Division of the Police Department and two members of the Child Welfare Bureau; the witnesses—Mr. Frederick Schmaltz, Mrs. Theresa Taborszki, and young Barney Taborszki; the accused—Police Sergeant O'Nolan; the uninvited—the Reverend James Morissey, who cheerfully pushed his way in despite protests, and cheerfully remained because no one cared to follow his suggestion that if they wished him removed it was certainly within their combined physical powers bodily to remove him; and two newspaper reporters, who possibly were so absorbed in the proceedings that they forgot to make notes, or possibly by a curious coincidence both lost their notes somewhere between the Municipal Building and their respective offices.

At home there was no crowding. There was a cold, fearful emptiness. Everywhere. In every room. In every heart.

Rose shadowed Brendan, stoutly maintaining that everything would be all right. She knew it. It *had* to be.

"None of these people *know* Father," Rosie said. "That's the only reason anybody could ever say any of those horrible things, or believe for one minute they could possibly be true."

"The Police Commissioner knows him," Brendan said. "They joined the Police Force together. A long time ago. Twenty-three years."

"Well *then*," said Rosie. "Anybody who's known Father *that* long . . . ! All he has to do is explain exactly what happened, and how, and why, and what happened after *that*, and the Commissioner will know at once that the whole thing is just something that somebody's trying to make sound nasty, when it's really something perfectly right and perfectly *good!*"

"He won't defend himself," Brendan said unhappily. "I heard Pat say he won't. Pat said he'll be too proud to defend himself, because it's debasing even to *deny* doing something that you wouldn't and couldn't have done."

"You will have to answer the question, Sergeant."

"Not will I. Do you ask questions concerning the fulfillment or nonfulfillment of my duties as a police officer, these will I answer. Do you ask questions concerning my private affairs, these will I not."

"You will answer all questions."

"Not will I answer what is outside the province of this Department to ask. What I do in my own home—what is between myself and members of my family, such as this one became the moment he crossed the line of my property— not are these Department matters, and not have they bearing upon Department matters. My private affairs am I not required to discuss."

"You are required to answer any question put to you. If you refuse, you can be dismissed here and now, without further hearing or recourse to appeal."

Coldly: "Do then as you please."

But Rosie's confidence was something to cling to, like a stout branch that could, if you held on, perhaps carry you safely through the flood of fear to firm dry land.

"Well," said Rosie staunchly, "Barney's there. And certainly Barney's going to speak up and defend him."

"They won't pay much attention to what Barney says. He's just a boy. They'll pretend to think he's been told what to say. Even that he's afraid to tell the truth."

"Well, Barney's mother. And that Mr. Schmaltz. He'll certainly be there, won't he?"

"Yes, but Pat doesn't think he'll tell the truth. Pat thinks they'll have made sure ahead of time that he'll say he wanted Barney taken into custody and Father talked him out of it."

"How can they make sure he says any such thing? That would be lying!"

"It's just a Police Department hearing. I don't know that anybody's under oath."

"But they're friends! He'd certainly never go in there and tell lies about Father!"

"No, sir. No. I didn't want that boy arrested. What I want a kid arrested for, he takes a little roll of bell wire and a flashlight bulb out of my store? I know all these kids, see? The whole trouble is, their parents got to work all the time, they got no time to mind the kids. You let a boy run loose on the street, sooner or later he gets in trouble. This ain't a bad boy. You look at him, you know all he needs is a man's hand on him once in a while to make him toe the mark. I know lots of times he takes stuff out of my store. Little stuff. But some day I know it'll be big stuff, somewhere. So this time I think I give him a real good scare.

"Sure, I know it's O'Nolan on duty. That's why I did it. Because you take a man with nine kids, he knows kids. He likes kids. So he looks this boy over and he says to me, 'Fred,' he says, 'all this boy needs is a father. If he was mine,' he says, 'I'd straighten him out in one lesson. One would be enough,' he says, 'because anyone can see this is a boy who would naturally rather do right than wrong,' So he makes his proposition about going along home with him to be just the same as one of the family, and he leaves

212

*it to the kid to decide. And the kid—he's a fresh one—he
says, 'Okay, I'll take you up on that; it's a deal.'"*

Rosie's confidence, boldly expressed, not only helped
Brendan get through the dreadful hours, but bounced back
from the sounding board and fed upon itself.

"Anybody can plainly see," Rosie said, "how much
Barney likes Father. And that makes the whole thing just
so completely ridiculous!"

"They can still take him away," Brendan said.

"How can they? His own mother is his legal guardian,
isn't she? And his own mother said he could come here to
live. She said she was *glad* to let him live with us!"

"The courts can do anything," Brendan said, not for the
sake of contradicting Rosie, because he didn't want to con-
tradict Rosie, he wanted to believe her; but because he had
read more and knew better how terribly far afield blind
justice can all too often stray. "The Welfare people are
very powerful. It would be just Father wanting to keep
Barney, against everybody else wanting to take him away."

"But his own mother!"

"They can say his own mother is unfit."

"Unfit!" Rosie became fiercely indignant. "How could
they say that? It's just that she has to work. Barney says she
does the best she can, but she just can't ever quite make
both ends meet. But that only means she ought to get
Relief," said Rosie, knowing children at school whose
families were on Relief. "That doesn't mean they'd have
any right to take her own children away from her!"

*"It seems very obvious," the welfare worker said, "that in
addition to the fact that Mrs. Taborszki is financially unable to provide for her children, her sense of moral responsibility for them is at best questionable. Else she would not
have committed her son to the care of someone she didn't
know at all; someone she had never seen before and for all
she knew might never see again; someone of whose background, whose intentions, whose character she knew nothing
at all. She had not even a common acquaintance who might
speak for him."*

"The priest was with him!" Barney's mother cried, over-
coming her fright and her awe and her bewildered tears in a
flash of indignation. *"The priest told me there wasn't a*

kinder or a finer man in his whole parish than Sergeant O'Nolan! Or a better husband and father! He told me it would be the best thing in the world for my Barney, going into his home. And I believed him. And I still believe him! Nobody has any right to say I'd let my boy go off with somebody I didn't know would be good to him, and help him grow up to be the fine, decent person he's got a right to be, instead of one of these no-account street loafers like the ones he was running around with!"

"And anyway," said Rosie, "Father Morissey said he was going along. He'll straighten everything out."

"Pat said they probably wouldn't let Father Morissey into the hearing room."

"Ha!" said Rosie. "I'd just like to see anybody keep Father Morissey out of anywhere he wanted to go in!"

"Well, even if they let him in, they might not let him say anything."

"Double ha! When Father Morissey has something to say, he says it!"

"Some very defamatory innuendoes have been wafted about this room, Commissioner. Wafted upward, mostly, since hot air rises—and I would say fortunately so for you worthy gentlemen, because otherwise on a midsummer afternoon with the air conditioner apparently out of order, the discomfort would certainly by this time have become acute. Now, much has been intimated in what has passed back and forth here, but very little of a truly factual nature has been brought out. Could that be, I wonder, because the intimations and the facts have little in common? Of you gentlemen who are assembled here not to bring charges but to hear them, and not to distort facts but to weigh them, may I request a few minutes' sufferance to ask our young friend Barney a question or two?"

"Please make it brief, Father."

"Thank you. Barney, it has been brought out that Sergeant O'Nolan detained you at the station house that afternoon until he went off duty at four o'clock. And it has been brought out that he took you home, that is, to your mother's house, before taking you to his own house. But there seems to be a considerable time lapse there—about *two hours—not accounted for. I think the Commissioner and these other distinguished gentlemen might appreciate being filled in on that. When you left the station house that afternoon, where did you go? Where did Sergeant O'Nolan take you first?"*

"To you, Father. To the church."

"Ah! Obviously a very sinister first stop in a very sinister itinerary. What was his purpose in doing that? Have you any idea?"

"So I could confess."

"Did he suspect how long it had been since the last time you went to Confession?"

"Yes, Father. He asked me and I told him. About three years."

"Now this seems to indicate that his first concern was to assure your return to a state of grace. Is that right?"

"Yes, Father."

"The natural concern, gentlemen, of a brutal and sadistic man. . . . Now, Barney, we haven't really heard any of the details of your first fearful night in Sergeant O'Nolan's house. Was anyone else there?"

"Yes, Father. Everybody."

"His wife?"

"Yes."

"His children?"

"Most of them."

"And how did they receive you? With protest? With pity? With horror? Revulsion?"

"They were all swell to me, Father."

"Well, I dare say some of them could afford to be, those already earning their own livings. But how about the younger ones? Sergeant O'Nolan isn't a rich man, you know. One more added to an already large family means a little less for everybody else. Surely the younger ones were resentful? Unfriendly?"

"No, Father. Like I told you, they all treated me swell. They seemed real glad to have me come."

"Well, tell the gentlemen exactly what that first evening was like, Barney. What did you do?"

"Well, after I'd met the family, the next thing was we had supper. The Chief and me."

"The Chief?"

"Him."

"Oh, Sergeant O'Nolan. Is that what he makes you call him? The Chief?"

"He doesn't make me. I just do."

"Oh. Well, you were having supper. It was bread and water for you, I assume."

"No, Father. Chicken potpie."

"Very unorthodox. What then?"

"Well, then . . . well, we'd made this deal, see? So the next thing was, we got that out of the way, and then——"

"Oh, now wait a minute, Barney. It has been established that you were beaten. It has been suggested that you were very severely beaten. Cruelly. This whole little meeting here today is based on that. Now, you can't skip casually over a serious matter like that, Barney, as if it were just some minor detail that you 'got out of the way.' Please try to choose your words more carefully, or you might create an impression that the reports of the brutal treatment you received were exaggerated. The Commissioner himself asked you, just a little while ago, if it was true that Sergeant O'Nolan promised to mete out certain punishment to you, and if he did, and you answered 'yes' to both questions. You aren't reversing your previous testimony, are you? It's true, isn't it—you were beaten? The gentlemen will like you to answer yes or no."

"No. No, I wasn't. Not what anyone would mean when they say beaten."

"Ah. You suggest that there are degrees of chastisement. Are you suggesting that what you received was in minor degree? He didn't hurt you?"

"Well, somebody hands you a few on your backside, Father, sure it hurts a little. But not anything to kick up a fuss about."

"I see. Well, go ahead, Barney. After you got that little unpleasantness out of the way, what then?"

"Well, then we all just had a good time."

"Extraordinary! Including yourself? You mean you weren't locked up somewhere?"

"No, Father. Bren, he sang some Irish songs, and when Peggy came home we danced a reel—Bren and Peggy, and Rosie and me. I never had such a swell time in my life. It was real late before anybody knew it. Midnight. So then we went to bed."

"And where were you forced to sleep? In the attic with the bats or in the cellar with the rats?"

"I slept in Bren's room, Father. He had everything fixed up to share with me, even before I got there. Everything. As if it was all as much mine as his. It's a swell room, Father. Bren's a swell kid."

"Who is this 'Bren' you keep talking about, Barney? Another poor unfortunate like yourself, lured to this House of Horrors to be subjected to cruel and inhuman treatment at the hands of this nefarious character whose first concern was the state of your immortal soul?"

"You know Bren, Father. He's one of your altar boys."

"Ah, yes. Brendan. The flaming sword. The bringer of light into darkness. . . I have had people tell me that just to watch Brendan light the altar candles is a profoundly inspirational experience. A most unusual boy. Most unusual sweetness of character. One naturally wonders how he comes by it."

"I don't see why anybody would wonder that, Father. Bren's one of the Chief's own sons!"

"There you go rollicking off again, Barney, with that impetuous, reckless use of words. I'm afraid you'll force upon the gentlemen a most untenable conclusion: You like Sergeant O'Nolan, don't you?"

"Like him? Jesus Christ, Father . . . !"

"And besides," said Rosie, "God rewards good people and punishes the wicked."

"That's in Heaven, Rosie. Or in Hell."

"It's right here, too. Barney's a good person, so God rewarded him by having him meet Father. And God wouldn't have somebody do a good deed, like Father bringing Barney here, and then turn around and let a lot of nasty people mess it all up. If He wanted the juvenile delinquent people to have Barney, what would be the sense of getting Father mixed up in it? The whole trouble with you, Bren, is you're scared. So you keep thinking of all the worst things that can happen, instead of the sensible, logical things."

"You don't understand, Rosie. There's somebody who wants to make trouble for Father, because of something that happened long ago. It's somebody with a lot of influence. Somebody who won't stop at anything. Pat says——"

"Oh, *Pat* says! Stop telling me what Pat says! Pat doesn't know everything! I'm tired of hearing Pat says this and Pat says that!"

"Rosie, let's go up to my room—Barney's and my room —and pray."

"All right. But only if you pray in English. I get mixed up and lose count when I hear you mumbling away in Irish."

"I'll just pray for Father and Barney in Irish. The rest in English."

"Who else are we going to pray for, for goodness' sake?"

"Father Morissey. Barney's mother. Mr. Schmaltz. And the Police Commissioner."

"What on earth do we want to pray for *him* for?"

"We just do," Brendan said.

"*You've wasted our time. You've wasted our time with the most arrant piece of nonsense that any conniving bunch of second-rate operators ever tired to ram down my throat with one hand while they pulled the wool over my eyes with the other. Tried to. How long do you think I've been around? Just the last five days? Don't answer. I know the answers!*

"*Sergeant, get back on your job in the morning. You'll draw your pay for the time you were off.*

"*One thing's clear. What this Department needs is a few more who think first of the kids and second of their own jobs. God knows we've got enough of the other kind. I can count four without turning my head! For the record— Don't put your pencils away, boys. Go ahead, quote me. I'm saying for the record, that if any more men in this Department want to take a kid off the street and into their own homes, they can do it with my promise of full immunity against the consequences of treading on anybody else's toes. For my money, one real father's worth more to a kid than a whole slew of Big Brothers. This is the luckiest kid in town.*

"*I'm running this Department! I'm not dancing on anybody's strings, and I'm a hard man to pressure. Sure, the Department can stand some improvement, but give me a*

218

chance, fellows, I've only been running it a year. We've got
some dry rot in the timbers. We've got some personnel
that's not pulling its weight, just trying to throw it around.
There's some the Department can do without. But not
O'Nolan. Hell, no. The ones we can do without are you
characters moonlighting on the side for some stuffed shirt
one floor up who thinks he can use me to do his little
hatchet jobs! Take back the word, boys. There's nobody
in this town big enough to use me. And when I get clear
through to the bottom of this jackass piece of skulduggery,
some skulls are going to be knocked together till they crack
wide open, and heads are going to roll all over the place.

"Okay. That wraps it up. . . .

"Father, you were right about the air conditioning. It's
hotter than hell in here, and the air's not fit for a man of
God to breathe."

"Don't think for one minute," Pat said that night, "that
the kid's in the clear. That crowd won't quit. They'll bide
their time, waiting for a chance to pick him up. If they
have to, they'll manufacture their own chance. All they
need is to see him standing on a street corner near somebody they can call 'undesirable'—and undesirables are a
glut on the market—they can be planted all over the place."

"Not will he stand on street corners," his father replied.
"Until school opens, he is forbidden to leave these premises, except in suitable company. They may look well for
their chance. Not will it be given them."

"Hell," Pat said, "you can't keep a fourteen-year-old kid
yarded for six weeks. You might as well have let them jail
him in the first place. It would be a good thing," Pat added
casually, "to get him out of town for a while, till things
blow over."

"Would it that," his father agreed.

He sat turning the thought in his mind. "Out of town"
was a vague phrase. A week at the seashore? In the moun-
tains? On the road? Eight of them, and such a vacation
costing many times what the cost would be for that same
week did they remain at home. More than a week could
not be thought of, and what good would a week do?

"Not will it blow over in a week," he said. "Nor yet in
many weeks."

219

"You're a twenty-year-plus man, Pop. You have your vacation coming up. A whole month. Four full weeks if you fly. Three if you take a fast boat."

Fly? Boat?

"Now Pádraig, what might it be that you have in your mind?"

"It's been a good long time," Pat said, still sounding very casual, "since you left that rock-pile. You haven't seen your mother for twenty-three years. Take the kid with you. I'll pick up the tab."

A long silence settled over the O'Nolan living room.

Anne, mending a torn shirt of Jimmy's, paused with her needle halfway through the cloth.

Peggy looked up in surprise from the evening paper, which she was searching with feverish certainty that there must—there *must*—be something in it somewhere to tell the world that her father had been cleared of those hideous charges. Because if there wasn't . . .

Rose also looked up in surprise. Her eyes went to Barney. Barney, in surprise, was looking at Brendan.

Brendan wasn't looking at anybody. After one swift, incredulous look, first at his brother, then at his father, Brendan had looked away again. At nothing. As if that single swift glance had been at something too bright, too blinding, so that when he looked away it was like turning from the glare of sun on snow into the dimness of a room where he could see nothing at all.

Brendan did not know, then or afterward, what his thoughts were. Only what they couldn't have been. He couldn't have wanted his father not to go to Ireland. He couldn't have wanted Barney not to go. But that his father might go without him . . . that was impossible. Go to Ireland? They had dreamed of it too much. Talked of it too much. Promised themselves too often. His father would not, would not, go to Ireland without him.

There had never been money to spare. Now Pat was offering the money. For his father and Barney. Not for him. Perhaps his father could afford enough for him.

No. What would the others do? What would they eat? How would they live? How would their mother buy the clothes they would so soon need for the opening of school, if his father spent two weeks' pay, three weeks' pay, taking him to Ireland?

No . . .

Never, never would his father go without him. But if he didn't, then it would be his fault, his selfishness, his inability to bear being left behind that would make his father deny himself the trip, deny it to Barney, when so much depended upon it—his father's pleasure, Barney's safety.

Oh, please, please, let me be able to look at my father and say, "Take Barney and go." Please don't let him see that I would never be able to bear it if he were to go, that I would die before ever he came home again.

The long silence ended with rejection of the offer.

"The good and generous one you are to offer it, Pádraig, but not is it a thing that can be done at this time. Yet as much do I thank you as if it were so that I could accept the offer."

"It strikes me pretty funny," Pat said, no longer sounding casual, but angry, "that you can suddenly elect to be too proud to take money from me, when you weren't too proud to get yourself in a mess like this in the first place! It's a little late to be so high-and-mighty stiff-necked, isn't it?"

"Not does pride enter into it, one way or the other, whether too little or too much. Other considerations govern what can or cannot be done."

"I'm damned if I know what other considerations have anything to do with it at all. You've got the time off. I've got the money. I'm sure Mother's all for it. If you're worrying about the kids, forget it. They'll keep in line and then some, while you're gone. I'll see to that."

"Not is it worry that prevents. Much trust have I in you, Pádraig, to assume responsibility for this household, were it so that I might be absent for a time. The good brother have you always been, and not would I look to see the day when this would not be so."

Pat grinned faintly and said, "Nice try, Pop. Well, think it over. There's no hurry. Just don't forget it's a one-way trip for this kid the first time he cuts loose to go even as far as the corner store."

The subject was dropped.

Barney and Rose started to play gin rummy. They wanted Brendan to play, but Brendan said he would rather

221

just watch and kibitz. He watched but he didn't kibitz, for he didn't see the cards. Or even the table. . . .

The gray sea was breaking against the gray limestone shelf that was Inishmaan, washing over the lower shores and pounding against the spray-drenched cliffs. Sometimes the road that led to the village from the place where the curragh had been beached was under water, and they stepped from one flat rock to another, over the water-filled fissures or the pools.

Everywhere around them, as they came up from the sea, were the rocks. Lichens and mosses laid patches of soft color on the grays, and here and there a little bright green grass was growing. Miles and miles of stone fences formed a patternless network, enclosing the barren fields.

The little house in the village was of whitewashed stone, two rooms and a loft under a slate-shingled roof. In the doorway, as they came up the last rise of the road from the sea, a woman stood waiting.

Tall and strong and beautiful she was, wearing the traditional homemade clothes of the Island, yet with the look of a queen. Silent, there in the doorway, she stood watching them come. . . .

A thousand times, awake or asleep, Brendan had seen himself walking up that road, to that little house, at his father's side.

His grandmother was sixty-five, and though his father said that wasn't old for the O'Rourke women, who thought nothing of living to one hundred, still it was not young. Suppose she were to die without ever seeing her son again. Her only son.

It would be his fault.

He was fifteen, but Peggy and Paul said he would never grow up. They said he wasn't as grown up as Rosie. They said John at nine was catching up with him. They said he acted like a baby. Or a girl. He still cried too easily. He was still afraid of his own shadow. He was always either wildly happy or wildly unhappy. He was immature, unstable.

If he could act fifteen . . . if he could be the way Pat had been at fifteen, the way Paul had been . . . if he weren't such a baby, such a coward, he could say to his father, without tears, with good-natured, genuine regard for them instead of pity for himself: "Please go, Father. Please don't pass it up on my account. Take Barney and go."

But he hadn't the courage even to try.

"Rose," he heard his mother say, "it's quite late, darling."

"We'll just finish this hand, Mother."

The evening was over. The beautiful evening, the evening that had started out so joyously because God had been so kind, because all the ugliness and fear had been wiped out —his father was cleared of the charges and Barney hadn't been taken away. The joyous evening had ended in this silent, suffocating grief that he could neither throw off nor give way to.

"Late it is for all of us," his father said. "After such a day as we have had, a bit of extra sleep could serve us well. But even better, I think, would an extra prayer serve us. Brendan, it would please me much did you say *An Phaidir,* as you used to do at bedtime when you were a very small lad, kneeling here at this footstool. Perhaps it is not a thing I should ask, seeing that you are no longer five years old, but fifteen. Easy it is to forget that boys grow up, though footstools remain the same."

Brendan knelt beside the stool. He was not deceived; he knew it was not coincidence that his father should speak so. His father had looked into his heart. He had seen the grief there, and the pain, and the shame, and the terrible longing to say the words that he was too weak, too cowardly to say.

He said the Our Father. When he had finished, he remained kneeling and whispered, without raising his head:

"Téir, má's é do thoil é 'Athair. Téir."

"Má théim, a mhic, raghair liom," his father answered. *"Téir a chodladh anois. Tá áthas mór indán dúinn."*

Brendan mounted the steps to the third floor as if each were a golden rung on a ladder to heaven. Joy and hope had blazed up in him at his father's words, and he was caught in the updraft, whirled heavenward like a burning leaf snatched from a bonfire by the wind.

The words he had thought he couldn't say, the unbearable words, had been said. Whispered, only, but it was enough, his father had heard.

And: "If I go," his father had answered, "you will go with me."

Oh, beautiful promise, beautiful hope, beautiful joy!

223

"Go to bed now," his father had said.

To bed? With this blazing light all around? How could he sleep?

"There is great happiness ahead for us," his father had said.

He meant—oh, he could have meant only one thing!

He meant that Pat was kind. Pat was good. Always, always, Pat had been so good to him. Pat had always been able to look, as his father looked, straight into his heart, straight through all the little lies, deceits, subterfuges, make-believes. Pat would know, he would not need to be told, that not to go to Ireland with his father would be more than he could bear. It would sever the thread of life that bound his soul to his body. He would wither like a plant cut through at the ground.

Pat was playing a game. He was trying to force his father to put into words the thing that lay in both their minds, the thing that needed no words.

"Go visit your mother," Pat had said. "Take Barney with you. I'll put up the money."

And his father, refusing to put in words the thing they both knew, had not said, as it was Pat's intent to make him say, "Not would I go to Ireland and leave Brendan behind." Instead, he had said vaguely that there were "other considerations," and Pat had pretended that he didn't know what those other considerations might be.

But when they had played the game to its finish . . . ? No matter who won . . .

They were talking again. Their voices reached Brendan, but not their words. Rapt and motionless, he stood at the top of the third-floor stairs, straining to hear.

Barney came back into the hall, to see what was keeping him.

"What's up?"

"We're going to Irleand!" Brendan whispered.

"The Chief said not," Barney whispered back.

"We are, though!"

"You think? *Both* of us, Bren?"

"Both of us!"

Brendan slipped off his shoes, indicating with gestures that Barney should do the same.

"Let's go down where we can hear."

224

"Bren, we're supposed to go to bed."

"I know. We will. Later."

They went soundlessly down to the second floor hall. They listened.

The talk downstairs settled into an endurance test.

Pat reviewed again and again the dangers to Barney, and his father repeated again and again the same assurances.

Pat made a sentimental appeal on behalf of his grandmother.

"Think what it would mean to her, Pop. I'll bet there's never a time when the steamer comes over from Galway that she doesn't half think you might be on it."

"That way it is with mothers," his father agreed.

"You'd never forgive yourself," Pat said, "if you waited too long."

"Nor would I," his father answered, "if I waited not long enough."

"Well, what are you waiting *for?*" Pat demanded.

This was putting it squarely. Dodge that one if you can, Pat's tone said. Upstairs, Brendan held his breath.

"I wait for circumstances to be such that what is joy on the one hand be not grief on the other," his father said, "as sometimes happens when a thing is done in haste, without regard of plans earlier made."

"*That's* a laugh," Pat answered. "Taking twenty-three years sure must be what they mean by making haste slowly. And anyway," Pat said, "you know how it is with plans. Something's always coming along to knock them into a cocked hat. It's smarter to be ready to jump when the chance comes your way than to be hog-tied by a lot of outdated plans."

The talk went on. Pat glowingly outlined certain pleasures of the trip, and his father said. "That is so. Much have we talked of it." And this was coming close, very close, to putting a name to those "other considerations."

At this crucial point their voices dropped and Brendan could no longer hear what they were saying. To creep down close enough to hear would be to invite discovery, for the lower part of the stairway was plainly visible to anyone looking toward the hall from the living room. In desperation he lay flat on his stomach at the head of the stairs and, ignoring Barney's whispered protests, inched his way downward, head first, until he brought himself even with the top of the living-room archway, through which the voices came.

Braced there on his hands, he was able to hear, but the position soon became unendurable. His arms and shoulders ached from supporting his weight. The head-down position made the blood throb at his temples. How he would get back to the upper hall he didn't know, for his paralyzed arms would never push him back, and he wouldn't be able to reverse his position without making some noise. Just when he thought he could endure the agony no longer— either the agony of his position on the stairs or the agony of the merry-go-round of talk—and was about to whisper to Barney to take a good grip on his ankles and try to pull him back, just at that moment he heard a change in his father's voice, a note of finality that said the talking was over.

"Now is it late," his father said, and Brendan could hear him getting to his feet, "and tomorow at eight must I be at the Station, thanks to God and Father Morissey. We have said, I think, all that we have to say on this matter, Pádraig, and useless does it seem to discuss it further. Though not would I wish," he added, "to seem ungrateful. Much kindness and generosity are in your heart, my son, that you offer so much, and shame would it be did anyone reproach you for that you have not offered more. Not would it be in your father's heart to do so, nor do I think in any other's."

Again there was one of those long silences, pregnant with every unspoken thing that lay between them.

It was broken by Pat, saying in a loud voice, angry on the surface, but only on the surface, for under it he was laughing:

"Okay, you win! I'll stake the confounded little cuss! But he'll shine my shoes for it every day till he's twenty-one, and the first time he misses I'll——"

The rest was lost in sudden tumult on the stairs.

Brendan, making a quick and reflexive move to rise, pitched forward, turned a full somersault, and skidded to the bottom of the stairway on his back, as if the remaining steps were a sliding board.

Battered and bruised and momentarily stunned, he lay there while his father and Patrick came running from the living room; his mother and Peggy from the kitchen; Barney

226

from the head of the stairs; Rosie from her room on the second floor; and Paul, who had also heard the bumping and thumping, from as far away as the third-floor front.

His father, after a quick feel for broken bones, helped him to his feet.

"Are you hurt?" his mother and Peggy asked together. "Are you hurt?"

He didn't know. He was too dazed and numb to feel anything. It didn't matter anyway, and it wasn't because he was hurt that he was crying.

They satisfied themselves that he wasn't hurt, at least that he wasn't hurt seriously.

Pat let loose.

"You slimy sneak! You creepy, spying little louse! You night crawler! It serves you right! If you had broken every bone in your body, it would still serve you right! That's one time you got what you had coming! And I'm going to look you over, boy, and if I find a spot on you that's not already black and blue, believe me, it's going to be!"

"Are you sure you're not hurt?" his mother and Peggy kept asking.

But all he could say, standing there sustained by his father's arm, with tears streaming down his face, was: "Am I going to Ireland? Am I going to Ireland?"

Pat let go with a second volley.

But his father's arm tightened around him, and his father's voice, warm with its rich laughter, assured him: *"Tá tú ag dul go h'Éirinn. . . .* You are going to Ireland!"

10

SOMETIMES one year slipped into another with little to mark its passing or little to remember it by. A new calendar went up in the kitchen. One or two letters or school assignments were incorrectly dated. There was snow and cold in January, and occasional false promises of early spring in March. One day ended and another began. The passage of time was so smooth, the changes so gradual, that sometimes it was only when the children were trying on last winter's clothes that a full realization came of how much change there had been. The year, like a bird's shadow over the grass, was gone before one had time to see what cast the shadow.

In some years, of course, there were certain significant milestones, things of transcendent importance, to which, as an aid to memory, other lesser things could be tried. These years were remembered not by their dates, or by the world events that marked them, but by the events that distinguished them at home. The year 1941, for example, was always The Year of the Trouble. The year Mary was born, 1948, was more frequently referred to as The Year Mother Was So Long in the Hospital. By unanimous recognition of its most important happening, 1953 was The Year Barney Came. Some years were marked by dual milestones: The Year Pat Joined the Police Force, 1950, was one and the same with The Year Katie Went into the Convent.

The year 1956, then, would be known for all time as The Year Brendan Joined the Navy; and even though it became, later, also The Year Peggy Was Married, the second event, for all its joy, could not overcome the strange

228

sadness, the never-quite-dispelled shadow that lay over the house after the glow that was Brendan had left it.

It was not according to any plan, or at anyone's suggestion, even a joking suggestion, that Brendan joined the Navy.

Plans, on the contrary, had been for something else entirely. It was his father's plan, had long been his father's plan, that he go to college. None of the others had, but then none of the others (except Katie, who was college educated within the Order) had wanted to.

Pat, for as long as he or anyone else could remember, had had only one plan. Everyone had known and accepted this as a matter of course, because Pat was so completely a projection of his father, that to follow in his father's footsteps had seemed the inevitable thing for him to do. After graduation from high school he had worked for one year as guard at a manufacturing plant turning out ordnance materials, and then, upon reaching the required age of nineteen, had joined the Police Department.

Peggy had thought of going to a State Teachers College, but had decided to work for a year in order to lay by enough money to see her through. Then she met Bill, and everything had changed. It no longer seemed worth the effort to prepare herself for the teaching profession, especially as she wasn't sure she wanted to teach, or that she had any aptitude for it. She had compromised, instead, by enrolling in evening classes at the university, to broaden her knowledge of languages and literature, history, the arts, and other cultural subjects—a preparatory course, in short, for being Mrs. William Kane MacCarthy.

Paul had scoffed at the idea of a college degree being indispensable to the Young Man Wanting to Get Ahead.

"Waste four years in college? Nuts. The woods are full of fellows with college degrees in mechanical engineering and stuff like that, lucky if they can get a job servicing electric refrigerators. What can they teach me in college that I don't already know for my line of work? Mathematics? That's what bookkeepers are for. Public relations? I get on okay with the customers and the union boys, and what else is there? Sure, my hitch in the military's coming up, and it's not with me the way it was with my unexpendable big brother—police brass knocking itself out to get him an occupational deferment. But I've got no kick. I'm on the volunteer list, in line to start the day I make it to eighteen and a half. And when it's over, just stand clear, folks, and watch my dust!"

But it was different with Brendan.

Brendan—as his father knew, and as his grandmother, the moment she had seen him, had remarked—was very like his paternal grandfather. His grandfather had been a school-teacher, a scholar, a man of letters. A gentle man. A man who needed, although this was never openly stated, some-one to stand between him and the world; someone strong and vigorous and, when need be, aggressive; someone like the O'Rourke women, who had fought shoulder to shoulder beside their men against every invader in a thousand years, and had died beside them at Drogheda.

Brendan had inherited from his grandfather, then, qual-ities that go to the making of a scholar: a fondness for books and study; a natural inclination to the academic; and, particularly, a ready grasp of languages. From being bi-lingual it was an easy thing for Brendan to become poly-lingual. In high school he had four years of Latin and three of French, and had picked up at the same time a fair amount of Spanish and German from classmates taking these electives. A special, non-credit, after-hours course in Greek had been offered during the last semester of his senior year and he had taken it. In addition, on his own initiative, at home, he had engaged in the comparative study of other Celtic languages—Scottish Gaelic, Manx, and Welsh.

Most of this, in the opinion of most people, was about as useful to him in the world of today as a knowledge of how to write on clay tablets with a stylus. Even if he planned to teach (and to some the idea of Brendan pre-siding over a schoolroom was ludicrous in itself), who, except for a few specialists (or nuts like Brendan, Paul said), would want to be taught dead or dying languages? Certainly to spend another four years pursuing the same futureless studies would be pouring money down a rat hole. Still—as even the critics of the plan realized—what was the alternative? Imagine Brendan going to work!

This was the first time the question of pouring money down rat holes came up. Anybody else's money, that is. If Pat or Peggy or Paul had decided to obtain a college edu-cation, it would have been obtained at their own expense.

230

There was no one else who could, or would, have put up the money.

But everything was always different with Brendan. Somehow, the money would be found to put Brendan through college.

It wouldn't come from Pat, although Pat offered it.

"Not is it in your place," his father said, "to provide for your brother while I am able to do so myself."

"I've heard it takes about ten grand to put a kid through college these days," Pat answered. "You make sixty-two hundred a year, and you live from one pay check to the next. But you're going to take a little chunk of twenty-five hundred out of the gross each year for four years, and still get by. Nice going, Pop. With that kind of reverse arithmetic, they need you in Washington. You could balance the budget in nothing flat. Look, for Pete's sake. I'm a guy with a bank account. Half my pay for five years is just lying there collecting its three percent per annum. If the O'Nolans are going to have a college man in the family, I want to be in position to slap him down when he gets fresh."

"Better will it be, Pádraig," his father said, "do you continue to collect the three percent. Soon enough will you marry and have your own to provide for, and not will your bank account grow so fast then, nor be as much as you might wish when your own are at an age for college. It is not you who must do for Brendan as shall be done, but myself."

"How?"

"Not is that clear to me at this moment. But it is a thing I am set on, and a thing I will manage as the time comes."

"Yes," said Pat, "you'll manage. You and the kids!"

Cold anger brought the conversation to an end.

"None will suffer for it. The younger ones will I provide for also, according to what is suitable for them, as the need arises."

It was inevitable that there be teasing. Peggy and Paul could no more help teasing than they could help drawing a normal number of breaths per minute. They did not mean to hurt. Brendan knew this; they never meant to hurt. There may have been, indiscernibly, the remnants of childhood jealousy carried along over the years, faint resentment toward one who (perhaps they had only imagined) was favored, held in special regard, always a little apart, a pet.

"Father's little pet."

The old child's word slipped into the teasing.

"*We* had to go to work, as soon as *we* finished high school. But Father's little pet is going to college."

"What will he know when he's through? Four times as much as he knows now. Four times nothing equals nothing!"

"Well, Father has to do something with him. He won't work, and he can't just sit around the house."

"It's just postponing the evil day. Because what do you suppose he'll do when he finishes college? Right. Sit around the house!"

"Mother will have to dust him every day, the same as the other ornaments."

"You call him an ornament?"

He was at loose ends, that summer after graduation from high school. He tried—halfheartedly, because he knew the futility of it—to find some sort of employment, but his attempts were without success. He spent most of his time reading. Sometimes he rode around with Father Morissey on his parish calls. Regularly every Wednesday afternoon they visited the children's ward of St. Andrew's Hospital, and there he had a part in the visit, entertaining with a story or a song. There seemed to be nothing of the summer to remember, when it was over, except those Wednesday afternoons.

He wanted to go to college, wanted it more than anything he could think of. But was it true, did he want it for the reason Paul said, "to postpone the evil day"? The day when he would be expected to start doing something useful? To earn his own living? To stand on his own feet?

Did he want to go to college to escape? Escape from what? From his own inadequacies? From the world?

What did he hope to find there? Surely something more than just a place to hide. A place where he could fit in? Where he would be too busy to be lonely? Where he might, among those thousands of others, find the person he was always looking for—the one-out-of-the-world friend he would meet someday, somewhere?

He missed Barney's companionship—Barney was working full time that summer for Paul, who was home again after two years of army service. But long before he lost Barney to Paul, he had lost him to Rose.

This was a hurt that he sealed away. It wasn't that he didn't want to share; it was only that he had wanted their friendship, their brotherhood, to be the special thing to Barney that it was to him. It was never, never for a minute, that he was unwilling to yield first place to Rose. That handwriting had been on the wall from the beginning; it was not that he didn't like what the hand had written, but only that as Rosie's name was written in, his own was with such finality inked out. Brendan and Barney. Those two names, for a time, had been linked on everyone's tongue. Naturally. Inseparably. One was hardly thought of without the other. But then somehow, subtly and surely, the linkage was changed, and the two inseparable names became Barney and Rose.

Rosie, as everyone knew, had steadfastly refused from the start to regard Barney as a brother, and it could have come as no surprise to anyone, that summer when she turned an incredibly lovely fourteen, to discover that Barney no longer regarded her as a sister, if he ever had. In mental outlook and moral responsibility, Rosie had always been mature beyond her years; it was no surprise that physical maturity, when it came, should be swift and complete and as rich-textured as the flower whose name she bore.

They had no wish to exclude him. Quite the opposite; they were willing, even determined, to form a threesome on any and every occasion. But he became adept at manufacturing nonexistent reasons why he couldn't go here or there, or, conversely, why he *must* go here or there, to the end that he did not by his presence, even though it was a welcome presence, create the proverbial crowd.

Looking back, he could see that he had really only had Barney, specially, to himself, for himself, during those wonderful first weeks, the weeks that had become, as the years passed, hardly distinguishable from a dream. He could look back and remember the exact occasion, even the exact moment, when he knew the loneliness was still there.

There was the junior play at school, and he was in it, but he hadn't told at home that he had one of the leads. In the first place, his father was working the late shift and couldn't come, and his mother hadn't been well that autumn and shouldn't come. If they knew he had a leading role, they would know it would hurt him not to have them there; but if they didn't know about the role they wouldn't know about the hurt, and that would make it easier for everybody, including himself. In the second place, he planned to keep it as a surprise for Barney and Rose, for whom he had reserved two of the choicest seats.

And then, the day before, a conflict of dates arose, through a last-minute shift in the scheduled time of the St. Andrew's Fall Festival. Rose couldn't go to the play—she had charge of a booth at the Festival; so there was Barney, twice committed, subject to a Solomon decision, about to be sliced in two.

It was (and this was comfort of a sort) Brendan himself who saved Barney from this unhappy fate.

"Oh, you go with Rose," he said at once. "That's all right. I know someone who'll be glad to buy the tickets"— he didn't, but he thought he could find someone—"because the reserved seats are sold out. And anyway, I know Pat isn't looking forward with any joy to the chauffeuring assignment—he has a date. So you'll get a vote of thanks from Pat, Barney, if you switch plans and go with Rosie instead."

And he knew. He knew by Barney's quick look of relief, by his quick smile, by his quick acceptance of the changed plans, that this was what he would rather do: go with Rose.

In its little sealed room far down inside of him, the loneliness, that had only been quiescent, came to life again.

Yet it was a strange thing, the way it worked out. Strange how that mischance about the dates, which had robbed him of something he had looked forward to for weeks, gave him, in trade, something that he never would have dared dream of.

On the night before the play, returning home late from final dress rehearsal, he did not shine Pat's shoes. The first time since the trip to Ireland. Regularly, every night without fail, for nearly three months, he had shined Pat's shoes. And had liked to, had been glad to. It wasn't that he forgot, that night. He saw them there, outside Pat's door, and he picked them up and rubbed the toes on the sleeve of his coat and set them down again. He would have known, of course, if it hadn't been so late, if he hadn't been so tired and so unhappy, that Pat would not be deceived.

In the morning Pat was angry, and a little rough. In the afternoon he was sorry.

"You had it coming," he said, "don't make any mistake about that. But I shouldn't have raised such a ruckus that the whole house knew. So I figure if I get slapped with a fine and costs, it ought to make us even up. You name it, kid."

Pat had his wallet in his hand.

But Pat's being sorry was enough; the account was already balanced and the slate wiped clean.

"Oh, it doesn't matter about this morning, Pat."

"The hell it doesn't."

Pat drew two ten-dollar bills from his wallet and held them out, but Brendan put his hands behind his back.

"No, Pat. Please. I don't want any money."

"Everybody wants money. Take it."

"Pat, I don't care about this morning. Honestly I don't."

"You cared plenty, this morning," Pat said, "and I care now. Here. Put this in your pocket. You'll think up a use for it later."

"No, Pat. I don't want money. I . . . don't like money."

"Who asks you to like it? I'm going to square myself, whether you like it or not. Take it!"

"Pat"—the undreamed-of thing came suddenly, like a shaft of light striking through a stained-glass window, spreading a many-colored radiance—"Pat, does it have to be money?"

"What do you mean, does it have to be money?"

"I mean, could it be something you would do?"

"*Do?* Now see here. I don't know what you've got in mind, but I'm not sticking my neck out."

"No." The light shifted, the radiance was gone. "No, you wouldn't want to. I wouldn't ask you to."

"What?"

"Oh, not anything, really. It was just a crazy thought I had, just for a minute."

"All right," Pat said resignedly. "It can't be any crazier that the thought *I* had—that I hadn't already stuck my neck out. Spill it."

"Pat, you know about Barney and Rose . . . not coming to the play tonight. . . ."

"Oh, Lord," Pat said.

"I still have the tickets. I . . . there won't be anybody there. I mean, any of the family. I just wondered"—he steadied his voice—"but it's all right. I know you wouldn't want to. . . ."

"How much of a part do you have in this play?"

"Oh . . . just a part. Pat, you wouldn't come, would you?"

"And drag the new girl friend to a high-school kids' play? It sure sounds like the end of a beautiful friendship."

An absurd hope: "They're very good seats. Fourth row, center."

"Great. We won't be able to miss anything if we try."

"Pat, do you mean—?"

"If that's the fine," Pat said, "I'm stuck with it. Are the costs included, or are you cooking up something more?"

"Only . . . would you come backstage afterward, so I can introduce you to everybody?"

"What in the name of all the Saints would you want to introduce me for?"

"Oh, I'd just like to, Pat. Nobody knows I have a brother like you."

It was part of the pattern of his life that grief could turn to joy, or joy to grief, in these dizzying reversals. With Pat there to watch, he gave an inspired performance, and had one of the happiest nights of his life. Years afterward, in times of loneliness, of fear or despair, he could reach back into the past and lift out the shining minutes of that night, like bright jewels from a treasure chest; and on whatever darkened stage he was performing, he could set up those moments and turn the spotlight on them, and feast on remembered joy through a weary, wakeful night when joy seemed gone forever from his world.

September came. Brendan enrolled at the university and Rose at St. Elizabeth's Academy. The drain on the fund that had been rigorously set by for these purposes was complete.

St. Elizabeth's had previously been the one extravagance which the O'Nolans allowed themselves. Tuition was two hundred dollars a semester, and without the money which had come to Anne when her father's estate was settled, Katie and Peggy could hardly have completed their four years. Now that money was gone, but here was Rose, and to deny Rose what her sisters had had would be manifest injustice. Somehow, therefore, money must be allocated to send Rose to St. Elizabeth's.

And, somehow, much more money to send Brendan to the university.

Pat made one more effort (everyone heard the argument, which ended in the usual stubborn refusal and the usual exchange of heated words) and then gave up, for he saw that it was a matter of pride.

That he had accepted the trip to Ireland, his father said, for himself and the two boys, was one thing. Not was a trip to Ireland a necessity. A matter of pleasure, for that he could accept. But for his children's needs, not so. For their needs he must himself provide. Did he fail to do so, then he failed in his duty as a father. What must be done, that would he find a way to do; not should the burden fall upon one brother to provide for another.

It was not suggested by anyone—the question was not even raised—that Brendan contrive somehow, as others contrived, to pay his own way. It was known and accepted that this was not within the narrow scope of his powers.

He could not, himself, oppose his father's determination to give him a college education. Opposing his father was not a thing he had ever done. He had never had the wish, and certainly would never have had either the courage or the competence. He ventured, just once, to protest that the cost was too great, that the idea should be abandoned, but his father crushed this incipient revolt with a look and the words, "Not will I hear of it," and the plan went forward.

He lived at home, but the wider world of the university opened to receive him, and the four months of his first (and only) term were, on the whole, very happy. The academic life, which seemed the only life he was fitted for, provided him with a sense of accomplishment. He formed no close friendships, yet he had nothing but friendly contacts on all sides, and these provided him with a sense of being accepted. No one seemed to find him especially amusing or especially different or especially anything at all. He was just another freshman, adapting himself to the life of the university.

Worry over the expense he was to his parents bothered him at first, but he found consolation in promising himself that he would eventually repay them. When he finished college and was earning money, he would turn back to them every cent he earned, above a bare minimum for living expenses, until the full cost of his education had been repaid. He would teach, probably, although he might do something else—write books, perhaps. Whatever he did, he would prove to everybody that the money hadn't been wasted, and he would make his parents proud of him, and glad that they had given him this special opportunity.

In the meantime, the obvious way to prove that the money wasn't being wasted was to do well. He worked hard. In his fields of interest he excelled, but in spite of working hard his deficiencies in other fields were unhappily apparent. He did fairly well in biology, but in mathematics he barely scraped by.

There was no sound reason, of course, why this should depress him to the extent it did, but then his reactions to things very often had little foundation in reason. When he received the transcript of his grades at midyear, it was not the A's that stood out, but the C in biology and the D in math. He felt that he had not lived up to his father's expectations. He had not done well enough. An irrational, consuming fear grew on him that he would never do well enough, never in anything, never his whole life long.

Then, on one of those days of vacation, he overheard a conversation. It was not this time between his father and Pat (who was maintaining a coldly expectant silence), but between his father and mother.

"Rose won't mind," he heard his mother say. "I know she won't mind, Tadhg. I know from things she has said that she would be just as well satisfied going to the diocesan high school; perhaps better, because that's where most of the girls from Saint Andrew's are. And of the two," his mother said, "it is so much more important for Brendan to keep on."

"Not is it a fair thing," his father said, "to deprive one in order to do for the other."

"But it isn't a matter of depriving Rose. Only of changing schools. She is so practical, so adaptable, it will make no difference."

"It will make the difference," his father answered, "that she will not have what her sisters had. Not would the wrong be less for that she is good-natured and of mature understanding and not of a disposition to complain. As for Brendan. . . ."

They were both silent for a long moment. To Brendan, listening, the silence told more than the frankest, most disparaging words. It told him that there was nothing, really, that could be said about Brendan.

"It will be a little difficult," his father went on, "for Brendan to find his place in the world. Not have I doubt that he will find it, but a while it may take, and the road, I think, will not be easy. This must we do for him, Anneen, at any cost. Beyond this, he must set his own feet on his own road. For this next semester's tuition, I will borrow; and for Rose also, that there need be no change at this time. Then must we try, hereafter, to set a certain amount aside out of each pay, for this purpose, so that when next September comes we are prepared. Had it not been for the need of the new furnace, this year well enough could we have managed."

At any cost.

The three words stayed with Brendan all morning. They were so loud, throbbing in his mind, that after he had slipped away and then made a second approach to the kitchen, walking with a firm step so they would hear him come, he imagined that his father knew he had been there before, listening in secret, hearing those words.

Nothing was said until his father asked, just before leaving for work, when must he register for the coming term.

"Arú amáireach, 'Athair."

His father smiled, put a hand on Brendan's shoulder and said, *"Tá go maith. Ná bíodh imní ort,* do not worry. By the day after tomorrow will the money be then in your hand."

But he worried. All morning he worried, and the words lay in his mind: At any cost. This must we do for him *at any cost.*

His father was going to borrow the money. Now, in addition to the costs of daily living, in addition to the extra, unpredictable costs—such as the new furnace or illness or any of a dozen things—now in addition there would be interest on debt. And the debt to repay. Yet they planned to set something aside for next year, robbing themselves, robbing the others. (Pat's voice: Yes, you'll manage. You and the kids!)

And if it all became too hard, Rose would have to leave St. Elizabeth's. But he would go to college. At any cost. Because he must be helped to set his feet on his own road, to find his place in the world. Because he couldn't do this without help, as the others had, as Rosie would. The road will not be easy, his father had said. . . . Because he was so useless, so weak, so dependent. That was why the road would not be easy, why he must be helped at any cost.

He was eighteen. Only the other day they had celebrated his eighteenth birthday as if it were an especially important event, somehow different, more significant than other birthday anniversaries. But it wasn't. Being eighteen hadn't changed him. He was still the family liability. The family joke.

"Bren's eighteen today."

"No kidding! Eighteen months?"

"Years, silly. Can't you tell?"

"Not till I see signs that a razor's been over that skin-you-love-to-touch. Don't forget, he was born on Groundhog Day. You only count the years he doesn't see his shadow. Because everybody knows Bren's afraid of his own shadow. Every time he sees it he runs back in his hole."

"And misses a year."

"That's right. It averages out, so what he really is—he's nine years old."

"Imagine that! And it seems only yesterday that he was in his playpen."

"What do you mean, only yesterday? He's *still* in his playpen!"

The house was very quiet all morning. He and his mother had it to themselves, everyone else was either at work or at school. He stayed upstairs in his room reading, when his thoughts didn't intrude across the page; the rest of the time he worried. When his mother called him to come down to lunch, he put on a cheerful front and kept her laughing with imitations of his French professor, a foppish little man who wore a small waxed mustache, a neat little Vandyke beard, and gold-rimmed pince-nez on a fine gold chain.

During the afternoon the weather, which had been rainy, cleared under a fresh bright wind blowing like the winds of March. His mother asked him if he would mind walking up to the post office to send a money order. She gave him the money and a slip of paper with a name and address, and he set off, glad of an errand to take him outdoors.

The wind lifted his spirits. He rode its bright stream into a world of promise and hope, a world in which he would, as his father said, find his place. It might not be easy, but he would find it. It was waiting for him. When he came to it he would know, he would recognize it at once, there would be something to say to him: *This is it, you are here.*

So small the things on which one's destiny depends.

A postal money order.

A high, clean wind, sweeping through the streets and tumbling the clouds across the sky.

If there had been only one or the other of these things, it never would have happened. A high wind always excited him, exhilarated him, swept him along like a leaf; but an aimless walk in the wind would simply have taken him around the block, or around ten blocks, and brought him home again. There would have been no incident. No incident, certainly, like today's, when he did not walk aimlessly, but on an errand to a fixed destination.

The post office.

Directly in front of him, as he mounted the three or four steps from the street, was a Navy recruiting sign. Across the top, in great letters, was the exhortation: JOIN THE NAVY. Under this was the picture. In the foreground was a portion of the deck of a ship, with a young man in Navy whites standing at the rail looking outward across a very bright blue sea. In the distance, beyond the rolling blue water, was a rocky shoreline that made him think of the coast of Connemara seen from Galway Bay.

The sign spoke to him. It was not without meaning, he thought, that it was there at that exact spot, at that exact time. His imagination leaped to the significance of its being there, of his seeing it at this moment of all moments, when he had prayed to be shown what he must do, prayed to be shown a road on which he could set his feet.

The sign was there for him. God had meant him to see it, had meant him to know that this was the answer.

Wonder and exultation filled him, and he went inside.

The mood of wonder and exultation lasted a long while. It lasted all the way home through the bright blowing wind. It lasted while he opened the front door and walked through the hall and on back to the kitchen, where John and Jim and Mary, home from school, were having cocoa and cookies.

His mother was there with them, at the table, and it wasn't until he saw her looking at him in a puzzled way—as if he had changed, as if he were not Brendan O'Nolan but somebody else, somebody who brought something strange and disruptive into that familiar scene—that the buoyancy of his mood began to dwindle and with sickening speed to let him down.

"Is it a holiday?" his mother asked, perplexed. "Was the post office closed?"

Looking down, he saw that the money she had given him, with the slip of paper folded around it, was in his left hand.

He looked at it, and he looked at his mother, and reaction set in. He hadn't been cold. Out in the wind he had been warm, his blood had been racing. But now he began to shiver.

"Darling," his mother said anxiously, "you weren't dressed warmly enough to be out so long in that wind. Sit down and have a cup of hot cocoa. Here."

"Mother . . ."

He hadn't planned to tell it this way. He had planned to wait until everyone was home, assembled at the supper table, and then, very casually, to astound them all with his incredible news. But he hadn't planned on the collapse of his high feeling, on the sudden coldness that went all through him, on the crushing realization of what he had done, on the rising panic.

"I've joined the Navy."

He imagined that his mother swayed a little bit and that the hand on the back of Mary's chair gripped it for support. She was very pale. Now, to everything else remorse was added, for she wasn't well, she hadn't been really well for years, and he had given her this shock.

The three children stared at him.

His mother asked, "Brendan, you aren't joking?"

"No, Mother."

She leaned forward, then, and kissed his cheek. Her hands pressed his arms.

"Well, it certainly comes as a surprise, darling. But, of course, you have a perfect right . . . and it's really a fine thing to do. Your father"—she faltered a little—"I'm sure your father will think so too."

242

Brendan would never know what his father really thought, or how he felt.

"Tell it me at once," he said, sensing the moment he entered the house that something was wrong, "that I do not torment myself with thinking it may be a thing worse than it is."

What, in his agonized search of his father's face, he hoped to see, after it had been told, Brendan did not know.

Approval? Pride? Reassurance? Or . . . forgiveness?

In that inscrutable face, that face that could be as impenetrable as carved stone, he could read nothing. Surprise, anger, dismay, pity, sadness—whatever was there, it was not revealed by the faintest sign.

Brendan thought he could neither endure waiting to hear his father's first word, nor endure the word when it came. For what could it be but bitter censure of an act so wild, so impulsive, so unreasoning?

Or—worse than any word that might be spoken—suppose his father said nothing at all, but in cold silence turned away from him, washed his hands of him, shrugged him off, indifferent, uncaring. *You have made your bed. . . .*

Neither of these unbearable things took place, neither the harsh upbraiding nor the cold turning away. Instead, at the end of a long silence, his father smiled.

Everything Brendan could want to see was in his father's smile: acceptance, understanding, comfort, love, and—for whatever cause—pride. All his life that smile had lighted his world. All his life it had banished every shadow, and with every shadow every fear.

"*A mhic!*" His father's arm, offering and sharing its own great strength, went around him. "Not is it a thing to surprise me, that the sea would speak to you and that in this way you would answer, for of the limestone of Ára Na Naomh are your bones made, and the sea water runs with the blood in your veins."

The pall was lifted. The state of shock which had gripped the house when he came home with his news released its hold. Normal activity was resumed. Normal conversation could flow in normal channels. His father, biding his time, asked for no explanation, but talked of the event as if, though unexpected, it was perfectly plausible. The two young boys were enthralled with the idea of their brother being in the United States Navy. It was something that no one ever thought of; it showed how anything can happen. Barney, full of admiration, longed to do the same, but unfortunately Barney was under age and had two years of high school still ahead of him, besides. Rose, who knew more of the financial problems of the household than anyone thought she did, said, "I know exactly why you did it, Bren. It's just like you to do something noble."

He knew he hadn't been noble. The desire to spare his parents the expense of putting him through college, the desire not to be the reason why Rose might have to quit St. Elizabeth's, had been in his mind, it was true; had been, in a sense, the springboard from which he had made his leap. But he knew he had not acted clearly, rationally, realistically, on the sound basis of those desires. He had acted on an impulse as sudden, as formless, as unthinking, as erratic, as his impulses always were. He had been carried away by a splendid dream: a dream of doing something responsible and decisive; of rising courageously to meet his own destiny; of making his father proud of him. But it was only a dream, as fleeting as it had been grandiose. Now the dream was gone. Only the reality remained.

Patrick and Paul, coming in together a little late, just at supper time, were pounced on by Jimmy with the news. Plainly, at first, they didn't believe it. Paul said, "Look, sprout, who do you think you're kidding?" But Pat exchanged a quick look with his father, and knew that it was true.

Paul said, "Never the Navy! Never our little pet, our precious lamb, in the Navy!" But something in the air, something in everyone's silence, told him that they were not, after all, being kidded. His tone changed, then, as he exclaimed, "Hot dog! Saint Brendan the Navigator in person!"

Brendan had known that Paul would laugh. Paul always laughed. But if Pat. . . .

And Pat laughed, too, but in another way and for an entirely different reason. Pat came over and clapped a hand on his shoulder and said: "So you foxed us! Damned if you didn't! I've got to hand it to you, kid, you're a smooth operator. A man's got to move fast to keep ahead of you!"

He knew that Pat didn't mean any of this literally. Pat knew very well that he hadn't done anything clever, wasn't a "smooth operator," hadn't intentionally got ahead of any-

244

body. But it was wonderful, just the same, to hear him say these things.

Paul laughed and made wisecracks and whistled "Anchors Aweigh."

But it didn't matter. Brendan didn't even have to put up his guard, the little smile that told them all to go ahead and laugh. Infinitely better than his guard was what Pat said: "You did just what I'd have done in your place."

Late that evening when everyone else had gone upstairs and he was alone with his father, he told the whole sorry little tale: his eavesdropping, his worry, his not wanting to be a burden; his walk in the wind; the Navy recruiting poster, the significance he read into it; the splendid dream, the act itself . . . then the aftermath, the full realization of what he had done. And the fear. . . .

With his head bowed in his hands he said to his father, *"Tá eagla orm, 'Athair. Tá eagla mór orm.* I'm so afraid."

"Until you are sworn," his father said, "there is yet time to draw back. If you wish," he added, and there seemed a sad question in the words.

Hope, like the fire that sometimes leaps among dying embers, blazed for a single instant, flickered, and went out.

"I thought I was proving something," Brendan said. "And I did prove something—I proved what a fool I am. To be a fool is bad enough; but what will I be proving if I draw back? No. No, I must go through with it; there is no other choice. . . . But how can I, Father, how can I? I can't leave here. I can't leave you. I can't. What am I to do?"

"For what you must do," his father answered, "God will give you the strength when the time comes. The courage you already have."

"Níl. Níl misneach orm. I have no courage. I am such a coward, such a coward."

"Not are you so," his father said. "Not is a man a coward, for that he is afraid. Fear is a natural emotion, put on man by God for the preservation of his life. Not is it the fear, but only the manner of meeting the fear, or of yielding to it, that makes of a man a coward. You will not yield. This I know well, for under your feet there is rock. For thousands of years the sea has beaten against that rock, and washed over it, and drawn back defeated—and there it remains. Not will it fail you now, my son, that rock of which God made you."

"No, it is you," Brendan whispered, "it is you who are my rock. Always, all my life. You remember, don't you, how I always ran to you? Long after I was too old, and the others laughed and made fun of me, but I didn't care. What will I do now, when I need to run to you and you aren't there?"

"In your heart will I be then," his father answered, "and there will you turn to find me. But first will you turn to God, and with God's help will you meet each day as it comes. And then in a while each day will be a little easier, for with each day will your strength be greater. It is so that a man may build a good life for himself, one day at a time."

"I have destroyed your plans," Brendan said. "I have disappointed you, yet you aren't angry."

"Disappointed am I in my plans for you," said his father. "That is so. But disappointed in you, not so. Not would I have had you do as you have done, yet is it much pride to me that you took matters in your own hands, to do for yourself. And it may be that what you have done for yourself will prove better than what I would have done for you, had my plans been followed. We cannot tell about these things, because in the end it is God's plan we follow. But it is better, I think, if a man find his own place in the world, than that a place be made for him by others and he be pushed into it, as if he were no more than a peg to be fitted into a hole. It sometimes happens that one who is too much helped passes beyond a point of learning to help himself, and so remains dependent throughout his life. It may be that God in His wisdom saw greater danger to you did you follow the easy course laid down, than did you strike out alone on a course which you may, for a time, find not easy.

"Right now," his father said, "it is the change you fear, the severance from all that is familiar and from those you love. But it is only for a time, it is not forever. And even in the change you will find much to gladden your heart, for you are young, and for the young there is much that is new and good and beautiful in the world, to be found in many places and in many ways."

Under the spell of his father's words he felt comforted, and some of his exhilaration returned. When he and Barney went to bed, they talked for a while of the sea and far places, until Barney fell asleep in his quick and easy way.

Brendan, still wakeful, lay thinking of all the places he soon would see, cruising with the Fleet: the Mediterranean, the Pacific, the Far East. In all those places, as his father had said, there would be much that was new and beautiful, and his thoughts reached out with eager longing to those things, across the great green distances of the sea. Thinking of them, wondering what they would be, where he would find them, who would be sharing them with him, he fell asleep.

He woke in terror sometime in the night.

Whether he had dreamed, he did not know. Whether he had cried out, he did not know. But he knew the terror. It was the old dream-terror of his childhood—the dream of the great empty waste through which he ran calling for his father.

Long ago, trapped in sleep, he used to scream, and his father would hear him and come, and the terror would end. Or, waking from the dream, he would run crying to his parents' room, to the one safe place in all the world, his father's arms.

As he grew older, he learned not to scream and he learned not to run. He learned to lie still in his bed, cold and stiff with the terror, but denying himself flight to safety, because he was too old, because he must grow up.

Now he was eighteen, and he had joined the Navy, and he must take his place in the world. There was no safe place now; time and his own folly had closed and locked the door. The terror was a cold hand on his heart, freezing his blood, a cold hand at his throat, shutting off his breath. Alone and in secret he must face it, fight it, endure it, somehow outlast it.

Barney hadn't wakened. Barney there beside him, the warmth of his body, the sound of his breathing, helped dispel the terror; but when it passed, there was left in its place the cold, oppressive weight of the future, from which there could be no escape.

With his own hand in one reckless moment he had signed himself away from everything that was his life. Like the dream-terror, this new terror must be borne. Not for an hour only—the duration of a two-o'clock awakening. For years. Alone in the emptiness of the years, he must follow the road on which he had set his feet.

He had brought disappointment to his father. Anxiety.

Sorrow, because his father, who loved him, would suffer for his suffering. But whatever he brought in the future, he would not, would not . . . ever . . . bring shame.

God will give you strength, his father had said, when the time comes.

The time was now.

Tabhair dom, a Thiarna, neart i gcóir an lae amáireach. . . . Give me, O Lord, strength for tomorrow.

The prayer brought quietness to his thoughts. But he did not sleep again.

When Katie left, six years before, she left joyfully, and behind her remained the traces of her joy, making the house brighter. It had been a summer day, and her father and mother, taking the three youngest children with them, had driven her to the Convent, and when they came home again, it was to the added brightness of a house which God had so especially blessed.

No such joy attended Brendan's departure.

It was a school day and a work day, and at the final moment no one but his mother was there; and Pat, who was driving him to the naval district recruiting station, from which place he would, within a few hours, be started on his way to the base. At his request his father had already gone, leaving the house early in the morning, before his usual time.

"Téir uaim, 'Athair," he had pleaded. *"Ní féidir liom imeacht uait. . .* I beg you, please go from me first, because I cannot go from you."

So, at the final moment, he had only to kiss his mother good-by, and promise to write, and walk through the front door and across the porch.

But he looked down, and there under his foot was the board with the hole in it, which he had made with the brace and bit one long-ago golden day; the board his father had never replaced, because it let a bright little ellipse of sunlight into the dark cave under the porch where the fairies lived through the winter time. . . .

So lost, so gone . . . all the bright years, all the joy.

"If you start to bawl," Pat warned, "I'll paste you one."

At home that evening, at the supper table, Pat did what he could to dissipate the gloom.

"The kid's all right," he assured them. "Nobody has to

248

worry about him. Anybody who thinks he hasn't got what it takes just plain doesn't know which end's up. You can't tell what's inside a package by the wrappings. Oh, sure, he's going to find the going a little rough at first. But he'll do all right. He'll do fine."

But these remarks, intended to be heartening, by some strange chemistry produced an opposite effect.

Peggy said, "It's our fault, Paul's and mine. He never would have done it if we hadn't teased him so much, all the time." And, unexpectedly, Peggy began to cry.

Rose, who never cried, looked with tear-filled eyes at Barney and said, "No. It's our fault. We made him feel outside."

"He used to keep asking me if I liked him," said Barney with a stricken look. "But he couldn't really have thought, could he, that I didn't like him?"

It was all too much for Mary, who said pitifully, "I didn't want Brendan to go away!" and fell to uncontrollable weeping, her head in her mother's lap.

Pat looked around the table with the expression of a man who suddenly finds himself the only sane person left in a world gone mad.

"Are you all clean batty? One time in his life that kid does something that makes sense, and everybody acts like it's the end of the world! He's not dead, just in the U.S. Navy! If he'd waited and been called up for military service, nobody would have thought anything of it! But because he has the guts to go ahead and sign himself in, it's a major catastrophe. Maybe I'm the one who's crazy, but that way of looking at it sure as hell seems upside-down and backward to me!"

He turned to his father.

"Why don't you get in the act? It's your fault, isn't it, for wanting to put him through college? Or is it mine for not clobbering enough sense into your head to let me foot the bill? Or maybe it's Mother's for sending him to the post office!"

Tadhg O'Nolan looked from one to another of his children, with pity and understanding, but with some sternness also, and with what sadness of his own, they could only guess.

"Not is there fault in the matter at all," he said, "either upon any here or upon any not here, and therefore are we without reason to engage in self-reproach. Much worry would it be to your brother, I think, did he know that he has brought sadness to this house where all his life before he brought nothing but joy. And with tears such as these— tears shed for thinking that he may have acted in self-pity, for some bit of teasing or for some fancied slight—with such tears you do him injustice. Not did he act as he did for such reason, but for reasons put in his mind by God, and therefore reasons good in themselves, and leading to good at the end, we may be sure. Better would it be did we now join in prayers for his happiness and well-being, than in tears for our own loss."

The plane had been flying above the clouds. Through that cover, which seemed no part of either heaven or earth, it came down in a long descent toward the U.S. Navy base at San Diego. A continent lay behind it. Ahead, five thousand miles of ocean curved away to those horizons where the new and beautiful lay waiting.

11

ANY TIME after two o'clock.

Anne knew, without turning her head to see the clock on the bureau, that she had six hours.

Tadhg had left ten minutes ago. It must now be twenty minutes of eight.

The children were at breakfast. One by one they would come upstairs, as they finished eating and before they left for school, to say good-by. It would really be easier that way, much easier than to have them all at home when she must leave, all standing at the gate waving good-by, as they so often had.

No, it was not these who had waved good-by. It was the older ones, the ones who were no longer children, the ones who were no longer here; and their good-bys had been waved when she was leaving for the hospital to have another baby, one of these.

That was the trouble with sedatives, they clouded one's mind. In these last few hours she did not want her mind clouded. She would not have taken that pill during the night, but the pain had been so bad and she had not wanted Tadhg to know.

It was Pat, Katie, Peggy, Paul, and Brendan who had waved good-by at the gate. Or welcome. But none of them would be there today. There would be no use looking back, when the car turned at the corner, for a last glimpse of them waving at the gate.

And no use looking forward . . .

Pat would stop by for Peggy and they would come to the hospital this evening, to ask how she was feeling and if there was anything she wanted them to get for her or anything she wanted them to do. They would stand there in the room for a little while, worrying about her, loving her, but feeling uncomfortable because a hospital room is such an uncomfortable place; and not knowing what to say, because what is there to say when one must avoid the truth?

Paul was now living in Boston, the eastern terminus of the transcontinental trucking line in which he had recently bought a half interest; and Winnie hadn't been well—she was in her third month—they wouldn't come unless they were sent for.

Katie was a hundred miles away upstate, teaching, and at the very end of the school year it would be hard for her to get away. Pat would telephone her as soon as there was anything definite to report.

And Brendan . . . dear Brendan . . .

As soon as the children left for school, she would ask Rose to prop her up with pillows and give her her writing things, so that she could finish her letter to Brendan.

Barney came in first. He tried to make his good-natured grin seem natural, but he wasn't a very good actor and the effort only increased his look of anxiety.

"I guess I've got to shove off now, Aunt Annie. I just wanted to say I sure hope they get you fixed up real quick."

"Thank you, Barney."

She took his hands and drew him down until she could put a light kiss on his forehead.

"You know, if you hadn't called me 'Aunt Annie,' I would have completely forgotten which one of my sons you are. But now I remember. You're the one next after Brendan. Sometimes," Anne confessed, "I get a little confused."

Barney grinned.

"Well, I get confused too. I guess I only call you 'Aunt Annie' so as to keep things straight in my mind. So I don't think I'm two people, or a split personality, or something. Because I sure feel as if that's who I am, the next one after Bren, I mean."

"Lucky, lucky day," Anne said, "when five sons became six."

Barney left and the two young boys came in, scrubbed and shining at the start of the day.

They came close to the bed, feeling a little awkward, she could see, because it was such an unusual thing to do.

252

Through the past week they had simply looked in from the doorway, or, in a hurry, had shouted, " 'By, Mother!" from the foot of the stairs. But today was the day she was going to the hospital, and their father would have told them to come in and say good-by.

She slipped an arm around the waist of each in turn, giving a quick hug and kiss. They stood side by side, then, waiting for her to say something.

"You look wonderful," she told them. "I don't even need to straighten your ties. You aren't forgetting anything? You have your rosaries?"

They felt their pockets.

"Yes, Mother."

"I feel so sorry—missing your last day of school exercises. But you'll know I'm thinking about you every minute, won't you, darlings?"

"Oh, sure, Mother. That's all right."

She searched their faces, storing the memory away.

"I never saw two such handsome boys in my life," she said admiringly. "There's no doubt about it, you're both going to be the image of your father when you're a little older. Good-by, my darlings. I'm not going to say 'Be good,' because you always are."

" 'By, Mother."

Mary came into the room as the boys went out. This would be harder. Anne closed her eyes for just a moment and prayed. When she opened her eyes again she smiled at her beautiful nine-year-old daughter, the last baby, the one she had never had to give up, the one particularly her own, the one to her as Pat to his father, a second self, and so close, so close.

"Dearest, you know you're to wait at school until Peggy comes for you, don't you?"

"Yes, Mother."

"We're going to drop your things off on our way; you won't have to come back here at all. And you'll do everything you can to help Peggy, won't you? She gets tired very quickly, the baby is so heavy now. You can save her going up and down stairs, and . . . oh, there are so many little things you can do to make it easier for her. I'm depending on you, darling."

"Yes, Mother. I'll help Peggy. When will you be home?"

"I can't say, dear. I hope it won't be very long."

"Mother"—Mary's voice was a whisper, and fear that was instinctive, for she hadn't been told there was anything to fear, put its shadow in her eyes—"I wish you weren't going."

"So do I, darling. It's very hard to leave you, even for a few days, or a week . . . but the time will pass quickly, you will have so many new things to see and do at Peggy's house."

"Mother, I wish you were going to the hospital to have another baby, instead of another operation."

"Wouldn't that be fun?" Anne said, smiling. "You were cheated, weren't you, never having a baby sister or brother. Rose always loved having a new one. She was lucky, wasn't she, having three?"

"Pat was luckiest," Mary said. "He had eight."

"Well, I *hope* Pat considered himself lucky. I hope he didn't think, 'Oh, my gosh, *another* one!' "

They laughed together over this, but the shadow didn't lift from Mary's eyes.

"Mother, will I be allowed to come see you at the hospital?"

"I'm not sure, dear. At your age it's best to stay away from hospitals if you can. But if I should be there very long, I think they will let you."

"I don't know how I can stand it," Mary said, starting to cry, "if you're there for a very long time. I was so lonely without you, the other time, Mother. I'll miss you so. . . ."

"Dearest, please don't cry. You will make it so hard for me, if you cry. I want to think of you being happy at Peggy's house, and not worrying. . . . There now, darling, the boys are waiting for you. Give me a kiss and a big, big hug. . . . Now you must go, or you'll be late for school."

Anne lay back exhausted. Listening, she heard the front door open and close, the click of the latch on the gate, the diminishing sound of footsteps.

That much was over. But it had consumed a great deal of her courage, and almost all of her strength.

Rose came, bringing a cup of tea and two thin slices of buttered toast.

"Please don't say you don't want it, Mother. Dr. Mallory said I must make you eat. I know, there's been a stir, everybody coming up to say good-by. But you'll feel better when you've had your tea. Hadn't you better take one of the pain pills, Mother?"

"No darling. Not yet. I'm quite all right. It was just——"

"I know," Rose said. "Mary takes it very hard. But she'll have lots to think about, at Peggy's. She'll be all right, Mother. Let me get this other pillow under you. . . . There."

"Rose, I wish you would go to school now. I promise you, I'll stay right here in bed until your father comes. You're missing one of your finals."

"It doesn't matter. They'll let me make it up. Anyway I'm not going. Please eat *one* piece of toast, Mother. Are you comfortable? Would you like another pillow?"

"I'm perfectly comfortable, but another pillow will help, because I'd like to sit up for a while. I must finish my letter to Brendan. There on the bureau, dear, the clip-board and my pen."

"First you must drink your tea, Mother."

Rose brought another pillow, and the writing things from the bureau.

Clipped to the board were several sheets of paper, the half-finished letter, and an envelope addressed in Brendan's hand. From the envelope Anne took his most recent letter. With it she had put the last allotment check, which had come a few days earlier.

From the very beginning, she had received his entire pay. He insisted there was almost nothing he needed money for; his needs were taken care of, he said, by his rich uncle. She had wanted to open a savings account in his name against the day when his enlistment would end, but Tadhg said no. "For his sake you must yourself keep it," Tadhg said. "An unkindness would it be to deny him such pleasure as it is to know that by this much are things made easier for you, Anneen. In a separate account in your own name, you might put it, and do you care to, well might it be termed the Saint Elizabeth Fund; for much will it comfort him, I think, to provide in this way for his younger sisters, that they may be assured of the same educational advantages which his older sisters enjoyed. And much need," Tadhg added, "has he of such comfort." But each month she sent him five dollars, for she found it inconceivable that he would not have use for that much.

She gave the check into Rose's care.

"And will you see if I have five dollars in my bag, dear?"
Rose brought the five dollars.

"What do you suppose Bren will do when he gets out of the Navy, Mother?"

"I hope he'll return to college," Anne said. "He'll only be twenty-two. Lots of young men start college today in their twenties, or even older."

"Well, maybe. But do you know what I think?" Rose asked. "I think he'll be a priest."

A priest? Anne tried to form a picture in her mind of Brendan as a priest. It was a beautiful picture, yet she could not make it come clear. She could see a young priest facing the altar, but when he turned, she was not sure that it was Brendan.

Rose said: "He's so . . . well, you know how he is. What else could he be?"

"But that isn't reason enough."

Was that why the picture would not come clear?

"Well, that's what I think he'll be, just the same," Rose said. "Father would like it, wouldn't he?"

"Only if——"

"And if he thought Father would like it," Rose went on, not waiting to hear the *if,* "that would be reason enough for Brendan."

But not for God, Anne thought. She could hear Tadhg say, as he said so often, "Brendan will find his place." Did he mean the priesthood? He had never said so. Again she tried to form a picture, this time of Brendan's "place"; again it would not come clear. Yet it would be a good place, she knew, a place of joy.

Let it be not too long, she prayed. Let him find it, dear God, while the candle lasts. He would be so lost and frightened, in the dark, without the candle. . . .

"Are you sure you feel strong enough to sit up, Mother? You look so very tired."

"Just for a little while. Just long enough to finish my letter."

"And then you'll try to sleep for a while, won't you? Until it's time to get ready? I'll go wash the breakfast dishes while you finish your letter, and then I'll be up to sit with you."

It was half-past eight. Not six hours now. Only five.

She reread Brendan's letter to her. His letters were always

very cheerful, full of assurances (either openly stated or artfully implied) that he was well, and that his daily life was a round of absorbing study balanced by equally absorbing activity, of contact with only the most interesting people, and of one amusing incident after another. All letters that came to her, to Rose, or to Barney, were like this. The letters that came to his father were, she suspected, a little different—perhaps a little more open, a little less artful; but these were written in Irish and possibly lost something when translated to her, for "Not are there always the words in one language," Tadhg said, "to express the deepest meaning of what is written in another."

She lay back against the pillows, lost in remembering Brendan's letters.

At first they had come from the training center at San Diego; later, when he was assigned to a ship, from places even farther away—so far away that she had found it almost impossible to believe he really was in those places, and that it was not all part of one of the fabulous stories he used to delight in telling the younger children.

He wrote humorously of his failings. Being born to the sea was not quite the same thing, he told them, as being born to sail the seas. There was some question about his usefulness to the ship's community. He was absent-minded, he forgot things; this made him a problem to the ship's officers. On shore leave, he had even less sense of direction west of the International Date Line than east; this made him a problem to the Shore Patrol. They were trying to teach him radar and other esoteric subjects like that; it was conceded that he would do better as cook's helper. It might be said that he was a boatman rather than a sailor; he was familiar with every cubic inch of the boat, below decks; he had rare (though profoundly inspiring) glimpses of the sea.

Dear Brendan . . .

After being with the Fleet only a short time, he had been given shore duty. Through the past winter his letters had come from various small towns, where he served as decoy, he said, at local recruiting stations. Since the beginning of April he had been in Washington, doing clerical work, "third assistant," he told them, "to the third assistant office boy on the staff of an admiral who was always sick at sea."

Over these jesting accounts which he gave of himself, awareness of failure lay like the thinnest of shadows, so

257

thin that it might escape notice. The light tone of the letters was meant to deceive, as the well-remembered, puckish little smile had been meant to deceive in the past; and almost succeeded. . . .

The silver lining was that he was close to them again. He could come home, even if he had only a brief leave. They could go to see him. A few weeks ago Pat had driven her to Washington, and they had walked under the cherry trees, on a lovely April day of soft wind and swiftly interchanging sun and shadow. So great had been Brendan's joy in their coming that it had seemed to surround them with light, and she had imagined that other people, walking by, had been aware of passing within the circumference of that radiant circle. She felt, now, that if she could reconstruct every part of that day, she would understand what God intended Brendan's place in the world to be; but in trying to remember, the only thing that came back with complete clarity was the look of rapture on Mary's face as he told her a wonderful story of the god Poseidon and the Horses of the Sea.

Had she waited too long to finish her letter? It seemed such an effort, now, even to hold the pen, and she could not think what else she had wanted to say. She took up the pages written yesterday and reread them.

"Such a nice thing has happened for your father. Captain Mike Shaw has been transferred to command of his District. Perhaps you don't know that he received his promotion at the same time Pat did. I'm afraid I was so taken up with telling you of Pat's wonderful jump from patrolman to captain that I quite forgot to mention dear Mike. He was here at the house just the other day, and asked about you, as he always does. I don't suppose you remember the year he lived here with us, just after he met your father. You were only two years old—it was the year before the trouble—but you undertook to teach him the Our Father, in Irish. You gave it up, finally, as hopeless, but he still remembers how earnestly you tried. That was such a happy year. Mike was like a younger brother to your father in those days, and, of course, stood by him at the time of the trouble, when so many others decided that it wasn't good policy to be too friendly. They have never worked together again, in the same District, since that time; and with things as they are now . . ."

Anne paused, frowning, to read the last line again, wondering how she had come to write it, and if it would not perplex him.

". . . with things as they are now, it seems a special act of God's mercy that they are reunited in this way, at this time. It is so wonderful to know that instead of hostility, which so often has gone with these changes, there is friendship. I pray that it may be the beginning of a better time for your father. I have always felt sure that someday there will be a turn-about, and justice will be done; that God in His infinite goodness will not fail to reward one who has so dearly loved Him and so faithfully kept His commandments."

The page blurred. She closed her eyes and tried to think what else she had wanted to tell him. The money. . . .

She wrote, unevenly, not at all like her own writing:

"The check came. Once more I say thank you, darling. Thank you for the money, and thank you for being the generous and loving person you are."

There were other things she had wanted to tell him. How well Paul was doing with his trucking business. How well Bill was doing as a junior partner in the law firm of Lippincott, Spencer, Kennard, and MacCarthy, and how any time she saw him he always asked how things were with "his favorite altar boy." How Katie would not be teaching next year, but would instead be going to graduate school for a year's advanced study in the physical sciences.

So many things she had wanted to tell him. But it was too late, she was too tired, she could not write all those things. She could only write, and even if he guessed, still she must write:

"Thank you for being my son. Thank you for all the joy you have given me, for all the beauty you brought into my life, for all the song and the laughter, for all the ways I can remember you, looking back. Thank you for all your love of all of us, but especially for your great and beautiful love of your father, and for all the pleasure it has been to him that you learned to speak in the language of his heart.

"May God bless you and keep you, my beloved child, and lead you to happiness. May the Mother of God watch over you, looking always upon you with love and compassion, and hearing all your prayers."

Anne folded the letter with trembling fingers and slipped it, with the five-dollar bill, into an envelope.

Nine-thirty. Four hours.

Perhaps she should try to sleep a while. She must gain some strength, she must be strong and calm when Tadhg came. But with only four hours left, there was not time for sleeping.

Think of something. . . .

In the evening weeping shall have place, and in the morning gladness. . . .

Bring the morning soon, O God. Don't let them grieve. Don't let me bring unhappiness to them . . . to him. Restore his loss, I beseech Thee. Let him find someone who will love him as I do, someone he will love, someone beautiful and good, who will bring him such joy that grief can never be a part of his life again. Don't let this be an end, but only a turning point for him, a new beginning. . . .

"Rose?"

"I thought you were asleep, Mother."

"No. Just resting. Dear, I finished my letter to Brendan. It's here, somewhere. Will you address it and make sure that it goes out today? And Rose . . . ?"

"Yes, Mother?"

"You are so strong, darling. You have always been so strong, even when you were just a little thing. . . . You look like me, but you are really much more like your father. You have never hesitated to face facts. You have always been so . . . realistic. May I talk to you, Rose? Frankly, I mean."

"Yes, Mother."

"You know, don't you, that there is less than one chance in a thousand of my coming back?"

"Mother . . ."

"I know. We cling to that one chance, whatever it is. We hope, but at the same time we don't try, foolishly, to deceive ourselves. Dr. Mallory hasn't told me, but I know he has told your father. Your father has known since last December, when I had the other operation. Have you known since then, too?"

"Yes, Mother."

"Has everyone?"

"No. Just Father and Pat and me."

"Yes. That's what I thought. . . . Rose, it will be very hard for your father. And for Mary. Harder for them than for anyone else."

"I know, Mother. If"—Rose mastered the break in her voice and forced herself to go on very steadily, very realistically—"if it should turn out as you think, I shan't go back to school. I'll be sixteen in August. If . . . that should happen . . . I intend to stay right here and keep house."

"Rose, you are too young. Your education . . . it isn't right that you should sacrifice yourself——"

"I wouldn't look upon it as a sacrifice, Mother. It would simply be the logical thing to do. My education doesn't matter. Barney will finish high school next year. If he has to go into the army right away, we'll wait until he's out again before we marry. If he doesn't, of course you know he's going on the Police Force. We don't intend to get married the minute he's working, though. We intend to wait at least another year, until we have something laid by to start a family. We planned it this way long ago, Mother. It has nothing to do with . . . now, except that it . . . simplifies things. I guess that's being realistic. It will certainly make things easier for Father. . . ."

"Yes," Anne whispered.

". . . and it will let me do as much as anyone can toward filling your place with Mary. At least I'll *be* here; the house will never be empty when she comes home from school. And I'll do everything as near as I can to the way you've always done—the same kind of meals, and making sure the boys always have clean clothes for school, and keeping things nice around the house. . . . Mother, does that help at all?"

"Oh, so much, my darling, so much."

Rose dropped to her knees beside the bed.

"Mother, you don't think . . . because I'm realistic . . . that I don't love you?"

"Never would I think it, Rose."

"Because I do, Mother. Oh, I do. But sometimes I've wondered if you know how much, because I think we've all shown so much more plainly how we love Father than we've shown how we love you. All but Mary. As if because he's so . . . so dominant, we all turned to him, one by one, as soon as we were old enough to run around, and in a way just took you for granted, just knew you were there, in the background."

"Never reproach yourself for that, darling. I was always exactly where I wanted to be. I wanted you to love your father. There was nothing else I ever wanted quite so much."

"But you were there, Mother. You were always there. And you always will be. You know that, don't you . . . that you always will be?"

"But not in sadness. I would rather be forgotten than remembered in sadness."

"You will *never* be forgotten!" Rose said fiercely. "All my children will know you, and my first daughter will bear your name. . . . Mother, I'm not as strong as you think I am. The only thing that lets me bear it . . . I know you are suffering, and I can't want you to suffer just so we can keep you. But I *will* hope, Mother, I *will* hope! God wants us to hope. It would be worse than cowardly not to, it would be wicked!"

Rose stood up, turning away from the bed, and with angry finality wiped her eyes.

"I'm going to fix you an eggnog. You need to build up your strength."

Ten-thirty.

The hands of the clock on the bureau moved with incredible swiftness. If she looked, and looked away again, and then in what seemed only a minute or two looked back, ten minutes had gone in a flash.

Rose came back, and obediently her mother sipped the eggnog. Rose had brought the morning paper. Anne glanced at the headlines, but everything was remote, unreal, already wholly severed from these last few hours.

They talked of neighborhood happenings, and of what the boys would do with themselves over summer vacation, and of Pat's off-again-on-again engagement—currently off, following another conflict of wills, which had convinced his charming but independent-minded fiancée that marriage to Patrick O'Nolan would not be on the American Plan of wifely domination.

Rose said, "Pat better watch out. Peggy and Paul both got ahead of him, and if he's not careful, so will I. Sometimes I wonder if a girl to suit Pat has ever been born!"

The hands of the clock whirled around.

Eleven-thirty.

Twice the doorbell rang and Rose went downstairs. Mrs. Moran brought over a pot of homemade chicken soup. Mrs. O'Shaughnessy brought a bowl of rice pudding. Mrs. Cavazini, seeing Mrs. O'Shaughnessy come over, came hurrying across the street with a little basket of fresh-baked rolls, still hot from the oven.

Rose told them her mother was resting. They all sent messages.

"That's it, now," said Mrs. Moran. "She needs her rest. But you tell her I'll be watching from the porch to see her go, and she should look over and give an old body a wave. It's that close she is to me as my own daughter."

"Tell her not to worry about a thing, dearie," said Mrs. O'Shaughnessy, "while she's in the hospital. Anything that needs doing, you just let us know, so we can help, the same as she always helps us."

"Tell your dear mother we pray for her," Mrs. Cavazini said. "Tell her I go to the church this morning at six o'clock and I pray the whole Rosary for her. Tell her I know God soon make her well and bring her home again. Everybody on this street, up and down, we pray for her."

Twelve noon.

A little of Mrs. Moran's chicken soup.

"Just try the broth, Mother."

A portion of one of Mrs. Cavazini's rolls.

"Mrs. Cavazini asked if the boys could come over there for supper. She's having pizza. They love it. I told her I knew they'd be delighted. Is it all right for them to go, Mother?"

"I shall love to think of them enjoying pizza tonight," Anne said.

Twelve-thirty.

Rose helped her bathe and dress.

"What dress do you want to wear, Mother?"

"The blue-and-white print, I think, dear. It opens all the way down; it will be easy to get out of, at the hospital."

"I love this dress," Rose said. "That little stand-up collar is so sweet . . . and you're so beautiful, Mother."

Beautiful?

The face that looked back from the mirror was pale and thin and lined with pain. The face of a woman of sixty, Anne thought, and I am only forty-five. No one can see me and not know . . .

Only her hair was the same. Pale gold and shining, it lifted from her temples like wings, and fell into soft shadow waves under the gentle strokes of the brush in her daughter's hand.

Tadhg had always loved her hair. He called it winter sunlight.

"I'll take one of the pills now."

The pain and the tiredness drifted away. How wonderful that a drug could create such an effect of calmness and strength, as if nothing could possibly be wrong, as if nothing could possibly happen except that which was good and to be desired. How beautiful life was. How God was to be thanked for all the years of joy.

"There's Father. I'll take your bag downstairs," Rose said.

Anne listened to his step coming up, coming closer, now in the hall, now at the door. The great, dear, familiar figure filling the doorway. The dear face.

She gave him a smile of welcome.

"Ready and waiting," she said.

He took her hands and helped her to her feet, as lightly as a child might be helped, so wasted and frail she had become.

The beautiful calm made it quite easy and safe to say, "Tadhg, dearest, at the hospital there won't be time . . . and there will be other people . . . and it isn't the place, anyway. I don't want to say good-by to you at the hospital. I want to say it here, in this room, our room."

He took her in his arms. So strong his arms, so gentle, holding her so close. . . . Twenty-seven years of loving, in his kiss. "*Áine Ní Bhriain . . . a chroí istigh, a grá . . .* my heart's dearest, my love . . ."

"Tadhg, we have always been honest with each other. It isn't possible for you to be less than honest in anything, ever, so I know you cannot wish to be less than honest now. Or wish me to be. . . . And you are so strong. You have always shared your strength with me, dearest—such great strength—I have depended upon it for so long. . . . Tadhg, there is so much I must tell you, and so little time."

"There is nothing you must tell me, Anneen. That well do I know your heart as you know mine."

"Tadhg, I must tell you—I have been so happy . . . for twenty-seven years I have been so happy."

264

"Yet there is so much," he answered sorrowfully, "that I have not given you."

"Yes," she agreed, "so much. You have never given me one unkind word or look. You have never given me one unhappy moment. . . . Tadhg, do you remember the day we crossed the strait to Inishmaan?"

"Not can I forget it while I live. Nor yet when I no longer live, I think."

"Such a glittering day it was," Anne said, looking at the picture on the screen of time. "The sky was so blue and the sun so bright, with only now and then a racing cloud across it, and for just a moment, while the cloud passed, the water changing from indigo to the most incredible green. . . . My father was there, in the front of the curragh, and there were three other rowers, but none of them was there, for me. . . . I sat behind you, Tadhg, on a mail sack that you were taking to the Island, and I watched you as you rowed. . . . It was a hot day, and your shirt was wet and clinging. . . . I had never before seen anyone so splendid, so strong."

"It is you who are the strong one now, my wife. Did I not have your strength to bear me up, not could I endure this moment."

"Tadhg, good will come to you soon, I know, I know."

"Good is with me now. Good is always with me when you are in my arms. Your heart is within mine, mine within yours. So beautiful you are, Anneen, that always has the sight of you been gladness; and so beloved that but to touch you, to hold you close, has each time been a renewal of my life."

"Kiss me once more, Tadhg, and wish me safe home."

"*Go dtéir slán abhaile, a mhúirnín.*"

"A few hours. A day, perhaps, at the most. I'm afraid her heart can't hold out any longer than that."

The words came from somewhere across a great, mist-shrouded gulf.

But she was not asleep. It was strange to be awake yet so far away. Strange to know that the operation, the useless operation, was over, and that time was running on like a dark river toward that place where it would slip at last over the edge of the world. Strange to know that others were

265

there, watching; to hear their voices, to understand the words they said, yet to be so far separated from them.

Tadhg was there. Waking or sleeping or in a half-state between, she knew that Tadhg was there. Always and forever.

Sometimes she could not be sure just where she was.

A hospital room. . . . But where? When?

Once, long ago, in a darkened hospital room there had been a silver parallelogram of light on the wall, reflected from somewhere outside. She could remember lying there in bed using it as a frame for the faces of the children. And for his face, smiling down on her out of the dark.

When had it been? How long ago? What child?

It was very late. Very dark. It must surely be past midnight, everything was so silent. . . . Why was the house so still? Was anything wrong? Half awake, she felt anxious.

"Are the children all right, Tadhg? It's very late, isn't it? Are they all in bed?"

"Sleeping well are they, Anneen. *Bíodh sos maith agat, a rún.* Rest easy. Soon will it be day."

Long silences and deep shadows, the mist-filled gulf and the slow dark rushing. . . .

She woke and opened her eyes and he was there beside her. She smiled at him.

"Is it time to get up? Must you be at work early? Will you help me, dearest? If you would raise me, just a little . . . I feel so weak, but once I'm up, it will pass."

He slipped an arm under her shoulders, raising her a little, holding her close.

"Not yet is it time, *Áine Ní Bhriain.* Do you rest but for a while."

She whispered, "The sun on the water, Tadhg . . ."

She lived an hour longer, in his arms.

The summer wind blew lightly down the slope. In passing it picked up the heavy fragrance of the massed flowers, and, slowed a little by this sweet burden, moved on down across the grass toward the river.

Somewhere a bird was singing.

"O God, by Whose mercy rest is given to the souls of the faithful, in Thy kindness bless this grave. Entrust it to

the care of Thy holy angel, and set free from all the chains of sin the soul of her whose body is buried here, so that with all Thy saints she may rejoice in Thee forever . . ."

The bird was still. There was no sound but the sobbing of a child.

"Eternal rest grant unto her, O Lord."
"And let perpetual light shine upon her."

Lightly the wind touched those who stood with bowed heads, around the grave.

"May her soul and the souls of all the faithful departed, through the mercy of God, rest in peace."
"Amen."

Slowly, with a last look, the bystanders moved away, until only two were left.

Down the grassy slope, on the curve of the roadway, they gathered in little groups in the path of the flower-scented wind. The bright sun of summer lay on the hill, and far down, caught motionless between two bridges, the river was a gleam of silver.

Exchange of little, prosaic, ordinary remarks brought comfort and reassurance.

"Did you ever see the church so crowded?"

"And at least a hundred outside."

"How's the trucking business, Paul?"

"Fine. The only thing that has us worried is income tax."

"Winnie, you poor dear, it was so sweet of you to come, feeling as you do."

"Look who's talking. You'd better get off your feet, Peg."

A door of a car was held open. Peggy, heavy with her unborn child, and Mary, pale and silent and spent of tears, got in.

"We might as well start."

"Might as well. We'll be right behind you."

"But you're all coming to the house," Rose reminded them. "Mrs. Moran and Mrs. O'Shaughnessy are fixing dinner. They're expecting everybody."

"Rose, I couldn't possibly eat."

"But you must *come* just the same," fifteen-year-old

267

Rose commanded. "They're doing it for Mother. It's the last thing they can do. No one's going to cheat them of it!"

Peggy sighed. "Very well. We'll come."

The MacCarthys' car pulled away.

Paul and Winnie, and with them Sister Mary Bernadette, who had been Katie, followed.

"Rose, darling, do you think we should wait? Your father . . . ?"

"No, Aunt Nora. Don't wait. But please go to the house. Mother would want you to."

"Your dear mother. . . ."

With a handkerchief pressed to her eyes, Aunt Nora turned blindly to the car. She and Uncle Paul drove away.

"You might as well dust, too, Sis. Take the kids. We'll stick around."

Rose and Barney and the two boys left.

"When's your leave over?" Pat asked.

"Midnight."

"I'll drive you down."

Brendan's eyes lighted with pleasure.

"That will be great, Pat. Only . . . it's such a long trip for you, and I can take the bus."

"I'll drive you," Pat said.

He glanced up the hill and away again.

Sounds of traffic reached them from a distant street.

"How are you and the Admiral getting along these days?"

"Oh, fine. He's noticed me. He told one of the Reserve officers the other day to tell that dumb so-and-so who brings the interoffice mail to put it on the other side of his desk, he's not left-handed."

"Nothing like bringing yourself to the attention of the top brass, kid."

White cloud-mountains formed around the edges of the sky, broke and drifted eastward.

"Pat, Mother knew she was going to die."

"So she knew," Pat said.

"In her last letter she said good-by to me. She thanked me for . . . being her son. Pat, I'm not sure I ever thanked her for being my mother."

"Stow it," Pat said. "They're coming."

Father Morissey had already started down the slope. A last moment, and the remaining mourner rose from his knees and followed.

"Pull yourself together," Pat said roughly. "What right have *we* got to let go?"

In silence the four of them got in the car. In silence the car moved slowly down the hill. Around the first bend the motor took hold, and they followed the long, sweeping curve toward the river.

Behind them the wind blew sweet and free.

AVON ◆ The Sign of Good Reading

The Novels of D. E. Stevenson

AVON ◆ The Sign of Good Reading

Frances Parkinson Keyes

Agnes Sligh Turnbull

AVON ◭ The Sign of Good Reading

Elizabeth Taylor
ELIZABETH TAYLOR V2164 **75¢**

Virginia Graham
THERE GOES WHAT'S
HER NAME V2153 **75¢**

Eugenia Price
BELOVED INVADER V2165 **75¢**

Lousene Rousseau Brunner
CASSEROLE MAGIC S253 **60¢**

Rosemary Taylor
CHICKEN EVERY
SUNDAY V2113 **75¢**

On sale wherever better paperbacks are sold
or order directly from the publisher, including cover price plus 10¢ for handling and
mailing.

AVON BOOKS
959 Eighth Avenue
New York, New York 10019